Wings or Tails

Larisa Blackledge

Hardback ISBN: 979-8-9936632-0-3
Paperback ISBN: 979-8-9936632-1-0
Ebook ISBN: 979-8-9936632-2-7

To the dreamers. Don't stop believing,
Embrace the slop.

Author Notes

There is a lot of talk about flowers, herbs, and poisons. Please do not attempt anything at home. It is simply fun information. Some of them I have made up and do not exist.

Also note, there is sexual content, and descriptions of torture and death.

Chapter One
Forget-Me-Nots

This small yet striking flower symbolizes enduring love, remembrance, and long-lasting connections. While the common house plant is generally considered nontoxic, there are a few look-a-likes in the same family that are toxic.

Zily

Knocking echoes down the plain, mustard yellow hall, illuminated by the occasional light powered by crystals hidden in the walls. A deep voice reverberates from the other side of the slate grey door giving me permission to enter. A chill runs down my spine, though the air down here is warm and stuffy. There's only one of two reasons to be summoned to this door, neither good but one more favorable than the other. At the moment, I'm the only one in this hall. Rubbing my shoulder, a forgotten pain resurfacing, I suck in a deep breath. I step inside, closing the door behind me, keeping my gaze down.

Dark oak bookcases line both sides of the wall, full of books I am in no way allowed to touch let alone read. The back wall is a plain, stale leaden blue with a large wooden desk where the man that has the hair on the back of my neck rising on end sits in a tall back auburn chair. The air is stagnant; no scent to it. It's like a vacuum sucked out the air, making it difficult to breathe. Despite the bright hangings lights that should make the room welcoming, the walls feel like they're moving in on me, trapping me in here.

I hate this room.

Sir Colin Eyler stands up from the desk upon my entry, moving deliberately slowly, back straight, hands folded behind him. He wears a deep red, almost black suit, reminding me of dried blood, clean and pressed. He looks down at me, his pale blond hair slicked back with gel to keep them out of his bronze eyes.

"Snow." He greets me with my code name, an obvious one based on my snow white hair, ears, and fluffy white tail. I would not have chosen it for myself.

"Sir." I place my fist over my chest, bowing, not quite out of respect, but one of necessity. I keep my gaze on his shiny black shoes, wondering if they ever smudge.

"I have a job for you." His voice the usual dull, serious tone. There's no fluctuation. The kind that leaves no room for questions. My ears perk up at his words, my body involuntarily relaxing. It is the more favorable summons, though I don't particularly like my job. It's been years since I've been summoned for punishment, but the scars on my back sting every time I come here.

"The Caraway family are becoming too friendly with the Zeneth Kingdom for my liking, all thanks to their meddling son. The ramifications a treaty between the two could have here is not in our favor. Your assignment is to make sure the son isn't crowned King." Sir Colin Eyler's narrowed eyes bear his intent. "Ever." It's the usual spiel when he doesn't want someone to continue living.

I cock my head slightly to the side, recognizing the Caraway name belonging to the family of the Yuseaa Kingdom. I have yet to venture almost straight north, my previous jobs taking me east. The region is predominantly Corvum, and they don't have an exceptionally good standing with Kitsune, if I recall correctly. I would be instantly suspicious if I'm spotted.

"How do I get in?"

Sir Colin Eyler's bronze eyes flash with irritation. My whole body stiffens preparing for a strike. He doesn't hit me. "That is up to your discretion. You have two weeks. Leave at dawn." He holds out a single leaflet.

My tail twitches behind me, the time frame I'm allotted exciting me. I step forward, taking the leaflet, folding it neatly and tucking it safely in my short's pocket. I bow once more before leaving.

I stroll down the long, never changing hall with a little skip in my step, tail curled up and swishing back and forth. The words 'two weeks' echo in my mind, though I don't dare say them out loud in fear of Sir Colin Eyler's superb hearing of my excitement and reassigning the job to someone else, followed by punishment.

The few I pass going about their business give me strange looks. They know who I am and what I do as I am the only white haired Kitsune here. It doesn't matter what they think of me. The ones cleaning the space, dusting the walls or on the ground scrubbing the floor turn their heads away if I so much as glance at them. Some whisper about the way I skip away from the door, the hall we all fear. They must think I enjoy my job, but it's the time outside I look forward to.

The walls in the mess hall are a similar color to that of the hall and our bedrooms. It's full of Kitsune quietly talking in small cliques. A Vampire guard eyes me while I pick up extra food to take on my journey. I show him the leaflet, dipping my head, feeling uneasy under his gaze. Taking my bag of rations, my hand drifts up, rubbing the back of my neck. It's only a rumor that they can control us, but we live in fear of it; a different kind of control that keeps us obedient, going out and returning as directed. I hurry to my room.

In the small room I've lived in for most of my life that I share with my best friend, I sit on my cot. The room is large enough for two cots to line one pale yellow wall, a small nightstand beside the head of each and a dresser we share against the wall with the door. The width of the dresser is about as much walking room we have. Plain eggshell white sheets and grey blankets cover the cots. Mine is a pile in the middle of my bed while Callie's is tucked in nice and neat.

I open my nightstand drawer, vials rattling. I pull out a small box with eight sections to hold small bottles of poison safely. It's always the first to go in my bag, on top of padding kept inside the bottom of the pack to better protect the glass. I add a few empty jars and pouches for if I come across any interesting herbs or poisons on my journey. A single change of clothes is rolled up, always traveling light. The rations I got from the mess go in last.

"You got an assignment?" Callie asks from the doorway, observing the routine packing process. Her cocoa brown tail gives a single swish

I nod eagerly, a broad grin on my face. "It's the usual expectation, but I was given two weeks!"

"Two weeks?" Callie repeats, shifting on her feet. A hand reaches up to twirl a brown curl around her finger.

"Yeah. It's probably 'cause of the distance, but if my calculations are correct, I should have about a week of free time. I'm heading straight up to the Yuseaa Kingdom." I add blank loose sheets of paper to my bag before zipping it up, hardly glancing up at Callie all the while.

"Will you be alright going there? Won't you be caught right away just by your looks?" Concern laces her voice. It always does when I'm about to head out on a mission. She sits beside me as I lean my bag against my nightstand.

"The point is not to be caught, but yes, this will be a more difficult job. I don't want to be caught anywhere in their region. Perhaps I should wear a cloak." I tilt my head, contemplating. I don't have a cloak. Could I get one before the morning?

"You can use mine."

"What if you need it while I'm gone?"

Callie shrugs, standing once more. Pulling it out from the top drawer, Callie shakes out her black cloak with a few stitches in it. "I'll be fine without it. Maybe it'll give you good luck." She holds it out to me with a smile.

Returning her smile and getting to my feet as well, I take the old cloak, hugging it close. Callie has never gone on a job without this cloak. Her job is less dangerous than mine. She's a spy, though she has done assassination work. Blending in to be the one everyone over looks is the key to her work. I fold it up, draping it over my pack. Turning around, I wrap my arms around her, pulling her in for a hug. We're about the same height.

"I promise to return it to you in two weeks."

She gives me a squeeze. "We should give Decan a visit. Let him know you'll be gone awhile."

"Right. Don't want to make him worry with a sudden disappearance." It happened before. I received a serious scolding when I returned from a job I neglected to tell Decan nor Callie about once. There was a lot of ranting and arms thrown about while he paced.

Looping my arm with Callie's, we make our way through the series of halls. Decan's workshop is halfway across the fortress and up a level. A loud, piercing ring resonates down the hall from behind a closed door. Callie and I exchange glances. Our ears flatten against our heads. With a moment between pings, I throw the door open quickly, calling inside right as Decan hits the metal. Flinching at the sound and covering my ears with my hands, I struggle to get his attention again. I can only take the blaring ting so many times. A headache is already creeping in.

The forge burns hot in the back of the room, filling the air with a mix of searing coal and an earthy scent. Decan stands at a table right beside it where he repeatedly hammers out defects in the metal of the swords and the occasional armor he makes. His head turns on my third attempt. He pulls a long metal piece out of the fire to not leave it in too long, closing the door to the forge. Pulling down the cloth covering his nose and mouth, a broad grin crosses his face as he puts his work down. Thick leather gloves made to protect his hands get tucked in his belt. He lifts the dark shades up onto the bandanna protecting his brown ears and covering his tightly braided, dark brown locks of hair.

"Well, well. To what do I owe the pleasure of this visit?" Decan puts his hands on his hips, his ombre dark to light brown tail curled upward.

I giggle, lowering my hands, strolling farther into the room, Callie following right on my tail. "Working hard as usual, I see."

Decan waves his arms around the room of an assortment of swords, daggers, other weapons and a few pieces of armor. Some are still works in progress. He's completely in his element. "Gotta make a living, right?" He winks, nose wrinkling at his own joke. Could our lives truly be called living? We each make the most of what we have; each other.

I roll my eyes. "I've just come to tell you I'll be gone for a while on an assignment."

Decan's arms drop to his side, tail pointing down. His gaze flickers to Callie by my side. She gives a nod, both frowning. There's always a feeling of unease when one of us has to leave. Decan became a blacksmith nearly eight years ago. He hasn't left since. Callie and I get assignments outside the walls. We've always returned, so far, but many other Kitsune haven't.

"A while? How long? Are you going to be gone for your birthday?"

"Two weeks," Callie answers, moving around the room so we all face each other.

I cock my head, the bottom waves of my hair brushing across the back of my neck, thinking. "Yup. Yup. That does fall within the time I'll be gone."

Decan and Callie exchange looks. Decan bows his head with a sigh, a hand running over the bandanna and braids. "Alright. I guess we'll do this now."

Walking around the worktable, he rummages through some items under a bench, moving some boxes of random pieces of metal around. He comes up to me, holding out a long, plain box, dusted with soot.

With a raised eyebrow, I take it, setting it on the table so I can lift the lid off. A finely crafted double edge short sword gleams up at me. The handle is wrapped in scraps of leather. Burn marks make a swirly design on the grip with tiny green and blue gemstones embedded randomly around the swirls. They're fake jewels, but beautiful, nonetheless.

"Happy birthday!" My friends chime together.

"Callie… Decan…" I whisper, tears welling in my eyes.

They never miss a birthday. The only ones who know it and attempt to do something every year. It's usually something small; a baked cake; a braided bracelet; the bag I currently use. It's not guaranteed we'll see the next one. I hold everything they do for me dear. The bracelet Callie made for me broke years ago, but I still have it in a baggy in my nightstand drawer.

They grin at me. "Oh, come here shorty." Decan wraps an arm around my shoulders, knuckling my head, messing up my hair.

I laugh, swatting his hand away, ducking out of his grasp, shoving hair out of my face. Callie disappears to the other side of the room for a moment. She re-emerges with a sheath and new belt in hand.

"We had Kern make these to fit your new blade. It should also be easy to get the sheath in and out of the loop too when needed." Callie beams, her cocoa brown tail swishing excitedly.

Giggles bubble out while I try on the belt. He may not have known my exact size, but Kern knows how small I am, adding extra holes to accommodate. Finally, I lift the sword, weighing it in my hand. It's lightweight, knowing I'm not an extraordinary swordsman, but a weapon is often needed in our line of work, if not simply for protection in the forest we travel through. I sheath the sword on my hip, resting my hand on the pommel, turning side to side to show it off. We all burst out. It's with them, my friends, that I can manage to laugh, that makes this life bearable.

I set out as soon as I wake the next morning as ordered, backpack on my shoulders, a grey headband keeping my hair out of my face, and Callie's cloak shading me from the sun. My hand rests on my sword as I stroll through the yard, my head held high, the rising sun casting long shadows covering half of the mostly dirt field. The gates are the only way in or out of Gateswood as it's surrounded by immensely large, smooth concrete walls with barbed wire at the top. Guards are posted at the gates at all hours. There's a lever on either side that has to be pulled simultaneously for the gates to slide apart.

I approach one side with confidence, handing over the leaflet Sir Colin Eyler gave me. The guard looks it over, stamps it on the top right hand corner and hands it back. He shares an uninterested glance and a mumble with the man opposite him, something I can't hear but the Vampires can. The metal wheels squeal as they pull the doors apart, groaning the whole way.

I salute 'goodbye' as I enter the woods surrounding the base. This is how it got its name; Gateswood. I pause to put the leaflet safely away in a pocket of my backpack and to pull out my map. It's not a detailed map, simply showing the forest, the major rivers and hills with names of kingdoms over their general region. After double checking directions, I sling my pack over my shoulders and set out around the wall to the right for a while before splitting off, disappearing into the trees.

A gentle breeze rustles the treetops. Squirrels scamper up trunks, chasing one another. The noisy bugs are making their buzzing music. According to my calculations, it should be a few days' journey, which means I will have a week to get the job done. Really, it shouldn't take that long. The main challenge will be getting into the palace. I'll worry about that once I get there.

The fresh air is calming, smelling of oak, cedar and maple wood. Sun shimmers through the canopy above, casting the world around me in various shades of green. Sometimes I stop, a plant catching my eyes. I have a collection of herbs and berries that could be of use or rare ones I may not come across again. Those are my favorites.

I stock up on little red berries that are great for minor burns when mashed into a paste and smeared across the afflicted area. Althaea officinalis root helps with sore throats and coughs. Arnica is used for sprains. Everything goes into the extra jars and pouches I brought along. Adding to my collection is the best part of traveling.

In the evening of day two, I come across an eggshell colored mushroom with brown polka dots growing from some moss on a tree. I gasp, doing a little happy dance in a circle. I've read about this mushroom in one of the few books I've gotten my hands on. The top is poisonous, putting the consumer into a never-ending slumber while the stem could be used to make the antidote. It's nicknamed Sleeping Beauty.

I carefully cut the mushroom to collect enough of the stem to make an antidote too. The thought of using it for this mission briefly passes through my mind. It's pushed away quickly. I tuck the pouch with my new addition safely in my bag. I'll save it for a more special occasion. It's what I often say, however a "more special occasion" never presents itself. I don't actually want to use my rare collection. Then again, I don't like using common poisons either.

The sun caresses my face through a small break in the leaves on the third morning. I should reach the outskirts of the palace grounds this evening. Early tomorrow I'll begin figuring out how to get in and dispose of the prince. I contemplate it a little as I follow a cliff side that drops down to a river. There's not really a point of thinking about it now when I don't even know the layout of the mansion or even what the prince looks like. The cliff side bends and I keep equal distance away from it. I don't want to risk falling. It's not the fall that scares me, but the water below does. I will eventually need to cross it.

The ground shudders beneath my feet, causing me to stumble. My ears flicker. I draw my sword, the glass jewels glistening in the sun. Cracking and crunching of trees falling in the forest gets louder. Birds flee overhead. I consider fleeing with them. I'm not notably skilled in combat. If only I had enough time to lace the blade with poison. My hesitation in deciding to fight or run costs me. A beast as tall as the trees breaks into the small clearing, bringing with it a strong sickly sweet smell of rotting leaves. Its knuckles drag on the ground by its side. Random patches of black fur cover its brown muscled hide.

It spots me right away, staring me down with its beady little black holes of eyes. I hold perfectly still, wondering if it'll leave me alone if I don't move.

A loud guttural grunt reverberates from its chest as its arm swings wide. I jump back, its fist barely missing me. A gash is left in the ground where I had been standing before. My eyes widen, heart pounding in my head. That one hit would have taken me out.

Wanting to protect the glass jars in my bag, I take several steps back, stowing my backpack by a tree. I wave my hands above my head, shouting at it to make it follow me away from my bag.

I toss the hood of the cape off, making sure I can see well. Gripping my short sword with both hands, I readjust my stance to attempt to mimic how I've seen others hold a sword. The beast's other arm swings toward me, its hand grooving a path through the earth. I wait for it to get close, jumping over its fist with a roll landing. It's strong, but it's slow.

Leaping forward, the sharp edge of my blade slices its thigh as I run past, deep red blood seeping down the thick muscled calf. The beast roars, spinning around faster than I expected. I keep moving. Don't stop. Speed is my strong suit. I leap over its arm again, dirt flying from the impact of his fist, leaving a small crater in the ground. The second fist is right behind it. I stumble back, holding my sword in front of me. The swing grazes my blade, evoking a pained growl from the beast.

Running around it, I smirk through gritted teeth. There's a problem. It's not getting scared off by my little cuts and I'm getting worn out. My legs are burning from the running and jumping around like a rabbit, heart ready to thump right out of my chest, pulse thrumming in my head.

Dodging another attack, I leap onto its fist, running up the arm. If I can severely hurt it, maybe it'll flee. My feet begin to slip on the ripple of muscles on its arm. I stab my blade into its biceps. Moving, I have to stay moving or I'll fall off. Too focus on trying to get to its head, thick fingers curl around my body, claws digging into my side. We make eye contact, the world freezing for a moment as hot fury and icy fear meet. By grabbing me, the blade is yanked from its flesh. Blood pours from the wound. It throws its head back with an angry, pained roar. Grunting, I throw the sword with everything I have a moment before the beast tosses me away.

I roll across the ground, leaving a trail of hot red liquid. Struggling to my knees, I wheeze through pain filled intakes of breath, clutching my side. Blood coats my hand, dripping from my fingers. My head spins at the sight of my own blood. Ears twitching, I'm alerted to the beast's movement. It's pissed off and swinging wildly. I have enough sense to roll out of the way.

With blurry vision, I see the dark brown of my bag in the sea of green. Maybe, if I can reach it, I can make a run for it. Or I can come back to it. Where did my sword go? I don't want to lose my new precious gift. I'll come back, if I can just get away. Stumbling, my feet have a hard time staying under me, supporting my weight. They scream at me while I argue with them to move. The beast growls at me and I know it's swinging its massive paw again. I do my best to jump out of the way.

The world tumbles around me. Trees turn upside down. The earth is the sky, and the sky is the ground. Then I'm falling, staring up into the vast blue with speckles of fluffy white clouds. Air ruffles through my hair, my tail, my clothes. The moment of weightlessness feels like time has slowed. I float between the earth and water, sharp pain in my side and aching throughout my body. The cliff's edge moves farther and farther away from my outstretched hand while the sound of rushing water gets louder and louder.

Then comes the splash cracking through my spine. I don't have the energy to cry out as the pain vibrates through my body. Instinctively, my body struggles against the pain and the current, desperately trying to keep my head above water. Short bursts of air fill my lungs, along with the water I don't mean to suck in. My arms flail about, batting at the water around me. I am so tired. The pain in my side reminds me of punishments I've endured. Which hurt more? The holes in my side or the way the whip shredded my back when I was twelve years old? The water turns red all around. I begin sinking, the sunlight shimmering on the water surface.

This is it. The words float calmly through my mind, eyes fluttering shut. I can't hold my breath any longer. I'll finally be free.

Chapter Two
Strelitzia

Also known as 'Bird of Paradise,' this flower is associated with freedom, joy, royalty and nobility, love, and passion. It is toxic that when ingested, it can cause nausea, vomiting, dizziness, drowsiness, and diarrhea.

Sylas

The gentle spring breeze carries me through the beautiful clear blue sky, the sensation a faint tickle through the feathers of my wings. I needed a break, to feel the sweet freedom only flying can bring. Tucking my wings in, I spiral down before fanning them out again, the wind catching and ruffling the black feathers as I glide some more, laughter escaping.

The crashing of trees in the forest below catches my attention briefly. A roar of an angry creature emanates through the canopy. I don't think much of it. The beasts in this section of the forest often like to fight each other for dominance. It's a piercing cry of someone in pain that has me flapping my wings to pick up speed.

Swooping down, I follow the gorge. A small body is thrown from the forest, followed by a beastly roar of triumph and a thump. They plummet to the rushing river below. Folding my wings in, I let gravity aid me in my descent. I don't reach the body in time, pulling up at the last moment, the tips of my boots grazing the water. The sunlight reflects off the sparkling water, little foam curls with movement. I watch the water surface, the ebb and flow, searching for any sign of the body.

A ripple in the water. A pale hand pokes out from the water, sinking back under. I rush, scooping down, pulling the girl into my arms, water spraying everywhere. I hold her still, cold, wet body to my chest, gently shaking her.

"Hey! Come on. Come on. Wake up!" I plea. Her eyelashes flutter, ears twitching, coughing up water. She goes limp in my arms, but her chest rises and falls with every shallow breath. "Hang in there." I whisper, ignoring the question of what a Kitsune may be doing in my territory.

I fly up to the ridge. Large grooves scar the earth where the beast hit the ground. The forest creature in question lay splayed out on the ground, its beady eyes left wide open. Blood pools under its neck where a short sword is embedded. It's hard to believe this tiny girl took down this beast. At a cost, it seems.

Laying her down for a moment, I assess her wounds. It's not good. A puddle of blood pools under her, thinned from the water, staining the cloak around her and coating my shirt. I fold her arms across her body, loosening the belt around her waist and moving it higher while also taking the sheath off. Tightening it, her hands and arms are pinned, hopefully putting pressure against the holes. Sliding the sheath onto my own belt beside my sword, I retrieve the one from the beast. In the brief moment the metal glistens in the sun rays, I can tell it's finely crafted, though how light it is surprises me. I wipe it off and sheath it.

As I kneel down to pick her up again, a discarded backpack near a tree catches my eyes. I sling it over my shoulder quickly, dismissing my wings and unfurling them again through the straps.

Tenderly, carefully, I slide my hands under the girl, pulling her up against my chest. My wings spread out, batting the air with strong beats, drifting up. I shoot across the sky as fast as I dared with the frail body in my arms, the air cold against the wet skin, the soaked clothes.

Thankfully I left the glass doors to my balcony open, flying right in on the second floor. I land briefly to open the door to the wide hall with high ceilings made to allow for flying in an emergency. My wings carry me down the hall, past my aide and best friend, Kai, who gives me a concerned wide eyed look. I know he only sees that I carry a Kitsune, not a girl bleeding out on me. We'll talk later. It may not even matter if the blood staining my shirt is any indication.

I drop to the floor, retracting my wings to the tattoos that reflect my wings on my back, bursting through the doors to the infirmary of my family's personal doctor. There are two beds with white linen, curtains pulled back against the wall that can encircle them if needing privacy. To the left is a large cabinet of medicines and herbs, a desk of paperwork and where Dr. Burgess sits in a powder blue shirt, round glasses on his face and his brown hair chopped short. His apprentice stands beside him, reading a paper he handed her.

Dr. Burgess stands quickly, eyes narrowing on the girl in my arms. I set her on the nearest bed, the white linens turning red almost instantly. It has leaked down, turning her once white tail a tint of pink.

"Help," I wheeze. I can't seem to get enough air into my lungs.

"But Sir…" Dr. Burgess hesitates.

"Help her." The order comes out as a growl. I step back, giving him space.

"Yes, Sir Sylas Ambrose." Dr. Burgess bows before examining the girl.

He undoes the belt, sliding it out from under her. I take it to keep it with her other belongings. Shifting her hands to her sides, he lifts her shirt to peek at the wound, the wet fabric sticking to her skin. I'm grateful to see her chest still rising and falling, breathing slowly. Sonya brings over a cart of medical supplies. Tools, gauze, alcohol and more. Sonya glances at me, her soft brown eyes holding empathy. The rings holding the curtain clink as she swooshes the curtain around them for privacy when Dr. Burgess starts cutting away the girl's shirt.

"I'll check back later." I leave since it's unhelpful to stand around doing nothing. I'm not sure they hear me, neither responding, but I know they will take good care of her because Dr. Burgess is the best and I'm the one who asked him.

I walk down the hall, adjusting the strange backpack on my shoulders, thinking about how I'll tell my mom and dad about our unexpected, unusual guest. First, I need to make a quick stop in my room. No need to alarm them with my blood soaked clothes. I'll throw these clothes away instead of having a maid struggle to clean them, which I know they would.

I set the girl's backpack and sword on my bed covered in jade satin sheets. I'll see if the blood can be cleaned from her belt or see if she'll accept a new one. A new navy blue shirt replaces the bloody one. I roll up the sleeves the same way I had the previous shirt, slipping on a pair of black, pressed pants and comb my fingers through my hair, fixing the short ponytail. *There, presentable again.*

I glance at the door across the hall. It's a guest room, but it's not used because it's right across from mine. It'd be a good place for the girl to stay while she recovers. It'll be easy to keep an eye on her and how she is doing. Even if we make sure it's known she's a guest, there will be those who won't accept her being here. If she's staying right across from their prince -me- then it should reduce the likeliness something will happen to her. She's been through enough.

My parents are in my dad's study on the other side of the palace. I straighten my shirt, making sure it's tucked neatly in before knocking. They know it's me by the way I knock. We have a coded way of knocking, just between us. Kai has his own as well. Dad calls for me to enter. It's casual, lacking the regal tone of his position.

I step into the spacious room; walls blue like the sky with a large wood bookcase full of legal books, policies, and regulations. The large blue with thin white lines cahmo crystal we use for long distance communication sits on the round base in the corner. Light shines in through the wide window behind the large work desk, cream curtains pulled to the side. Somehow his office always smells like the forest outside. Mine only smells like work.

Dad sits at his desk, short black hair parted to the side, wearing a deep green button down, pen in hand with only a couple pieces of papers in front of him, the rest of his desk is clear save for the pen holder and stapler.

Mom looks up at me warmly from her seat in the cushioned cream chair right beside the desk, a novel in hand. She often sits with my dad while he works. They love the simple company of each other and she's right there if he needs help. He does the same when she's the one working, though his reading material is often work related.

Mom sets her book down at the edge of the desk, sitting up properly, her hands smoothing out her deep, forest green dress. Her long brown hair is half up today, the sides twirled and pinned in the back.

"Hello, Sy." She's the only one that calls me that. "Did you have a good flight this morning?" Dad finishes writing his thoughts before looking up at me. He gives a stern nod in greeting, though his eyes are warm like chocolate, curious about the answer as well.

I debate how to start this. "I found a girl floating in the Baxpon Canyon river. She appeared to have been severely injured by a forest beast. Dr. Burgess is seeing to her now."

Mother's eyes grow wide, covering her mouth with a soft gasp. "Dr. Burgess is a wonderful doctor, surely the girl will be alright?"

"I'll see to her later in the day. I was hoping we could have a room prepared for her to stay in while she recovers."

"Certainly. Rest is important for recovering. I'll see what rooms are available." Dad agrees, opening a drawer.

"I do believe room two-eighteen is available." I suggest nonchalantly.

Dad raises an eyebrow. Mom tilts her head slightly. I smile innocently. "Yes… I can make that arrangement."

"Wonderful. Since that is settled, I should check on her progress." I turn to leave, chewing on one bit of information. "Oh, and by the way, she's a Kitsune." One foot is already out the door.

"Wait a minute," Dad calls before I can get my body to follow the foot. I sigh, closing the door again. Dad's face is unreadable, his hands folded on the desk. Mom glances between us, looking shocked. "What is a Kitsune doing in our lands?"

"I don't know. She wasn't conscious and if it'd been a second later, I probably wouldn't have seen her, and she would have drowned." I explain more, describing the muscled forest creature, watching her fall and discovering her injuries next to the dead body of the beast.

"The poor dear." Mom sympathetically puts a manicured hand to her chest, her light blue eyes, the same as mine, peer at dad.

Dad runs a hand through his short black hair, the hair falling perfectly back into place. "I know you said she came close to death, but it concerns me that a Kitsune was in our borders, so close to our home at that." Mom's gaze drops. It's not talked about, but the distrust between our kind and Kitsune happened when my mom was a young girl.

"I'll take full responsibility for her." I put a fist over my chest. "If she does anything suspicious, I'll accept the consequences. If she does turn out to be dangerous, I'll figure out what to do with her."

Dad crosses his arms leaning back in his leather chair. He stares at me while contemplating the situation. "Very well. I would like to meet her when she is able to join us for a meal. I'll pass the word around of our… unusual guest."

My shoulders relax. "Thank you, father, mother." I bow. I don't need to look to know dad rolls his eyes. Grinning, I exit the study.

Waiting in the hall, Kai pushes off the wall, walking with me. "They didn't actually allow her to stay, did they?"

"They did." My gaze drifts to him, slowing my pace. I want to check on the girl, but I don't want to take Kai to her. He's my best friend, but he'd make a terrible first impression.

"Please tell me they warned you of the dangers."

"We all already know the dangers of strangers."

"Not just a stranger. A Kitsune. What is she even doing here? What if she's come to kill you or His Majesty?"

"She won't." I don't know why I have confidence in this. It is a possibility. Even if she wasn't a Kitsune. There's plenty who aim to take our lives. We don't have good relations with the Kitsune of Viararia Kingdom, but I haven't considered it that terrible. Others, like Kai, would disagree with me.

"You think saving her will change whatever she's set out to do?"

"I'll deal with it if the time comes. It'll be fine, Kai. It's not like I haven't dealt with assassins before. I'll keep an eye on her."

"Just don't make me say 'I told you so' over your corpse." Kai sighs heavily, shaking his head, short strands of his auburn hair brushing across his forehead.

I playfully punch his arm, smirking. "You can write it on my tombstone."

"Not funny." He glares, making me laugh.

Finally, I ditch him at my room. He has training to get to. I know it's not right, but I rummage through the backpack. There's paper, a set of clothes, dried flowers, little black pouches, and a box with jars safely sectioned off from each other. Peering at the writing on white labels, I recognize a few names, leading me to believe they are all poisons. I replace the box, bags, paper and clothes back into the backpack.

I sigh heavily, slumping onto my bed, knowing Kai is right. This supports his assassin claim, because why else would she have these in her bag? Her target is either me or my parents. Yet, I can't bring myself to say anything. It'll be our little secret. I'll keep my word, take responsibility for her, and protect my parents.

Heading back out toward the infirmary, I peek into the room across from mine. There's a desk in the corner, a night stand by the four post bed that lays bare, and an armoire with its doors left open, revealing an empty inside. I should see about filling it for her. Leona is going to be ecstatic about having a new girl to dress up.

I knock on the doctor's door before entering. The room smells of alcohol and sanitation. The girl is lying on the bed, eyes closed, lips slightly parted as slow, steady breaths pass through them. There's a concerning pink to her pale cheeks. Her hair nearly blends into the fresh white pillow and the tip of her tail pokes out from under clean sheets. Her shoulders are covered by a baby blue shirt they must have changed her into. The soaked cloak is hung on a hook beside the bed.

"Did everything go well?" I cross the room to the bed.

Dr. Burgess sits at his desk, filling a prescription I assume is for the girl. Sonya isn't in sight. He swivels around, his chair squealing. He stands politely with his hands folded behind him. "I believe so, Sir. She's lost a lot of blood, but appears stable now. The stitches should dissolve in a few weeks, and as long as she doesn't strain herself too much and takes proper care of the wounds, she'll be fine. It's all up to time now on when and how fast she recovers." His gaze drifts to the unconscious girl with a hint of disgust.

My fingers lightly brush hair from her forehead, hair now dry. Warm with fever. "That's better than I initially expected." Her ears twitch, bringing a smile to my lips. She looks peaceful sleeping there.

Dr. Burgess watches me with curious, old eyes, readjusting his glasses. "She's quite lucky you were there. She would not have made it on her own."

I pet her head, enjoying the way her soft, snow white ears fold back. "Will you send for me when she wakes?"

"As you wish, Sir Sylas Ambrose." He bows respectfully.

I should go to my own study and start on the pile of work I know is waiting for me there. Intending to waste time, I snatch the cape from the hook and cross back through the manor, passing my study to find the bedroom has been seen to. New violet, silk sheets and comforter cover the bed with fluffy pillows at the head. I drape the cape over the chair at the desk to continue drying, slipping across the hall to grab her other belongings from my room. I think she'll be pleased to see them.

Having run out of excuses to avoid work, I head to my study, passing paintings on either side of the wall that I've seen hundreds of times. There's a different theme in each hall. We rotate them every few months with ones in storage.

A young maid steps out of a room, carrying a basket of linen. She gives me a respectful nod and a small curtsy, continuing on her way. Maybe I have one more task that can distract me from my work a little longer. I call out to her. She pauses, glancing over her shoulder.

"Good day, Sir Sylas Ambrose." She beams, her bubbly personality radiating from her as usual. It's hard for anyone not to return her smile. She's the youngest maid working here, getting the job thanks to her sister's request

"Good day to you, Miss Marie. Are you very busy?" I peer down at the basket.

"I only have a few chores today. What can I do for you, Sire?"

"Could I borrow you for a moment?"

"Let me drop this at the wash and I'm all yours."

The scullery is in the back lower side of the manor. I wait outside the door while she does what she needs to, the sound of other maids working and giggling coming from inside. When she comes out, she dips her head, letting me know she is ready. We walk down the hall in quiet company, pausing before a cyan colored door. I knock twice, not receiving an answer. Cracking the door open, I excuse myself before slipping in with Marie.

The spacious room is brightly lit. One wall is covered with rolls of fabrics of all colors and textures. A short round platform sits in the middle of the room, and a section is blocked off in the back for changing. Leona's distracted, bent over her desk, sketching a new dress. Sketches cover the wall in front of her, some notes pinned around them. Beside the desk are prongs protruding from the wall holding various ribbons and thread.

She finally turns around, startling at the sight of us as we approach her. Her face starts to light up. "My, this is a surprise. What brings you to my little workshop, Sir Sylas?" She stands, sticking the pencil in her dark brown bun with others. She politely curtsies as is custom. She glances at Marie with kind eyes.

"I have an unexpected guest who will be staying with us for an uncertain amount of time. She is currently recovering in the infirmary, so I asked Marie to come here in her stead." She peers up at me curiously. "I believe they're about the same size, at least to get something for her to change into. I can bring her by when she is well enough to get more accurate measurements." I hold my hand out, estimating the girl's height from how she fit in my arms, trusting Leona can figure something out. She's wonderful at her job and has been our seamstress since I was a baby.

Leona's golden brown eyes brighten excitedly. "Certainly! What style of dress does the young lady like? Short, long, poofy, straight? Does she enjoy sparkles? What about lace?"

I chuckle, taking a step back, rubbing the back of my neck. The shorts and plain shirt she wore gave little to no indication of what kind of fashion she may be into. "Let's keep it simple for now. Would you mind making a dress for Marie as well? A thank you for assisting."

Marie gasps, blush seeping into her cheeks. "Oh, no. It's no problem. I'm happy to help."

"Nonsense! What girl doesn't love a new dress?" Leona grabs Marie's hand enthusiastically, pulling her to the platform. She hasn't ever turned down an opportunity to create something new for someone.

An easier smile slips across my face. "I'll leave you to it then. If you could take the dress to room two-eighteen, please. Thank you, Leona."

She gives a dismissive wave, a cloth tape measure in hand. I reluctantly head toward my study to wait for the mysterious girl to wake.

Chapter Three
Snowdrops

These flowers symbolize hope, purity, rebirth, and new beginnings. All parts of it is toxic to consume, causing nausea, vomiting, diarrhea, abdominal pain, drooling, and in-coordination. It is used in folk medicine for pain and headaches.

Lily

      Warmth envelopes my body, a thin fabric draped over me. The bed is firm, but comfier than my cot. I'm not in my room. My head feels heavy, cloudy. My body isn't much better, like immovable lead. Pain throbs at my core, giving me a sense of dread. *Where am I?*

      The light isn't directly overhead, but the room is bright, causing me to squint. The ceiling is white. The walls are cream. I don't recognize it. It takes all my will to get my body up on my elbow, groaning with groggy effort. I press the ball of my palms against my eyes, head spinning.

      "So, you're awake."

I flinch, sitting up quickly, too quickly. Cringing, I curl into myself, clutching my side. With the pain comes my memory. The beast, the cliff, the water. I thought I was dead.

"You shouldn't move so suddenly. You'll open your stitches." The male voice scolds, laced with irritation.

I peer up, finding a short man with glasses in a doctor's uniform, glaring at me. I blink, trying to clear my head. Taking in the rest of my surroundings, I've come to the conclusion I'm in an infirmary. The question is where. The closest place was… I stare at the man. He walks over, making a gesture with his hand that he wants to look at my wound.

I attempt to be subtle when I sniff to see if I'm right, sitting back and lifting my shirt enough to reveal my stomach and side where the gouges are. He pokes around my wounds, three hole up my left side, one at my ribs and the lowest one on my hip. A whimper escapes as I wince. The man starts going over care treatments in a chiding manner. I know all this already, but I stay quiet while my mind swims.

Panic bubbles within. He's a Corvum. I've found my way in, but what are they going to do to me? I also don't have anything on me anymore. How do I expect to carry out my mission? I should have died. I'm dead anyways if I return without carrying out the assignment. *What punishment will I receive?* Tears begin to swell in my eyes.

A scent unlike anything I've smelt before wafts into the room with a young lady carrying a couple bowls. Steam comes from the food within the bowls. My mouth instantly waters, stomach growling. Soft brown eyes flicker to me. I snap my mouth shut, pretending I wasn't just drooling.

"Oh! You're awake. Are you hungry?" Her voice is sweet, a long ponytail of wheat colored hair swishing behind her. She hands a bowl to the doctor. My body stiffen as she approaches me, making my new stitches ache. "Here, have it. I can get myself another bowl."

I peer at the soup giving off a savory scent, then up into kind brown eyes, brown like the earth. There's no hate or disgust in the way she's looking at me, not like the doctor. I hold out my hands, and she places the warm bowl in them. Hesitantly, I take a bite of something round and doughy. It's good. So good. I can't contain my tail thumping happily under the sheet, almost forgetting about the pain in my side. Almost.

The girl giggles. "I'm glad you like it. I'll get myself another serving." She turns to the doctor who is watching with disapproving eyes. "Should I inform Sir Sylas Ambrose as well?"

"Yes," The doctor drawls.

I indulge myself in the mysterious food, savoring every bite. It's thicker than soup I've have before. The spices are like nothing I've tasted before. It's creamy and there's chunks of chicken in it. I can't get enough of the dough lumps. If this ends up being my last meal, I would not be mad about it.

Ears twitch with the sound of the door opening, a woodsy yet papery scent drifting in. I feign disinterest, but goosebumps prickle my skin in anticipation. A weird reaction. Focus on the food. The bowl is nearly empty. *Do I eat weird? Stop thinking.*

"Glad to see you're still kicking." The voice is light and playful.

I tear my gaze from the bowl, peering up into blue skies that take my breath away. Pursing my lips together, my gaze drops to the collar of his navy blue shirt. The shirt along with his black pants are clean and pressed. Different from the casual attire Sonya is wearing.

He must be someone of importance. I hide the fear of wondering what they're going to do to me.

"Who are you?" I force a cold sharpness into my voice, setting the spoon down.

"My name's Sylas. Will you tell me yours?" He cocks his head ever so slightly, curiously, the midnight black hair pulled into a low ponytail brushing across the back of his neck. The name sounds familiar. I debate the consequences of giving him my name.

I turn my head with a "humpf," returning to finish the delicious food in front of me. I don't think I have much time left with it and who knows when I'll taste something like it again, if ever. He lets out a soft exhale I barely catch, but it sounds like a chuckle. My cheeks begin to feel warm. *Do I have a fever?*

"You should show more respect to someone who saved your life." The doctor scolds, glaring at me through his round glasses that make his whole face look round like an egg. I return the scowl, easier than looking at the man standing at my bedside.

I spare Sylas another glance out of the corner of my eyes. My code name is on my tongue. An easy disguise. "It's Zily."

Sylas' smile grows, shining in his eyes and warming the air around him. "I have a room prepared for you during your stay here." He turns toward the doctor.

My head spins with his words. A room? Not a cell? Stay? Like I'm a guest? Not a killer. Mixed emotions flood my chest, coursing through my veins. Excitement and relief; I won't be tortured and maybe I can taste more delicious food. The mission can still be carried out, which in of itself brings waves of emotions. Relief and dread. It would have been better if I drowned. I rub my forehead, a headache growing. I definitely have a fever.

"She should be fine as long as she takes it easy." He gives me a stern look, one of a doctor to their patient, not a Corvum to a Kitsune.

Sylas nods, the back of his broad shoulder to me. The shirt doesn't do much in the way of hiding the toned muscle down his back and forearms. He holds out his hand and the doctor passes over a bag with small bottles and gauze in it. Medicines. I wonder if he gave me something for the pain in there. Antibiotics most likely, but pain pills would be a blessing.

Sylas turns to me again. I look away, flinching when he reaches down, taking the empty bowl from my lap. I don't know what I expected.

"Oh, Sir Sylas Ambrose! Don't worry about that. Sonya can get it when she gets back." The doctor rushes to take the bowl from him.

My head snaps up as I stare at the man with bright blue eyes and a pleasant face. The name clicks into place in my memories. The way the doctor talks to him with respect. I want to laugh. Or shake my head. My target, the one I am to dispose of, is none other than my savior. Oh, the irony. How he will regret saving me.

"Thank you." He shifts his gaze back to me, his eyes trailing over me. I stiffen. "So, what do you say? Should I escort you to your room now?" He offers me his hand.

I stare at the open palm. Do I want to get up and move with the pain in my side and the way my head feels like it has rocks in it? Absolutely not. Do I want to stay here with the doctor glaring at me? Also, no. I've dealt with severe pain before and was forced to move while experiencing it. The pain is bad, but not crippling. I can stand on my own.

Ignoring the hand, I slowly shift to the edge of the bed, feet dangling over the edge. Sliding down, I assess my body. I feel sturdy enough that I take a step toward the door with a smirk.

The room spins so fast. Sharp pain shoots up my spine, causing a moment of darkness. I blink hard, staring at the floor. My feet are beneath me and I'm still standing. A strong hand grasps my arm. Another arm around my waist, hand splayed out against my stomach in case I go down again.

Aware of my surroundings again, blush burns my cheeks. I pull away, releasing his shirt that I grabbed on my descent, careful not to trigger another wave of dizzy nausea. I steal a glance up into worried, concerned eyes. A different color, but they remind me of Callie when she worries, and I don't like that. He opens his mouth to question. I continue to walk toward the door like nothing happened, grateful it doesn't happen again. One hand remains pressed against my side, holding pain and nausea at bay. I do not want to puke up the amazing food I just ate.

The hall is bright. A painting of a single rose in a vase on a windowsill at dusk stares back at me. The details, all the little strokes on the petals leave me in awe. I've never painted, but I do sketch. I can appreciate the work put into this. The door to the infirmary closes. I force myself to turn, to look up at Sylas. He's really tall. No. I know it's me that's short. Perhaps it's a combination to make the height difference. He waves his hand down the hall.

"This way."

There are more paintings lining the hall he escorts me down. I look at each one, slowing our pace to keep the pain from flaring up. He doesn't rush me, admiring paintings he's must have looked at every day of his life. I pretend not to be overly aware of his presence behind me, or that the reason his shirt is now untucked is because of me. The pictures change as we round a corner, becoming more abstract and losing my interest.

Finally, he stops in front of a door. "Are you doing alright?" He asks in a low voice, eyeing my side. I drop my hands, rolling my eyes in response. An amused smirk forms on his lips. "This will be your room during your stay here." He opens the door, gesturing for me to go in.

I step past him into a spacious room, as large as Decan's workshop. I have never seen a bedroom so big before. There's a desk with a pretty little lamp with purple orchid design on the lampshades on top in the corner near the door. There's a vanity in the back alcove where another door is open on the side. A mahogany armoire sits across from the bed. The bed would take up the whole space in Callie's and my room. It's covered in beautiful violet satin sheets. A fruity perfume fills the air.

My eyes land on the oddity in the room. A worn dirty brown backpack lays on top of the bed beside a short sword. I gasp, unable to hide my joy, forgetting the pain and the one beside me. A squeal escapes as I run, staggering to the bed. I hug the gift I thought I lost, my tail swishing uncontrollably behind me.

Shuffling reminds me of his presence and that he must be the one who grabbed it for me. I spin around, beaming at him. He watches me curiously, eyebrow twitching. I don't know how to thank him. How awful it felt thinking about having to tell my friends I lost the gift they worked so hard to make me only days after receiving it. Dread hits me like a brick. This man saved me. Found my most beloved gift. My collection. And I will have to kill him in order to keep it all. Does he know about my collection sitting inside my bag?

I settle back into myself. "Thank you." It's all I can offer.

"Is it special to you?" His eyes flicker to the sword. I wonder if it's safe to share this piece of me with him. He'll be dead within the week. It'll be fine.

"Yes. My friends made it specially for me." I glance away, feeling my cheeks heat up. "That's why it's not as heavy as a normal sword." I quietly confess, hinting at my lack of skill, eyeing the sword on his belt.

"It's finely crafted." He remarks.

"It's double-sided to help make up for the lack of weight." I laugh nervously. "I'm… I'm not great with swords, but as you know," I gently place my hand over my side, "it's dangerous out there."

Sylas chuckles, understandingly. "That it is, but you did manage to take out the beast, and you are still around. You're safe here, so get some rest." He reaches out, patting my head. I flinch, squeezing my eyes shut. He places the bag the doctor gave him on the nightstand before heading for the door. "Have a goodnight. I'll wake you for breakfast in the morning."

He strolls out with ease, hands in his pockets. My energy goes with him. I stare down at my sword, processing his last words. Did I really manage to kill it? I really need to thank Callie and Decan again for the sword. Giving the sword another squeeze, I silently send a message through the universe that I'll return to them.

The sword slides under my pillow. It's a habit to sleep with a weapon within reach. Digging through my bag, I check to make sure the jars in the bottom of my bag are intact. The bottom drawer of the night stand is just big enough to house my pack.

Clutching my side, feeling woozy, I rummage through what the doctor sent me with. A heavy sigh of relief comes with a bottle of pain pills. He took the time to write me instructions. There's plastic with some kind of adhesive I can stick over my wounds to be able to bathe with ease. He may not have liked me, but he's a good doctor. I respect that.

The door in the back of the room leads to a bathroom. Everything sparkles. The counter is made of white, shiny porcelain and the floor is marble separated into large squares by dark wood with a glossy finish. A shower stands in the back corner with glass doors so clear it's hard to tell there are doors at all. In the center of the room is an iron footed tub with a spongy charcoal outside and white inside. I gape at it. I haven't ever taken a bath before. Showers in taverns I've stayed in, sure. I've bathed in shallow creeks before. But not a hot bath. There are short shelves with little bottles of shampoo, conditioner, soap and other additives on the wall directly above it.

I hold my side. I'd love to give it a try, but I'm exhausted and riding the line of nausea. The blood in my fur needs to go, so a quick shower is in order. Once my tail is snow white again, and my hair feels fluffy soft, I venture back into the bedroom, a towel wrapped around me. A silk green nightgown is sprawled across the foot of the bed. I wonder if I can wear it. Sitting on the edge of the bed, I pick at the edge of the plastic. The adhesive does well sticking to my skin, making me wince as I peel it off. The wound is tend and sore. Thankfully, the nightgown slips on with ease. It's smooth, a new texture against my skin.

As my hands glide down the new fabric, I notice something on the chair by the desk. A giddy feeling bubbles up inside upon closer inspection. It's Callie's cape. It's here too. I didn't lose anything. I truly can't believe it. Holding it up, there's no sign of it being stained either. Did they wash it? I pull it close, breathing in deeply, coughing afterwards. It smells strongly of cleaner and perfume to try to cover the cleaning scent. I bet it was that girl. She seemed really nice. I have to remember to thank her when I see her again.

Leaving the cloak on the chair, I climb into the large bed, sinking into the comfy covers. The pillow is cool against my warm face. It's like laying in a cloud. I don't remember the last time I've slept so well.

Chapter Four
Chamomile

It's commonly used to make tea that has a calming effect. It is also used in lotions and creams to help with irritated skin like sunburns and eczema.

Sylas

Groggily, I peer at the maid standing just inside my bedroom. The morning knock woke me, and she told me how much time there is before breakfast. Now she waits patiently to be dismissed. She won't leave until I do so while sitting up, a way to make sure I won't simply go back to sleep. If I roll over, she'll move to the other side of the bed, continuing to stare at me. They were ordered to do this when I didn't get up one morning as a teenager. After all these years, they continue to do so.

Sitting up, I wave my hand toward her. She curtsies, wishing me a good day, and leaves, the door clicking shut behind her. I rub my face, memories of the previous day returning. Quickly, I toss the sheets off, getting to my feet.

I step into the hall in my satin blue pajamas. I knock on the door lightly. There's no answer. Cracking the door open, I peek inside. Zily is curled up in the middle of the bed, blanket tucked under her chin. She looks so at peace, ears laid back, lips slightly parted, face relaxed. I quietly close the door, deciding to let her sleep a little longer.

In my room, I cross the spacious area to a large white oak door. The private restroom is off to the right, and the wash goes off to the left. There's a rack in the corner to hang clean clothes to keep them dry, a basket on the floor for dirty clothes. Towels hang on the wall near the bath embedded in the floor full of water constantly being cycled and cleansed.

I dress casually for breakfast, pressed pants and a maroon button down. Most days are a simple pair of pants and a button down. There's not a need for more when I'm not attending meetings and it's not audience day. I fix the collar before rolling up my sleeves. It helps during the warmer months. It drove my father crazy, but after years of disputes over it, I continue to shorten my sleeves. The same with how long I keep my hair. A compromise is to pull it back into a neat, low ponytail. My sword gets fastened to my waist last, a constant companion.

With a glance at the clock above the short couch by the small bookshelf, I cross the hall, knocking on the door. Once again, there's no response. I ease into the room. She's rolled over, only her white ears poking out from under the blanket. It feels a shame to wake her. She should eat and I promised to introduce her to my parents.

I reach for her shoulder to give her a little nudge. A hand suddenly flies out of the covers, grabbing my wrist. Black marbles glare up at me. A heavy sigh escapes her lips. Releasing my wrist, she rubs her hand down her face.

"Good morning. Sorry, I didn't mean to startle you. I knocked." My smile slips noticing the way she's hugging herself. Is she in pain?

"I know." She pushes hair out of her face, tilting her head back to peer up at me with tired eyes. There's a soft pink to her cheeks. My hand automatically reaches toward her forehead. She swats me away before I can feel it. "If you would leave, I can get dressed."

"Do you need help changing your bandages?" I offer, taking a step back to give her space.

She shakes her head, pushing her hair out of her face again. It lays disorganized around her ears. She glances around the room like she forgot where she was. "No, I can do it. Thank you." A mix of hard and soft edges curving her tone. I chuckle. It's hard to believe she may be here to kill me. I resist the urge to reach out and touch her again. It's strange how much I want to run my fingers through her hair, fix the strands for her.

"I'll wait in the hall then. Don't forget to take your medicine as well." I raise a hand, turning to vacate the room. Leaning against the wall outside, a few servants pass by, going to begin their daily tasks. I give small nods, putting on the charm in response to their polite greetings. Their eyes dart to the door beside me, to the girl they know is inside. Rumors quickly spread thanks to the servants.

I straighten with the sound of the door opening. Zily walks out, holding her side, ears drooped. Her hands slide down the yellow summer dress as she inclines her head to look at me, hair falling away from her face. Her tail looks like a fluffy white cloud twitching behind sunshine. The bright color compliments her fair skin. Under the skirt, she's wearing her short brown boots. It doesn't seem to bother her that they don't match, but I'm sure Leona will find her some shoes once she sees her.

"You look lovely." Zily glances away, ears perking, trying unsuccessfully to look cold. Her cheeks color like blooming roses. The subtle movement of her tail tells me she's happy. "Shall we go to breakfast?" I offer her my arm. She tilts her head, eyebrows scrunching together, confused by the gesture.

Zily ignores me, walking down the hall a ways before waiting for me to take the lead. I let my steps linger, aware of her shorter legs. She pauses before a painting, staring at a field of flowers at dawn, a cabin on a hill in the distance. Another distracts her a little farther down, this one a large tree with blossoms changing to apples.

"Do you like paintings?" I stop behind her, gazing at the picture as well.

She doesn't answer right away, starting to turn and continue down the hall. "Maybe."

I fall in beside her, walking casually with one hand in my pocket, the other on the pommel of my sword. "Do you like flowers?"

"Yes."

My lips curl into a smile. "I know where I should take you then," I say more to myself.

On the ground floor, at the end of the main hall, past the foyer, we stop in front of a pair of double doors. I open them with one hand, waving my other hand for her to go in first, following right behind her.

I nearly run into her. Zily freezes right inside the dining room. For me, it's the usual sight. Dad is at the head of the long dark oak wood table, mother to his right. My seat is across from her.

When we have guests, I take the seat at the other end of the table from father. From her perspective, two powerful royals are staring her down. I wonder if I should have warned her. It's too late now. I put a hand on the small of her back, encouraging her forward.

"Good morning, father, mother. I trust you slept well. Let me introduce you; this is Zily. Zily, my mother, Lady Eleanor Marrilynn Caraway and my father, His Majesty, Reuben Esther Caraway." I meet my father's gaze, silently telling him to be nice in the same way he usually tells me to behave around guests. Zily presses back against my hand. I grab the top of the full back cherry wood chair next to my seat, pulling it out for her. Her gaze darts to me. I can't read the look of pitch night eyes.

"Good morning, Sy. Good morning, Zily." Mom looks friendly, though her crystal blue eyes observe Zily's every movement cautiously.

"G-good morning!" Zily squeaks, giving an awkward bow before dropping into the cushioned charcoal grey leather seat. Her face turns a strawberry red. I push the chair in for her. Her tail wraps around her while she strokes it nervously.

Dad doesn't pretend to smile for our guest, gaze focused on her. He didn't turn her away because of her injury and I vowed to take responsibility for her. I'm grateful for their trust in me, though I haven't decided what to do about the poisons I found in her bag. Zily keeps her head down. There could be another explanation for the poisons.

Servants begin to bring out our plates. Mom continues attempting to speak with Zily. "I trust Dr. Burgess has taken good care of you, yes?" Her voice is light and sweet like honey, laced with curiosity. She probably hopes to gain information as to what Zily was doing when the incident occurred. Zily looks like she would like to hide under the table. This may have been a mistake.

She swallows, lifting her gaze. "Yes. Yes, he's a good doctor, I believe." The genuineness in her voice surprises me. I saw the way Dr. Burgess looked at her.

"He's the best there is. That's why he's our personal physician," Dad states with an air of warning.

I shoot a look at my dad who turns his head away to thank the butler setting a plate in front of him. Zily shifts uncomfortably, the tips of her ears drooping slightly. She quietly thanks the butler. The main dish is two round puffed up dough, suspending sausage, bacon and baked eggs in the center. On the side is a small plate with a slice of cheese quiche and a tiny bowl of berries.

Father and mother don't delay, picking up their utensils. I use my fork to cut a small piece. Zily hesitates, giving the food a funny look. She mimics my cut, taking a bite. Her eyes sparkle, taking another bite eagerly. The delight on her face is nearly as bright as her dress, her tail softly patting against the seat beside her thighs.

"Do you like it?" Worry slowly slips away. She nods enthusiastically, looking at me with a pretty little smile.

My parents' stare, shocked by the sudden openness on Zily's face. The more she ate, the more she relaxed. She's not good at keeping the walls she pretends to have up. Mom makes small inquiries throughout breakfast. Nothing too suspicious that would change the mood. Mostly she asks about breakfast itself, foods Zily has had before and what she normally likes.

Zily hasn't had breakfast like this before. She's never even heard of quiche. She ate bacon twice in her life. The best food she remembers was at an inn she stayed at during her travels; it was a breakfast bowl with eggs, ham, peppers and potatoes. A look is exchanged between mom and dad at the mention of traveling.

"Do you travel often?" Mom asks innocently.

"As much as I can." Zily's voice lowers, a bit of shadow creeping back in. I change topics, wanting to keep the sparkle in her eyes.

All in all, breakfast is rather pleasant. Dad kept his political polite face on. They wish us a good day as I escort Zily out of the dining room first. I half expect her to rebuild the wall, but she looks up at me with her dark eyes full of glimmers of starlight, smiling. She brushes hair from her face, her tail curled upward.

"Now what?" She asks, eagerly curious.

Pleased and taking advantage of the opportunity, I make an offer. "Would you like a tour of the grounds?"

The subtle tail swish answers me. I chuckle, motioning for her to follow. She falls in step beside me, a little bounce to her stride. I decide to start with the upper floor. I want to make sure she remembers how to get back to her room. I motion toward my room in case she needs to find me. Her head swivels between the two rooms, raising an eyebrow. A small frown forms.

Yes, I've made it easy for you to kill me. Should I mention I don't have guards at night either? Mom and dad do. They probably added to them with a Kitsune in the mansion. Guards don't generally follow us around the grounds, but they are everywhere and constantly on alert. We've passed a couple on our way here, their gazes taking note of the Kitsune beside me.

I glance down at the girl with the night eyes in her sunshine dress, admiring paintings on the walls. I want to believe she won't do as expected. I'd rather become friends. It's my first time meeting a Kitsune. It's this optimism that has led to talks with the Zeneth kingdom. Perhaps I should speak with mom about the Viararia Kingdom. She used to have a friend there when she was a girl.

At the end of the hall, I open a large door. "And this is our library."

The light blue walls are lined with bookshelves filled with all kinds of books, from history to fairytales. One wall has a large window bringing in sunlight. There are a few velvet wingback chairs and a small maroon couch with a couple decorative pillows in the center of the room. A long, short glass table sits in front of the couch.

Zily's eyes grow wide for a moment before they cloud over. Her ears droop, flickering back for a moment and she turns to leave. "You may come here whenever you feel like," I add quickly.

She spins back, ears perking up again. "Really?" She whispers like she couldn't stop the question from escaping.

I grin with a nod, watching her reevaluate the library. Her tail wags. It's not slow and subtle. It's pure open excitement, gaze darting around the room, cataloging where she may start. I make a mental note of the new information. She likes flowers and books, and maybe paintings.

Continuing the tour, I lead her to my study. It's smaller than my dad's, but I have it set up similarly. There's a short bookshelf to the right with a few decorations on top. A statue of a fiery cat-like creature. A blue crystal held up by glass prongs given as a gift from one of my uncles, a Duke, for my twenty-fifth birthday. Last is a brown vase with darker brown swirls going around it. On the opposite wall is a small couch the color of chestnut. There's a light blue pillow and a throw blanket on it. My desk faces away from the window, my high back black chair turned away from when I last stood from it. Papers litter the top of the desk. Heat rises up my neck.

"If you're looking for me, this is usually a good place to start." I close the door quickly. She raises an eyebrow, but doesn't say a word.

I take her down the other set of stairs than the ones we used for breakfast, casually mentioning the paintings we pass since she has already shown an interest in them. Most of them have settings at dawn or dusk, my great-grandmother's favorite time of day. She adored painting, creating nearly all the works we have decorating the halls. Zily stares in amazement, brushing stray wavy strands of hair from her face.

My dad's study is on the ground floor almost directly below mine, a couple of guards standing outside of it. They watch Zily with narrowed eyes. She seems to nod her approval, her dark eyes lifting to me. I wish she would voice her questions. Her eyes practically say her thoughts. Why don't I have guards watching me? My hand rests on the pommel of my sword in answer. I swear she snorts.

A little farther down the hall, I open the doors to the throne room. It's a large room with tiles of sparkling white and powder blue. There are three seats at the end of the room, each of equal size but decorated differently for both of my parents and myself. Dad has emeralds lining the headrest, the back engraved with a sword through a crown. Mom has rubies with a round shield with a fiery bird etched into hers. I chose blue topaz for mine, and wings in the clouds on the back. Unoriginal, but I love the freedom the sky provides us. Each has colored cushioned seats.

Zily lingers in the doorway, gawking. I like watching the way she takes in everything, finding the things that interest her most. We glance into a few other rooms, a couple small sitting rooms, a drawing room and a lounge, so she can learn her way around. I point out the aquamarine crystals embedded in the walls every so often. If you touch them, a servant will be summoned to help.

I pause outside of Leona's work room, mentioning she should visit her later to get accurate measurements. Zily runs her hands down her dress. "Are they only going to be dresses?" Her voice is soft, drained of energy, cheeks flushed pink.

"I'm sure she will make you pants if you request it." She dips her head, a hand lifting to rub her eyes, the other one wrapped around her. "Are you alright? Should we take a break?" Worry that this may be too much walking for her and guilt that I hadn't considered her injury or fever while dragging her across the mansion washes over me.

She shakes her head dismissively, waving a hand in the air for added effect. "I'm fine." She's obviously hiding her discomfort. She points down the hall to a set of large, embellished double doors. "What's that?" Her attempt to distract me.

With a flourished wave, I let her believe she won, walking close to her. "Those? They lead to our ballroom."

"Ballroom?" She repeats as we reach the doors.

I step in front, placing my hands on either door, a beveled gold design running down them mirroring each other, shoving them open simultaneously. It's the largest room in the mansion, second being the throne room, third the banquet hall, and finally the formal dining room, different from the dining room we normally eat in.

Round tables with simple white clothes covering them scatter the outskirts of the dance floor. Three thrones sit atop a platform where my parents and I can observe our guests. I don't spend much time there, often walking around or dancing. There's a section to the side open for the live band. On the other far side of the room, the wall is covered in drapes of royal blue, sky blue and forest green, our family colors. There's a couple sets of glass doors that lead out to a quiet little courtyard with a couple trees and benches under them and a gazebo.

Zily steps into the room, slowly spinning around, taking it all in. I wonder what she's thinking about. I take advantage of her momentary distraction to press my hand against a diamond shaped aquamarine crystal in the wall right outside the doors. A maid shows soon after, curtsying out of respect. I request to have lunch for two taken to the sitting room. When I return my attention to Zily, she's staring up at the sparkling chandelier.

"Do you like to dance?" I meet her in the middle of the dance floor.

She turns back to me, a blank expression on her face, like she had been somewhere far away. She blinks a few times before shaking her head. "I don't know. I've never danced before." She looks sad, taking the room in once more.

"I can teach you." I hold out my hand, hoping the stars will return to her eyes.

Zily peers at me over her shoulder, one ear down, hands folded behind her back. I inch closer, thinking she may take up my offer. Her dark eyes flicker down to my hand. She frowns.

"No." The word is soft, reluctant but definite. She strides past me with brisk steps. "Where to now?"

I frown, wishing to know what's going through her mind. I close the doors. She refuses to look back at them, like it pained her. "Now we stop for lunch." Her ears perk up, but she continues avoiding looking at me.

I lead her down the hall, opening up a door to the room I had asked for lunch to be brought to. I'm pleased to see a tray waiting for us. There's a pair of bowls of zesty chicken salad with a cup of pudding for dessert and a pitcher of lemonade with a couple glasses on a silver base glass table. Two cyan blue chairs sit angled toward each other and a matching short couch.

Zily sighs into one of the seats. I stand in front of her, staring down. She tilts her head in question, brushing hair out of her face. She flinches when I reach for her, pressing my hand to her forehead. Warm. The fever is still there. She swats my hand away, glaring at me.

"I'm fine," She growls, though there is no bite to the sound. She picks up one of the bowls, sniffing it.

I ease into the other chair, shifting my sword to the side, watching her carefully. Maybe I should call it a day. It might have been too early to give her a tour of the whole mansion. There's paperwork I didn't finish yesterday waiting for me too. I want to show her the garden, though.

Her tail casually thumps the seat, the corner of her lips curving up. I pour us some lemonade, grabbing my own bowl. "We'll go outside after this, alright?" Her head bobs. I'm not sure she even heard me, eyes trained on the food.

We walk at a leisurely pace. I don't want to push her too much. We pass by a tree with a bench beneath it. A lady on break is reading a book there. She glances up, giving me a polite smile. I return it. She does a double take, spotting Zily beside me, clear distaste and judgment filling her eyes. Zily scowls back. She huffs, marching ahead.

We round the corner to the side of the building where our garden grows. Zily gasps, hand shooting up to cover her mouth. A grin spreads across my face, pleased with the reaction. She runs ahead, slipping around the brush. Her hand reaches out to touch orange petals, moving further in, trailing fingertips delicately across the rainbow of flowers she passes.

My feet follow at a slower pace, hands tucked in my pockets while she enjoys herself. I love watching the way her face glows, like sparkling powder snow in the early morning sun, moving from plant to plant, rattling off names. This is the perfect spot to end the tour.

"You have chamomiles, feverfews, marigolds. Oh! And nasturtiums!" She spins around, calling to me over a couple rows of flowers. "You have a garden full of medicine!" She throws her arms in the air, her tail wagging giddily.

It's not terribly surprising that she knows the properties of some of the flowers, considering what is in her bag, but it's interesting to know that that's what excites her. Perhaps there is another explanation to the poisons inside her bag after all. I frown, noticing how her breathing has quickened, the flush in her cheeks darkening. She catches sight of a potted flower on a pedestal tucked into the bend of the garden. I meet up with her there, taking a different route. One small hand rests on the edge of the stone pillar, the other wrapped around her, pressing against her side. She peers up at me, her dark eyes lighter than I have yet to see them.

"These are midnight daffodils!" She says ecstatically. "I heard they're just discovering all the things you can do with them! The nectar they produce can be used in a multitude of medicinal remedies. The seeds are actually quite poisonous if ingested improperly, but if crushed and mixed with honey, they are great on cuts! Or if crushed with the stem and some rose petals, it could cure serious illnesses, but it has to be the right balance of ingredients. I heard they're doing research on the properties of the sweet scent they produce too." She stops, sniffing the beautiful seven blue with yellow veins petal flowers.

"You sure are knowledgeable about what I thought were simply pretty flowers." I praise, a little more than amazed by the new information. "It's hard to believe a small, pretty, little flower could hold so much wonder within it."

Zily turns toward me, beaming. "Nature is a wondrous thing. There is always something new to learn."

I chuckle in agreement. "Will you tell me more another time?"

"Sure," Zily replies cheerfully. Her smile remains, but her tail's happy swishing slows, lowering toward the ground. Her other arm snakes around her, subtly hugging herself.

"Shall we return inside?" I wave my hand in a gesture back toward the entrance. "You can come back out whenever you like." I make sure to tell her, remembering her hesitation with the library. She nods, her ears starting to droop.

We walk back to her room. I expect -hope- she takes it easy. I'll check on her in a few. Kai is seen leaving my study. I groan, knowing he must have dropped off more work for me. He waits for me, shifting his weight to peer around me.

"Where's the Kitsune?" His voice is deep, laced with malice. He's being his usual untrusting self.

I roll my eyes. "In her room. She's sick and needs rest." Papers cover my desk. I can't even tell what is new. I run a hand over my hair, messing up the neatness of the ponytail.

"Does she have guards watching her?" He follows me into the room, setting a hand on the papers he brought in. I'm silently grateful for him.

"No." I pick up the top paper. There's only two pages regarding applications to join the royal guard from new candidates that'll be graduating soon.

"You shouldn't let your killer roam free." He crosses his arms.

I sigh, wanting to dispute his paranoia. I glance out the window. It looks out on the garden. Zily's face comes to mind, making the corner of my lips twitch. I think I'll pick some flowers for her room. *Would she like that?*

"Are you listening?" Kai scolds.

I wave my hand dismissively. "It'll be alright. Zily is a nice girl."

Chapter Five
Jimson Weed

Jimson weed is highly toxic, though death by it is rare. It causes a multitude of symptoms ranging from nausea, vomiting, hallucinations, fever, blurry vision, to seizures.

Lily

Searing pain radiates from my back from the first lashing. My hands are tied around a post in the middle of the room. Stains from previous occupants cover the cobble floor. I cry out as the whip bites into my back again, tearing through my shirt and drawing blood. My blood will become another stain in this room.

I gasp for air, sobs wracking my small body. "I'm sorry!" I scream futilely. Sir Colin Eyler isn't even in the room anymore, and the man with the leather whip won't stop until he has given out the allotted punishment.

The whip whistles through the air before impact, causing my body to tense with anticipation. Another scream is wretched from my burning lungs. Tears soak my face, snot dripping from my nose. Spit flies as I cry out with another slash across my back, cutting into my shoulder.

My head begins to swim, vision blurring. I feel sick. Bile rises in my throat. I try to swallow it back down, but as fresh pain burns into me, I can't hold it down anymore. The man behind me laughs at my misery. An acidic rancid smell fills my nostril. Darkness starts to creep into my vision.

I jerk awake, sitting up quickly, new pain making me curl into myself. It's not from my back; it's on my side, reminding me it was only a dream. This time. It's the first time I felt the sting of the whip that haunts my dreams all these years later.

The blankets are soaked with sweat. My hand runs along the sheets, grounding me to the present, though if I don't accomplish my assignment, my nightmare will become my reality. Again.

Recentering myself, I glance around the room, pausing to stare at the new fixture on the nightstand. A small white vase with an assortment of brightly colored flowers. A rose, poppy, marigold, and baby's breath. It's not organized in any way, but they're beautiful and give off a nice fragrance. I stretch my hand out, gently touching the rose. Sylas must have come to check on me while I was out. The corner of my lips tug upward. How thoughtful.

I shake my head.

The idiot. Sometimes I think he understands why I'm here. Other times he looks at me with the concern and worry of a friend and does things like this. The fool.

Slowly, I slide off the bed, digging into the nightstand for some pain meds. I enjoyed the tour, but it left me sore. Sucking in a deep breath, holding my side, I walk to the washroom. Sweating during my nap left me feeling gross and sticky. Using a white cloth soaked in cold water, I rub the remnants of the nightmare away. At the door, I peek into the hall before I exit my room.

It's not like I have to sneak around. I am a guest here. A simple guest walking down the hall with no idea of where I am going. A tall man with broad shoulders, short messy auburn hair, and brown eyes hard and sturdy like a tree trunk strides down the hall opposite me. He's in a military uniform, a sword on his hip. I've seen a few guards patrolling around during the tour. His hand wraps around the handle.

I keep my head down. Everyone I've passed today has given me not so welcoming looks. He is no different. In fact, his gaze is the harshest yet, more than even the King at breakfast this morning. The King tried to be intimidating, but his eyes are too kind. Like his son's.

"Hey, you," A deep voice growls. I look back. Menacing indeed. "Stay away from him, you hear me?"

I cock my head to the side. "Or what?" I ask innocently, hands folding behind me.

He lifts his sword, a sliver of metal glistening in the light. His brown eyed scowl stabs into me. There's no doubt he could take me down easily. I'm not a swordsman; I'm a poisoner. He stalks away, ending the staring contest.

I breathe out, pushing hair from my face. My hand moves around my waist to the bandages under my dress. Guilt and regret already chill my veins for being here, but I need to return to my friends and thus I have a job to do, even if Sylas had saved my life.

I stare at the man's back, watching him disappear down the hall. I nod my head in approval. I like this man. He may very well hunt me down afterwards and dispose of me like the filth I am. I swallow, pushing away the feelings that like to creep in from time to time.

Remembering about the room Sylas told me to visit, I work to find my way to the door he pointed out. The paintings help. I didn't pay too close attention to which way we turned or how far down a hall we walked, but I remember the paintings we passed.

I'm anxious to meet the one who made this pretty yellow sun dress, my first dress I can ever recall wearing. Sylas indicated she'll make me whatever I'd like to wear. I hope whoever this Corvum woman is tolerates me enough to make another pretty dress. Does she know she made a dress for a Kitsune?

The door is on the ground floor, across from a painting of a rose laying on a window sill with a setting sun in the backdrop. My knuckles rasp against the door, soft at first with hesitation, getting louder with the realization she probably couldn't hear it. The sound becomes louder than I mean it to be, the sound of confidence that I do not feel.

"Come in!" responds a voice like a songbird, beckoning me in.

"Excuse the intrusion," I say politely, poking my head in. A strange scent hits my nose; dyes.

The room is alive with shades of every color in fabrics in a multitude of textures. I want to touch them. Where I live, every room has the most basic furniture, walls so plain and the atmosphere always cold. Here, every room has a voice, a life of its own, warm and welcoming and this room is like a glowing rainbow. My tail begins to hesitantly swish back and forth, eyes not knowing where to settle.

A woman stands in the middle of the room with her back to me. She wears a deep green, sleeveless dress with the tattoos of her blue wings poking out the top, a black apron tied around her waist. Her hair is up in two messy buns. Shiny black shoes with green flowers on the toes completes her attire.

A mannequin sits on top of a short pedestal dressed in a pretty, bright blue, summer dress. The woman is fixing the sleeves. She glances back, doing a double take, nearly dropping the pin between her teeth. I give a sheepish smile, freezing halfway across the room to her. Disappointment is ready to settle in, thinking I may not get a new dress after all.

"Oh! You must be the one Sir Sylas mentioned!" The woman mumbles around the pin. She removes it, bounding to me in a few quick strides. "I'm Leona Lancaster. Pleasure to make your acquaintance." She beams, extending her hand. With her comes the scent of tea and honey.

I relax, tail lifting slightly. The warmth of the room, her voice and smile, seeps into me, not seeming terribly phased that a Kitsune is in her room. Maybe I will have a new dress. "Z-Zily." I stumble over my name, taking her hand.

"Zily!" Leona repeats enthusiastically in her singsong voice. She places her other hand over top of our joined ones, holding on a little longer than comfortably acceptable. I wonder if I should try to pull my hand away.

Suddenly she yanks me to the small platform. I wince, sharp pain shooting out from my side. "How do you like the dress? It is a bit big on you. Not to worry! I can fix that easily. What kind of dresses do you like? Long? Short? Ones with frills? Oh! What about sequins?" In a single motion, I replace the mannequin's spot.

I grit my teeth, resisting the urge to press my hand to my wound. My fingers twitch. I can't answer her right away, though I do consider her questions. Long always looks elegant. How I would love to wear a ball gown one day. I don't think anything too tight and restricting; I like freedom of movement. I can't think of any reason I wouldn't like frills and sequins, though I've only seen them a couple of times.

A tape measure appears out of the pocket of Leona's apron. She rattles on about different material and styles of dresses. My heart pounds, carried along the excitement of her words. I'm giddy with the offer to try on and wear dresses made specifically for me.

"I don't know." I tell her honestly, matching the glow in her eyes with the swish of my tail.

It won't last, but I can be girlie for a short while. I'll tell Callie about it when I return. A fleeting thought of sneaking a dress back for her passes, but consequences chase the thought away. I never take anything back. They'll only be taken away and burned. Then the whip would return.

Leona pulls a tiny notebook and pencil out of the apron, taking down measurements. I hold my hands out for her, shifting how she asks me. Her hands run down my side, testing the looseness of the sundress. I cringe when she brushes over my wound, making her jump back.

"Sorry. Did that hurt?" Her eyes flicker over me.

I hold my side. "I have stitches here." My voice comes out breathy.

"Right. Sir Sylas mentioned you were in the infirmary. I'm sorry. I'll be more cautious." She moves closer again to finish measurements and notes. Her fingers flutter just above my skin. In order to get my waist and hip measurements, she asks me to hold the tape measure in place to avoid hurting me again. She wasn't kidding about being more cautious.

She insists I put on the blue dress, so she can make the proper adjustments. Leona likes to talk, telling me about dress ideas she has for me, for my body. She uses some words I don't understand, but I giggle along. I inform her that I won't be staying very long, to which she tells me to change a few times a day. I laugh, which feels strange with where I'm at. She suggests taking a few with me. I purse my lips together.

Leona inquires about my boots, insisting I need matching footwear. It tickles when she measures my feet and has me try on a few different kinds of shoes. She catches me when I trip over my own feet with high heels on. I have to sit for a moment after, the movement straining my side. Leona apologizes repeatedly. I run my hand over the bandages. Doesn't feel like I pulled a stitch, so it's ok.

Around dinner time, I find my way to the dining room, passing a painting of a tree in autumn losing its crisp orange leaves. I wait outside the door, hoping Sylas hasn't gone in yet. Fiddling with my blue dress, Sylas comes into view. He grins at me with his bright eyes shining.

His gaze washes over me. Feeling a little exposed, I tuck a foot behind the other, wearing white flats with tiny bows on the heels that match my dress. He stops before me, not even an arm's length away, slouching a little with his hands tucked in his pockets. He's staring at my face so intensely, his eyes don't track my hands. I go through the motion as if I had the ingredients, pretending to cover my nails with a nearly invisible liquid. All I would have to do is touch him. A cut would work best, but he would eventually touch his face, poisoning himself.

Shifting my weight, I fold my hands behind me. "Don't you know it's rude to keep a lady waiting?" I attempt to sound annoyed, but even I hear the teasing in my voice, the corner of my lips curving up. *It's because I'm anxious being in enemy territory*, I tell myself. I certainly don't want to enter the dining room alone.

Sylas puts his hands up apologetically, suppressing a chuckle. "Sorry, I was trying to finish some paperwork. Forgive me?" He slightly quirks his head to the side, reminding me of a puppy. I bet the look allowed him to get away with a lot as a kid. Was he a mischievous child? I shouldn't think about such things.

I turn without answering him, not knowing how to respond. He reaches around me, making me all too aware of his closeness at my back, the scent of paper surrounding me and opens the door. That's another moment. All I would need is a small knife and his sword would be useless. I could have stabbed him before he even drew it at this distance. I suck in a deep breath to calm my pounding heart before entering, hoping my cheeks aren't pink or that they'll believe it's from the fever.

Eleanor and Reuben are already seated, leaning toward each other, gazing with love in their eyes. They stand to greet us as we enter. Once again, Sylas pulls out the chair for me, pushing me in. Heat rises to my face, and I know I can't pretend it's the fever. I force my face into a pleasant greeting for Reuben and Eleanor. Eleanor is wearing a different dress, long and regal, a ruby red with the sleeves draped off her shoulders. I'm glad to see she also changed for dinner, feeling silly when Leona insisted I wear a different dress. Though, I wish I wore something a little fancier.

The meal comes out in three courses. They are extravagant plates that smell delicious. I shift in my seat, staring at the piece of meat before me. I wait for the royals to take the first bite, unsure what is proper, but guessing that's a safe bet. My toes curl, keeping a moan from escaping. This is becoming my favorite job assignment. I love the dessert course the most. It's a triangle slice of crunchy layers with cake filling, chocolate drizzled over it with a solid, swirly chocolate piece on top. I ignore how easy it would be to reach over and poison the whole meal, simply pretending to be reaching for the salt.

Reuben and Sylas casually discuss their day, talking in vague code. I'm not surprised there are subjects they wouldn't want me hearing. Reuben keeps glancing at me, eyebrows furrowed into a glare that won't stay in place. His eyes seem to ask if I'm ok more than anything negative. Eleanor inquires about my day. I compliment their library and garden, a little more guarded with my words as well. She's pleased to hear that my fever isn't bothering me at the moment since my nap. We giggle about Leona's enthusiasm.

Eleanor and Reuben exit the room with us this time, continuing a conversation with their son. I don't contribute much, nodding my head here and there when they glance at me. The motion is making me sleepy. I rub my eyes, daydreaming about the bath. A hand touches my forehead. I jerk back instinctively, peering up into concerned blue eyes.

"Are you doing alright?" He asks, a worried crease between his eyes.

"Yes. I'm just tired." I tell him honestly, wanting to ease the worry in his eyes. I feel my own forehead, wondering what he felt and if my fever is coming back. A little warm. I'll take more medicine when I return to my room.

"Perhaps you should go to bed early?" Sylas suggests. A lovely idea.

"You should take it easy. Pushing yourself will only prolong your recovery." Eleanor comments, taking note of the interaction.

"You are right. If you'll excuse me, I think I will retire to my room." I give a little head bow and a curtsy. *Did I do that right?* They each wish me a good night.

I gasp when I get back to the room. The armoire was left open. I can't believe Leona already dropped off a few dresses for me to choose from. A long deep green dress that sparkles. A soft pink one that's shorter in the front and longer in the back. Last is a white dress with black flowers embroidered down it. There's a pair of black flats at the bottom, next to my old boots Leona promised to return for me.

There's a new nightgown waiting for me on the foot of the bed as well. Digging through the medical bag I was given, I pull out the plastic patches to protect my wound from the water. I skip a few steps to the bathroom, instantly regretting the action. Steaming water fills the tub, floral scent floating into the air from the drops of liquid I dripped into the water from one of the bottles on the shelf. It takes on a milky color.

Sighing while slipping down into the water, I understand why baths are enjoyable. I can feel the stress melting from my muscles. The shampoo and conditioner smell wonderful too, leaving my hair and tail fluffy and shiny. I use two pure white towels to dry, wrapping one around my tail. The nightgown is silk again with a lace trim.

I make sure to take my medicine before climbing into the large comfy bed, snuggling under the covers. This job isn't like any other I've been given. I'm enjoying all the luxury I'm given with the clothes, the bed and bath, and, oh, the food. I'm grateful for this assignment, but I know it's going to haunt me for the rest of my life.

Recalling the different times and ways I could have killed Sylas today keeps me awake, staring at the ceiling. They are all of course "if onlys" and "could haves." If only I had this on me, I could have done it. I could be more prepared tomorrow. Though I do need to keep my recovery under consideration, so tomorrow probably isn't the best idea.

I wonder what my friends are up to. Has Callie been given a job? Will she be there waiting for me when I return? Is Decan remembering to eat? Sometimes he gets so engulfed in perfecting his work, he forgets to eat. He would love the food here. They both would. The meals we receive in the mess hall are always bland and flavorless. Callie and I get to try new things while out on missions. Poor Decan doesn't have an idea what bacon or quiche tastes like. Food shouldn't be too terrible to sneak back. We could eat the evidence and avoid punishment. I close my eyes, hoping the nightmares had their fill during my nap earlier.

I reach for the pain pills as soon as I wake up. Prickles of pain around the holes tell me I slept wrong. The stitches are starting to itch. The skin is pink and tender, but it looks like it's healing nicely. I put fresh layer of salve and bandages on, laying back down with my legs dangling over the edge to wait for the medicine to kick in.

Staring at the wardrobe's open doors, I peer at the dresses from under my arm draped over my eyes. I picture myself wearing each. A knock startles me into a sitting position. Curling in on myself, I grit my teeth. I really should stop doing that.

"Morning! Are you awake? Breakfast will be served soon." Sylas' voice comes through the door. The handle jiggles slightly, indicating his hand is on it.

"Yes! Alright! I'll be right out!" I call back, a bit panicked that he'll barge in. Again. I really didn't expect him to just walk in yesterday when I decided not to answer. Either time.

He doesn't enter, thankfully. I groan, sliding off the bed. The pain is numbing, but I wish the medicine would work faster. Shuffling to the wardrobe, I pluck the pink dress from the hanger. I giggle, feeling the flow of the fabric. It's like the dress has a tail like I do, the back hem brushing low on my calves, my tail slipping through the fabric at will. With the flats on, I run the brush through my hair really quick, it bouncing against my shoulders, wetting it to keep the bangs in place and the longer front strands out of my face for the time.

Sylas waits for me leaning against the wall beside the door. He nods, looking me over. For a moment, I think he disapproves of my choice of attire until I realize he's staring at my hand clutching my side. I drop it, smiling at him reassuringly. *Stop looking at me like that. I'm not unfamiliar with pain. Stop worrying.*

After a delicious breakfast where I should stop counting the ways I could have killed him since I've decided to focus on recovering for now, Sylas tells me he has some business to take care of, leaving me all alone. I watch him disappear down the hall, sighing, shoving my hair back. They need better security around here. As if summoned by my thoughts, the man with the reddish-brown hair passes by, scowling at me, heading in the same direction Sylas walked off in. I resist the urge to give him a rude gesture. I respect him, the only one that seems to actually see me as a threat. In the twenty-four hours I have been mobile, I've counted eleven times I could have poisoned Sylas and another three or so times I believe I had a chance at using other means.

Larisa Blackledge

With having free time, I venture upstairs to the library. I gaze once again at the rows of books lining the shelves against the wall. Where to begin? I freely wag my tail without anyone around to see. Trailing my finger down the spines of books as I read the titles, I pick out a couple of books.

I curl up in one of the comfy chairs, feet tucked to the side, tail draped across my lap. The book I chose is of no surprise, an herbalist's journal. A small stack of other books about poisons, herbs and flowers wait their turn on the table. I soak up the information, new and old. I want to get through as many books as I can while I'm here. Who knows when I'll have the chance to read freely like this, if ever again.

Chapter Six
Myrtle Spurge

It's a noxious weed that excretes milky latex compound that causes severe skin and eye irritation that may lead to blindness. When ingested it causes nausea, vomiting, and diarrhea.

Sylas

Stretching in my swivel chair with one arm behind the other, I glance at the clock noticing it's about lunch time. I wonder if Zily's ate yet. I attempt to fix my ponytail after raking my fingers through my hair so many times while working. I begin my search for Zily by peeking into the sitting room I took her to yesterday. She's not in her room either.

Marie dips her head in greeting, her face beaming with the joy she always carries around, a tray with an empty tea set in her hands. I stop her.

"Have you seen Zily, the white Kitsune, anywhere?"

"Oh, is that her name? I've brought her tea in the library. She drank it, though I don't believe she really noticed my presence. Her nose is deep in some books." She giggles.

Recalling her reaction to seeing the library, I should have known to check there. "Thank you, Marie."

She curtsies in her expert way with the tray in one hand to lift her skirt with the other. I make a trip to the kitchen to pick up lunch. All the chefs do a double take at my presence, spinning around quickly. Almost in unison, they bow. "Sire." I wave them off, smiling politely at them.

Our main chef isn't on lunch duty today. I approach one of the others, Bran, inquiring about lunch. Bran excitedly rings his hands, asking what kind of lunch I would like. He could make me anything I like quickly. Disappointment crosses his face when I simply want sandwiches. I watch him prep to put it together. He makes an open faced sandwich, piling ingredients onto a baguette.

"Could I have two please?" I stop him before he puts it into the oven to melt the cheese.

"Certainly! But won't you need three?" He asks, laying out more bread.

"The other is for Zily."

He turns his head staring at me with a blank expression, not recognizing the name. His eyes darken, facial features hardening. He doesn't dare say anything as he figures out who I'm referring to. He doesn't speak for the rest of our interaction. As he goes to hand me the tray, another comes up, grabbing the handles first.

"I can take it for you, Sir. Where do you want it taken to?" He's younger, an apprentice, wanting desperately to be recognized.

"Thank you, Mykal, but I can take it. It's really not a problem." I pick the plates up off the tray. He's too stunned that I know his name to move or reply. I know all their names. I slip out of the kitchen carrying the plates of sandwiches quickly before another could offer their services. There's no need to subject Zily to unnecessary scrutiny.

Zily is exactly how Marie described her in the library. Her back is against the armrest of the couch, legs tucked to the side with her feet hanging off the side though her flats are halfway under the couch. Her head is back, holding the book in front of her face, completely engrossed in what she's reading. Two small stacks sit on the table in front of the couch. I peek at some of the titles as I set the plates down. *Encyclopedia of Flowers. Herbal Medicines. Death by the Garden.* Lovely. She doesn't hide what she is, does she? And the one she is currently reading; *Bloom Across the Lands.*

Zily jolts up at the sound of porcelain against glass. I chuckle, sitting on the other side of the couch, angling toward her, crossing one leg over the other. She glares at me, though she doesn't actually look upset. Her features are too soft, the way her bottom lip sticks out in a pout, and the tips of her ears curl down.

"I thought you might be hungry." I nod toward the table.

Almost on cue, Zily's stomach growls. Her face turns a deep red, gaze darting back to me. I pretend not to notice. She uses a scrap of paper she found as a bookmark, setting the book down. She shifts, dropping her feet to the floor, leaning down to grab a sandwich. I take the other one, watching her carefully. She always has interesting reactions to foods, like she's never had any of this before. She takes a bite, closing her eyes. It's a simple sandwich, but she acts like it's the best lunch in the world.

"What are you reading?" I shoot for small talk, wanting to learn more about her. She pauses mid bite, dark eyes flickering up to me. There's specks of gold in them. Like stars in an endless night sky. I forget to breathe.

"About rare flowers and herbs." She continues with her bite, chews and swallows. I stop staring at her lips when her fingers touch them briefly. "It's a book of more recent discoveries."

"Sounds about right." The corners of my lips pull up, imagining her bright face in the garden. Zily cocks her head, raising an eyebrow. When I don't say more, she goes back to eating. I wait till we finish our sandwiches to break the silence again. "What got you interested in flowers and herbs?" *and poisons*.

She tilts her head in the other direction, brushing hair away that falls into her face. "That's a good question," she says quietly. A glaze covers her eyes as she drifts somewhere in a memory. I wish she'd share it with me.

"Zily?" I gently say her name, bringing her back to the present. Would she tell me if I asked where she went? Probably not. Why would she? I opt for a slight change of subject. "What kind of plant are you reading about now?"

Zily's ears perk up and she sits straighter. "It's about a new species of glowing mushroom. It was found to grow on dead bamboo. I find plants and fungi that glow fascinating. It's remarkable the things the world grows."

"You find all kinds fascinating." I tease with a grin.

A faint blush crosses Zily's cheeks. She looks down, retreating into herself again. That's not what I wanted to do. I had hoped to hear more. Though I should take this opportunity to leave and get back to work. I doubt she'll mind, wanting to return to the book. I internally groan, wishing I could stay on this couch with her while she reads.

I uncross my legs. "I'll check on you later. Maybe you can tell me about the new discoveries." I encourage, standing, taking the plates. "Glad to see you're taking it easy for your injury's sake."

Her head bobs, staring up at me. It's an assessing gaze that makes me wonder what she sees when she looks at me. It's a rare moment when she actually makes eye contact; it feels like she's always looking somewhere other than my eyes. I don't move until she breaks the stare, reaching for the book.

Like being released from a spell, I take several steps backwards. My chest feels tight, wrapped in a tangle of vines. Every step out of the room is like trudging through mud. But I unfortunately have work to do. She just had to appear during an extra busy time.

After dropping off the plates in the kitchen, I run into Kai on the way back to my study. He walks with me up the stairs, his brown eyes watching the hall ahead. He appears unobservant with a narrow focus, but he is seeing everything around him. He'd notice a fly on the wall. It's why he's one of the best knights in the royal guard, my personal aid. For other reasons, he's my best friend.

"Where's the Kitsune?" He asks in a low voice. I know he's expecting her to simply pop up out of nowhere. I sigh.

"She's in the library, and her name is Zily." He scoffs, rolling his eyes.

"I can't believe you're letting her do as she likes. You should have a guard watching her at all times. You should have a guard watching you at all times."

It's my turn to roll my eyes. "Do I need to come down to practice to remind you why I don't need a babysitter?"

"So, you think you can beat me, eh?" A smirk forms, glancing at me sideways. No, I can't, but he knows that's not the point. I give him the side eye.

"If she is a danger, I'll handle it." I repeat previous words. "She needs to heal first, anyway." He doesn't accept this as a reason to let her wander freely. At my study door, I warn him, "Don't make trouble with her."

"If I don't have to, I won't." He raises his hand as he walks away.

I return to the mess on my desk with a groan, running my fingers through my hair. I take the ponytail out. It takes me ten minutes to find the papers I've already gone over and signed, making a stack to take to my dad later. I wonder how he keeps his study clean. For the life of me, I can't keep my desk in order. It's frustrating. I put a page down and suddenly I can't find it again. My fingers find their way in my black silk hair over and over again, having to redo the ponytail a few times because I pull my hair loose with the action.

Taking a short break, I stand, staring out the window to the garden. The sun is refreshing on my face. The view has always been my reset break when I can't escape the work for longer than a few moments. I chose this room so I can gaze out at the rainbow of flowers. Flowers and a bright smile with sparkling eyes, arms stretched wide.

I shake my head. Memories of her have already planted themselves and taken root in my mind. I don't think I can look at another flower again without thinking of her. If I can make time, a picnic in the garden would be nice.

I abandon my work a little before dinner, making my way across the mansion to the library. Zily stands by a bookshelf staring up at an open spot. A book in hand, she lifts up on her tippy toes, trying desperately to get the book onto the shelf. She's so tiny and cute. Standing behind her, I push the book into place. She drops back onto her heels, letting the hand that was holding her side fall away. She turns around slowly, back against the shelf. Her eyes grow wide, a soft pink leaking into her cheeks.

"Thanks," she whispers. I nod, lingering a moment longer, my hand still on the book.

I take a step back, gesturing toward the door. "Ready for dinner?"

Zily doesn't say anything, her arms wrapped around herself, but her tail swishes a couple times indicating her excitement. When we reach the hall of the dining room, a bit of a skip enters her steps. I chuckle, earning me a glance with a tilt of her head.

"You really like food."

Zily gasps, her ears dropping back, glaring at me. "And what if I do? I don't get to have fancy dinners all the time." She turns her head, picking up her pace. I laugh more, keeping up easily.

"I didn't mean anything by it. I'm glad you're enjoying yourself." I tell her genuinely. "Do you like caramel?"

"What's caramel?" She peeks at me again.

I blink. Where is she from that she doesn't know what caramel is? Have there been other foods she didn't know too? I open the door to the dining room for her. She gives a friendly greeting with a "Hello!" I'm glad she's relaxing around them a little.

"Hello dear." Mom returns the expression, amusement dancing in her eyes. Dad simply nods. Mom and dad sit. Zily reaches to pull her seat out at the same time as I do. Her cheeks flush, taking a step back. Mom watches from her seat across from us, her gaze drifting between us.

"How was your day?" Mom asks once we are seated, curious, while the first serving is brought out. Little plates with three small brown crispy balls and a tiny dish of a dipping sauce are placed in front of us.

"It was good." Zily stares at the fish balls intently.

Dad cuts one in half, lightly dipping it into the sauce. I smother mine in the sauce. With a subtle nod, Zily mimics the process, taking her fork. A quiet moan of delight escapes. The balls are made of fish caught in the river, mixed with cheese, onions, peppers and seasonings, then fried. The sauce has a little spice to it, complimenting the meatball nicely. It's an appetizer we have often, but it seems to be her first time.

"You have quite an amazing selection of books." Zily finally continues speaking as she finishes the last fried seafood ball.

"You like to read?" Mom sounds surprised, delighted. "What do you enjoy reading?"

Zily's face lights up, and not due to the duck platter placed in front of her. "About different herbs. It's amazing how different properties of a single plant, say a rose, could be used. It could be used for medicine or cooking or perfume. It just depends what parts you use and what you mix it with. There are so many different teas, poisons, creams, and lotions that can be made from simple flowers. I have made my own lotions for years." Zily peers up from her plate.

Going quiet, blush entering her cheeks, she drops her gaze again. Her ears droop to the side, pulling her tail around to her lap. I pull my attention from her, glancing around the table. My parents are having a silent conversation with their eyes. They're not as interested in what she's saying as I am. They're analyzing her words while I enjoy the way she glows while talking about plants and books.

"Did you get through the work Charles should have left on your desk?" Dad raises an eyebrow. By telling me who dropped it off, it tells me what policies he's asking about.

I glance at Zily poking at her duck. She's gone quiet again, but appears to be enjoying the duck. "I looked at it. I haven't gotten through it completely, yet." I shift back towards Zily while Mom leans in to talk to Dad. "When did you start?" Her dark gaze lifts to me, her fork freezing halfway up. "Your interest in herbs. When did it start? When did you learn how to make your own lotions?" I keep my voice low.

Zily's eyes widen. I thought she may like to continue the discussion, but she's looking at me with complete horror on her face. She turns her head away, taking the bite on her fork. Hair falls, hiding her face. Several minutes pass without a word from her.

"Nine or ten." My gaze flickers to her. She pushes the hair out of her face. "I was nine or ten when I started to gain an interest in herbs. I was about eleven when I first attempted to make lotion, though I wouldn't say I perfected it until around fourteen. I didn't have many opportunities to practice with lotions." Her voice is soft, light, and quiet. My chest warms with the idea that she may be opening up to me.

"What was it that piqued your interest?" I persist, hoping she won't shut down.

She bites her lip, refusing to look at me. Another couple forkfuls later, she's finished the duck. "I was collecting flowers like a normal child. As I was sneaking them back inside, a doctor stopped me. She ended up taking me to her room, telling me about some of the things they could be used for. In the end, she kept the flowers, so I wouldn't get in trouble."

In trouble… The words echo in my mind as dessert is finally brought out. What could a little girl be in trouble for bringing flowers in? I back off, watching her as the small, round pastry tart, topped with nuts and filled with jam and caramel is placed in front of her. I want to see her reaction to her first taste of caramel. I hope it'll lift her spirits.

It comes out on tiny white plates. The custard is cold and smooth, drizzled with a light brown caramel. Zily takes the little fork, slicing through it with ease. Her gaze darts up to me in question. Slowly, she takes a bite. Her ears perk up and then lay back against her head, delight spreading across her lips. She looks at me with sparkles in her eyes.

I grin, giving a single nod. This is exactly what I was hoping for. She takes her time indulging in the little dessert. A glaze covers her eyes like when she gets lost in thought. The stars dim in her eyes. She peers down at her empty plate. I take a small quick bite of my own, sliding the small plate in front of her.

She lifts her head, looking at me confused. My gaze flickers to the pastry, encouraging her to take it. Her mouth opens to speak, but nothing comes out. A flash of emotions cross her eyes. I can't make it all out. Joy, sorrow, excitement, pity. She smiles sweetly, a little strained. Her tail thumps beside her as she enjoys the second serving.

We leave the dining room first, Mom and Dad quietly speaking together. "How are you feeling today?" I reach for Zily to check her fever. She swats my hand away before I can, glaring.

"I'm fine." I don't trust those words.

"Alright. Would you like to take a walk in the garden? You could tell me more about the flowers we have."

She hugs herself, looking away. "Not tonight," she says quietly, that glaze returning to her eyes.

A frown threatens to slip onto my face. "Another time."

I walk her back to her room, wishing her a good evening. I'm hoping what's bothering her doesn't have to do with the bottles in her backpack. As the door closes, I hear her whisper "Stupid."

Chapter Seven
Philodendron

This plant represents peace, growth and joy. It is poisonous to consume, causing symptoms such as burning sensation in mouth and throat, swelling of the mouth and tongue, nausea and vomiting.

Zily

Eyes as dark as the night stare back at me in the reflection of my blade. I hold it carefully across my lap. I miss my friends. I wish I could talk to Callie. She'd understand. My assignments are not something I desire. When I'm sent out, someone dies. I don't like killing, but it's always been them or me. I have scars from the punishments for disappointing Sir Colin Eyler.

I've learned to get in and out quickly and unseen. It's rare that I've seen the eyes of the one I kill. There was one that had green eyes with tendrils of brown. She was a Witch traveling through the Euthoria Kingdom. It was hard to track her down. We happened to stop in the same inn. If she hadn't spilled her drink on me, I wouldn't have known she was there. She apologized repeatedly, dabbing a napkin to my shirt. I smiled, taking the blame for running into her. I bought her a new drink, adding a little extra to keep her from waking the next morning. We sat together, talking and drinking, her with that dark liquor and me with water. Her name was Serena. She liked to dance. Sir Colin Eyler didn't like the secret messages she'd carry for high officials across borders.

This man with sky blue eyes, kind and caring, who asks me about my interests, though I'm not sure he really cares, who gives me extra dessert, always smiling, will have to die at the end of the week. I can feel the days counting down. I'm running out of time. He's running out of time. Yet, for the first time since the last time I felt the sting of the whip, I consider not carrying out the act. It would be so easy to accomplish; the easiest killing I've done. Add a bit of poison to some food and offer it to him. He'd take it without question, I have no doubt. It'd be Serena all over again.

I remind myself that my friends are waiting for me. What would they think? What would they do if I didn't return? Would Sir Colin Eyler punish them in my stead? That's my fear. It happened once before. Callie didn't return within the time given. Decan and I had hot rods pressed into our flesh. That scar mirrors the new one. Callie apologized for days, sobbing. She even tried to ask to be punished. They never did. Sometimes the worst punishment is seeing those you care about in pain.

I picture bright blue eyes dulling as the life fades from them. Shaking my head, I slide my sword back into its sheath, giving it a hug, a cold replacement for my friends. It gets tucked back under my pillow.

I need to stop thinking. Either way, I have a few days to figure out how I'm going to do it, but my wound is still healing. The stitching itches like crazy. The salve Dr. Burgess gave me has really helped the healing process. I think I can recreate the salve for future injuries. I'm curious what the scarring will look like. I've gained many scars over the years, though I'm lucky with the way they fade into my skin.

Desperately trying not to think about it, the thoughts of my work carry into the next morning. I can't look at Sylas as he escorts me to breakfast. Not when he compliments the deep green dress I chose to wear, not when he offers me the tiny pastry we have for dessert, though I don't turn it away.

I retreat to the library as soon as breakfast is over, speaking up first before Sylas could invite me to whatever he had in mind. I pause, seeing the man with the red-brown hair, the color of changing leaves, approaching Sylas. We exchange scowls. He calls Sylas by name, no prefix of "Sir" or adding "Ambrose" to it like I've heard everyone, but his parents do. I watch them curiously. He wants Sylas to train with new recruits today, to boost morale. Sylas groans. I learn the man is called Kai.

The books I left on the table are thankfully right where I left them. I get settled into the chair, leaving my flats on the floor, tucking my feet under me. I want to get through as many books as possible since I don't know if I'll ever have the chance to get my hands on this many books again. Sir Colin Eyler doesn't like it when we read, though it's how a learned about the poisons he likes me to use on my victims. I've snuck books out of the few rooms I've seen them in, such as his office. There's been a couple times that I was caught. The beatings I received were worth it to me. Borrowing books only called for bruises, not enough to permanently mark me. I learned to read quickly due to those short moments with the books. I taught Callie to read a little after we were given a room together.

Decan knows his letters, but struggles in sounding out words. We didn't have as much private time to work on it together.

Time passes too quickly.

My stomach tells me to look up at the clock on the wall near the entrance. I put the paper I'm using as a bookmark in, stretching out my legs. My foot tingles, having fallen asleep. I stretch my arms up, careful not to irritate my side.

Hesitating, I touch the crystal in the hall that Sylas said would summon a servant if I need help. Toying with my dress while I wait, I wonder if word has spread about my visit. Would they be willing to help me after seeing I'm a Kitsune? A few servants cross through the halls, going into different rooms. None come down toward me.

Sighing, I smooth out my dress. I venture down to the kitchen to ask for lunch myself. Hopefully they will if I ask really nicely.

The smell of the kitchen makes my stomach growl. I hesitate in the doorway, looking around at the cooks. It amazes me. I've never seen the kitchen at Gateswood, but there are six distinct stations, each with a double oven, a stove top and lots of counter space on either side of the stove as well as an island. Half of them are being used. A savory, herbal scent comes from one of them.

I approach that one, putting on my friendliest expression, politely asking what they are making and if I could possibly have a portion. The man glances over his shoulder, looking me up and down with narrowed eyes. Others whisper, moving away, leaving this chef to deal with me.

"This meal is for His Majesty and Her Majesty. It is not for the likes of you." He growls. My shoulders slump, tail dropping.

"Can I make a sandwich?" He scoffs, turning back to the stove, mixing an orange sauce with vegetable frying in the pan.

I sigh in defeat, turning to leave. I can't blame them. I'm a Kitsune. I'm unwanted. Shaking my head, I remind myself that I'm a guest as far as they know. They should make food for their guests. Are they afraid of getting in trouble for not serving a guest? I try not to let it bother me, not having the courage to talk back to them. I can make it till dinner.

Instead of going back to the library, I head out to the garden. The flowers are blooming beautifully in the spring sun. Sucking in a deep breath, I enjoy the fresh air and pretty scents carried in the soft breeze. I make my way through the little maze-like paths, stopping in front of the midnight daffodils. Would they notice if I snipped a little off for my collection?

Movement catches my attention. Sylas raises a hand, reaching the edge of the garden. I watch him, wondering how he found me. I don't particularly want him around. He makes my chest tight, heart fluttering within its cage. He comes around a hedge carrying a basket.

"Getting some sun?" His eyes shine. *Does he smile like that at everyone?* I haven't noticed.

"Simply enjoying the colors." I pointedly stare at the basket in his hand.

"Care for a bit of lunch?" He holds up the basket. I blink, my tail twitching behind me.

He sits down on the grass. I fold my dress under my knees, sitting back on my ankles. He pulls out a few small containers, a large glass bottle filled with a pink colored liquid, followed by two round glasses, plates and silverware. I don't want my eagerness to show as he serves me. I tilt my head curiously. How many people does the prince serve food to?

The bottle makes a loud pop sound as he takes the cork out. He looks up, handing me a glass with the strange sparkly drink in it. I hate the warmth his presence causes, spreading throughout my body. When he looks down to pour his own glass, I sniff the drink. It kind of reminds me of sniffing a flower. There's a hint of orange blossom, strawberry, rose and something sweet. I take a sip, cradling it in both hands. The array of flavors is mystifying. It's light and crisp, perfect in the warm spring air. How can a drink taste dry? There's a hint of citrus, maybe lemon, in the second sip.

"So, were the books all new plants and discoveries or did you come across things you already knew?"

I peer up, staring for a few moments, gaging if he's simply trying to make conversation or genuinely interested. He meets my gaze when I don't answer right away. The clear sky above doesn't compare to his eyes. I take another sip, a blush seeping into my cheeks.

"Both. One was made just last year that is full of new species and what has been discovered about them thus far. I read a few others that did contain some information I already knew, but I don't mind reading about it again. It's like a refresher." I break eye contact, glancing at the ivy geraniums beside him, still a little nervous about talking openly.

"What is your favorite flower?" He picks up a tiny sandwich. There's three of them on both of our plates, each looking a little different.

I follow suit, plucking one up. The crunch surprises me. Who thought of putting cucumbers into a sandwich? "What is this?" I finish it off quickly, excited to know what the others have. I wash it down with the pink magic drink. "And this?" I finally decide to ask, holding up the glass. If I can, I want to get some back in Gateswood.

Sylas' hand freezes with the glass to his lips. "The wine?" I bob my head, feeling a little dizzy in a strange good way. "You've never had wine before? Have you had alcohol?" My hair hits my face as I respond, a giggle escaping. "Maybe you should put it down." He reaches for my glass.

I move it out of reach. "It's hard to say." I answer his question, though his eyebrows draw together. "It's hard to pick a favorite flower. I like so many. There's dahlias which come in a multitude of colors, and they look like fluffy little balls. I like Mr. Fockers." I giggle, taking another sip. "They have a funny name but are a beautiful vibrant blue. I like kalmias, the pink and white ones or the red and white ones. They're pretty, but very poisonous to consume. No making tea out of them." I wag my finger.

"Clivia miniatas are a bright orange like the sunrise or sunset. But I think my favorite is…" I pause again, closing my eyes. My head feels light and bubbly as if I could float away. "Balloon flowers," I declare, holding my empty glass up in cheer. "Their real name is Platycodon Grandiflorus, but balloon flower is a funner name."

"Balloon flowers?" Sylas grins to himself. "Any reason for those?" He moves the bottle of the magical pink drink behind his back, leaning back on his hands, legs bent, one knee pointing to the sky, the other on the ground. He sits like a prince, relaxed and effortlessly handsome.

"I mean they do have medicinal benefits, but really I just like the way they look. They're a type of bellflower and are a pretty purple color." I briefly wonder if I'm boring him, but I feel too good to care. I can't stop giggling and fiddling with my dress.

"Good to know." Sylas smiles to himself, a stray black hair falling in front of his clear blue eyes. I can't look away. "Is purple your favorite color?"

"No." His eyebrows raise at my quick response. I continue without hesitation. "Blue. Blue like your… sky." I catch myself before I share my thoughts. It feels like the world is spinning around me. Is this an effect of the drink? Like a poison. *Did he drug me? It's supposed to be the other way around.*

"I see." He leans forward, an arm resting across his knee.

"Thanks for bringing food out. I thought I was going to have to wait until dinner to eat." I try to regain control of my tongue, to make the fog lift from my mind.

I glare at the ground where his hand presses into the grass. My gaze follows the hand as it takes the edge of the cuff on his other arm. Strong fingers begin rolling up the sleeve in practiced habit, tanned muscles gleaming in the sunlight, pausing above his elbow, teasing the edge of his bicep. He shifts to do the other side.

"You could have asked a servant to bring you some, or gone to the kitchen to get yourself something if you preferred." I blink, dragging my gaze back up to his only for it to drop again as he undoes the top button. His eyes never leave me, setting a fire inside my chest. *Why does he have to look at me like that?*

I force myself to look at the flowers behind him. My vision is so unfocused, I can't distinguish what flowers they are. "Nuh uh. The servants ignored me and the cooks wouldn't make me lunch, nor could I make my own."

"They what?" He growls.

It startles me. I have yet to hear his voice drop like that. My head dips, peering at him through my eyelashes. He sighs out his frustration, raking his hands through his hair, glimmers of blue shimmer in the sunlight, pulling the strands back together to redo his ponytail. It's not as neat as it was at breakfast. I wonder why he keeps it in a ponytail. *I would like to run my fingers through it.* No. Nope. Get rid of the thought.

"I will have a word with them." He sucks in a breath. I feel a little bad for the cooks. "In the meantime, would you like a small dessert?"

My ears perk up, tail swishing across the grass behind me. He chuckles, holding out a yellow tart on a napkin. I hold my hands cupped together for him to place it into. I take small bites, enjoying the lemon flavor. I close my eyes, savoring it. My head is slowly clearing.

"Have you ever thought about making your own field journal?" Sylas suggests, appreciating his treat.

I stare at him. "When would I do that? I don't get much laid back time. It would also be a very large book." I want to lick my fingers after finishing the treat.

Sylas cocks his head. "What do you do that keeps you so busy?" I pause mid lick, looking up at him. His smirk dares me to say it. Raising an eyebrow, I begin to think he knows what I do. I frown, chest tightening. "You could start one while you're here." I angle my head to mirror him.

"I suppose I could, though I wouldn't get very far." He frowns at my response.

He begins putting the dishes back in the basket, along with the pink bottle of the mysterious liquid. I can't decide if I like it. It tasted good, but I think it messed with my head. He tucks a leg under the other, standing smoothly. Sylas holds out a hand to help me up.

For a moment, I think of declining, but I slide my small pale hand into his, feeling the calluses of a sword master. I'm less graceful getting to my feet, even with help. My legs had fallen asleep under me. Sylas holds onto my waist until I've steadied myself. Heat floods my cheeks as I stare up into the face of a clear spring day.

I take a step back, straightening my dress, looking anywhere, but at him. Nausea makes my head hurt.

"Are you going back to the library?" He picks up the basket. I can feel his eyes on me, like burning rays.

I nod, brushing hair from my face. "Uh huh. I'm trying to read as many books as I can while I have the time."

"Well, you have a lifetime to read all the books you like." Sylas encourages.

I snort, earning an eyebrow raise. "No. This is a rare chance to read freely."

For a moment I think he's going to inquire more, that maybe we'll broach the topic again and maybe, just maybe, I'll tell him why I'm here. What will he think? Will he still look at me the same? The thought that he might not, hurts more than I expected.

The man with the autumn hair, Kai, if I remember correctly, walks out the front door as we are going in. His sharp brown eyes narrow on the basket Sylas sets inside the door on the floor, looking up to me. My ears flatten against my head as I return his glare. My skin prickles with defensiveness, senses telling me to find safety. Another part of me says safety is a step to my right. I ignore that call, crossing my arms.

"Do you remember what we discussed this morning?" Kai tears his gaze from me to look pointedly at Sylas.

"Yes, I do." His voice is lower than when he talks to me, reminding me of when I told him about the cooks, but not quite the same. It's a warning, I realize, making me curious what they discussed this morning.

"You're going to outright ignore it?" Kai criticizes in a similar tone. Sylas doesn't scare him, and he doesn't back down despite being his subject. What kind of relationship do they have? Sylas shrugs, sliding his hands into his pockets, the sword shifting at his hip.

Curious to see how this goes, I speak up. "Let me guess, it was about me, no? If you have an issue with me, you can say it to my face. Don't be a coward." Sylas' head snaps in my direction with wide eyes. I doubt anyone has ever called this man a coward. His muscles struggling under his black uniform, broad shoulders and strong jawline scream strength, power, and command. I would compare his aura to that of Sir Colin Eyler, but Kai's eyes are kind. He cares greatly for Sylas. Friends, I conclude. Not just a random guard, but his friend.

"I was simply trying to play nice." Kai growls through gritted teeth

"I'm not here to play games."

"What are you doing here?"

There it is; the question. Had I been egging him on to reveal the truth? If he knows, he'll stop me. Sylas will be safe. The end result will be the same if I fail to kill him. I blink, mentally shaking the thoughts from my head. Sylas steps between us, his towering figure shielding me from his guard. Another opening. It'd be so easy to kill him. It makes my stomach turn.

"That's enough. You know how she got here. She is my guest, and I expect you to treat her as such." It doesn't answer the question, but his words are final. Kai scoffs, continuing on his way, purposely bumping into me. Sylas' strong hand on my back keeps me from stumbling back. "I'm sorry about him." He watches me carefully. I stare at Kai's back.

With a quick glance at our surroundings, I angle my head back to look at him. His warm eyes sink my heart. I lower my voice. "He's right, ya know." A frown forms on his lips. "I am here to kill you." I whisper the words out loud holding his gaze.

Sylas raises a hand, making me flinch, squeezing my eyes closed. I've decided to accept whatever he deems appropriate to the confession. His hand gently rests on my head, patting me. "Heal first, then you can attempt to kill me as many times as you like." I open my mouth to respond, but nothing comes out. "I have work I need to finish. See you at dinner. Remember to take your medicine. We don't want the fever returning."

His hand lingers as he walks around me, heading down the hall. I stare at his receding figure speechless. I've never had a target tell me to try to kill them. I wish I could tell him more. Tell him how much I hate killing. How I really don't want him to die. How I have friends waiting for me. There's consequences if I don't succeed. But I can't say the words. Even thinking about it gives me a headache.

Tears unwillingly slip down my cheeks.

Chapter Eight
Balloon Flower

Platycodon Grandiflorus; nicknamed the balloon flower for its balloon-shaped buds. It represents endless love, the return of a friend, sincerity, honesty and elegance. It has roots in being used to help with coughs and sore throats.

Sylas

I didn't expect her to be honest with me like that. I hoped -still hope- that being here will change her mind. I hold by what I said; if the time comes, I'll deal with the consequences of hosting my own assassin. Though, how can a killer light up like she does when tasting new foods? The way she glows, a soft pink blooming in her cheeks when she talks about books and flowers swells my heart. I wish to know more about her. Where has she been in her travels? Why can't she read whenever she likes? Why would picking flowers get her in trouble? If I asked her to stay, would she?

I refuse to let others know until it can't be hidden any longer. The servants already look at her with disdain prejudice from some kind of disagreement with the Viararia Kingdom during my grandmother and grandfather's rule. Mom once said we were close with them when she was just a kid, but then her mom forbid her from seeing her best friend ever again. Relationships with my grandmother had always been strained. I have a few fond memories with my great-grandmother when I was a little boy before she passed. I don't believe she understood the sudden hate towards Kitsunes, but all the servants and citizens followed my grandmother's lead. It's always been normal for me, though mom had to adjust to it and taught me to get to know the person first before full judgment. It's why I can't bring myself to dislike Zily.

Instead of going up to my study, I stay on the ground floor. Across the entire mansion, near the servants' quarters, I knock on a door, entering into a room that smells strongly of leather and candles. Mr. Haider Torres makes an assortment of leather items, including our belts and sheaths. His wife, Hellen Torres, is our jeweler. I haven't personally visited them before, but I'm hoping Mr. Torres will be able to bring an idea to life.

Mr. Torres turns around from taking measurements of a slab on his work bench. His grey and brown eyebrows shoot up, startled by my presence. I give my usual princely smile.

"Sir, is there something I can do for you?" He rings his hands nervously, old voice crackling.

"I was hoping you could make something for me." As if that isn't obvious. "It's a bit of an unusual request."

"Certainly. What would you like me to create?" Relief floods his old eyes. I wonder what he thought of my presence.

"A book."

"Sir?" His eyebrows scrunched together. Hellen comes out of the back of the room, glancing between us with wide eyes.

"If it's possible, could you make a leather bound book?"

"Oh. Yes. It's been a while, but old habits should kick in easy enough. Would you like anything in particular on the cover?"

The thought that the cover could be personalized hadn't occurred to me. My lips curve up, knowing the perfect thing to have on it. It'll match the book's intended purpose as well. "A balloon flower. Do you know it?"

Mr. Torres begins to shake his head, wringing his hands again, but Mrs. Torres interjects, "Yes! I do. I can help."

"Thank you." Joy and excitement flutter inside my chest. "And the letter Z in the bottom corner, if you would please. When do you think I'll be able to pick it up?" I don't want to rush them, but my eagerness slips through.

Mr. and Mrs. look at each other, having a silent conversation the same way I've seen my parents communicate without words. "If we're able to gather supplies tonight, we can have it ready in the morning."

I grin, already planning on stopping by before I wake Zily for breakfast. "That would be fantastic." I give a slight bow of my appreciation, startling them again. They have no idea how much their speedy work means to me. With the matter settled, I turn to leave.

"Oh, Sir?" Mrs. Torres calls. I glance back. "Do you have a color in mind to accent the flower?"

"Blue. Blue like the sky."

My chest bubbles with anticipation of when I'll be able to give her the gift. I imagine the expression on her face when she sees it. There's no doubt that Mr. Torres will make it look exquisite. The thought helps me get through my work.

After finishing the policy I was going over, I head outside to meet up with Kai, having promised to help with the recruits this afternoon. Kai is ordering the recruits through a drill. Jumping jacks, down into push-ups, up and again to jog in place, then repeat all with their wings out and swords strapped to their waists. He gives me a long side glance. I roll my eyes.

"What was with the basket?"

"We had a picnic for lunch." I mimic his stance, crossing my arms, looking over the men. They've made remarkable progress in their training since their first day three years ago. Kai is an excellent instructor and pushes them just to their limits to encourage growth but not to break them. This is his second batch of recruits he's trained. Soon they'll decide where they want to go after all this.

"How can you be sure she didn't poison you?"

"I think it was the other way around." I mumble, thinking of her reaction to the wine. Kai raises an eyebrow. "She had wine for the first time. I don't think she's ever had alcohol before. The effects were… interesting." She bloomed like the flowers behind her. Snow-in-Summer.

"Ah. I'll get her drunk and she'll spill her guts."

"You will do no such thing."

Kai chuckles. "Kidding." The grin tells me he is only partly joking.

Kai instructs the recruits to run around the mansion. I usually welcome any chance to not be in my study, but I wasn't expecting this kind of work out. The run gives me time to think, and despite seeking a resolution for a silly dispute left on my desk, all I can think about is Zily. She admitted what I already suspected, but she looked so sad saying it. Stars enter her eyes when she talks about flowers or enjoying new foods, but her eyes were like cold black holes when she told me she's to kill me.

Then the way she flinched when I patted her head. Did she think I was going to strike her? It's not the first time she's reacted that way. My stomach twists thinking about the kind of horrors she may have endured to have a reaction like that. It makes my blood boil that someone would purposely wipe her beautiful smile off her face.

Kai gives me a funny look at the end of the run. Sweat coats the back of my neck, soaking my untucked shirt. My chest rises and falls while panting, trying to fill my lungs with air and breathe out the loathing I feel for a stranger. I rid my mind of those thoughts, taking my hair out of its ponytail, combing my fingers through to calm myself.

Kai asks me to take the men through aerial maneuvers. Practicing speed, the men follow me in a dive and a quick, sharp turns. Kai hovers in the air, watching from a distance, judging each of the men's performance. Faster. My wings flap, shooting me through the air, the breeze cool against my face. Adrenaline pumps through my veins when I finish, leading them back down to the ground. Kai gives out pointers while I take a breather.

The day's practice ends with a bit of sword play. I forge the unrequited anger into my movements. Kai and I face off, our little sparring match becoming a bit of a show for the trainees as it often does. I don't have to hold back against Kai. There is a reason he trains those aspiring to be among the royal guard.

His blade comes from the side. I block him, pushing the attack off and pressing forward. The clinking of metal on metal fills the air as we repeatedly attack and defend. I swing down. Kai steps to the side, thrusting out his sword. I pivot, dipping my blade to block while moving out of the way.

As it often ends, Kai defeats me, the tip of his blade pointed at my throat. He smirks, sheathing his sword. I roll my eyes, doing the same. The men watching clap. We bow in unison. The first time new recruits see Kai brutally defeat me, they are completely speechless. They're usually afraid to face off against me, afraid of unknown consequences of harming their prince. Once, Kai left a small cut on my cheek and I clapped him on the back for a good match, breaking the fear holding them back. Now there's a few that give me a hard time when I spar against them. Soon, there will be a new rotation once these men graduate and get their assignments.

I return to my room for a hot bath before dinner, wanting to get the sticky sweat off me. Feeling refreshed, I don a deep blue button down, debating on rolling the sleeves up again. I left them down during my meetings with father in the morning, but it became too much out in the sun. The fabric folds up past my elbows, figuring it's just a normal dinner with my parents and Zily. It's crazy how comfortable I've become in only a few days of knowing her. I leave my hair down to dry, putting a hair band on my wrist.

Expecting her to be in the library, that's where I head to pick Zily up for dinner. I've barely started down the hall when I spot her walking toward me. She raises an eyebrow, but doesn't say anything to me as she passes by, disappearing into her room. Leaning against the wall across from her door, I tie my hair back, waiting for her to reemerge.

Zily steps out, gaze on the floor, her cheeks as pink as the dress she wears, the skirt a puff of scrunched up roses down just past her knees, a red ribbon around the waist, tied in a bow in the back. Red hair clips hold her hair out of her face. It's only then that I realize how much her hair gets in her face. Short red heels adorn her feet. I drag my gaze back up to her night eyes. She's staring at me.

"Do you like hair clips?" I ask, reaching for them, gently running my fingers down a strand of hair. I like the way it makes her blush. She doesn't flinch this time, gaze never leaving mine.

She nods. "I used to have a headband to keep my hair out of my face, but I must have lost it in the river. These are prettier anyways." She starts down the hall, expecting me to follow. I watch her for a moment longer, her tail curled up, indicating her pleasant mood.

"You're beautiful." I tell her before I start after her. She shows no indication of hearing me.

Mom compliments Zily's dress as soon as we enter the dining room, receiving a grin and a quick swish of the tail. As with every meal, I pull the chair out for her, wait for her to sit and push her in. She seems to be getting used to the routine. The looks she gave me the first few times made me want to laugh.

Zily appears happier during dinner, engaging more in idle conversation than she had the first night. It's good to see her giggling, her face lit up like the sun on freshly fallen snow; blinding. It's hard to believe that that's the face of a killer.

After supper, I escort her back to her room. She skips the whole way back. She waits for me at the top of the stairs, her bounding taking her up the steps faster than normal. I chuckle.

"How is your side doing?" She's been moving more.

"It's healing faster than I expected; faster than any injury I've nursed before!" She says excitedly, raising her arms up, twisting back and forth slightly, showing her range of motion. Her arms drop back to her side. "I've made note of what I think was in the salve, so maybe I can recreate it. I don't want to push it yet, but I think his estimation of two weeks is a good one. I didn't trust it at first."

I nod along. "Dr. Burgess is the best around. You could ask him how he makes it."

Zily gives me a look like she doesn't believe my statement. "I don't think he would give it to me very willingly."

I shrug nonchalantly. If she really wants it, I could ask for it, but she'd have to voice that to me. She turns, opening her door. She glances over her shoulder. "Goodnight, Sylas."

Zily leaves me alone in the hall, my name on her lips leaving me completely speechless.

I'm up before the morning wake up knock comes. I startle the maid, hand out to open the door at the same time as I'm leaving. With an apologetic smile, I hurry to out the door and down the hall. Hopefully it's not too early, but they did say in the morning. Servants pass through the halls, heading toward their daily chores, some have already started.

I knock on the door to Mr. and Mrs. Torres work room, silently praying they're in there. Mrs. Torres answers, her face brightens when she sees me. She beckons me inside with a wave of her hand.

"Good morning, Sir Sylas Ambrose. We didn't expect you this early, but we have the book ready for you right over here." She walks over to the table where her husband stands.

"Forgive me. I wasn't sure how early would be appropriate. I'm a little eager." I confess, feeling heat rise up my neck.

Mrs. Torres giggles in response, wrinkles forming around her eyes. Mr. Torres picks up the book, larger than expected, and shows it to me. Front and center is a balloon flower embossed into the leather. Embedded in each of the four corners are little blue stones. A curly Z is in the bottom right corner next to the stone. I take it from his hands, holding it to my chest.

"Thank you! She's going to love this." I give a slight bow of appreciation. The elderly couple share a glance, raised eyebrows and a smirk. Rushing from the room, keen to get back upstairs to give the book to Zily.

Zily responds to my knock instantly, telling me to wait. Little does she know how much of a struggle that is for me right now. When she finally opens the door, she's in a pretty soft blue dress with sparkles shimmering in the skirt. The top forms to her curves, the sleeves hanging off her shoulders. A sparkly headband holds her hair out of her face, nearly blending in with her snow white hair. She looks absolutely beautiful, but there is no light in her eyes.

"Are you alright?"

Zily sighs, running a hand over her head, ears lying flat. "I'm just tired."

"Did you not sleep well?" Tell me more. Talk to me. Open up.

She shifts as if debating on what to say. "I had a dream- a nightmare really."

"Do you want to talk about it?" I offer. For a moment, she looks up at me, and I think she considers it.

She shakes her head. "Not really. I… I miss my friends." She looks down, arm strung across her body, holding the other one.

Friends. I feel like an idiot for not thinking there might be people she wants to return to. Does she have family waiting for her? It's probably a question for another time.

"Here. Something to show your friends." I hold out the book.

Zily hesitates, eyes fixated on the book. Slowly she lifts it out of my hands, running her fingers over the cover, down to her initial, before leafing through all the blank pages inside. "For me?" I almost don't hear her speak. She closes it, hugging it to her chest, her dark eyes staring up at me. "Field journal?"

"Yes. Or whatever you would like. I know you said it'd be a large book if you created one, so why not get started?" An easy grin makes its way onto my lips. I relax when the tiny hints of stars begin to dance in her eyes, blurred by tears that threaten to spill out.

"Thank you." She gives it a squeeze, turning back to her room to leave it behind. Once again, she leaves me speechless in the hall, and I know I'm in trouble by the pounding in my chest. If she truly intends to kill me, I don't think I could bring myself to stop her.

Chapter Nine
Gardenia

These generally symbolize purity, love, trust and an expression of admiration. The sweet scent is popular for perfumes, oils and other beauty products.

Lily

    I didn't expect to be holding back tears this early in the morning. There's still time before breakfast, yet Sylas knocked on my door sooner than previous mornings. It kind of annoyed me after a restless night. I already had the dress I wanted to wear picked out and had to quickly slip it on so I could meet him in the hall. Then he hands me a present. I told the man I'm going to kill him, and he decides to spoil me. I don't understand him.

    Tears begin to slide down my cheeks. My legs give out, and I lean against the bed, quietly crying into the comforter hanging off it. I don't want him hearing, nor can I take too long because I don't want him to worry. It's silly, this circle of worrying about him worrying about me. I wipe my face, resting the book on my pillow. I'll come back for it after breakfast.

Hoping cool water will help, I wash my face, staring in the mirror hoping my eyes aren't too noticeably red. With a deep breath, I plant a smile on my face because that's what I want him to see. Time to head to breakfast. I focus on that thought, letting the curiosity, the joy of tasting new food fill me as I throw the door open. My hand automatically reaches for his, pulling it back before it has a chance to touch him. I fold my hands behind my back.

"Shall we go?" I hope my face isn't betraying me with the swirl of emotions waging war inside my chest.

Sylas waves his hand for me to go first, a gesture he often makes, falling in step beside me. I take my seat beside him at the long dining table. I know the routine, but I'm not quite used to the treatment. Makes me feel like a princess. His parents greet me with friendly expressions. Eleanor tilts her head in question that I cannot read, so I don't respond. I'm afraid of what she may see on my face.

Breakfast does the trick, lifting my spirits. Today is a kind of toast filled with a strawberry cream. I skip out of the dining room. Sylas' hand brushes my arm, catching my attention, but Reuben calls him, reminding him of some business they have together. Sylas' head drops back, groaning. I watch the way he straightens the collar of his blue shirt, buttoning the top button, my chest tightening. Seeing him become professional in a blink of an eye is magical. Without a word, he nods and waves goodbye.

I return to my room, fetching my new book, digging through the night stand for a pen. There's none. I check my bag, usually carrying a couple pencils with me, but it seems I've forgotten to pack them this time. Wandering down the hall, clutching the leather book to my chest, I consider asking a servant for a pencil, but most avert their gaze. A little discouraged, I back track to a dark wood door. If I remember correctly from the tour, this is Sylas' study.

I knock once, though I don't expect him to be in there. I poke my head in. It's a cozy room. Not as bright as I expected, but it gives a warm and welcoming feeling. There's a couch that surprises me, a small bookshelf, and the messiest desk I have ever seen. I glimpsed it the day of the tour, but has it grown?

My hands automatically reach for the papers, wanting to organize them. Quickly, I put them back down. I should not be reading these. Opening and closing drawers quickly, a cahmo crystal of blue and thick white swirls smoothed into a ball rolls about. I grab it, holding it still while closing the drawer in fear of it shattering. I've only seen one once before. I don't know how breakable they are, and I don't intend to find out. Finding what I came for, I snatch up a pencil in another drawer with more papers with scribbles on them, spinning to leave. I glimpse outside, a gasp escaping. It's the garden. The beautiful colors create a rainbow. There is no individual flower way up here. They swirl and blend together like an art piece.

I pull myself away from the window, before someone catches me inside the study. With a pencil in hand, I stroll out to the garden. I plopped down on the ground in front of a bunch of balloon flowers. Of course, I have to have these as the first sketch in my book. I steal a glance up at the window I now know is Sylas' study.

Sketching has been a secret hobby. It has helped me through many nights outside of Gateswood in more ways than one. I've never dared have my drawings inside the walls. I don't know how I'll keep this hidden, but it'll be fun to be able to share these with Callie and Decan. Thinking about my friends makes my chest ache missing them.

Callie would like it here. She'd be just as delighted about the food as I am. We'd run through the halls of the mansion, sit in the library, drink tea and enjoy bathing in the sunlight in the garden. Decan would be a little more wary. He'd start by following us around, a little behind like an overprotective big brother. He'd get along well with Kai. I laugh at the thought. Fighting back tears, I push back the image of what will never be as I start writing little notes around my sketch about the properties and uses of a balloon flower.

I move on to the midnight daffodil, the mystery behind it drawing me in. One day, I'll experiment with it. Being one of the ones to make a new discovery fuels my fantasies. The pencil pauses mid-stroke. Feeling like I'm being watched, I glance around. I incline my head, peering up at the window.

Sylas gives a little wave. I grin, waving back, pencil lodged between my fingers. It looks like his hair is down. I've noticed his hair becomes more disheveled as the day goes on. It makes me wonder, once again, if he ever simply leaves it down. I've seen it down briefly, but he pulled it back quickly. He turns back, returning to his work. I go back to sketching.

The day passes faster than any of the others previous. My stomach growls at me, mad that I completely spaced lunch. Four pages are filled with drawings and notes on the side. The names of the flowers are in curly writing at the top of the pages.

I drop the book off in my room, continuing on to Sylas' study. He's always come to get me for supper, besides the one day I met him outside the dining room doors. It's my turn. I knock on the door, waiting for a response. He sounds tired when I'm given permission to enter. Sylas instantly gets to his feet, an easy smile crossing his lips. His hair is pulled back again, but his shirt is untucked.

"Ready for dinner?" I ask, my tail swishing behind me expectantly. His gaze snaps to the clock on the wall.

"That time already?"

"Did you forget about lunch as well?" I shift, averting my eyes as he retucks his shirt in, having to undo his belt to do so.

"No, it merged with a meeting with my uncle. Did you forget to eat?" His raised eyebrow scolds me. I giggle, promising to show him my drawings sometime, something about that prospect makes me nervous.

He tells me about his day as we walk down to the dining room. He had to attend meetings with his parents. Since he's taking over the crown in mid autumn, he needs to be aware of everything, more than before. He gives me a daring look, silently saying if I don't kill him first. I return it with my most innocent look, batting my eyelashes. He laughs, the sound resonating in my core.

The following morning passes even faster than the last, dread forming in the pit of my stomach. I wear a floral gown, blending in with the garden I wander. I spend the morning sketching, deciding to add notes at a later time. Referencing books in the library will be a great way to double check my memory.

I finish drawing a Lily of the Nile when my stomach lets me know it's about lunch time. I don't want to skip it two days in a row. Glancing at the window, I wonder if Sylas has had lunch yet. I stroll inside toward the kitchen. Remembering how they looked at me last time, I hesitate outside the doors.

Sylas said he'd talk to the cooks. I suck in a deep breath and walk in. It's quieter than I expected. I must be early. It looks as though the chefs are just setting up at two stations. There's about five of them at each station, pulling out ingredients, firing up the stoves, and getting plates ready.

"May I have something for lunch?" I ask one of them.

They look me up and down. Without a word, he makes me a plain sandwich. Bread, cheese, ham. It's better than nothing, though it means I'll be eating alone. I don't want Sylas to see. A man with a curly blond mop on his head bumps into me as I'm leaving. He's not terribly taller than I am. He looks at me, looks down at my pitiful sandwich, not even on a plate.

"Nuh uh. That won't do. I can't let you leave with that thing." He points a disgusted finger at the sandwich, grabbing my arm and hauling me back into the kitchen.

The section straight ahead from the door is the smallest area. He drags a stool over for me to sit on in front of the island, tying an apron around him. He begins to hum while he cooks. Rice and chicken fill a pan. A white sauce thickens in a pot. The delicious smell fills the air. I swallow, trying not to drool.

The man serves the food onto four plates. My tail swishes slowly, patiently. He sets one of the plates on a tray with a cup of fruit and a meringue cookie. I stand, fiddling with my dress, working up the courage to ask.

"Could I have two?"

The man glances at me curiously. "Two?"

"Yes, please. One for Sylas too. Please," I ask, being extra polite. I don't want this chef turning against me as well.

Something sparks in his hazel eyes, lips curving. "Sir Sylas?" He repeats. I nod quickly.

He transfers a second of everything onto the tray, adding a couple tea cups, a sugar cube jar and a teapot. He picks up the tray, then looks at me and my book. "Are you able to carry this? Should I have someone take it for you?" He begins to look at others in the kitchen.

I quickly step forward, sliding my arms under, balancing the tray on my book. He hesitates to let go. I curl my fingers around the edge of the tray. "I got it. Thank you so much!" I attempt a small curtsy. How does it go? One ankle behind the other and dip. He walks me to the door, holding it open for me.

The tray is heavier than expected. A good portion of the weight comes from the teapot, centered on the tray. I take the stairs slowly and carefully, feeling each step and making sure my foot is firmly planted before continuing.

There's a problem when I reach the door to Sylas' study. Unable to knock with my hands full, I use my foot to tap the door. I wobble a little. *I hope he heard that.* My arms are getting tired.

A grin spreads across my face, meeting sky blue eyes. They grow wide with surprise. "Hungry?" I lift the tray a little. My arms start to tremble.

His eyes light up at the sight. "Here, give me that."

He takes the platter, setting it on the short table in front of the couch. I close the door, sitting beside him on the couch, setting my book on the table as well. I lean forward, pouring us each a cup of tea.

"How many sugars do you like?" I drop several cubes into my cup, losing track of how many.

"Only two." I'm not surprised.

We talk idly while we eat. My tail thumps happily beside me as I mix the chicken, rice, and sauce for another bite. I keep eyeing the cookie, waiting until I finished my food first. Sylas laughs. I give him a sideways glance, wondering what's so funny. He simply shakes his head.

"Have you made progress?" He dips his head toward my book.

My ears perk up, swallowing hard without meaning to when I go to answer. I switch the empty plate on my lap for my book. I open it to the first page, excited to show him. "Yes! I've been busy!"

"Wow." Sylas breathes in amazement, heating my cheeks. He pulls the book closer, leaning in to stare at my pictures. "I didn't know you could draw. These are beautiful." He turns the page to a new flower.

A little giggle escapes. "They're not that good, but you can tell which flower is which and that's what counts." My face burns with the compliment.

"No really. They're good." Sylas restates, handing the book back. A part of me wants to tell him about drawings I would do for people during my travels.

I hug the book to my chest, unsure what to say. He doesn't say anything more, simply stares back at me with a warm expression and clear eyes. I wonder what he sees when he looks at me like that. I'm the first to look away, reaching for the cookie I still have left to eat, hoping it's not obvious how my heart is pounding wildly in my chest. It's an unusual feeling, like a caged bird looking for freedom. I slide the book to the couch beside me, nibbling on the cookie. It's so good! I sigh, quietly, enjoying the treat.

"Here." Sylas gets my attention again. I glance down at the half a cookie he offers to me. The bigger half, I notice. A smile tugs at the corner of my lips, our fingers brushing as I take the cookie.

"Thank you," I whisper.

I don't flinch this time when his hand moves towards my head. He's gentle when he pets my head. My body relaxes on its own, like my subconscious knows I'm safe with him. I want to lean into him.

"You really like sweets, don't you?"

I simply nod, savoring the cookie, my hair a curtain around my face. It's not like I get good food often, let alone sweets.

"I suppose I should try to get this finished today." He sighs heavily, getting up to return to his desk, running his hand over his hair, a few strands starting to come loose from the ponytail. That's how his hair always becomes a mess by the end of the day. How many times does he comb his fingers through it while it's bound? How many times does he redo the ponytail throughout the day?

"Can I stay?" I ask quietly.

Sylas' eyebrows raise. A grin sweeps across his face. "Sure. I'd love the company."

I clean up the dishes, so they are neatly stacked on the tray, quietly humming to myself. Leaning against the armrest of the couch to face Sylas with knees bent and skirt draped over them, my book rests against my legs. I scribble down notes about the flowers already drawn. It doesn't take me long. I should go to the library to find more information, but I don't particularly want to leave.

I peek up at Sylas. He's leaning on his elbow, fingers in his hair that he's decided to let down. Sensing my gaze, he peers up for a moment, giving me a weak smile. I return it. Looking down at my book, I contemplate what to do. I consider drawing another flower from the garden, but inspiration isn't hitting me.

Twirling the pencil, I look up again, Sylas hard at work. Flipping to the back of the book, lines glide across the page, shading for the changes of color. The picture comes to life before me, easier than anything has ever come to me. Sylas leans back, stretching. I blink, staring at his hair falling over his shoulders.

"Is your hair longer than mine?" I hadn't meant to voice that out loud.

Sylas chuckles, automatically running his fingers through his hair. "Maybe. Yeah, I think so. Why?"

I ignore him, erasing the bottom edges to make it longer in my sketch. "I never noticed before. You always have it pulled back." My eyelashes flutter, hiding my assessing gaze, wanting to get the length right. His hair looks soft and the kind of sleek black that has a shimmer of blue in the sun. I would like to try my hand with colored pencils some time.

"Why don't you leave it down?"

"My parents aren't particularly fond of the longer hair. I keep it pulled back as a middle ground." He looks down at a paper.

"Well, I like it." I move on to drawing the desk.

Sylas stares at me, mouth open like he's going to say something, but nothing comes out. He looks down at the papers covering his desk, shuffling them around. A knock comes.

"Come in!" Sylas calls, his voice pitching.

I quickly flip the pages to one of the flowers. It doesn't matter who comes through that door; it's too embarrassing for anyone to see what I was drawing. I swallow, keeping my face neutral even as my heart pounds rapidly in my chest.

"What are you doing here?" Kai's deep, irritated voice comes from beside me.

Inclining my head, I stare up at him. I definitely don't want him seeing what I sketched. "I'm writing. What are you doing? You're so noisy." He isn't, but his eyes flare, bringing a smirk to my face. He scowls.

"What is it, Kai?" Sylas brings our attention to him, probably hoping to stop a fight. I enjoy teasing this man.

Kai drags his gaze away from me, walking to the desk. Sylas stares at the small stack in Kai's hand. "Please, no," he whispers.

"It's this week's training report." Kai confirms. He leans down, hands splayed out on the desk, lowering his voice. "What is she doing here?" *He does know I can still hear him, doesn't he?*

"Calm down. She's just keeping me company." Sylas doesn't pretend that I can't hear them. "She brought lunch and is using the couch to do her own work."

"What if she tried to poison you?" I roll my eyes, but he's on to something there. I'm up to thirty-two times I could have poisoned him, not only at meal times. Today also confirmed that he would eat anything I give him.

"She didn't, Kai. I'm fine. It's fine. Is there anything else?" Something passes between them silently. Sylas raises an eyebrow.

Kai turns to leave, eyes narrowing on me. I wiggle my fingers goodbye at him. He huffs, storming past. "See you later."

"Next time, don't bring paperwork with you." Sylas sighs, moving the new stack of papers to the corner of his desk.

I wait a moment, listening for movement outside the door in case he decided to eavesdrop. Satisfied that Kai is really gone, I speak up. "Thirty-two times." Sylas raises his head, meeting my gaze, eyebrows drawn together. "Approximately thirty-two times I could have poisoned you."

His eyes grow wide, the number taking him by surprise. He leans forward, elbows on the desk, chin resting on interlocked fingers. "You should know I have built a tolerance for poisons."

"Not for what I have," I say confidently.

"I guess we'll just have to try them."

I cock my head, pretending his words don't hurt. He scribbles on a paper, moving it to the side. I watch him in silence for a moment. His eyes scan words, flipping between sheets, eyebrows drawn. It looks like boring tedious work.

"Sylas?" His pen freezes mid-stroke, his blue eyes lifting to meet mine. I hold it before continuing. "Do you like this? Do you like being a prince? Are you happy being born into royalty?" It seems like a lot of stress and work to be worth it, plus the number of people who want him dead, not only Sir Colin Eyler. He's sighed so many times during my time with him in the study.

A spark lights in his eyes. "It's not always easy, that's for sure. There are way too many days like this spent on paperwork, but even on days like today, there's always something that seems to make it worth it." He pauses, head dipping down a little, looking through his eyelashes, smiling at me. "I don't think I would be the man I am today if I were born into any other family. I want to do what I can with the power I have to make things a little better. Though, I would like to think I would do that no matter what family I was born into."

"Is that why you're aiming for peace with the Zeneth Kingdom?" I'm genuinely curious. I don't know why he would want to make an alliance with Vampires, my own experience with them being unpleasant. It does raise the question of why Sir Colin Eyler wouldn't want this alliance.

He blinks. Once. Twice. "How do you know about that?" I don't answer, fearing I may have crossed a line. "Is that why you're here?" Slowly my head bobs, testing to see how much I can give away before the pain comes. There's a little prickle at the back of my head, but it's fine. "Do you think that I shouldn't?"

"Not me." I clench my pencil, hiding the sharp needle of pain that shoots through me. "I don't know if it's a good idea."

He watches me for a minute. "You don't like Vampires, do you?"

A headache is growing as a warning inside my head. I need to choose my words carefully. "I… haven't met a good one."

He looks at me with consideration. He speaks slowly, gently. "I don't know if it'll change your mind, but there are some good ones out there. The Antionelli family is actually quite nice. They take good care of their people. I'm sure there are some rotten apples, but doesn't that go for any race? It's like how everyone thinks every Kitsune is trouble, but we have a sweet one here."

I roll my eyes, blush seeping into my cheeks. My arms cross in defiance. "But I am trouble; I'm an assassin."

Sylas laughs. "Sure, but you're an adorable little miss assassin." He winks.

I huff, pouting. "I'll poison you." I threaten in the same teasing tone he's using.

He dips his head, staring down at me. "Do you want to poison me?" His voice shouldn't be so light for such a serious question.

I look down at my book. "No."

No other word is spoken. Questions hang in the air like a thick fog that rolled in. Sylas doesn't push, returning to his work, a crease set between his eyebrows. I can't concentrate to think about plants or to sketch. I want to keep talking. I like talking to him, hearing his voice, just not about the inevitable end.

Closing the book, I set it on the table, swinging my feet off the couch. As casually as I can muster, I approach the desk. He watches me out of the corner of his eyes when he should be reading the document in his hand.

I place a hand on the desk. "Why is your desk such a mess?"

Sylas gasps, putting a hand over his heart like I stabbed him, leaning back in his chair. The paper that was in his hand, now abandoned on the left side of his desk. "It is not a mess! I know where everything is." He tries to sound dignified. I can't tell if he's being serious or not.

I nod my head. "Where is the paper you were just reading?"

Sylas glances down, scanning sheets. He doesn't spot it. I sigh, reaching across him, stretching a little to grab it for him. The stitches in my side get a little irritated with me, aching and becoming itchy. I hand him the paper, rubbing a hand down my side in attempt to alleviate it some.

"Thanks." He whispers, blush bleeding into his face.

There's a few papers with the same symbol on them that I pick up, putting them in order. I pause. I started this once before when I was in here searching for a pencil. This time he's here and he doesn't seem bothered by me reading these, so I continue. There's plenty of documents that have symbols or key words at the top I use to group them together. A few require a bit of skimming.

Sylas watches me, holding on to that single piece of paper, while I get the rest of his desk in order. I have it organized by dates and what sounds kind of important. I do my best not to read too much as I am an enemy of the court and really shouldn't have my hands on these. He makes no objections, however.

One paper catches my attention as I lower it to a stack of similar type documents. I can't help, but read this one, eyebrows furrowing. It's a dispute between a couple of ranchers. Each accused the other of stealing their horses. The complaint has been filed multiple times and has been going on for months.

"Do you really have to deal with things like this?" I wave the paper, handing it to him.

Sylas glances it over, sighing heavily, his fingers finding his hair again. I do enjoy seeing his hair down, the way it frames his face, his sharp jawline. "Yeah. When they can't agree upon a solution themselves."

"Why don't they just mark which one is theirs?" It seems like a simple solution. Why get the crown involved?

"They would say the other removed their marker and put their own."

"What about branding? That's what they do with cows, don't they?" I don't know much about ranching, but I can't imagine keeping track of which animal belongs to who is that hard.

Sylas leans over, putting his face in his hands. "I hadn't thought about that. Why didn't I think about that?"

I roll my eyes, a smile tugging on the corner of my lips. "There, there." I pat his head. Suddenly with an excuse to touch his hair, strands run between my fingertips. It's as soft as expected.

Sylas writes down the suggestion, stamp the corner, and lays the paper on top of a very small finished pile. I take up another few papers, forgoing any reserve I felt before. Questions come out with ease, steering him to solutions while also trying to understand the importance of the documents. As the finished pile grows, there's a little more room on the desk. I slide on to the edge, keeping my tail tucked to the side to not disturb the papers.

I hardly notice the time passing, until there's a knock on the door. I bristle, half expecting it to be Kai again. Suddenly aware of how close I am, leaning in to read together with Sylas, I sit up straight. Hair falls in front of my face. I fix the headband holding my hair back, pretending my heart isn't pounding out of control.

A young maid walks in, startled into staring at the floor when we make eye contact. "Excuse the intrusion, Sir. Dinner will be served soon."

"It's already that late? Alright, thank you." He dismisses her.

I shift, ankles crossed, daring the maid to make eye contact again. Her eyes flicker to the tray from lunch, then to me. My chin remains held high. Her eyes narrow on me, darting to Sylas behind me scribbling on the last sheet I handed to him. She leaves without a word.

Sylas hands the papers back and I staple them together, adding the stamp, and putting them on the stack. He stares at the pile, my hand resting on top of it. "I doubt I would have gotten through all this on my own today. Thank you. You were a big help."

I watch him out of the corner of my eyes, his fingers raking through his hair like he is going to put it in a ponytail, only to drop it again. Picking up one more stack of papers, I look up at him standing. "What is this about?"

He glances at them briefly, groaning. "Those are Kai's weekly reports about how training the new recruits are going. I wish he would tell me in person, but he insists on making it official. I think he likes giving me extra work."

I giggle, sliding off the desk, straightening my dress. "I can summarize it for you, if you like." I pick up my book on the way out. We make a detour to my room to drop off my book.

"That would be great. You're a faster reader than I am. You went through documents like nothing."

The compliment has me beaming. "How do you think I got through all those books in a couple days?"

I developed the fast reading skill out of necessity. I could only read in secret. I had to finish them quickly and return them before they were noticed as missing. It's another thing I don't tell him. Maybe I will. What's the harm in sharing a little when he won't be living long?

Chapter Ten
Lotus

Lotus represents beauty, enlightenment, rebirth, and purity. Nearly every part is edible. often used in stews, stir-fries, turned in to sweet paste, candied or made into tea.

Sylas

I knock a little too enthusiastically on Zily's door the following morning. Switching out of my pajamas, I don't really care what I have on. It's right before dawn. I almost didn't get out of bed, but I want to surprise her, a small thank you for the help she gave me yesterday. Knocking again finally gets quiet movement from inside the room. The door swings open. Midnight eyes glare up at me, messy white hair framing her face.

"What do you want?" She growls. I tear my gaze from the thin pink nightgown, one strap hanging off her shoulder. A floral scent wafts out of her room with her. Swallowing hard, I silently tell myself not to back down.

"Come with me." I grab her hand before she has a chance to object. She gasps, stumbling along behind.

I drag her into my room, crossing to the balcony, the door left open from earlier. The stars are starting to fade as day approaches. She's rubbing her eyes, staring out across the yard to the forest. I lower my voice, grinning. "Do you trust me?"

She squints up at me with sleepy eyes, ears dropping to the side. "Yes."

I'm delighted by her response. No longer hesitating, I lean down, scooping her in my arms, one supporting her back and the other under her legs, bare skin touching, the nightgown too short. She gives a little yelp, staring at me wide eyed, pink staining her cheeks. My black feathered wings spread out behind me, ruffling as I prepare to fly.

"Sylas?" she murmurs.

With a couple powerful beats, we're lifted into the air, wind whipping through my hair. A soft gasp escapes her lips. Zily's hands ball into fists on my chest, clinging to my shirt, eyes squeezed shut.

"It's alright. I'm not going to drop you," I coo to her. "Come on. You don't want to miss this."

Zily peeks an eye open, peering up at me. I smile reassuringly. Slowly, she turns her head to look out. We hover high above the mansion. The early morning breeze is cool against my face. The only sound coming from birds far off and the occasional whoosh of my wings flapping.

In the distance, a golden light begins to illuminate the sky. Zily lifts her head more, ears perking. Purples and pinks shoot through the few puffy clouds. Blue creeps its way across the sky.

Zily leans against me, finally relaxing. Her lips form an O before spreading into a smile. After a few short minutes, the top of the sun pokes up out of the horizon.

"Do you like it?" I whisper.

She angles her head to meet my gaze. Little gold flecks sparkle in her dark eyes. "It's beautiful." She sighs, resting her head against my shoulder, watching the sun finish its ascent.

"Yes. Beautiful." I repeat, looking down at her glowing face, radiating like the rising sun.

Blue takes over the sky, the sun shining across the lands. We return to my balcony. I carefully set her down, my hands lingering on her waist until she has her balance. Blush coats her cheeks, her nightgown riding up her thighs. I pretend not to notice as she tugs it back down.

"I'm glad you liked it. I was hoping it would be a good start in thanking you for yesterday." I brush a stray strand out of her face.

Zily tries to fix her hair, fingers combing it repeatedly, ears back. I like the way she blushes. "Ah, yes. It was really nice. And I forgive you for getting me up so early." I laugh. It seems to be contagious as a broad grin slips on to her lips, giggles escaping. "I suppose I'll go get dressed now." She shifts awkwardly. I make a point not to look down.

She peeks into the hall to make sure no one sees. I stand in the doorway, watching until she's in her room. It's ridiculous how jealous I am at the mere thought of someone else seeing her in the little nightgown. Slipping back into my room, I go about my morning routine.

The hot water of the shower that usually helps to wake me up, does nothing to slow my pounding heart. I can still feel Zily in my arms, the way she leaned against me, her body relaxing, how her hands clung to my shirt. I linger in the shower longer than normal, letting the water wash away thoughts of her and how she makes my heart stutter.

I pick out a maroon button down to wear for the day, rolling the sleeves up after feeling how hot the day is going to be already. Summer will be here soon.

The maid that comes to wake me this morning is surprised to see I'm already up and fully dressed, towel draped over my shoulders to keep my dripping hair from soaking my shirt. It's the second day in a row. She leaves quickly. A second knock comes a short time later, confusing me. Did the maids get the schedules mixed up? They don't enter on their own like they do for wake up calls.

Opening the door, Zily stares up at me. She's in a breathtakingly beautiful knee length violet dress, a pair of short black heels bringing her barely past my shoulders. Her hair is brushed, a purple headband with a bow holding it out of her face, though the bangs drape across her forehead. A large black bow decorates her tail, something I haven't seen her do before.

I force myself to meet her gaze. "You know there's still time before breakfast, don't you?" I step to the side, inviting her back into my room.

"No. I haven't gotten up this early before." She looks around the room, spotting the clock above the little couch. "Well, not since coming here. I normally get up around dawn."

I rub the towel over my head, distracting myself with drying my hair. "Do you have any plans for today?" I slip into my bathroom.

"I don't know. Probably go back to the garden." She rocks back and forth on her heels, her back to me when I come back out brushing my hair.

"Do you like horses?"

She twirls a white strand around her finger, glancing back over her shoulder at me. "I've never been up close to one before. I've passed them. They're pretty, but kinda scary."

"Scary? Why do you think they're scary?" I debate putting my hair in a ponytail or leaving it down. My dad gave me a funny expression at dinner last night when I left it. Mom didn't say anything about it either, though there was a sparkle in her eyes.

"Because they're huge and pure muscles! And do you see how small I am? I've heard of people getting trampled by them. It wouldn't take much to flatten me." She waves a hand over herself. I don't remember the last time I laughed so hard, I clutch my stomach. She waits patiently for me to finish, hands folded behind her back, rocking back and forth on her heels.

"Okay. Okay." I chuckle, grinning back. "We can start making our way to breakfast if you like. Walk slow." Her tail swishes. As we walk to breakfast, I silently plot our day. I thought about having a horse prepared for her, but I'm thinking we should ride together after that reaction.

She keeps her hands folded behind her as we walk down the hall. Her head is turned gazing at the paintings. When we reach the ground floor, she strolls over stopping before a painting. It's of a golden wheat field with a rising sun in the background. A girl stands in the middle of it, arms outstretch, head back and wings spread wide.

"This is new." Zily's head swivels, looking up and down the hall. "So's that one." She points to the next painting. This one is a forest scene at night. Small animals poke out from behind tree trunks.

"It looks like they're switching them out with ones in storage. You may want to take a walk around to see all the new ones over the next few days." I comment.

"Next few days..." she whispers.

We walk the last little bit to the dining room. My parents are near their seats chatting mildly. Zily gives a cheerful wave as "good mornings" are exchanged. As breakfast drags on, mom and Zily lead the conversation. Zily inquires more about the rotation of paintings. Mom talks about her grandmother, the paintings and telling some stories from when she was a girl. As much as I enjoy watching them getting along and bonding, I'm eager to get to the next surprise, to see her face.

She innocently eats her dessert slowly, taking small bites to savor the flavor. I eat half of my parfait, giving her the rest. Her eyes shine, taking it without question. It's subtle, but she's had a hand wrapped around her waist through the whole meal. Is her stitches bothering her? Had I hurt her during our flight this morning and she's been hiding it? I frown, making a mental note to be cautious of it for the rest of the day.

Before she has a chance to head towards the stairs after breakfast, I grab her hand. She looks at me in question. I simply smile when she doesn't pull her hand away. "This way. You'll see."

We make it about halfway to the stables when she yanks her hand free of mine. I glance at her, making sure she isn't going to run away. She's staring at the ground ahead of her, her face red. I flex my fingers.

The stables is a long building beside the mansion. Men and women bustle about their daily routine of taking care of the horses.

Zily freezes as a mare is brought out, being taken to get some exercise. Her wide eyes watch it in horror. I bring an arm around her shoulders, ushering her inside.

"Shouldn't I change? Won't the dress get dirty?" Her voice squeaks. I gently squeeze her shoulder.

"I thought you said you trust me." I smirk down at her. She shrinks, tail tucked in. "It'll be fine. I have you." She nods, pressing into my side.

Horses rest in individual stalls. A few are being brushed. Some stalls are being mucked out. A horse neighs at the same time as a loud bang of something being kicked. Zily flinches, looking around, her hand clutching my shirt. I pause near a stall, looking in at a mare. I glance down at Zily.

"Wait here." I pull away. Her hand lingers in the air, reaching for me.

A stool was left a little farther in. I place it in front of the stall door. Turning back, I offer a hand to Zily still standing in the middle of the aisle. She steps onto the stool, coming up to my height. I stand behind her to keep her from suddenly falling backwards. Tearing her gaze away, she peers inside.

The pretty mare with a pure auburn coat laying inside the stall on a bed of hay, raises her head to stare at Zily. Zily gives a weak smile, hands on the edge of the door. She turns her head, noticing the auburn foal with a black mane and tail and white speckles on its back trotting up to the gate. It whinnies up at Zily. A breathy laugh comes out with a little grin. Encouraging her to do the same, I reach in to rub the foal's nose, standing beside her.

"Do you want to pet him?"

Zily's eyes grow wide. "Won't she get mad if I reach into her territory?"

I chuckle, shaking my head. "No. They're friendly. This little one here is S'more and that's his mom, Maple." Zily raises an eyebrow at the names.

Hesitantly, she sticks her hand in, bending over the door more so her palm is near S'more. He presses his snout into her hand. She strokes his nose, trying to rub his neck like I am, but she can't reach.

"He's small like me," she says softly.

Maple suddenly stands, strolling over to the window. Zily jerks back at the quick movement, the stool wobbling under her. I press a hand against her back to keep her from toppling over. Maple sticks her head out of the opening, blowing air through her nose.

"See? I told you she'd want some pets. There's no reason to be afraid." I keep a hand on Zily's back.

With my hand over hers, I press it to Maple's neck, guiding it down. After a couple times, she gains confidence, face glowing.

"Wanna feed them?"

"Absolutely not." She responds quickly, smiling while she cautiously touches Maple's mane.

"Wait here." I take a step back, making sure she's alright before I go farther down the aisle to a handler. I get a few carrots while I instruct him to prepare my horse for a ride.

Dangling the carrots, Zily glances at them and quickly shakes her head. Maple catches sight of the carrots, throwing back her head and neighing. I laugh, laying a carrot out on my palm for her to take. Maple snatches it with her teeth. Zily stares at me. Again, I offer her a carrot. She holds it out the same way I did. Maple's nose rubs against her hand, teeth nipping up the carrot.

Zily giggles, the sound like music. "It feels weird." S'more is given a couple of small carrots as well. "Did you name them because of their coats?"

"I didn't name them, but I suspect so."

"I suppose it's a little more creative than 'Snow,'" she says quietly, lifting onto her tiptoes to reach down to pet S'more some more. He whinnies excitedly. A soft smile forms on her lips. "At least it's a cute name."

I cock my head, staring at her white hair and tail. "Do you go by 'Snow'?" I ask curiously.

Her head snaps to me, onyx eyes boring into me. "Don't call me that."

My eyebrows shoot up at the edge in her tone. I take a step back, though she's returned her attention back to the mare and foal. Her smile is weaker, more forced as Maple nudges her. I make note of the reaction as I look for something to bring her real smile back.

"Sir Sylas Ambrose, Jupiter is ready for you." *Just in time.* The handler stares at Zily with harsh eyes. I don't know if she doesn't see or if she disregards him. I take the reins from him, shooing him away quickly.

Zily turns around, hopping off the stool. She looks up, and up at Jupiter, my black and white stallion. Her eyes grow as wide as saucers. "What is that?" She squeaks.

"This is Jupiter. He's my personal horse. He is very friendly. Come here. I'll show you." I hold out a hand for her to take. She doesn't step any closer.

"No. That's okay. I'm quite comfortable over here with Maple and S'more." She pats Maple's neck, who has her head through the window and is looking for more carrots.

I raise an eyebrow, a warning that I will go to her if she doesn't come to me. Her dress bunches in her hands, sucking in a deep breath. With an eye on Jupiter, she walks to my side. Jupiter pays her no mind as I pet him lovingly.

Zily lifts onto her tippy toes, her hand following below my hand, petting him. Slowly the fear dims from her eyes. Once she seems more relaxed, I move behind her. She turns with the motion, watching me.

"How is your side?"

"It's fine." Her eyebrows scrunch together.

"Good." I grab her waist, lifting her up. A sharp shriek escapes as she tries to grab onto me, but I get her into the saddle.

Zily stares at me wide eyed and speechless, lips parted. The color completely drained from her face. I'm second guessing myself if this is a good idea. I instruct her to hold onto the saddle horn. Facing her all the while, I lead Jupiter out of the stables. Putting a foot in the stirrup, I hop onto the saddle behind her. We readjust to sit comfortably.

"Ready?" I smirk, unable to hide my excitement.

Zily closes her eyes, sucking in a deep breath. She looks up at me, matching my grin with her own wary smile, both hands on the saddle horn. "Yes."

I coax Jupiter into a trot, working up to a gallop. Zily stares ahead, ears down and tail curled around her. Her back presses into my chest, a hand holding onto my arm around her. I really hope she likes where I'm taking her. We enter the forest.

The ride is about an hour before coming to a river. We begin following it. Zily has finally relaxed, looking around at the scenery, the array of green surrounding us. The earthy scent of the forest surrounds us, pines and maples. The canopy is too thick for someone like me to fly in from above, but thin enough that the light is warm, friendly and inviting. The river flows calmly in the opposite direction beside us. Small creatures scurry out of our path to their homes while birds chirp around us.

"This is technically the same river you fell in before." I inform her.

"I don't want to do that again." She eyes the water.

I half laugh. It feels like a lifetime ago already. We're nearing the spot, flowers popping up here and there. Zily turns, wanting to get a better look at one. I should have let her grab her book. I tap her shoulder, pointing ahead. She finally looks, covering her mouth with a gasp.

The river narrows to a small creek. Flowers bloom everywhere, on land and in the shallow water. A large old tree stands in the midst of small white flowers, soft pink ones growing on its branches. Zily's tail starts wagging.

I bring Jupiter to a halt, sliding off first. I raise my arms up to help Zily down. She practically jumps off, catching me off guard, her arms wrapping around me. I set her down, reluctantly letting her go. She hops around, face beaming with pure joy. She crouches down by the flowers along the water while I tie Jupiter to the tree.

Kneeling down beside her, I tear my gaze from her face, looking at the flower she's staring at. Yellow fan flowers lay on the water surface. She gasps with excitement when it closes around a water bug.

"It's a carnivorous plant!" she exclaims, taking a moment longer to stare at the flower. I wait for her to say more. "It eats bugs! Instead of getting its nutrients through its roots, it gets it by eating bugs." She explains bright eyed.

"What's this one called?"

"I don't know. I've only read a little about water plants, and none of it had pictures." Her shoulders rise and fall, face glowing, clearly pleased with the new sights. She waddles sideways a few steps to stare at a flower drooping at the tip of the stem with yellow-orange curved petals and purple stamens. The individual one she observes isn't even a foot tall while others of its kind reach a couple feet high.

Her arm is wrapped around her, hand pressing against her side. "Is your side ok?" I told myself I'd be careful with her.

Her gaze flicker to me, a soft smile on her lips. "It's a little tender, but it's healing well." She reaches out to touch the yellow flower, giggling. "Don't worry about it," she says distractedly.

Smiling, I stand, stretching my arms towards the sky. I walk over to the massive tree, sitting down against it. My hands find themselves tucked behind my head as I slide down to a more lying position. The grass is thick in this area, making the ground soft and comfy. I've laid in this same spot against this tree hundreds of times over the years. It's like the trunk has formed to my body. A tiny opening in the trees reveal a clear blue sky. The birds sing their songs in the branches overhead. The peace and quiet seeps into my muscles.

Zily joins me, sitting on the grass beside me, twirling a small red flower between her fingers. I watch her beautiful face. "Welcome to my secret little getaway."

"It's a beautiful spot. How did you manage to find this way out here?"

I look up at the green leaves shading us, little pink petals falling from the tree. "When I was a teenager, I tried to run away."

"You tried to run away!" She repeats.

"I wasn't a fan of having my life being controlled by everyone around me." Her head bobs with understanding, looking away. I frown, wondering who could be controlling her life. "But you know what I learned as I got older? I still get to choose my own path. My life is my own and I decide how to live it."

Zily stares at me. I cock my head in question. Bangs brush across forehead as her head slowly swings back and forth, chin down. After a few moments of silence, my eyes drooping, I catch her lips curling into a small smile. One comes across my lips as well as I close my eyes, the heat of the day soaking into my bones, relaxing my body.

Chapter Eleven
Cardinal Flower

Flower of distinction and beauty. It's toxic to ingest, resulting in symptoms such as nausea, vomiting, diarrhea, weakness and convulsions.

Sylas

Emerald and gold shimmer above in a haze, making it difficult to distinguish between dream and reality. There's a warmth at my side drawing me in, telling me to hold on to the dream, sleep longer. Groggily, I rub my eyes. I don't recall falling asleep. Glancing over, Zily is at my side where I remember her, though she's now slouched against me, head resting on my shoulder. Her eyes are closed, mouth slightly parted, ears curved down. Her hands lay open at her sides, the red flower resting in her palm. Completely undisturbed.

She looks so peaceful, sleeping, white strands obscuring her face. The headband hangs around her neck. I gently brush hair from her cheek, lightly grinning when it falls back to place. A fruity scent comes from her. This is the most relaxed I've seen her, and the most at peace I've felt in a long time.

"Can things stay like this?" I whisper. Zily's eyes flutter, her face turning to rub against my chest.

I reach for her again, but she sits up, rubbing her eyes with little curled fists. She looks around confused, blinking repeatedly. She peers down at me with half open eyelids. "You fell asleep," she accuses.

"You fell asleep." I sit up, stretching.

"That's what happens when you wake me up early." She raises her arms, back arching. A groan escapes that has me biting my lip. Shaking herself, she stands up, smoothing out her dress. "That was a good nap. I don't know about you, but I slept quite deeply." She giggles, face vibrant.

Following her up, I take a final look at the creek. I will never look at the river the same again, not since rescuing her from it. Zily pushes the headband back onto her head, trying to fix the hair that folded funny. I slide my fingers through her hair, helping out. Pink blossoms in her cheeks as she stares up at me.

"Ready to head back and get some lunch?" Zily nods, holding her stomach.

Jupiter's been a good boy, grazing the grass the whole time. He nudges me while I untie his reins. Zily stands beside the stallion, looking at me expectantly, a little more prepared this time for me to lift her into the saddle. I tease her about how small and petite she is. She huffs, crossing her arms and turning her head away from me when I climb up behind her.

Zily faces the river during our ride back. She watches it get deeper, the flow quickening its pace. She presses more against my chest. I bring my arms in closer to comfort her.

"You're really afraid of the water, aren't you?" I peer down at her.

She looks up at me with her big round dark eyes. "Well, I almost drowned, you know. That wasn't even the first time." She admits.

I glance at the water. The strength of the current isn't obvious from the surface, but I know it, having swam in it before. I think about her falling in again. "Maybe we should teach you to swim sometime."

Zily shakes her head vigorously. "No thanks. I'm good with just avoiding water."

"What if there's another accident? It'd help, you know." I worry what will happen if no one is there to save her next time.

She shrugs as if it's no big deal. "Then I drown."

The nonchalance she speaks of her own death tightens the cage around my heart. I shift the reins to one hand, wrapping my arm around her waist, careful where I place it. I squeeze a little extra hard, wanting to keep her with me. "I won't let you drown."

She meets my gaze with shock in her eyes. Her eyes quickly dart away, face turning red. "Okay. Swimming lessons it is." She quietly agrees. I give her another tender squeeze, loosening my overall grip on her.

We continue the ride back in comfortable silence with only the sound of padding hooves on the ground. Her head rests against my chest. When I check on her, her eyes are closed. She breathes slow and steady, face calm with the ever so slightest hint of joy on her lips. Sensing me looking at her, she opens her eyes, raising an eyebrow. I smile at her, returning my attention to the trail ahead.

I'm all too aware of body against mine. Would it be strange to think she fits perfectly here in my arms? Perhaps, but I enjoy it. I don't know why she hates the name 'Snow,' but I do agree it's ill fitting. She's too bright and warm, more like the sun, but not so harsh. A star. Yes, she's like a star on a clear summer night. Shining bright in the darkness, and warm when you get close.

In the stables, I help her down again. She remains quiet and I can't tell if she's stuck in her head or if there's simply nothing to say. I tell the handler that comes to retrieve Jupiter to give him a treat and a good brushing. He deserves it.

I automatically want to reach for her hand on our way back in, heading for the kitchen, but she has them folded behind her back. She's not even looking at me, gaze on the forest behind the stables.

Zily's hesitant to come into the kitchen with me, making me wonder if my threat to the cooks didn't hold. She peers around me, frowning at the different chefs at their stations. Her ears droop, staying close to my side. Lunch is already made for me and my parents, someone already taking my parents' lunch to them. I scowl at Tristan that has to put together another serving for Zily. She stares off at an empty station.

I get Tristan to carry the tray for us. He knows better than to look at Zily. I direct us to the second sitting room we have. It has a couple of sky blue felt couches and a round glass table in the middle. There's a glass display case up against the back wall with little glass figures and my mom's favorite vases. A window allows the sun to shine in, lighting up the whole room. The man sets the tray on the table, leaving us be.

Zily plops on the couch, sitting on the edge, examining the food. There's two deli sandwiches, salads, and two lemon drop cupcakes along with a pitcher of lemonade and a couple glasses. I take a seat beside her, leaning forward to pour us each a glass of lemonade, picking up one of the plates of salad.

Zily takes a sandwich, biting into hers, her tail swishing excitedly behind her. She takes another bite before opening it up. I pause mid bite, watching her pick black olives off, placing them in a pile on the plate. She puts her sandwich back together and continues eating.

"Did we actually find a food you don't like?"

Zily side glances me. "I don't eat just anything." She takes another bite.

"You could have fooled me." She shoots me a glare. I laugh, choking on the food in my mouth.

She switches to her salad. "What are we doing for the rest of the day?"

I enjoy the way she says "we," my mind spinning to come up with something fun. "I'm not sure. Any requests?"

She doesn't finish the salad, grabbing the cupcake. A few moments pass, both savoring the treat. "Got any other secrets you'd like to share?" Her lips quirk up at the corner.

I chuckle, resting my head against the back of the couch, thinking. "Not really. If I can't afford to be away for a few hours, I hide out in my study or the music room."

"Music room?" Zily repeats.

"Yeah. The music… did I not show you?" The blank expression tells me I didn't. "Well, I think I know where we should go next."

I wait until Zily seems ready to go. She sighs happily, enjoying the last tiny bite of cupcake, washing it down with lemonade. She sits quietly content for a moment. When she turns towards me with shining eyes, I stand. We pass a maid, Nina, in the hall. I politely ask her to retrieve our dishes from lunch.

The music room is down the same hall as the ballroom. I remember why we passed it up. We went to lunch after visiting the ballroom. Zily gazes down the hall to the double doors now, that sad longing look in her eyes. I clear my throat, ushering her into the room.

The walls are an off-white, showcasing lines of string instruments hanging on the wall. Wind instruments hang on another wall. Drums rest in one corner of the room. In the far corner is our white polished grand piano that is sometimes used at balls.

Zily slowly spins, taking it all in. She walks up to the string instruments. Her hand reaches out to touch one, pulling back quickly. I join her, running fingers across strings, lightly plucking a few, showing her they're safe to touch.

"Do you play an instrument?" *Tell me more.*

She scrutinizes me with a look. "Do I seem like the type that would know how to play anything in this room?"

"I don't know. Maybe you had lessons when you were little."

Zily glances away, suddenly hugging herself, visibly closing herself off. "No. I've never had access to any instruments." She quietly responds.

She's starting to shut down. I quickly scan the instruments on the wall, pulling a violin down. "Want to give it a try?" I hold it out in offering.

Her gaze lifts, peering at me through her eyelashes. A tiny smile returns, reaching for the violin. "How do you play it?"

I step around her, showing her how to hold it under her chin, placing the bow in her other hand. With my hand over hers, we gently glide the bow along the strings, a soft pleasant sound reverberating from the violin. After a couple more instructions, I step back, letting her give it a shot on her own.

Zily's eyebrows scrunch as she tries to get her fingertips in position. She brings the bow up, sliding it across the strings. It makes a screeching sound. She cringes, ears curling at the sound. She looks at me in horror. Before I have a chance to say anything, she bursts out laughing, more beautiful than the melodies any instruments could produce. More. I want to hear it again and again.

She attempts another pass of the bow over the strings with a big grin on her face. Another horrible sound comes out. She laughs, not stopping. I smile, my fingers curling in response to the awful high pitch sound, but I don't move, only to keep listening to the laughter accompanying it.

She hands the violin back to me. I put it back in its spot on the wall. When I turn back to Zily, she's standing by a drum set, staring at me expectantly. When I get closer, she starts to beat the drums, a low thrum vibrating from them. She giggles, hitting them in a rhythmic pattern. I slide my hands in my pockets, watching her bang on different drums. Her tail wags freely behind her, her star filled eyes keep glancing at me as if to make sure I'm still watching her.

"Come this way." I nod for her to follow me to the back of the room. She skips to my side.

I slide onto the bench at the piano, patting the space next to me for Zily to sit. She does, eyes never leaving me, waiting expectedly. I press a key. She copies me, giggling. Licking my lips, I tear my gaze away from her, resting my fingers above the keys.

My fingers dance along the white keys, playing nothing in particular; freely, following the feel of the melody and where my emotions take my hands. It's a sweet lively tune, matching Zily's bubbly aura. I peek at her, her eyes watching the way my hands flutter across the keys, mesmerized. I slow, leading to the final notes.

"That was… amazing." She sighs, breathlessly happy.

"Why don't you try?" I encourage.

"Oh, no. I cannot play. You heard what I produced earlier." Blush seeps in her cheeks. She fiddles her fingers.

"This one is a little easier to pretend you know what you're doing. Try it." I wave at the keys.

She sucks in a deep breath, nervous. She splays her fingers out like I had, struggling to reach the keys. I snicker. She shoots me a look I pretend not to notice. Slowly, she presses down. A pretty sound grows her confidence. She moves her hands up and down the keys, testing the different tones. She lowers her hands, glowing when she's done.

"Would you like me to teach you the names of the keys and how to read sheet music some time?" I thought the offer was a shot in the dark, like the dancing, but her eyes shine.

"Yes!" The word comes out fast with eagerness. "Please." She breathes out the second word.

"Alright then." I have to remind myself to breathe.

She stands first, taking another lap around the room. I run my fingers through my hair, knowing full well this woman will be the death of me, one way or another. I've come to accept that.

In the hall, I mention needing to check my study to see if anything new has come in. Zily says she'll meet me there after she picks up her book. She wants to draw the new flowers she saw today while the image is fresh in her mind.

I like the way she walks in without knocking when she comes to the study. It startles me at first. She simply smiles at me, taking her seat on the couch like this room also belongs to her. The pencil glides across the paper.

Only a couple items have reached my desk. I spend some time making notes for my parents, for Kai, for anyone who might have to deal with the work after I'm gone. I lock them in the lower drawer of my desk that also has a false bottom. I don't want them accidentally discovered, keeping Zily safe, but I want my affairs in order to make life easier for others.

I sit next to her on the couch, her bare feet poking out from under her dress pulled over her knees, her heels abandoned on the floor. Once she finished the sketch she's working on, she turns the book around to show me. A whole page is covered in the flowers we'd seen today. My eyebrows raise, somehow even more amazed by the beauty she captured here than the sketches she's shown me before. It's like the flowers are coming off the page. *Will she cease to amaze me?*

"They're beautiful," I breathe. A soft pink creeps onto her cheeks as she stares at her creations.

"I don't want to forget today," she whispers.

"Me either." I whisper back. Her starry gaze lifts to me. I get to my feet, holding out a hand. "Shall we head to dinner?"

Zily takes my hand without hesitation, something she would not have done only a few days ago. She doesn't let go of my hand until we reached her room and she goes in to drop off her book. I consider taking it again, but she skips ahead, playing with her skirt.

As we settle into our seats, mom inquires about our day. Zily and I share a glance. "I introduced her to Maple and S'more."

"Oh, that sounds lovely." Mom beams. "How is Maple and her little foal?"

"They're doing good. Both Maple and S'more seemed to take a liking to Zily, though she was terrified of them at first'." I glance over with a smirk.

Her mouth drops open. "I was not!" I raise an eyebrow in challenge. "Horses can be a little scary, but I wasn't terrified." She huffs into a pout. I chuckle, nudging her playfully. Her tail rises and falls once on the seat.

Dad smirks. "Did you show her Jupiter?" Food is brought out.

"Yes. We took a ride actually."

"You cannot tell me that huge beast of muscle is not scary upon first glance." Zily attempts to justify herself. The whole table laughs. A cute grin finds its place on her lips.

"We spent some time in the music room after lunch. She may have a natural talent for the piano."

Zily nearly chokes on her food, face turning red. "No… It just didn't sound completely awful, not like the other thing."

"Violin."

"Sy could teach you. He's had many years of practice with excellent tutors." Mother offers.

"I already agreed to teach her." I glance over at Zily, smiling while I wait for her to finish her dessert.

I slide another half slice of cake to her. She beams, glowing brightly beside me. Mom watches, a pleasant smile on her face. She and dad exchange glances, his hand resting on top of hers, giving a tender squeeze.

I'm not ready for the day to end, but I can see the exhaustion creeping into her eyes. Despite having a nap this morning, it turned into a long day, and she is still recovering. We walk slowly to the stairs, milking the time.

"Did you have fun today?"

Her head bobs, rubbing her eyes absently. "Yeah. It was the best birthday I ever had."

I stumble at her words. "What? It's your birthday? Why didn't you tell me? I would have gotten you a present."

She rolls her eyes, a soft blush creeping into her cheeks. "You already got me a gift. My book. Besides, it's not a big deal." She fiddles with her dress sheepishly.

"That wasn't a birthday gift." I counter.

She rolls her eyes again, shaking her head. She fixes me with a smile. "Thank you for today. I'm going to go back to my room and relax a little."

"Happy birthday, Zily." I call after her.

She looks at me over her shoulder a few steps up, one hand on the rail, the other wrapped around herself. "Goodnight, Sylas."

I walk down the hall. Of course I'm going to get her a birthday gift. I pay Mr. and Mrs. Torres another visit, hoping they have an idea what I can give her. I'm grateful to find they're not busy and haven't turned in for the evening. I'd feel awful if I interrupted their usual work. They're clearly shocked to see me again.

"What can we do for you this evening, Sir Sylas Ambrose?" Mrs. Torres inquires.

"Well, I found out it's Zily's birthday today, so I'm hoping you could help me figure out something to give her?" I give an apologetic look for asking for yet another gift to be made quickly.

Mr. and Mrs. Torres glances at each other. I wonder if the rumors of Zily have made it down this far. The older couple don't venture from their corner of the mansion too often.

"Do you have something in mind?"

"She doesn't really have any jewelry; I don't even know if she likes jewelry, but I was thinking maybe hairpins? Her hair tends to fall in her face if she doesn't wear a headband or hair clips. Do you have something?" I stare at Mrs. Torres hopefully.

She waves me over to her desk. Different stones of varying sizes, some for earrings and larger ones for necklaces are separated by color and shape into sectioned off boxes. She has a few already made hairpins, but none of them are matching. Then a rose gold crescent moon with little onyx gems catches my attention. I pick it up to get a closer look. The black would stand out against her snow white hair. A rose gold star would kind of match. Both are about an inch wide.

"Can these be made into hair clips?" I hold them out.

"Certainly! It won't take me long." Mrs. Torres takes them, sitting down at her desk to begin work.

I stand around waiting since she said it won't be too long. Mr. Torres occupies my time, showing me how he presses and cuts the leather. I don't tell him how the oily, earthy smell is starting to give me a headache. The process is fascinating, however.

Mrs. Torres presents me with the hairpins in a pretty little black box with a bow on it. I grin, taking the small box, thanking them repeatedly for their expedient help. "I hope she likes them." Mrs. Torres sees me out with crinkles around her joyful eyes.

I knock on Zily's door, hoping she's not asleep yet. She doesn't answer. I crack the door open, dim light streaming out, sliding the box inside. I return to my own room, flopping onto my bed, feeling exhilarated. If today was my last day, I would die happy.

Chapter Twelve
Lactarius Indigo

This edible mushroom bleeds blue when you cut into the cap. The color disappears when you cook it, turning more grey.

Zily

I thought I heard the door while I dried off from my bath. The room is empty when I poke my head out. I suppose it doesn't matter if he was in here or not. I'm wearing a thin violet nightgown, similar to the one I had on this morning. My face heats, remembering the way he picked me up and held me. I peek into the hall, just in case.

My foot brushes against something when I close the door. Picking up a little black box with a cute bow on top, I sit on the edge of the bed. I gently pull on the ribbon, thinking I could use it in my hair or maybe my tail. The box opens with ease, revealing beautiful hair clips. A crescent moon is covered in tiny black jewels, perhaps onyx or black diamonds. A rose gold star sits as the moon's mate.

"I thought I told him he didn't have to get me anything." I set the box with the hairpins on top of my book on the nightstand, gaze lingering on the hairpins a moment longer.

Laying in bed, my hand touches my short sword. I pull it to me, hugging it close. I miss my friends. Their voices, their laughter ring in my head. I would love to bring them here, share this little piece of the world with them, but that's not possible under Sir Colin Eyler's control. I can feel the tiny ping of pain in the back of my head reminding me I can't tell Sylas about him, Gateswood and *it*. If the rumors are true, I may be forced to carry out the act anyways if I return without killing Sylas.

My vision blurs as my eyes begin to water. I've made my peace with death. It may come sooner than I would actually like. My main fear of it is the pain it will cause others, my friends, Sylas. However, whether or not I complete my task, death will find me soon after. Tears stain my pillow

The hair clips snap into place easily. I vigorously shake my head, impressed that they stay in place. They don't slip at all. I grin at my reflection, wearing a white floral blue dress that flows around my ankles. I love the way the bottom flares out when I spin. Touching the moon one more time, unable to believe something so pretty could be mine, I head out into the hall.

Sylas exits his room at the same moment. He's wearing a forest green button down, adjusting the sleeves. His biceps flex under the smooth material, wanting to roll the sleeves up. He will later. His hair is slicked back into a ponytail that I know will become a mess as the day drags on. A part of me wants to mess it up here and now. I prefer it when he doesn't look so clean and polished. He smiles at me and I beam back.

Putting my hands on my hips, I attempt to scold him. "What did I say about birthday gifts?" My tail twitches behind me.

"That I should get you more?" He smirks, eyes bright like midday clear skies. I roll my eyes, giving an exaggerated sigh. "Do you like them?" His fingers brush the star, following the strand of hair it's holding back, trailing down my cheek.

Heat rushes to my face. I nod, looking down, quietly speaking. "Thank you. They're pretty."

"Good." He puts a hand on my back, escorting me down the hall.

Sylas removes his hand when we reach the stairs, lingering warmth reminding me of his touch all the way to the dining room. I greet Eleanor and Reuben as naturally as I can, hoping my face isn't as red as it feels. My heart pounds wildly in my chest, skipping a beat every time I steal a glance at Sylas throughout breakfast and his gaze meets mine.

Disappointment settles in my stomach when Reuben begins discussing a trip he and Sylas need to make to Sylas' uncle. It's not appropriate for me to object, so I keep my mouth shut, but there's not much time left. I don't want to spend it alone. I would have preferred spending the day in Sylas' study, helping him with work than watching their wings unfurl behind the two men.

I had seen Sylas' wings once before, yet in this lighting of full day, they are more beautiful than I remember. The feathers are a deep black like midnight, that shift like waves. Sunlight reveals glimmers of blue and purple. Beautiful. His wings are beautiful. He glances back at me once before his wings spread out, flapping once, shooting him into the air beside his father. Guards fly with them, surrounding them for protection.

Once the men are only specs in the sky, I return to my room to fetch my book. I go to the library, deciding to find the names of the flowers from yesterday. There's a book specifically about riverside flowers. I find all the flowers from the creek but one. The yellow one. I make notes of my favorite details next to the flowers. I don't have as much room for notes since I drew them together instead of on individual pages.

My stomach growls, telling me it's time for lunch. I debate taking my book with me, hugging it to my chest, but leaving it on my bed since I pass by my room on the way to the kitchen. Peeking into the kitchen, I see the usual suspects that typically glare at me. I walk a little into the room, standing in the middle of the small open space.

"Could I have some lunch?" I don't ask anyone in particular.

"Sure thing, hun. I'm making pierogi with broccoli and sausage in a white mushroom sauce." The man from the other day grins at me over his shoulder. Relief floods me. He waves me over, motioning to the stool behind him.

I nod eagerly, trying to contain my tail from wagging too much. He stirs the pan. The smell makes my mouth water, sucking in a deep breath. He serves two plates, handing one to me. He stares at me expectantly, waiting for me to take a bite. I oblige, ears perking. Delicious!

He chuckles, wiping his hands on a towel. "Glad you like it. I'm Zachary." He holds out his hand. I shift the plate to one side, shaking his hand. "If you want something to eat, come ask me. Don't mind the others." He gives a pointed scowl at the other cooks. They all quickly turn their backs.

"I'm Zily. Thank you so much! The food you make is always so wonderful! Do you make our dinners as well?" I take another bite. It burns my mouth, forcing me to let it cool before continuing.

Zachary nods once, hands on his waist. His apron is tan with a brown dog face on the chest. "Yes. Dinner is my main job. Lunch is on occasion."

"Well, I'm glad you were here today. Thanks again!" I wave goodbye, carrying my plate out. I bump into a maid. She glares at me, scolding Zachary for giving away some of the Queen's food. He argues back, standing his ground.

I wander up the stairs, wondering where I should enjoy eating lunch. Before I know it, I'm standing outside of Sylas' study. It should be fine. I know he won't mind and I should have privacy. The tall back chair makes me feel like a child, my feet dangling. Playfully, I swivel back and forth. Taking a bite of my lunch, I moan in delight at the delicious dish.

I scan the papers on the desk. There's notes of a meeting Reuben was in that Sylas missed, and a couple sheets going over details about the coronation in a few months. He won't live to see the day.

I stand suddenly, looking out the window to the garden, not wanting those thoughts to taint my day. It's another warm day, but the sun is hidden behind clouds. It looks like it'll rain soon. I think it'll be good for the flowers. Men jog by on the outskirts of the garden. I spy Kai among them, pointing and yelling at a few. I stick my tongue out at his unsuspecting form.

The door opens behind me. I dive under the desk instinctively. A confused maid picks up my plate. She lingers for a moment until the door finally clicks shut again. I sigh, crawling out. I don't really have a reason to hide. Sylas lets me in here. I doubt he'd be mad that I'm here without him. Still, I peek into the hall, stepping out before anyone can see where I emerged from.

I walk down the hall, intending to go back to the library. If it didn't look like it's about to rain, I'd go to the garden. A thud from behind a door makes me jump. Out of curiosity, I poke my head in. It's the lounge Sylas pointed out during our tour with two brown chairs in front of a round, wood table with cards stacked neatly on top in the center and a small bar in the back corner. A man stands there, pouring himself another glass. He's wearing the same navy blue uniform the men Kai trains wear.

He turns around, a square glass with a brownish liquid in hand. His eyebrows shoot up upon seeing me. I debate leaving. He sets the glass down, swaggering over to me with a cocky grin, gaze roaming over me.

"Well, hello there, gorgeous." I wrinkle my nose. He reeks, bitter and stale.

"You must be Neil." I remember the name from Kai's reports.

"You know my name, but I don't have the pleasure of knowing yours." He reaches for my head, for my ears. He's never seen a Kitsune before. I take a step back, glaring at him. "Oh, don't be like that, babe. Come have a drink with me."

He tries to grab my hand. I yank it away. A dark cloud envelops his features. "I said come here." He growls, lurching for me. I slap him, my nails clawing his cheek.

"No, and if you know what's good for you, you won't try that again." Blood tricks down his cheek. I spin on my heel, making my escape before the situation escalates more. I recognized the look in his eyes, and it scares me.

Marching outside through the back courtyard, I glance at the grey clouds. I pick up my pace, lifting the hem of my dress, not wanting to be outside when the sky decides to break.

Kai stands with his back to me, hands on his hips, instructing the lot in front of him. They run in place, drop down to a push up on command, then back up again to repeat. Their wings are out, but tucked in tight. I don't know if he senses me, but Kai's hand shifts to his sword, glancing over his shoulder at me. His eyes narrow.

"What brings you out here, little miss?" He stares down at me. I raise an eyebrow at the greeting, but he doesn't say more.

"I thought you would like to know where Neil is today."

Kai closes his eyes, throwing his head back to the sky, quietly swearing. "Let me guess, he's drunk?"

I blink, unfamiliar with the term. He looks at me again, waiting for me to say something. "Brown liquid in a funny glass?"

"Ah. Right. You don't know alcohols. I didn't really believe Sylas when he said you hadn't had wine before."

"Alcohol is for cleaning wounds," I say confused, a little defensive.

I've seen the liquid Neil was drinking before in the inns I've stayed in, but I've never learned what they were, nor tried it for myself. I know people act funny when they drink it. Serena dropped her guard because of the liquid. I don't understand why they'd drink it. Was this 'alcohol' in the wine I drank with Sylas? It tasted so good, though.

Kai groans, pressing his palm to his forehead. "I am not about to give you a drink lesson. Where is Neil?"

"The lounge on the second floor."

"Great. Myka, you're in charge while I'm gone. Go through the drill three times. I'll be back." He spins, marching back to the mansion. I have to speed walk to keep up.

"Also," I debate on telling him. His gaze stares me down as we walk. "He may have a slight injury… to his face."

"Probably deserved it."

"Oh, he did." I confirm. He sighs.

"Thanks." He gives my head a quick pat, a little rough before taking the stair's steps two at a time. I rub my head, glaring at his back.

Sighing, my fingers graze my hairpins, wondering when Sylas will be back. With one foot on the bottom step, a door opens down the hall. "Oh, Zily! Perfect! Would you come here a moment?" Leona calls, waving her hand, a measuring tape draped over her shoulders. Her hair is up in one massive messy bun with pens and pencils sticking out every which direction.

Curious, I stroll over to her, not expecting her to grab my wrist and drag me into the room. She briefly explains how she wanted a live model for a dress she's working on. She shoves me into the changing area, throwing a dress in after me. I do as I'm told.

Stepping out, I have to hold the bottom of the shiny emerald green dress to keep it from dragging on the floor. Leona jumps up and down clapping her hands together. I look down sheepishly at her enthusiasm She helps me onto the pedestal, fixing the dress to fall around it.

"Hold still for me a minute, k?" She starts placing pins here and there.

A minute turns into an hour. I don't mind. I don't have anything to do and at least I'm being helpful this way. Leona isn't a quiet worker either. She likes to gossip, going on about a number of Sylas' family members who have requested dresses to be made by her specifically for different events, the most recent being the upcoming coronation. Some are the picky sort, sending dresses back, but not explaining what they do or don't like. It's infuriating. Leona complains that she hasn't had a chance to discuss Her Highness Eleanor's dress yet.

Leona fluffs the dress, checking some stitching before moving around to the back. "Do you have a dress in mind?"

"What? Me?" I squeak.

"Yes! It's a big event with a ball following it. You'll need a beautiful dress for the ceremony and a ball gown for the dance. Perhaps you'd like to match Sir Sylas?"

My face heats up, imagining wearing a pretty ball gown, dancing in the ballroom with Sylas. It reminds me of his offer to teach me to dance. He'd be patient with me, even if I step on his feet. His eyes would only be on me, spinning me around, the pretty dress flaring out. What would others think if they saw us in matching attire? A Kitsune and their newly crowned king. My heart thunders in my chest as my imagination runs wild. I suck in an unstable breath.

"I… I won't be here," I whisper.

"Why not?" She smooths out the back, walking around, examining her work.

"I'll be going soon." I force a smile, hiding the pain the words cause.

"That's a shame. I've never had someone stand so long without complaint." A grin slips onto my face. "I'm glad your side is doing better. I was worried about touching it again, but you didn't seem bothered by it."

I shake my head, putting a hand on my waist over the center healing hole. "It's healing quickly. It itches like mad, but it doesn't usually hurt anymore."

"That's good to hear. Here, take this and change into it, would you please?"

She hands me a new dress, one that's black with white stars, falling about mid-calf. The sleeves hang off my shoulders. The sweetheart chest is a bit big on me. Leona gets me back onto the pedestal. She brings in the fabric to fit my body better. A deep blush rises at her complements, specifically the ones about my chest. I touch the back, feeling where the fabric lands. It's not terribly low, but lower than the ones I've chosen to wear thus far. She doesn't say anything about the exposed scars peeking out the top.

The sound of a whip resounds in the back of my mind. The tear it leaves on my back. The chuckle from the man on the other end. The burning of hot rods to flesh.

I look around for a change in subject, needing to bury horrible memories threatening to fill my mind. She turns around to fetch something from her desk. A hint of a tattoo can be seen across her upper back. "Hey, Leona, if you don't mind me asking, what do your wings look like?" I don't know if it's rude to ask or not, but I am curious.

"My wings?" She repeats, looking back at me, a needle in between her fingers. She seems happy enough to answer. "They're blue." Unprompted, Leona releases large blue feathered wings from her back. They are not simply blue. They are cobalt and lapis with hints of indigo. The wings stretch out to their full length before she folds them in behind her, turning around to face me again. The tips of the bottom feathers brush the floor.

"They're gorgeous." I breathe. "Why does everyone hide them?"

"They can get in the way. Some can hardly make it through the doors with them resting out. Our doors and halls are made a little wider than most, so we can fly through them if need be, but it's still not the easiest thing to do in close quarters. They're not comfortable to sit with either. Do you like sitting on your tail all the time?" She tries to help me relate.

My tail curls up, dropping a moment later. "No, I have trouble sometimes, depending on the chair."

Leona nods her understanding. She adjusts the sleeves of the dress next. She steps back once she's finished. "It's really a shame you'll be leaving." Her eyes glaze over, looking truly disappointed by the prospect. "You're done. Thank you again."

"Should I change?" I hop off the platform, turning toward the changing room.

"Nope! This one's for you. Thought it'd match your hair clips." She tilts her head thoughtfully, staring at the moon and star in my hair.

"Thank you, Leona." The corner of my lips tug upward, blush creeping into my cheeks. There's no way she doesn't know who gave them to me.

I head upstairs to my room, thinking about the dress Leona used me as a living mannequin for. It has me wondering what kind of gown I would wear if I could attend a ball. A dream. It's only a dream I know, but as I sit on the bed, my book in my lap, I sketch lines down the page. Notes like with my flower drawings point at different sections of the dress. There'd be a lot of tulle to puff out the skirt. Flowers. It has to have flowers, maybe in a lace. I've come to favor the heart shape bodices, straps hanging off the shoulders like the one I'm wearing. Deciding on a color is the hardest part. Blue. It'd be shades of blue, because Leona is right; I would want to match Sylas, and he would wear his family's colors.

Chapter Thirteen
Jasmine

This flower symbolizes purity, love, and grace. In some places, it's been used as an antiseptic to prevent and treat skin infection. It's also known to be used in aromatherapy.

Sylas

I hit my balcony with a heavy thud, exhausted from a long flight after hours of playing my role as the crowned prince, soon to be king. They're family, but it's still politics. Sighing, I release my hair from the ponytail, not bothering or rather not thinking about bringing my wings in, simply wanting to flop onto my bed for ten minutes. Halfway across the room, a knock comes that has me groaning until I see hair of snow white, meeting midnight eyes. My spirit instantly lifts.

Zily steps in, closing the door behind her, eyes shining. I glance down at the star covered dress. She giggles, touching the star hair clip in her hair, meeting me in the middle of the room

"How was your day?" We ask simultaneously. A wide grin spreads across my face.

"I had a meeting with my uncle. A duke. Formalities. Nothing exciting. How was your day?" I count the stars in her eyes. Her hands are folded behind her back as she bounces on the balls of her feet.

She pauses, looking off into the distance. "It was fine. Leona made me a new dress." She gives a quick twirl, the skirt flaring out.

"I see that." The dress hugs her upper curves quite nicely. She's back to bouncing when she looks at me again. "Are you sure that's all that happened?"

Zily begins rocking back and forth on her heels, eyes going distant again, thinking. "Mmmm. I spent some time in the library. Ate a delicious lunch Zachary made. You have more work on your desk, by the way. Got a man in trouble with Kai. Then spent hours standing still for Leona."

I'm momentarily taken aback by the whirlwind of information. "Zachary is our head chef. I'm glad he made you lunch." *That he's not one of the ones I have to yell at.* "You were in my study?"

"Zachary is really nice. I ate lunch in the study." Her gaze shifts again.

"You didn't happen to do some work while you were there, did you?" I joke, running my fingers through my hair, already dreading whatever it is that's landed on my desk.

"I read a bit of it." Zily grins at me.

"Is that all that happened? You seem pretty excited for a 'fine' day." I laugh. Her bouncing ceases.

"I'm just glad you're back." The earnestness of the words with the soft smile shoots right through my heart.

"Did you miss me?" The urge to reach for her, to cup her face, pull her in, hold her is stronger than it's ever been. How would she react?

"No." The word comes out too fast, clipped, at odds with the glow of her face. I watch her, not saying a word. Her ears twitch, returning my stare, periodically glancing away. "Hey, Sylas?" The way she says my name sends my heart thundering. Her face begins to turn a deep red.

"What is it?"

"Would it be ok if I touched your wings?"

I blink, stunned by the question. My wings, like all Corvum's, are sensitive. No one has touched them other than for healing. I look her over, her tail slowly swishing behind her. A smirk grows on my lips with a thought. "Sure… If you let me pet your tail."

"What?" Zily squeaks a gasp. Her tail curls around her. She holds it, stroking the fur. "No… It's sensitive." She answers quietly, blushing deeply.

I cross my arms. "And you think my wings aren't?" I'm not going to press the deal. If she really wants to touch my wings, I'll let her, but I wanted her to have an understanding of how intimate an action it is.

"Fine." My arms drop with shock as she turns around, her tail curling upwards.

Zily peeks at me over her shoulder, her cheeks a beautiful rose color. I swallow, not having a clue what I'm doing as I reach for her tail. One hand caresses the bottom while I gently comb my fingers through the soft fluffy fur. A shiver runs through her. I start higher up, slowly trailing my fingers back down to the tip, my heart thundering in my chest, watching her reaction.

"That's enough. My turn." She spins around, goosebumps along her arms, face bright red.

"Alright. A deal's a deal." I stretch out my wings for her, sucking in a deep breath to calm myself and get my thoughts back in order.

My composure dissolves as soon as she touches me. She raises to her tiptoes, lightly trailing a finger along the bend of my right wing. Her hand flattens, grazing down then back up, feathers slipping between her fingers. I cover my mouth, heat flooding my body. My wing twitches, earning me a curious glance.

"It… tickles." I tell her, hoping she's done.

Zily cocks her head innocently, though her eyes burn. Without breaking eye contact, she pushes both hands up through the feathers, fingers splayed out, catching and ruffling as many feathers as she can with the motion. I grab her without thinking, moving my wings out of reach, her hands outstretched toward them. Her giggles are delightful, but my thoughts are anything but innocent, clutching her waist.

I fight with myself between pulling her in and pushing her away. In the struggle, my fingers slide up her sides, evoking a squeal as she jerks back. Understanding enough, I exact my revenge. Her legs give out under her as I tickle her relentlessly, shrieks of laughter filling the room. I'm over top of her, her hands clutching my arms. I love her laugh.

"Okay! Enough, enough!" Zily pleas for mercy.

I stop my persistence, watching the last of the giggles bubble out. She wipes tears away, a big grin on her face matching my own. Slowly, I let her sit up, her legs tucking under her. Her tail swishes happily behind her. There's a glow in her cheeks, her hairs a mess and stars twinkle in her eyes. She's absolutely beautiful.

I take the star clip out, brushing her hair back and replacing it. I repeat the process with the moon. She doesn't move at all during all this, her arms wrapped around her waist.

"Your side, is it alright?" My hand drops to hers pressed against her side, afraid I had been too rough.

Zily twists her hand to take mine. "It's alright. I'm fine really. I forgot about it. They haven't been bothering me lately aside from being super itchy at times."

She shifts, getting ready to stand. I help her up, not releasing her hand. She doesn't seem to mind. I bring my wings back in to simple tattoos that she can't tickle. Zily gives a wicked grin that has me rolling my eyes. One more minute. I want one more minute of this. Just us. That smile.

I take the chance, yanking her to me, wrapping my arms around her, feeling her small body pressed against mine. Her ears flatten sideways as I rest my chin on top of her head. Staring off at nothing, I feel her warmth seeping into me, my chest swelling. Hands ball into fists, clinging to my shirt.

"I can hear your heartbeat," she whispers. I squeeze her, not allowing her to think the thoughts I know haunt her. "One more minute." She echoes my own wish.

It doesn't feel completely right when she takes a step back out of my embrace. She stares up at me. The stars are gone in an unreadable expression. "Shall we head to dinner?" I offer her my hand again. She doesn't return the smile this time, but she does take my hand.

It's at the dining room doors when she takes her hand away. She doesn't want my parents seeing. I could care less what others think if it keeps her by my side. She greets my parents a bit strained.

Dad has relaxed more around Zily. He openly discusses our meeting with my uncle and cousin in front of her. She seems as shocked as I am, though she remains quiet. My cousin is in a similar position as me on a smaller scale. He'll be taking over for his father soon, but my uncle has been creating some strife in their lands that my cousin wanted help with. I need to see them in a few weeks to make sure everything is progressing nicely.

Dessert is a simple chocolate moose with a vanilla cookie delicately placed on top to not sink in. I engage in conversation, keeping an eye on Zily at all times. As always, she takes little bites, savoring it. I take the cookie, dipping it once into the chocolate, before swapping her empty bowl for mine. Her eyes flicker to me, tail quietly thumping the chair beside her thigh. I give a subtle nod. She hums happily sucking the pudding off the spoon.

After dinner, I invite her for a walk in the garden. We didn't have a lot of time together today. We often do our own thing, but being away from the manor all day feels different. More time. I always yearn for more time with her.

Zily doesn't object, though she seems surprised. We say goodnight to my parents, walking through the foyer. The sky is lit up by the billions of stars twinkling, a half-moon shining down on us. A lamp posts shine the way down the path, dimly lit by fire crystals. Zily skips beside me, hands behind her back, face to the sky.

She pauses to admire a bush of blue flowers, her fingers gently rubbing the petals. The evening breeze ruffles her hair, the clips keeping it out of her face. I wonder if it tickles her ears with the way they flicker. She glances at me when I chuckle. I shake my head dismissively, sliding my hands into my pockets. Turning, she wanders farther into the garden, peeking back to make sure I'm following. Of course I do.

"Zily?" She's sniffing little white flowers. Night phlox, if I remember the name correctly. Her dazzling eyes drift to me. "Do you like it here?"

Her head tilts contemplating the question, tail swishing. She stares up at the sky, voice but a whisper. "It's like a dream."

I step up behind her, wrapping my arms around her. With a tender squeeze, I hope to ease some of the pain that seeped into her eyes. I'm a coward for not simply asking her to stay with me. She has people waiting for her. I know my fate and I've accepted it. But for tonight, I want to forget all that.

I brush my fingers down her cheek, crooking my finger to turn her head toward me, dipping my head down to capture her lips with mine. The touch is soft, testing her response. My heart thrums in my ears. She doesn't pull away, so I press, deepening the kiss. I make it brief, not wanting to overwhelm her.

I stare at her face for any sort of reaction. Pink blossoms in her cheeks. Her eyes are wide, stars swirling in the black depth. She twists, hands clutching my shirt, resting her head against my chest. She said earlier she could hear my heart like this. Can she hear the way it gallops now?

"Let's go in," she quietly says, stepping out of my embrace. I frown when she avoids looking at me, but she takes my hand, lacing our fingers together. She doesn't let go until we're at her door and she says goodnight.

Zily greets me with her usual morning enthusiasm. She wears a pretty, long green dress that hugs her torso, her ass, and her thighs before loosening. It's different from the dresses she has chosen thus far. I don't comment on it, but I definitely admire it. She readjusts the moon hair clip, bringing attention to her eyes with the motion. They're red rimmed as if she'd been crying. I open my mouth to ask her what's wrong, but she grabs my hand.

"Let's go!" She drags me down the hall, tail swishing excitedly. I laugh, the sound strained like it didn't want to come out of my chest. The dress restricts her movement. Maybe it's better not to bring it up and ruin her current cheerful mood.

Her hand slips from mine as I open the door to the dining room. Her smile is forced through breakfast. She hardly speaks. When my mom inquires if she's alright, Zily simply says she's tired. It's the first time she doesn't come close to finishing her plate.

"Is there anything you would like to do today?" I ask her when we leave the dining room. I reach for her hand, a gesture that is starting to feel natural, but she steps back, folding her hands behind her back.

"I'm going to grab my book." She doesn't wait for me to respond, walking to the stairs.

My heart sinks, fearing the worst. I hope I'm wrong. I hope we have more time. I stroll out to the garden, expecting her to either go there or to the library if she is grabbing her book. I stroll through the garden, thinking about last night.

When it doesn't seem like she's coming to the garden, I pick a few flowers. I need to check the work Zily said landed on my desk. Stopping by her room on the way, I knock, peeking inside when she doesn't answer. The room is empty. Her book sits on the nightstand, her sword laying across her pillow and her bag is half under the bed. I close my eyes, sucking in a deep breath. So, this is it. I leave the flowers on the pillow beside her sword.

Kai strolls down the hall toward me soon after I leave Zily's room. He has that usual annoyed expression on his face, glaring at the world around him. He's going to be so pissed when this is over. If I beg, would he not go after her?

"What's wrong with your Kitsune?" I blink, staring at him. "It looked like she was crying. It was… unnerving." He crosses his arms. The look he wears is all too familiar, but it's unusual to see him worrying about someone other than me.

"I don't know. I think she's having a bad day." Not a complete lie.

"Are you going to the study?" I nod. "Will she be there again?" I shrug. He looks annoyed. "You really need to keep better track of her." There's not the same bite to the words as they had at the beginning of the week.

"I let her do as she wishes."

"That's dangerous."

"I know."

Chapter Fourteen
Hydrangea

The meaning behind this flower varies by their color, but often convey gratitude, apology, heartfelt feelings, and abundance. All parts are toxic and contain a compound that releases cyanide.

Zily

Walking back from the library after skimming books about poisons, I wipe my eyes, keeping my head down in case I pass anyone. The ones in my bag won't do. I have ingredients for paralysis. One's that make the target so incredibly thirsty, they inadvertently drown themselves. There's the ones that induce vomiting, seizures, the feeling of skin being on fire and the long term ones where the target gets progressively sick, passing days later.

None of them will work. Not for this job. I don't want him to suffer. Just go to sleep. But I don't have access to ingredients to make one that'd be quick and painless. The thought that I may not be able to use my normal poisoning method crosses my mind, making me nauseous. I've only stabbed someone a handful of times, but is that the quickest method I currently have access to?

I duck my head, spotting Kai walking in the opposite direction. For once, I wish my hair could fall in front of my face, to hide behind the white curtain. A hand wraps around my arm, turning me back. On instinct, I look up. Kai is staring at me, eyebrows scrunched together as he searches my face. If he figures it out, he could stop me.

"What-" He begins. I yank my arm away, glaring at him the best I can. Before he can continue, I hurry down the hall, my hands balled into fists, clutching my skirt. I hate the concern that filled his eyes.

Flowers lay on my pillow, the leaves touching my sword I left out. I pick up the little bouquet, smiling to myself as fresh tears slip down my cheek. The idiot. He knows why I'm here and yet he gives me his desserts, leaves me flowers, and kisses me. By the Moon, he kissed me last night.

Sucking in a deep breath, I go into the bathroom to splash water on my face. If this is going to be our last day, then I'd like to spend it together. I pick up my book, hugging it close to my chest. He said if I was looking for him, I should check his study. I told him about some papers on his desk yesterday, so it seems like a good bet.

I open the door without knocking, forcing myself to look happy. Sylas jumps, slamming a drawer shut. We stare at each other. I cock my head in question, tail swishing behind me. He smiles nervously.

"Would you like some company?"

"Sure. Yes. Of course." He shifts in his seat.

"Did you hide something?" I cross the room, sitting on the edge of the desk as I had before. It's a bit of a struggle with the dress I'm currently wearing restricting my movement. I wanted to try a new style. It confirms that I'm not a fan of tight fit dresses, though I do enjoy the way Sylas looks at me in it. My gaze drifts down, wondering which drawer it was he closed.

"No. It's nothing." I raise an eyebrow, letting him know he isn't a good liar. Clouds enter his eyes.

"Do you have a lot of work to get through?" He shrugs, lifting a few pieces of paper, letting them flutter back down into their neat little stack. "Are you able to keep your desk in order if I go sit on the couch?" I tease.

"Yes. I think I can manage." Sylas rolls his eyes. I grin at him. He smiles back.

Sliding off the desk, I take my spot on the couch. Funny how I've come to consider certain spots as mine, like I fit perfectly there. I'll miss it here. *No, don't think about it. Don't think about tomorrow.* I'm going to enjoy today.

I flip to the back of my book of the single drawing I have of Sylas at his desk. Starting on a new one, I imagine his wings. I sketch and erase until I get the texture of his wings right, soft and smooth. I glance up when Sylas leaves his desk, sitting with me. Angled away from him, I make sure he can't see my sketch.

He stares at me openly, unapologetically. He angles his body towards me, an elbow propped on the back of the couch, one leg on the couch, bent so his foot dangles. My cheeks begin to heat up, my gaze flickering up to him repeatedly.

"You're beautiful," he says out of nowhere.

I lift my book, hiding my face. "You can't just say something like that," I squeak, closing my eyes. The warmth of his words spread with every beat of my pounding heart.

"Zily." I peek over the book. He leans forward, his hand petting my head, gentle and sweet. "It's ok. It's going to be ok. I promise." His blue eyes are clear as he speaks.

I sigh, closing my book. I managed to finish the wings, but couldn't draw his legs. Oh well. Swinging my feet down, I twist so that I can lean on him. His arm slips around my waist. His touch is tender, worried about my injury. I rest my head on his chest, listening to his heartbeat. I don't notice the passage of time, sitting here with him.

"Are you hungry?" He asks at some point, his voice low, fingers playing with my hair, sending goosebumps across my skin.

"It'll be dinner soon enough."

"We did sort of miss the usual lunch time."

"Can we stay like this a little longer?" I whisper.

"Yes." He kisses the top of my head.

I close my eyes, fighting back thoughts from streaming in. My mind remains blank. If I think about anything, good or bad, it'll lead to tears, and I don't want that. If I think about Callie and Decan, how much I miss them, the stories I'll tell them, it means the job is done. If I think about not returning, the unknown of what will happen to my friends scares me. I can't be sure Sir Colin Eyler won't do anything to me, to them, to Sylas if I disobey. Rumors of the total control he has over us scare me.

So, the beating of the heart I listen intently to becomes my world. I breathe in the scent of paper, wind and wood, holding me in place. Like a blanket of comfort, his arms wrap around me, keeping the fear temporarily at bay. There is only this. This couch. This scent. This body. This heart. It's selfish, but I silently make a claim to it. Mine. All of it is mine.

Supper comes sooner than I would have liked. My stomach yells at me for not eating lunch. Sylas keeps an arm around me as he helps me to my feet. It stays there while we walk down the hall. Cold seeps in when I step away into my room. I change into a different dress, black with tiny white polka dots, long and flowy. The flowers Sylas left still lay on my pillow. Wanting to keep them, I lay them out on a blank page in my book, pressing down with everything I have.

Leaving my book beside my sword, I head back out into the hall, seeking warmth like the winter melting into spring. Sylas gaze travels over me, taking in the new dress. I do a quick spin for him, giggling. He slides his hand in mine, and I skip beside him to dinner. I almost hold on, but our fingers uncurl from each other. He opens the door for me. Eleanor and Reuben greet me pleasantly. I don't think about the disappointment they'll feel when they learn I've killed their son. They're good people; I've come to like them, having breakfast and dinner with them daily. They don't deserve it.

I snicker while Eleanor tells a story of how Reuben fell asleep during work one day, drooling all over his desk. Reuben's ears turn red, eating his meal without looking up. No, he steals a glance at his wife, the tiniest hint of a smile on his lips, a loving gleam in his eyes.

I peek over at Sylas, considering mentioning his messy desk. He's staring at me with clear blue eyes shining. My face heats up, and I quickly look away, pretending not to notice. Eleanor is watching us. I want to tell her, *'No, it's not like that.'* But it is and it'll end tonight.

I drop a hand to my lap, bunching fabric in my fist, keeping the smile planted on my face. Sylas' foot bumps mine. I swallow, turning my head to look at him again. His eyes ask what's wrong. As subtly as possible, I shake my head. I nearly laugh when I feel his foot against mine. We can't hold hands, but we can still touch in this small way.

Saying goodnight to Eleanor and Reuben, I wonder if they can tell I'm saying goodbye. Sylas' hand finds mine when we're halfway up the stairs, his fingers lacing with mine. I squeeze with everything in me, not complaining when he squeezes back a little too hard. I face him, my bedroom door at my back. My throat feels dry.

"Goodnight, Zily." He speaks first, taking a step away toward his room. My hand lifts with his, not ready to let go.

"Goodnight." I quietly reply, my hand slipping from his.

I enter my room first, leaning back against the door. The tears flow freely down my cheeks. Every awful thought, every wish, every emotion wreaking havoc on my body. Sliding to the floor, legs unable to hold me up anymore, shoulders shaking, I cover my mouth to muffle the sobs.

That was our last "goodnight." Our last dinner together. Our last day. The last time I'll ever hear his voice. All the firsts followed by the lasts race through my mind. There's so much I wish I could have done.

When my body stops shaking, feeling hollow, I crawl to the bed, using it to help me stand. I change into my shorts, feeling like a foreign object, and the shirt I was given after being stitched up. The stitches haven't completely dissolved yet, but I'm not too worried about them. My boots don't feel right after the flats and heels I've worn for the past week. It's really only been a week. How could my life have changed so much within a week?

I've never had a week of leisure like this before. Everything about being here is truly like a dream that I wish I didn't have to wake from. However, the thing that keeps me from speaking of Gateswood and Sir Colin Eyler pushes me towards completing the task. It's a constant prickly pang in the back of my head whenever I think about disobeying, about speaking out. If rumors turn out to be true, I'll be forced to do this either way, or another will be sent to complete the task. I would rather do it myself and make it as quick a death as possible. I know my friends will be sad, but I accepted my own demise back in the river. It hasn't changed. Only the method.

I sit on the edge of the bed, waiting for the right time to cross the hall. My sword lays across my lap. I've never used a sword to complete the job before. A few times I did stab my target. The stabbings were usually out of panic.

There was this one time I was sent out to kill Duke Ryder of the Euthoria Kingdom visiting the kingdom of Atelyra. I was tasked with making sure he didn't make it to the king of Atelyra. It was an unusual set meeting since Sir Ryder was a Werewolf in lands dominated by Vampires. It was one of my longer jobs, another where I was given two weeks, though that was hardly enough time to get there, do the task and get back.

I sped walked through the forest, over hills, getting a lift on the back of a carriages from traveling merchants to get to where I needed to in a timely manner. I've seen so much of the lands during my jobs. Every shade of green the trees and grass can offer. The orange, red, and yellows of the falling leaves. The tans and browns of vast fields. I've slept on hard dirt as well as muddy terrain after its just rained.

Wagon rides were the best, especially on this mission. I could sit on the back, rest my feet while I watched the world pass by. If the road wasn't too bumpy, I would sketch the landscape. Over the years, a few have offered to buy my drawings. I earned money by sketching portraits for those who asked. At first, I only sold them for a couple curpem a piece. Then a man handed me an arenti, telling me I was under charging, and I should know my worth. It was strange when I was approached by those who specifically requested portraits done by me. Once I did some sketches for an event. It seemed like a big deal for a couple. I was paid aurem. Finding out Sir Colin Eyler didn't care what money we had or how we got it was a blessing.

My drawings became a good cover. No one paid attention to why I was there if I had pen and paper in hand. It made info gather easier to, casually talking to those requesting I draw them. Sir Ryder would be passing through the town I was scouting before reaching his final destination. I needed to get to him there for more reasons than one. There would be less guards and obstacles. If I could learn what inn he planned to stay at, I could form a plan.

Luckily, people like to gossip. As I handed over a portrait to a middle aged couple, they informed me excitedly that someone very important would be staying at their establishment. He's supposed to arrive that night. Perfect. If I rushed, I could make it back with a little time to spare and avoid punishment.

The town was decently lit during the night. Fire crystals rest on top of posts, lighting up the walkways. Between the buildings, shadows roam. I lurked through them, zigzagging my way to the inn. It was the middle of the night, and you would think most everyone would be asleep by this point, especially someone who had been traveling for days on end.

I prepared my poison of choice below the window of where the duke was staying. The window was dark. I put the poison on a little knife the size of a pen. The objective was to give him a little paper cut without waking him and get out.

The window slid open with ease. I climbed in, crouching in the darkness against the wall. But it wasn't completely dark. There was light seeping through the crack of the bathroom door. Just as I registered that he's in fact not in his bed, the bathroom door opened. I dove under the bed, my heart pounding.

Sir Ryder sat on the bed. His bare feet rested on the floor on the side of the bed right in front of my face. I took my little blade and did a quick little slash along the side of the heel. A little trickle of blood dripped from the wound. A hiss came from above as he quickly stood.

Before I had a chance to attempt to scoot out from under the bed, the Duke looked under the bed. The moment his dark eyes met mine, he flipped the bed. I gasped, jumping to my feet. Spinning, I dashed for the window. Luckily, I left it open. Unluckily, the Duke grabbed me by my tail, dragging me back. A shriek escaped with the sharp pain.

"What the fuck do you think you're doing?" he demanded. His hand locked onto my hair, lifting me up in front of him.

I kicked my feet dangling a couple of inches off the ground, tears streaming down my face. I tried to pry his hand out of my hair. The blade cut up his hand, forcing him to let go. He called me some names, taking a step back. Trying to get my bearings, he stepped forward again. Screaming, I swung down, stabbing the blade into his shoulder, right by his neck. He yelled in pain and blood sprayed everywhere.

While he was busy pulling the knife out, I ran to the window, leaping out and spraining my ankle. Still, I ran for as long as I could manage. That was one of the worst jobs. I don't know if he bled out or if the poison took him. Bleeding out might have been the better option with the amount of poison that ended up in his body. It was not a friendly poison.

This time will be different. I won't let Sylas suffer. If I shove the sword through his heart, it'll be a quick death.

I shake myself from the memory. Just like that time, it's the middle of the night and most everyone should be asleep. I pack my book safely inside my bag. As much as I love my hair clips, I put them away in the front pocket, finding the plainest headband I have in the room to keep my hair out of my face. My bag is left by the door, ready to go. I buckle my sword belt on, touching the pommel.

Turning off my bedroom light, I slip into the hall silently. The hall is dark save for a single dim light at the end of the corridor and the faint glow of the aquamarine crystals embedded in the wall to call servants. I stand there in the open for a moment, waiting, half expecting someone would come around the corner and see me. Stop me. A little hope flickers that someone will stop me, that he'll stop me. I know it's useless.

Taking the five steps across the hall, grabbing the door knob to his room. I push all thoughts away, retreating to the darkness within myself I would hide during previous missions until it's over.

The door doesn't so much as creek when I crack it open, peering into the room. Moonlight shines through the glass door to the balcony, curtains pulled back, illuminating half the room. My eyes have already adjusted to the dark thanks to the moments I took in the hall. Every detail is clear to me. The target lays in a bed of violet silk sheets, unmoving, presumably asleep. Easing in, the door makes the smallest click closed.

I circle the room, getting out of the moonlight as quickly as possible. The short sword glides from its sheath silently. I've done this before. This is no different than the others, yet the little voice I shoved into the darkness cries.

The target shifts, rolling over in his sleep. I freeze in the shadows. His chest rises with steady deep breaths. Slowly, not to disturb him, I climb onto the bed. I know I've woken him when his body stiffens under me. My legs straddle his waist as I hold the sword above his chest with both hands.

His eyes open, nearly breaking me. For a moment, I'm glad. He'll throw me off. He can stop me. I know he can. It goes without saying; he's stronger than I am. I press the tip of the blade against the blue silk fabric of his shirt over his heart. He doesn't move, watching me quietly.

"I told you I'm here to kill you." I prompt him to take action. He continues to lay unmoving under me.

"I know." His lips curve up.

I close my eyes, unable to look at him, at his smile. It's breaking me. I can't do this. It was just a facade. "Why don't you fight back?"

"I can't." He repeats the words that echo in my head. What have we done to get here? Both accepting death so easily. He caresses my face with one hand, my eyes opening, fighting back tears that I thought I ran out of. His thumb brushes my cheek, his other hand reaching up to cover mine on the hilt of the sword. "It's okay. If it's something you have to do, then I'm glad it's by your hands." He pulls the blade down, the sharp tip puncturing his skin.

I stare at the tiny blotch of blood soaking through his shirt. My head begins to spin, my breaths coming out in quick heavy succession. I can't keep my grip on my sword, hands shaking. Sylas pushes himself up, shoving the blade away to not stab himself anymore. The sword clatters to the floor.

Sylas cups my face with both hands, forcing me to look at him, into his eyes of clear sky. I've forgotten how to breathe, lungs gasping for air. My head thrums. His hand glides up, petting my ears back, fingers running through my hair, cooing to me, but there's a ringing in my ears that drowns him out.

"I'm sorry." I don't know if the words make it out.

He smiles at me, that sweet, affectionate one I've come to know and love. His lips land on mine, stealing the air I've been attempting to suck in. Everything goes quiet. The ringing stops. The prickly feeling in the back of my head fades. Heat floods my body.

I slide my arms around his neck, my lips parting for him. He sighs against me, his hand sliding to my back, pulling me closer. Our bodies press together. His tongue teases mine and I nip at it. My fingers find their way into his hair. I love his hair down.

He groans against my mouth, hands searching for payback. He strokes my tail, following the curve up. A sound, a whimper, I've never made before slip past my lips, a shiver running down my spine. Sylas breaks the kiss, lips brushing along my jaw, down my neck. Tilting my head to give him better access, consequences of our actions poke their way into my mind.

"There'll be others," I whisper. He growls in response, my nails dragging across the top of his back. I wonder if I should undo the buttons or if I can pull the shirt off of him. His fingers tease my skin above my shorts. "They'll come. They-they'll kill…" I cut off, whimpering, my body jerking as he strokes my tail again, gently tugging. I bury my face in the crook between his neck and shoulder. He smells like fresh air and trees. Intoxicating.

The world flips. I blink, stunned, staring up at Sylas grinning down at me. The light in his eyes is breathtaking. He leans down, kissing my forehead sweetly while a hand roams up my side under my shirt. "They won't. I'll keep you safe. I promise." He touches his brow to mine. "Trust me."

There's so much he doesn't know. So much I can't tell him, even though I want to. A headache threatens to creep in. Fear wants to take over, but it's pushed away by the light in his eyes, the gentle touches and kisses. I wrap my arms around him again, pulling his shirt up to bunch up in my hands.

"I do."

His eyes flare when my nails scratch bare skin. He pulls back enough for me to finish pulling off his shirt. My fingertips skim down his chest. I pause over the little hole made by my blade, a little trickle of blood seeping out. I press my palm flat against the spot, feeling the beat of the heart under it.

Sylas takes my hand, kissing it. *Don't think about it,* his tender touch says. It's just us right now. Later. Later we'll talk and I'll find a way to keep him safe. I wrap my arms around him, once again playing with his hair, using him to lift my body so his roaming hand can pull my shirt off, discarding my under garments with it.

I shiver, my bare skin exposed to the air. He plants kisses and nips down my chest, between my breasts, across my stomach down to my navel. His fingers curl around the seam of my shorts. He hesitates. Without using words to tell him what I want, my fingers tangle in his hair, pulling him back up to me. I press my lips to his, biting his bottom lip, forcing him to open up to me. My tongue slides in between his lips. A deep groan escapes, sucking on my tongue. He makes quick work of my shorts, struggling with his own pants, making me giggle.

Sylas' gaze trails over my body, making me a little self-conscious, though I stay still for him. He traces a finger across the forming scars of my wounds. He kisses each sealed hole sweetly.

The one on my hip is the most healed, followed by the one by my ribs, though that one had hurt the most. He moves to kiss old scars on the other side, long silver tone markings along my side. New and old; my worlds colliding.

A hand slips under my ass, squeezing and massaging. I whimper, his fingers combing through my tail. He towers over, pressing the heat of his body down on me. I hook my legs around his waist.

"Not fair," I breathe in his ear, lightly trailing my fingers over the tattoos of his wings on his back.

He growls, obliging to my request, his wings unfurling like a curtain around us. I stretch, our bodies rubbing together as I brush my fingers through the feathers. So soft. He bites the crook of my neck in response. His hips lower pressing against me. I can feel his desire as great as my own.

Sylas kisses me deeply, hand supporting my back as he adjusts our bodies, angling himself at my core. A gasp escapes as he presses into me, slow and steady, taking his time. I moan against his lips. Heat courses through my body.

Time is lost in the steam of kisses, scratches and the grinding of bodies. Sounds I would normally be embarrassed by fill the room. I don't hold back. It seems to encourage Sylas with the way his hips roll, pressing deep into me before pulling out and diving back in, his large hands caressing my back. I bury my face in his neck when the pressure inside grows to be too much, a blissful pleasure taking over everything. His body stiffens, arms locked around me when his own release takes him.

Sylas pets my head as I cling to him, sweat coating our bodies. He kisses my forehead, rolling off of me. Holding me against him, he tucks a wing under me. I squirm on my feather bed, resting my head on his chest. He hisses through his teeth. I peek at him, grinning. Despite what we just did, there's a heat in his eyes that makes me consider climbing on top of him.

His wing wraps around me like a cozy blanket. "Sleep. There's always tomorrow."

Tomorrow. The word echoes in my mind, a shining promise. I can't believe it will be so bright. There's darkness and fear on the edges, but the joy consumes me along with a new determination. A new plan.

Tomorrow, I'll still be in his arms. I'll tell him what I can before the pain becomes unbearable. Tomorrow, I'll tell him all about Callie and Decan and maybe we'll make a plan to rescue them together. Can we really be rescued from his clutches? I don't dwell too long on the thought. Tonight, I will believe in a future I never thought I could have before, on the slim chance that it can exist.

"Sylas," I whisper sleepily.

"Hmm?" *He too is falling asleep.*

I sigh happily listening to his heartbeat. "I just wanted to say your name."

"Zily," He breathes my name, tickling my ears. I relax, curled into his body, touching in as many places as possible.

Chapter Fifteen
Feverfew

This symbolizes a connection to health and happiness. It can be used with medicine to help relieve migraines.

Sylas

The morning knock comes all too soon. I'm barely conscious enough to pull the blanket up over our naked bodies. Zily remains asleep, nestled against my side, mostly hidden by my wing. I can count on one hand the number of times I've slept with my wings out. If she asked, I'd sleep like this every night.

The maid steps in, curtsying and cheerfully informs me how much time there is before breakfast. I sigh, raking my fingers through my hair, grateful the maid today is Marie. She won't gossip with others about this, though her eyes are wide as she takes in the scene. Her gaze flickers to my wing, to the blanket. I shift enough to show her Zily's snow white hair and ears. They twitch, my breath tickling them.

Marie grins, putting a finger to her lips, promising to keep our secret. That is until we're ready for the world to know. I don't want to keep our relationship a secret, but we should probably talk before word gets around. There's a lot that needs to be discussed.

Zily rubs her eyes sleepily, waking to the sound of the door closing behind Marie. The stars shine in her eyes as she peers up at me, brighter than I've ever seen. Cupping her cheek, I kiss her deeply.

"Would you like to bathe before breakfast," I ask while she runs her fingers through my hair over and over. I kiss her again, unable to help myself. A wall has come down between us and I'm struggling to contain myself.

"A bath would be nice. I may have gotten a bit sweaty last night." My lips curl into a smirk while she giggles, a pretty blush blooming on her cheeks. Her hand falls to my chest, resting over the puncture wound. Dry blood has crusted over it.

Before her thoughts have a chance to linger on that subject, I slide from the bed, putting my wings away. Keeping an arm around her, I pull Zily with me. She squeals when I pick her up, carrying her to the bathing room. I love her giggles. She has her arms crossed in a modest manner, even though she let me see every bit of her last night.

Zily gasps loudly. "What is that?"

I pause in the middle of the bathing room, following her gaze. "The tub?"

Zily looks at me, a hand pointing at the square bath in the floor, clear quartz making up the walls with red jasper dotted in. "That is not a tub. It's like a mini lake!"

I laugh, stepping down into the warm water, slowly sinking onto the seat. The water swishes around us. I take the soap massaging it across her pale skin. She tenses, shifting, hugging herself. It's not in modesty. Her hands are trying to cover scars. They've always been hidden under her choice of dress, but her back is covered in old lacerations, silver marks on her pale skin.

I kiss her shoulder, a shiver running down her. "You're beautiful," I tell her when she peeks back at me. The corner of her lips turns up.

The shampoo lathers into bubbles around her soft tail. Zily shivers as I comb my fingers through the fur. She shoots me a glare my way, not out of anger, but a warning. I kiss her deeply, cupping the back of her neck, petting her tail while washing the shampoo out. She moans, her fingers finding their way into my hair.

Maybe bathing together wasn't a good idea. The thought that we may be going too fast disappears as she straddles me. I groan, taking her slender hips in my hands, pulling her close. She rolls her body, her breasts rubbing against my chest.

I suck on her tongue, lifting her, lining myself up with her entrance. She seats herself. I slide in with ease, devouring her moan. My hands explore her body, up her waist to her breasts. I circle her nipple with my thumb. She whimpers, her head falling back as I kiss down her neck, nipping at the crook of her neck. I want to mark her, but perhaps not somewhere visible.

My hands continue memorizing her body, sliding them around, rubbing down her back, feeling the grooves of the scars. Whoever did this to her will pay. But right now, I'm only focused on her. One hand pauses on her lower back, the other cupping her perfect little ass. Her back arches, nail digging into my shoulder. I groan, biting the inside of her breast, sucking hard. I'll mark her here. Her hips roll, rising and falling, sending a wave of pleasure through me.

I hit her most sensitive spot repeatedly without mercy, raking my fingers through her tails to drive her over the edge. Her body trembles in my arms. I hiss at the sting her nails leave behind on my back, marking me in her own way, I know and I love it. She's not loud with the delicious noises that escape her, but I do adore them, the way she does a sharp gasp, burying her face in my neck as she climaxes. I hold her against me, trailing my fingers up and down her back, attempting to catch my breath.

"Zily," I whisper.

She giggles, lightly kissing me. "Sylas."

"We're supposed to be getting ready for breakfast."

Her head falls back with breathy laughter. "This is not my fault." I shiver as she slides off me, moving to my side.

I chuckle, grabbing the soap again. She pours some shampoo onto her hand, reaching up to my head. I've never had someone wash my hair for me like this before, her fingers massage my scalp. A sound close to a purr escapes. She giggles some more, catching her breath. I return the favor, gently rubbing her ears, discovering another sensitive spot. She dips her head, making soft pleasant sounds.

I start to dry her off, but she pulls away, wrapping a towel around her tail. I openly admire her body, watching the way she twists and bends, the cream colored towel caressing her skin. Turning away, I stride back into my room, crossing to my closet.

I have pants on when Zily emerges with a towel, wrapped around her body. I run my fingers through my wet hair wondering what I'm going to do. I didn't expect to fall like this. The worry I have for her, what she's been through, the fear she tries to hide, and the anger toward those who hurt her and inflict those fears makes my blood boil. I won't let them get to her.

Zily pokes her head into the hall. I nearly pull her back in, but she slips out before I reach her. She gives me a smirk from across the hall, closing the door. Right. She needs to get dressed too, just like I need to finish. I button up a light blue shirt, rolling up the sleeves, tucking it into my pants. Deciding my hair is dry enough, I run a brush through it, leaving it down. I collect Zily's clothes, putting them in the hamper with my own. It takes a moment to find where her sword went to. It somehow ended up under the bed. I return it to its sheath, leaning it against the nightstand.

Knocking on Zily's door is almost a morning ritual, yet it feels different today. My body craves her touch. She calls, telling me to enter. She's at the mirror, fixing her hair clips into place. She catches my gaze in the reflection as I cross the room to her. Her bag lays open on the bed, her book on her pillow.

The dress she chose is like a poofy light blue cloud, a built-in petticoat fluffs the skirt just above her knees, the sleeves hanging loose over her shoulders. White wedges bring her up past my shoulders. They're taller than other heels she's worn thus far.

I slide my arms around her. She sighs happily, relaxing into my embrace. "How did you know which dress I was going to wear?"

"I just thought I should match the day." Our clothes are nearly the exact same shade of blue. I lean around, kissing her cheek. "Ready for breakfast?"

"Yes! I'm starving."

"I'm sure." A grin creeps across my lips. Zily's face turns a deeper red. She shoves me. I laugh, taking her hand.

We walk hand in hand down to the dining room. My arm pulls back when Zily suddenly stops walking. She stares at the door, peeking up at me. I know what she's going to say before she says it, fear in her eyes, ears drooped to the side.

"We should tell them." Her voice is quiet. Excitement is already bubbling up in me. "Do you think they'll… hate me?"

The question surprises me. "No. No, they won't. We'll talk and it'll be fine." I squeeze her hand reassuringly. "You should know everyone suspected you, so it won't be too much of a surprise."

"Are you going to tell Kai he was right?" Her lips curl.

I tilt my head back, looking at the ceiling. "I'd rather not." She giggles. A delightful sound. "Here's the plan. We're going to enjoy our breakfast, and we'll talk after. Then we'll make a plan with everyone. Alright?" She nods with a shy, wary smile. "But we'll tell them this now." I lift her hand to my lips.

A cute pink flush washes over her. She looks nervous, but her hand remains in mine as I open the door. My parents stand by their seats, finishing a conversation. Morning wishes are exchanged as always. Mom's eyes flicker down, not missing a thing, a big beaming grin on her face. I'm sure dad notices too, but his face remains neutral, pulling the seat out for mom. Zily pretends not to notice the look mom is giving us, keeping her gaze down, but her deepening red face gives her away.

Breakfast is served. "Reminder: we have a lunch meeting today, Sylas." Dad picks at his eggs. Of course I remember, but he's saying it because of my rolled up sleeves and hair.

I sigh, glancing at Zily. We have a long day ahead. Dad informs me of the expected arrival time of our guests. I'm grateful he doesn't mention that our guest is the King of the Zeneth Kingdom. The little I know of why Zily was sent here is because of them. I don't want her mood to sour over breakfast. I'll ask her about it after.

"I'll meet you in your office a half an hour beforehand," I tell dad, taking Zily's hand to leave. He raises an eyebrow. Mom gives a short nod. She'll be there too.

Zily and I walk to my study. There's a bounce to her step, not quite a skip with the wedges on. Her tail swishes behind her. I wish she always smiled like she is now, but I know it'll have to fade while we talk. I close the door behind us, pulling her to the couch. She giggles falling onto my lap. I wrap my arms securely around her.

Though she continues to appear cheerful, some of the stars have dimmed in her eyes. "Can you tell me about who sent you?"

Zily closes her eyes, taking several long, deep breaths. I play with her hair, waiting patiently. "Sir Colin Eyler is in charge of Gateswood." She winces. With another shaky breath she continues, "he and the others we answer to are Vampires, which is why I questioned if it's a good idea to become friends with the Zeneth Kingdom. I don't know why Sir… doesn't want you to; he only tells me what I need to know, and that's who he wants dead and the time frame I have, so maybe it is a good idea." She speaks quickly, trying to get the words out. Her legs pull in as she starts to curl into a ball on my lap, her fingers press into her temples.

I rub circles on her back, slowly soaking in every word. "He sends you on jobs without much information." I clarify, needing to make sure I have everything straight for when I take the information to my parents and Kai.

Her head bobs, peeking at me, eyes dark voids. "We don't even get a description of our target. It's better to not ask questions… lest we get punished." My arms tighten around her at the thought of these punishments. The scars.

"Are all the jobs he sends you on like this one?" I'm trying to be gentle with my words.

"Mysterious deaths all over." She confirms with a humorless laugh, looking at her fiddling fingers. "I've gotten good at my job."

I kiss her cheek. "It's ok. You don't have to do that anymore. You're not going back." A little smile returns. "Are there others? You've mentioned your friends before."

Her ears perk slightly. "Callie and Decan. They're my best friends. We've been together since we were little. Decan is a blacksmith. He made my sword for my birthday. He's often quite serious, but is relaxed around me and Callie. Callie helped with the hilt of the sword and asked another to make the sheath. Callie… She works as more of an informant, but has been given a few jobs like mine. I started like her, until he learned of my interest and skills with poisons." Zily's ears droop again. She rubs the back of her neck.

"Could you tell me more about this Colin Eyler?" The more info the better. I can tell this isn't easy for her. She keeps rubbing her temples.

Her head bobs. "He… I don't know how long Gateswood has been around. It's south. We have to get written permission from… Sir… Colin Eyler to leave. I was given two weeks." Her voice fades a little more with every word. "If we don't do as told… We get punished. I'm told he can…" Her head falls against my shoulder.

"Zily? Zily!" I shift her, her head falling back. I cup her cheek. Panic fills me until her eyes flutter open. She blinks a few times confused. I press my brow to hers. "Are you alright?" She nods, her forehead rubbing against mine. She still seems out of it. "I think that's enough for now, ok?" I hold her close, stroking her head.

"Okay," she whispers.

Her shoulders begin to tremble after a moment, a soft sob escaping. I squeeze her, rocking back forth, not saying a thing while she cries. My chest is tight, trying to reason out what had just happened. I thought she was whispering because she was nervous about talking about it. I did not expect her to black out for a moment. What kind of control does this man have over her?

"Do you think Callie and Decan can stay here too?" It surprises me when she speaks again, voice small.

"Of course. We'll save your friends, I promise. Callie can have your room and there's an unoccupied room down the hall Decan can have."

"Where will I stay?"

"With me. If you like." I kiss the top of her head.

"Yes," she breathes. "It won't be long before they send another to finish the job."

"It'll be fine. I won't let them hurt you. Don't think about it right now." She nuzzles against my chest. "Do you want to nap?" It might be a good idea after last night and whatever is going on with her now.

"You should talk to Kai about guard rotation. He's the one in charge of that, right? Or does he only train the new recruits?" Her eyes drift close, breathing deeply.

"Shhh. Don't worry about that right now. Rest." I coo, petting her head.

Soon Zily's body relaxes against me, her chest rising and falling in a slow and steady rhythmic pattern. I hold her for a while longer before slipping out from under her, laying her on the couch. Her ears twitch at the change, but she remains asleep. I cover her with the throw blanket on the back of the couch, slipping out the door as quietly as possible. There's plenty of time before I said I would meet my parents. Though I did plan to tell them first, I head out in search of Kai.

Kai is in the training grounds, rather above it, yelling instructions at the recruits. They swing their swords in unison. I fly up beside him. In a low voice, I tell him I need to talk to him. He waits for me to speak, not moving. I drift backwards, motioning with my head that this is a private matter. Kai's golden brown wings push him backwards. He reluctantly turns his back to the men, but not before giving them a death glare for if they even consider slacking off. He crosses his arms.

"Do you think they're ready if we put them on the guard rotation?"

Kai raises an eyebrow, glancing back. "Yeah. They'd know what to do. It'd probably be good for them to shadow some of the veterans. Only a couple of them plan to join the Royal Guard, but the experience will be good for all of them." He brings his steely gaze back to me. "Why?"

"We should expect some… unwelcome guests."

"Like the Kitsune you've been doting on?" There's a teasing in his voice I'm not used to.

A smirk creeps across my lips. "Exactly."

Kai stares at me, running a hand through his auburn hair. "Explain from the beginning."

I sigh, launching into yes, Zily was here to kill me. No, she's not going to. Yes, I'm sure. Then about the place she referred to as Gateswood and Colin Eyler. Kai bites back an "I told you so," letting me finish the explanation.

There's a moment of silence when I finish. "That's it? She didn't tell you anything else about this man? What they want or where they're located?"

"She blacked out." Kai's eyebrows shoot up. "I don't think she can, for whatever reason. It was like talking pained her and at a certain point she just… passed out. I left her to rest in the study."

Kai nods, staring off, gears turning inside his head. "So out of all the ladies in the world, you fell for a Kitsune, your assassin?"

I roll my eyes, giving a little shrug. "What can I say? I like them deadly." That got a laugh out of Kai.

"Seriously though, that sounds like a huge mess that's a little too close to home for my liking."

"Agreed. I'll be speaking with my parents shortly. I don't know how much of a plan we can currently make with our guests coming and not knowing the location of Gateswood, but if you have an idea, let me know. And can you talk to Brawns about increasing security without giving him too many details?"

Kai sighs, bowing his head. "Sure. I'll tell him it's for training."

"Thanks. One more thing," I hesitate, "could you help keep an eye on Zily when I'm unable to. She believes they'll send someone to replace her, and I worry what will happen when they discover she's defected."

Kai rakes his fingers through his hair again. "What? Am I supposed to worry about both of you now?" I grin. "Sure. Once I get the boys set up with Brawns, I'll have more time. I owe her anyways, and I want to get to know her if you're really serious about her." He raises a single eyebrow in question.

I nod, unable to stop smiling. "I am."

Kai glances back at the men training, eyes narrowing. "I need to get back. You need to speak with your parents."

I return to my room, flying in through my balcony window, fixing my sleeves, making sure my shirt is neatly tucked and adding a blazer. I smooth my hair back into a ponytail, checking my reflection. The conversation with Kai was like a warm up. My parents have warmed up to Zily, so I'm not worried about that, but we need to prepare for the danger that's coming.

I peek into my study, heading down to my dad's. Zily is gone, the blanket folded and draped over the back of the couch. I make a quick stop by Leona's room as well, asking her to take dresses for Zily to my room from now on. A wave of emotions flashes across her face. A little smirk, sparkles of excitement, realizing how much space she has to fill now, making me laugh. Then her expression settles on something that says she's happy for me. Heat rises up my neck.

At my dad's office, I knock and enter quickly, both of my parents standing while waiting for me. My attire, though smooth and professional, is more informal than his. He's in a suit of navy blue, black hair combed down, shining with some kind of product.

"Does this have to do with Zily?" Dad gets right to it, mouth set into a tight line, concern in his eyes. Mom stares at me with a small frown, her hands clenched together, tighter than usual, in front of her.

"Yes. She'll be staying with us." I leave no room for questions in my statement. That is one subject I won't budge on, though with my parents, I don't suspect it'll be an issue.

"Then what is the problem?"

I suck in a deep breath. "The problem is Zily was sent to kill me and the person who wants me dead will send others like Zily that'll probably hurt her as well."

"So, we shouldn't have trusted her?" Dad raises an eyebrow, eyes darkening. I open my mouth to respond.

"That can't be true." Mom covers her mouth in shock. She turns to dad.

"I'm surprised Kai didn't do something with her. He kept mentioning not trusting her."

"She seems so sweet at dinner."

"Are you sure she should stay here?"

"She's not going to kill me," I state plainly.

"How can you be sure? She's only been here a week. I know you've become infatuated with her, but you need to take threats against your life seriously." Dad stares at me with narrowed eyes. My ears can't believe what they're hearing.

"It may be hard to hear, but perhaps Kai is right. She seems sweet, though it seems like it's been a lie." Mom sounds disappointed.

"We should let Kai interrogate her."

"She's not going to kill me!" I interrupt. It's not often I have to force someone to listen to me, and I've never had to use this tone with my parents before. I cross the room, preparing to stand my ground. They stare at me; dad with a harsh gaze; mom with worry and pity. "Kai will do no such thing. She told me what she could. Another will be sent to replace her. I've already spoke with Kai about increasing security."

"What did she end up telling you? You know I trust you and your judgments, that's why we're stepping down to let you take our place, but how can you be sure what she says is true?" Dad's voice remains low. His fingers flex. The only sign that he's irritated.

"Because it caused her pain to the point that she blacked out on me." I meet his gaze.

Mom's eyes widened. "What? What do you mean she blacked out? Is she alright?" Mom's soft heart gives me hope. I do not take my gaze away from my father's.

"She passed out in my arms in the middle of telling me about Colin Eyler. He's the man that sent her. I think he's done something to her that prevents her from going into too much detail." Shock crosses both my parents' faces. I take their moment of speechlessness to forge on. "She referred to the place she came from as Gateswood. I don't have much info on that; I wanted to let her rest after what happened. According to her, Eyler isn't too keen about me making alliances with the Zeneth Kingdom." I let out a breath, wondering if I got everything that needed to be said out.

Dad touches his chin in thought. "When should we expect another attempt on your life?" He raises an eyebrow, silently asking if Zily did try to take my life.

I will not be sharing anything that happened last night with them. "I don't have a time frame yet. I'll ask her when I can."

"Sy," Mom says gently. I let my gaze drift over to her. "You care a lot about Zily, don't you?"

I can feel heat rising up my neck as I picture her pretty smile, her giggles, the way she savors every bite of food, how excited she gets about flowers, and the way she felt next to me last night. "Yes. Yes, I do."

Mom and dad exchange looks, having a silent conversation. "If she can't speak in detail, could she point on a map where this Gateswood is located?" Dad still doesn't look pleased with me.

"I'm sure Zily wouldn't mind, as long as it's not too much of a strain on her."

"Then in the meantime, you have another kingdom to win over."

As if on cue, a maid knocks on the door, announcing the arrival of our guests. Time to make unlikely friends.

Chapter Sixteen
Calendula

This little flower means happiness, simplicity and healing. It's said to have anti-inflammatory properties that could help with skin conditions and wound healing. It can be added to lotions and balms or made into teas and oils.

Zily

I spy them from the library window. I'm trying unsuccessfully to pull a book down from a high shelf without pulling a chair over to climb on. It's right when I place a foot on the chair that I look down at the carriage that's just arrived, a couple of men dressed in finery step out of the carriage, surrounded by guards. One with swooped back blond hair in a maroon and gold suit turns his head in my direction. I drop down. If he wasn't a Vampire, I believe he wouldn't have seen me. But their eyes are sharp and even my speed isn't fast enough.

I peer over the chair, ears pinned back. The blond has his back to me, speaking with a man with short chestnut hair in similar color, though his attire matches that of the guards that came with them. A maid comes out to greet them, curtsying low. The men nod a greeting at whatever she has said. They both shoot a look up to my window before following her inside.

The library is my sanctuary; I decide not to leave. Sylas will find me here after his meeting. I settle down to read, wondering how long the Vampires are planning to stay. I know this is a good thing, that it'll be good for Sylas' kingdom, but my personal experience with their kind puts a sour taste in my mouth.

The books don't do much in the way of distraction. My thoughts keep wandering back to Sylas and those Vampires. All the things that can go wrong wage war against all the good this meeting could bring.

A hand waves in front of my face, the smell of something delicious reaching my nose. My tail begins to wag before I look up. Zachary's staring down at me. A dish with a small slice of meat drizzled in brown gravy with a side of steamed vegetables. My mouth waters.

"For me?" I sit up properly.

"I don't see anyone else in here, do you?" Zachary grins.

I lean over the short table, cutting a little bite. Moaning with delight, I press my hand to my cheek, savoring the juicy bite. Wonderful as always. Zachary relaxes into the couch beside me, his arms spread along the back of the couch.

"I figured you hadn't eaten when I found out you weren't at the meeting with Sir Sylas."

My head snaps to him. "Did you see him? How is it going?"

Zachary shakes his head. "No, I didn't go in. I asked one of the butlers serving them if they'd seen you. I knew how many plates to make and the numbers weren't adding up."

"That's sweet of you to think of me." A genuine smile slips onto my lips. I think I've made a friend without realizing it.

Zachary shrugs, a casual gesture. "Are you going to be at dinner?"

I glance at him sideways, chewing on a carrot. "Yes… Why?"

"Well Sir Jasper va Antionelli and Sir Stafaan de Voges will be at dinner, and I thought it was weird that you weren't there at lunch."

I freeze at the new information. Swallowing hard, I nearly choke. "How long are they staying?"

"A couple of days. I don't know the details; I only make the meals." He raises an eyebrow.

"It's nothing." I go back to my food, ignoring the knot forming in the pit of my stomach. Zachary waits until I'm finished, taking the plate back with him. It's really sweet of him to bring me food and keep me company the whole time.

Pacing around the room, I tell myself that they're different. Just because they are Vampires, doesn't make them like Sir Colin Eyler. My nerves prickle on my skin, my stomach turning. I can feel my body slipping into survival mode, walking with light steps. Can't speak in fear of them hearing, not knowing where they are ever. School my face and voice into neutrality.

The library door opens, making me stiffen. Sylas walks in looking like the prince he is. He's not in a full suit like I had seen the Vampires wearing, but his pants and shirt are starch and pressed, the blazer buttoned up professionally. His hair is the slickest I have ever seen it pulled back. His eyes glow like the midday sky.

He lifts his arms in invitation. I quickly cross the room, nestling myself against his chest. His arm envelops me. Safe and warm. That's how I feel with him. *And more.* I sigh, relaxing a little. He strokes my head, my tail wagging.

"Did you eat?"

"Zachary brought me lunch." I peer up at him, clinging to the front of his blazer, wondering if I'm wrinkling it.

"Good." He kisses my forehead. "The first part of the meeting went well."

"But not the second?" I frown.

"Lunch was the first part. Then we have dinner tonight and an official meeting tomorrow." I nod, averting my gaze, hiding the panic riling inside. He notices. "It'll be alright; they're nice."

"Don't say anything you don't want them hearing while they're here," I whisper.

Sylas squeezes me. "Try not to think about it. What have you been doing? Were you reading?" I glance around the room, catching on the book I worked so hard to get sitting on the table, mostly unread. It's a struggle not to think about it. "Father is entertaining Jasper va Antionelli and Stafaan de Voges right now. How about we take a walk in the garden?"

I weakly smile, knowing he's aiming to cheer me up. Now that I've made my decision to be with him, fear courses under my skin. He suggested fetching my book, but today I simply want to enjoy the flowers with him. I hold his hand, not caring about the looks the servants or the guards give us as we pass by. They keep their faces in a neutral expression, but their disapproving gazes have me lifting my chin. Despite his status and what I am, Sylas chose me. He's holding my hand, not another's.

Sylas keeps questioning me about the different flowers in the garden. I don't know if he's genuinely interested or hoping to keep me distracted. Maybe it's both. I enjoy it, nonetheless, sharing my knowledge of herbal uses for healing, poisons, and teas.

Since I had a late lunch, I'm not terribly hungry when dinner rolls around. That's what I tell myself when I begin to feel sick at the thought of dinner. Sylas squeezes my hand in comfort. He opens the door to the dining room, but instead of letting me walk in first, he stays by my side. Jasper va Antionelli and Stafaan de Voges are already in the room near the door with Eleanor and Reuben. Eleanor politely giggles at something that was said, fingers covering her mouth.

My body stiffens as their gaze turns to me. Sylas bows slightly. I dip into a curtsy, not knowing how low I should go, movement jerkier than I would have liked. Sylas' hand moves smoothly across his body, gesturing to me.

"Sir Jasper and Sir Stafaan, this is Zily." My heart skips on my name.

"The girl from the window." The man with chestnut hair smirks at me like a cat, head slightly crooked.

"Oh, yes, hello." My voice pitches. I forgot about that, my face heating up.

Reuben signals us to sit by pulling Eleanor's seat out for her. I glance at Sylas when we don't sit in our usual seats. Reuben and Eleanor are in their expected chairs. The seat Sylas normally sits in stays empty while Jasper sits in my seat, Stafaan across from him. With an empty chair between me and Jasper, Sylas pushes me in, taking the end seat. We mirror his parents.

I fidget with my dress as dinner is served, keeping my head down. Conversation is as casual as it normally is, just with two extra voices. Jasper has a thick, rich laugh. His slanted eyes glance at me frequently. There's a silent questioning in the room. Who am I?

What is my significance? What am I to Sylas? Sylas responds by gently talking to me, bringing me into conversation and holding my hand, his covering mine on top of the table, fingers lacing through together. I'm afraid they can hear my heart pounding out of control.

Stafaan is the quieter type. His voice is deep, and he speaks only when spoken to. There's a constant smirk on his face, like he thinks everything is amusing. He has hardly set down the glass of wine, constantly swirling it around while he observes the room. His eyes are rounder than Jasper's, but he has a sharp jawline and strong muscles in his neck that I'm sure goes down beneath his clothes where we cannot see.

Sylas slides his little piece of cake to me after taking a single bite. Stafaan raises an eyebrow. I eat it quietly, a mix of joy and nerves. Sylas leans back in his chair. "I know we'll be discussing terms of the agreement tomorrow afternoon, but would you like a tour of the grounds in the morning?"

I glance over at him. His thumb brushes against my hand, his gaze never leaving Jasper's. I force my lips to curl into a pleasant smile, facing Jasper. "The garden is beautiful."

Jasper and Stafaan share a look. Stafaan answers, "Sure. Sounds lovely." It's odd that Stafaan answered for them.

Dinner finally comes to an end, and we wish everyone a good night. Sylas doesn't let go of my hand as we return to our room. I don't notice right away that I walked into Sylas' room. He turns to me, cupping my face.

"Are you ok?" He asks gently. My head bobs. "I know this is hard, but I want to believe it's good."

I slide my arms around his neck. "Me too." Sighing, I lean on him. "I know we bathed this morning, but I think I'm going to take a bath."

"Do you normally take a bath at night?" I nuzzle his chest, silently confirming. "Should I join you?"

With an eyebrow raised, I peek at him. He smirks mischievously at me.

After breakfast, Sylas leads a similar tour he took me on during my first day here. It's the same halls, though he skips many of the rooms he pointed out to me, such as our room, his study, his parents' study, Leona's workroom and the music room. He does show them the ballroom. He talks more on the significance of the colors, the history of the sparkling chandelier, and those who have come to their balls before.

The blues represent the sky; their domain. Light for day and navy blue for night. The green represents the forest they fly over. The chandelier was made as a gift to Sylas' great-great-grandmother for her wedding. The list of names that comes out of Sylas' mouth goes over my head.

I take a longer look at the wide open space, imagining the dance floor filled with fancy suits and pretty gowns, moving with the music. Last time I was in here, I couldn't imagine being among the dancers. That future isn't that far off now. If we can make it through this.

I close my eyes, remembering how trying to tell Sylas about Sir Colin Eyler went. For a moment, I thought I could fight through the raging headache, the sharp pain inside my head to get the words out. Then the next thing I knew I was waking up to Sylas panicked expression. It caused a new wave of fear of what Sir Colin Eyler might be able to make me do. I can't even express it.

I shake my head, shifting my thoughts back to more pleasant subjects. Leona is going to enjoy the drawing I made. A ballgown; I'll get to wear a ballgown. Spinning back around, hands folded behind my back, I catch Sylas' eye. His head bows subtly, knowing what I'm thinking. He'll teach me how to dance.

My gaze drifts to our guests, momentarily forgetting about them. Both men have their arms crossed. Stafaan leans in, whispering to Jasper, staring up at the wall of tapestries. Jasper nods his head absently, watching me. My cheeks flush. Even though it takes me closer to them, I retreat to Sylas' side, lacing my fingers with his. He casually invites the pair to his coronation ball. If all goes well here, he'll send a formal invite.

We head out to the garden next. My ears flicker, seeking to hear what Jasper and Stafaan may be whispering about. Jasper's face is glowing and Stafaan has an amused expression on his face. The outdoors is warm, but not too hot, a couple clouds in the sky. A breeze brings the scent of rain with it. It'll probably rain tonight.

"Zily could tell you a fact about any flower or shrub here," Sylas suddenly says, looking down at me with admiration. I shoot him a panicked glance.

"Is that right?" Stafaan steps away from the group, touching a round, orange flower with a lot of little long petals.

Sylas pulls his hand from mine, pressing it to my lower back to lightly shove me forward. I glance back, smoothing out my dress as if I could wipe my nerves away, I walk up beside Stafaan. I peer up at him. He towers over me, green eyes shining with mystery and curiosity. Goosebumps threaten to cover my arms

"This is a calendula. It's a part of the marigold family. Mixed with honey and oils, it can be turned into a salve for cuts and burns."

Stafaan raises an eyebrow. "What about this one?" He points at a small bunch of pink and yellow flowers.

"All of those," I make a big gesture to incorporate the purple, blue and yellow flowers around where he pointed, "are primroses. They can be steeped into a tea that can help with headaches."

That's how our time continues. Stafaan and I walk through the garden with me spouting random facts I know, a smile slowly growing. I can't help it; I love sharing my knowledge of herbs and flowers. There's a hint of growing excitement in Stafaan's voice with each plant he points at. He reaches for a purple bell shaped flower. I grab his wrist. His eyes narrow on me.

"That's called angel's trumpet. Highly toxic." I remove my hand. He nods his appreciation, eyeing the pretty flower.

"I never knew a garden could kill or heal a person." Stafaan gives me a look of appreciation and respect. Blush creeps into my cheeks.

Jasper turns to Sylas. "Stafaan finds flowers fascinating, but his knowledge isn't anything like hers."

Both of them watch us, pride in Sylas' eyes. My face burns deeper. Sylas turns. "Shall we go in for lunch?"

I skip to Sylas' side, slipping my hand in his. Stafaan walks close to Jasper, their fingers hooking together. Once inside, Jasper's hands slide to his pockets, while Stafaan's returns to their usual crossed position.

We go to one of the sitting rooms, the one with the cyan chairs and little couch. A couple of servants bring in platters of salads and pastas, placing them on the glass table. I'm disappointed noticing there isn't a dessert this time.

Sylas and I take the couch, our thighs pressed against each other. He leans over, talking casually with Jasper, comparing their lives as royals. Jasper was crowned King nearly five years ago when his father died suddenly. I gather his dad didn't die of natural causes. Stafaan remains quiet in his chair, sitting up straight, watching Jasper. It's like he expects us to hurt Jasper right in front of him. Sometimes, he reminds me of Sylas in the way he watches Jasper.

The meeting happens after lunch. As much as I would like to know what is happening and being discussed, that's a boundary I'm not ready to cross, though I have a funny feeling Sylas would let me sit in on it. He'd probably ask me for my opinion. Instead, I retreat to his study. It's a quiet place where I don't expect anyone to find me.

I spend several minutes on the couch, willing my body to relax. I've been tense all morning. Sighing, I pace around the room, peeking at the desk. There's a small stack of papers front and center on Sylas' desk, paper clips and folders separating the different documents. I slide into the chair, having to get back out to raise it to a comfortable height for me to use the desk. My feet dangle off the floor.

It won't hurt to read through them now. There's a chance I'll read them later if I help Sylas again. I find some blank papers in a drawer, making notes summarizing the documents and my thoughts on them.

The door opens, startling me. Peering up, I meet Kai's hard gaze. My eyes narrow at him, wondering what shit he is going to say about me doing Sylas' work. He strides across the room after closing the door behind him, a large parchment rolled up under an arm. He stares at the papers in front of me and the pen in my hand.

"Making yourself at home?" I open my mouth with a retort, but he continues, "I don't think I've ever seen his desk this clean."

A smirk takes over my features, my chest warming with satisfaction. "He does have a certain talent for chaos, doesn't he?"

Kai grins down at me. I put the pen down, folding my hands in my lap, sitting up straight. "Is there something you wanted, Kai?" My tone is friendly since it appears he hasn't come here to start a fight.

"I came to see if you could attempt something. I understand if you want to wait for Sylas, but then we'll have to wait for Sir Jasper va Antionelli to leave." Kai sets the item on the desk, rolling it out. "Even if you can give me a direction to start looking, it'd be helpful."

It's a large detailed map, covering most of the desk. It shows the mansion, a village nearby, the long stretching forest, the river, roads and more. I know instantly what he's asking of me. I let my mind wander, testing the prickle of pain simply thinking about telling others what I know of Gateswood causes. It doesn't feel too bad, so I nod, looking up at him.

"I can give it a try." I put my finger on the mansion, moving it west to the river. "We're here, and Sylas found me here." My heart rate picks up, a fuzzy feeling starting to cloud my thoughts. I can't say the name; it won't form on my tongue. I swallow hard. "I came from this way." I move my finger south-west. I pull back before I can point out the spot where Gateswood lies, putting my head in my hands. "Sorry." I whisper, breathing heavily.

Kai surprises me by coming around the desk and rubs circles on my back. "It's alright. You did good." I put my head down on the desk, nausea spinning the room. "Are you able to tell me what prevents you from discussing that place?"

I press my cheek against the cool wood, ears flat against my head. "Definitely not. Simply thinking about... *that*... hurts." I wince, closing my eyes. My hand massages the back of my neck.

Kai sighs, rolling the map up. "Well, this is a start. We'll find the place. How much time do you think we have before they send someone else?"

I slowly lift my head, trying to sit straight again, but my vision blurs momentarily. "Another day or so. It should take them about three days to get here from leaving if they move at the same pace I do."

Kai crosses his arms, the map lodged under his armpit. "At least Sir Jasper va Antionelli will be gone by then."

"When do they leave?"

"The day after tomorrow." Kai is making his way to the door.

I sigh, not wanting to spend another day with them. "Hey, so if Jasper is the King of Zeneth, who is running the kingdom in his absence?"

Kai turns back. "You know a kingdom doesn't crumble if their leader is gone for a few days, right?" I shrug, not knowing a lot about royal life besides the little I've witnessed. "If he was married, it would have been up to his wife. I'm sure he has a trusted adviser or someone keeping track of the paperwork for him, sort of like you're doing for Sylas now."

A small smile creeps onto my face. The nausea is finally subsiding. I lean back in the chair "What do you know about Stafaan'?"

A deep hum comes from Kai as he thinks. "He's head of the royal guard unit. He's Jasper's personal guard. In a lot of ways, he's like me."

I stare at him, my head bobbing. I can see that. The protectiveness. The build. The looks. I cock my head to the side, eyebrows knitting together as a brief memory flashes through my mind. Didn't I see them holding hands? And the way he'd stare at Jasper during lunch. Protective, yes, but there was more.

"And me," I whisper.

"What?" Kai raises an eyebrow. I wave my hand dismissively. "I have work to get back to. Thanks for this." He motions to the map, leaving the study.

I sit back in the chair, staring absently at the door. Something about my realization gives me a sense of connection with Stafaan. Perhaps, just maybe, I could be friends with a Vampire. He likes flowers too, and he admires his King in the way I do Sylas. The other word makes me blush deeply. If I use it for them, I may have to face it myself.

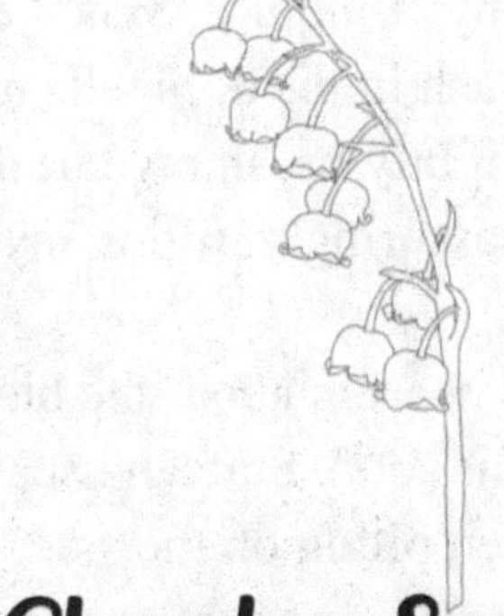

Chapter Seventeen
Lily of the Valley

It symbolizes purity, humility, happiness, and the return of happiness.
This toxic flower can cause abdominal pain, blurred vision, drowsiness,
and reduced heart rate when ingested.

Zily

Stafaan spots me staring at him during dinner. *We're not so different.* A smile forms on my lips. I work a little harder to engage in conversation, taking Sylas by surprise with how quiet I have been around them. Holding my head high, I'm enjoying myself, and I adore the way Sylas' eyes shine when he glances at me. They don't like talking business during supper, but there's a brief mention and agreement that discussions are going well. Tomorrow, they should have the agreement on paper.

Defying Sir Colin Eyler scares me inside, my body remembering previous times of disobedience, though the aches that usually come with the memories isn't there. Knowing he couldn't stop this, fills me with pleasure. They'll have the final meeting tomorrow morning. Sylas suggests going for a walk after lunch tomorrow, to some nearby ruins.

"The ones a little south?" I inquire. Sylas' eyebrows raise. "I saw them on the map." The flash in his eyes tells me he knows why I looked at a map. His fingers lightly brush my cheek, silently asking if I'm alright. I look at him reassuringly, tilting my head to follow his touch.

"I have been enjoying hearing about the history here." Jasper agrees to the idea, poking at his food. Stafaan uses his fork to steal the mushrooms Jasper had been piling on the side.

It's settled. We retire to our room after supper. I go into our large walk-in closet, picking out the dress I want to wear tomorrow. I giggle looking between his side and my side of the closet. The use of the word 'our' feels foreign, summoning butterflies in my chest. Sylas leans against the door frame, watching me pull an earthy brown dress with thin straps off the bar. I hang it on the outside of the closet door.

Climbing into bed, Sylas shows me a little surprise. On his side of the bed, there's a notch in the mattress where he keeps his sword. One has been made for my short sword on my side of the bed. I kiss him deeply, grateful to have it close and for the old habit of sleeping with a weapon under me. Curling up against Sylas, my head on his chest, he plays with my hair while telling me all about the meeting. I mumble about the work on his desk, smiling when he groans, enjoying the way he squeezes me when I tell him I've gone through it already. He can just read my notes if he wants.

I'm not surprised when Sylas decides to match my dress with his own silk brown shirt. It's cute. He starts to put his hair into a ponytail. With a finger, I motion for him to come close. He leans down and I steal his hair band, turning to run away. He laughs, trying to get it back, picking me up from behind. In the end, I win, though he wears the band on his wrist. Sitting on his lap, he allows me to run my fingers through his hair few times before heading to breakfast.

I greet everyone as I do every morning, with the extra guests included. Stafaan and Jasper exchange a look. Jasper shrugs, taking his seat. I don't participate in conversation as much, enjoying the egg on toast and ham we're served, my tail quietly patting the seat.

Sylas kisses my cheek when it's time for him to finish his meeting with Jasper. We hold hands until his feet take him too far away that my hand slips from his. I sigh, an odd kind of bliss filling my chest even as I watch him disappear down the hall. Riding the high, I skip up the steps to our room, tearing a page from my book. The ballroom reminded me of my dress sketch that I'm hoping Leona can bring to life.

Leona jumps around excitedly when I show her. She rambles on for an hour, recreating my sketch with shadings to indicate the right materials that'll be used and coloring it. It's beautiful. It almost doesn't feel right to have it be made for me. Leona wants to start on it right away, though she has others she needs to finish first. She takes me over to her wall of fabrics to satisfy the urge. My hand glides over silks, cotton, lace, satin, and more.

"This will be the main fabric, and we'll have this lace flower pattern over top. Do you want it in just the skirt or on the bodice as well?" Leona points at a light blue satin, then to a black lace that's hard to tell has flowers in it with the way it's rolled up. "Probably white, though. What do you think?" Her eyes shine with excitement.

My heart flutters. "Just the skirt. I think white would look better. Black would make it too dark."

"It'll look like a cloud garden in the sky." Leona makes notes in her little notebook.

I giggle, staring at the lace some more. Reaching up, I brush my bangs, ears twitching. "Do… Do you think white would blend in too much?" I ask cautiously.

Leona's eyes flicker up, trailing down me in an assessing gaze. "You've warn white before."

"Not fully."

"This isn't fully either."

I sigh, giving in. I haven't been one to worry about appearance, but if thousands of eyes are going to be on me, judging me, I want to make sure I can stand up next to Sylas without embarrassing him. "You're right. I'm over thinking this."

She puts a hand on my shoulder. "Don't worry. My job is to make clothes to look good on you. All you have to do is be your pretty self."

My cheeks burn, but I smile at her. Reluctantly, Leona returns to her previous work. I walk down the hall, lost in my thoughts. Dresses and balls. What does a live band sound like? My imagination conjures possible decorations, food and lighting. It'd be dim with the chandelier sparkling overhead. I wonder how many people will actually be there. What does Sylas do during the entirety of a ball? What will his coronation look like?

"So, you're not invited into the meetings either?" A deep voice makes me jump.

Stafaan leans against the wall around the corner, arms crossed. The corner of his lip twitches. I openly glare at him for scaring me. The hair on the back of my neck stands on end.

"Why would I be a part of them?"

He shrugs, pushing off, strolling to stand in front of me, staring down at me. "I don't know. I thought you were Sir Sylas' lover." My face burns at the title. It's not something I've been called before. My heart melt.

"Then why aren't you in there?"

"Guards aren't allowed in political affairs."

"But, aren't you…" I drop the question, eyebrows furrowing, reevaluating what I learned yesterday. "It's a secret," I whisper. He raises an eyebrow, not following my thoughts. I shake my head. "I was going to have some tea. Would you like to join me?" The other eyebrow raises with the first. He shrugs nonchalantly.

Zachary isn't in the kitchen, however, the kitchen aid takes one look at the pair of us and makes us tea. They don't want to piss off the visiting King, though their eyes narrow on me. I hold my head high, asking one to carry the tray to the nearby sitting room, the one with the baby blue couches. They don't dare tell me no. It's nice having another that scares them with me. I wonder if I show confidence if they'll respect me more.

Stafaan drops onto one of the couches, slouching down. I carefully pour us each a cup, offering one to him, before sitting on the other little couch. Picking up my own cup cradled in both hands, I take a couple sips, trying not to burn my tongue.

"They don't like you here," he says flatly.

I nearly spit out my tea. It's not something I didn't know, but his forwardness catches me off guard. I wonder what he's heard since his time here. No one is as careful around Vampires as I am.

"No. Many do not. They see a Kitsune and think ill of me without even knowing me." The tea swirls around in the little cup, careful to keep it from spilling over. "I'm not too different, so I want to apologize. I haven't had good experiences with… Vampires." I stumble over my words, but I offer a friendly smile.

Stafaan's shoulders rise and fall. There's an ease to the movement, like he's used to doing it. His posture and the way he's acting is different than when he's watching over Jasper, and yet it doesn't feel quite right either. It's another mask. *How many does he have?*

"I don't think there's a harm in being wary of others." A moment of silence passes as we sip our tea. It's finally cool enough that it doesn't burn. "Does it bother you that they don't like you even though you're their prince's lover?"

I blink, staring at him. A quick laugh escapes, tea threatening to splash over the rim of my cup. I have to set it down to laugh harder. "Honestly, it used to. Only days ago, actually, but as time goes on, I only care about the way Sylas looks at me. You know what I mean? Despite the prejudice of many here, I have made a couple of friends that I trust will stand by me if I need them. Sylas and those friends chose me." I pause, folding my hands in my lap, staring down at them. "I do worry what that title entails. I'm new here, and I don't have much knowledge of a royal's life and responsibilities. I can't even say I'll be more than I am now. It's all too new." Stafaan's head dips in understanding, leaning forward to pour himself more tea. "How long have you been with Jasper?"

"I started training to be in the royal guard when I was only a kid. It was fifty years ago when I made it into the unit, and about seventeen years ago when I got assigned as Jasper's personal guard." Stafaan explains in a rehearsed fashion. I stare, stunned by the numbers. I bite back the question of *'how old are you?'*

Then I realize he didn't answer my question. "That's not what I asked. I was curious how long you've been with Jasper."

Stafaan freezes, the color draining from his face. His narrowed eyes lift to meet mine. It sends a chill through me, but I keep it from showing on my face, tilting my head to the side. Slowly, he sets the tea cup down on the table. "Nearly eight years." He's watching me carefully, analyzing my reaction. My heart races like I'm under attack.

"That's still pretty new for you as well then." I do math in my head.

Stafaan looks down at his lap. "We haven't told anyone. There's a lot of pressure on kings when picking their life partner. There's… a few reasons why we wouldn't be accepted."

"Who cares." The words fall out unexpectedly. His gazes flicker back to me. "Seriously. Ignore those who look down on you like I did the chefs and the other servants. Yes, they can be mean, and it had bothered me, but I've figured out what I want and have decided to not let anyone get between me and that future." I can see it, bright behind my eyes. At the moment, it out shines the fear that it won't come true. The will to fight for it grows.

He's at a loss for words, simply staring at me, lips slightly parted. He's probably figuring out which mask to put on now, choosing what careful words to say next. I pour myself more tea, cringing when I burn my tongue again.

"I think I'll talk to him." He takes up his cup again, deciding not to put on a mask. There's a new kind of calm to his features. The way his lips curl is different than the smirk he wears at dinner. "Did you ask me to tea to corner me?"

"No. Maybe." A grin spread on my lips. "I don't know royal customs. Is this inappropriate?" I don't actually care if it is or not, though maybe I should if I'm considered Sylas' lover, his partner. I haven't considered what my position will be by being with Sylas. First, I have to keep him alive and deal with Gateswood.

Stafaan laughs wholeheartedly, leaning back on the couch, crossing a leg over his knee. "You'll get the hang of it."

"I already help with paperwork."

"Then you're off to a good start."

"How did you two end up together, if you don't mind me asking?" My ears flicker curiously.

"It was slow. We've known each other since we were kids. We had regular sparring matches. There was a time during my training and work when we stopped, and I hadn't seen him in many years. We picked it back up again when I became his personal guard." Stafaan takes a long drink, attempting to hide his nerves. I wonder if he's ever told anyone this story before. "One day, while we were sparring, I told him how I really felt about him. It was awkward as fuck at first until he finally stammered over himself, saying he felt the same. I nearly walked away, ready to resign as his guard." A chuckle escapes.

I grin at him, enjoying watching him relax. "How does no one know about you two?"

He leans back with his arms draped across the back of the couch, one leg crossed over the other, foot bouncing. "Oh, there's a few who suspect, but no one has actually said anything, and we've certainly not said or done anything publicly."

"Shame." I tilt my head. "I haven't spoken about my relationship with Sylas, but we hold hands everywhere now. I think everyone knows."

"We were questioning it at dinner." Stafaan nods his head. "How did you end up here? You said you've only been here a short time?"

A smile slips easily onto my lips. "Sylas saved me from the Baxpon River. I nearly drowned and bled out from fighting a forest beast."

Stafaan's eyebrows rise. "What were you doing in the forest?"

"That is the question." I giggle at his perplexed expression. "I came here to kill Sylas. You could say the plan has changed a bit."

Stafaan laughs hard, a hand running over his hair. I cock my head, wandering what he thinks of having tea with an assassin. "I'll say it changed a lot."

I tell him a little more of my days here, the food I've never had before, the music room and Sylas' messy desk. He chuckles some more, sharing maybe a little too much information about the papers that cross Jasper's desk.

Stafaan's eyes flicker to the door. Trusting his hearing, I turn to the door just as it opens, Sylas and Jasper walking in. Both of them are beaming.

"There you are. I wondered where you wandered to." Sylas holds out his hand. I instantly stand, going to his side. My arm snakes around his till out hands connect with laced fingers.

"Are you hungry? We talked about having lunch and then going to the ruins Sylas mentioned last night." Jasper stares at Stafaan, eyes flaring with I think excitement. His hand twitches before sliding into his pocket. They must have learned to communicate with subtle gestures and looks to keep their secret hidden for so long. It makes me sad for them, reminding me how I'd pull away before dinner. I don't do that anymore. It would be nice if they could be open around us as well.

Stafaan's gaze drifts from my hold of Sylas, to my eyes, finally landing on Jasper. "Sounds good to me."

Reluctantly, Sylas pulls free. "I'll step out and request lunch to be brought to us." He looks down at me, silently telling me to behave, leaving me alone in a room with not only a pair of Vampires, but the King of another kingdom.

Spinning, I sit back on the couch shoulders back, hands folded in my lap. I watch them curiously, waiting to see if Stafaan will take advantage of our previous conversation. Jasper sits on the same couch as Stafaan, though as far away as physically possible. It's awkward. How can anyone not figure them out? I share a look with Stafaan, raising an eyebrow. He mimics me, leaning back, arms stretching along the backside of the couch again.

"So, how long have you been with Sir Sylas?" Jasper attempts small talk. Stafaan snorts, earning a pointed look from Jasper.

"You can drop the 'Sir'. He doesn't particularly like the formality of it." Stafaan shifts a little closer to him. "I've been here two weeks. Almost."

Jasper shoots Stafaan a warning look. I smile innocently as if I can't read their expressions. Stafaan's neck muscle tics, the only indication that he's nervous. Without breaking eye contact with me, mischief in his eyes, he slides closer to Jasper. His arm wraps around his shoulders.

Jasper's head swivels, panic in his eyes. He glances between Stafaan and me. There's a moment of silence, waiting to see what I say. I keep the smile planted. "Did you tell her?" he whispers. My ears twitch, barely catching the words.

Stafaan shakes his head. "She figured it out."

"We've kept it a secret for years from an entire mansion full of people, and you guessed in a couple days." He sighs in defeat.

"I saw you hold hands in the garden briefly, though I actually didn't think much of it at the time."

Jasper slowly relaxes into Stafaan. Their bodies seem to fit together, mold together as one, the looks they exchange full of love. It makes me curious what Sylas and I look like from an outsider perspective.

Sylas returns, speaking as he opens the door. "Lunch will be brought to us shortly."

The King tenses, watching Sylas with hawk eyes. Stafaan's hand slides down Jasper's arm, giving a light squeeze. Sylas doesn't give the men a second look before dropping down beside me, wrapping an arm around my waist. He adjusts his sword on the other side of him, getting comfy.

"Playing nice?" Sylas asks playfully, pulling me against him.

I exchange looks with the other two. All of us start laughing. Sylas glances back and forth utterly confused, though he appears amused by the interaction. I lean into him.

Soon, three servants bring in a few platters of food. I recognize Zachary's handy work, steam coming off of creamy white sauce on thick long noodles with mushrooms mixed in. Slices of toast are stacked on their own small plate. Three salads and a small bowl of soup are our starters. I'm saddened that there isn't a dessert again.

Stafaan releases Jasper, taking the soup. It's a deep red, and when he blows on it, an earthy savory aroma comes off it. I stare at it curiously, wondering what kind of soup it is, wanting to taste it someday. The rest of us pick up our salads, eyeing the main dish. It's a comfortable silence as we eat, something I wouldn't have expected in this company.

Casually, Sylas announces they finished writing up the treaty between the kingdoms and it'll be put into place immediately. After Jasper and Stafaan make it home. He talks in the way he would tell me about it later, openly, the only acknowledgment of Stafaan's and Jasper's closeness, though they don't know it. I love knowing little things about Sylas.

Chapter Eighteen
Magnolias

This represents endurance, beauty, nobility; a balance between strength and gentleness. Some places use the flower to make medicine. The bud has been used for common cold symptoms, headaches, and toothaches.

Sylas

"Well, hello to you too." Zily giggles as Maple sticks her head out the stall door, looking at Zily for pets, or treats. Probably treats. S'more whinnies inside.

Zily's body stretches over the stall window, tip toes pushing her up, all in an attempt to reach the needy foal as well. Holding a hand up, I motion for Jasper and Stafaan to wait here. I pass by Zily, affectionately pressing the palm of my hand to the top of her head, her ears flickering back with the touch. Her sweet voice follows me as she introduces Maple and S'more.

Finding a handler, I request a few horses to be prepped for riding. He asks me to pick out two for our guests. Pebbles, a dapple grey mare, is an easy ride. She gets along with just about anyone and follows directions well. Pax, a deep brown stallion, is more stubborn, but he hasn't been out in a while. He would love the long ride. Stafaan should be able to handle him. The handler bows his head, scurrying off to get help saddling the three horses.

I return to the others with my hands in my pocket. Zily has pulled the stool over to Maples' stall. She laughs, face glowing as she talks with Jasper. I'm glad to see her getting along with them, that she's not afraid anymore. The first day was difficult seeing the fear in the darkness of her eyes. I'm not sure what changed it, but it warms my heart watching them interact.

"Has she told you about the first time I brought her here?" My hand rests on the small of Zily's back as I stand behind her. She looks at me over her shoulder, making sure I see her eye roll. "She was terrified of horses. Even Maple here."

Stafaan looks to her and laughs. Jasper gives her a side eye, eyebrow raise. Pink blossoms in her cheeks. "She didn't mention being terrified, only that it was her first real encounter with horses, and that you took her for a ride."

I chuckle, tenderly rubbing Zily's back. "She did not want to come in here. Kept calling them 'muscled beasts'." I adore this story, this memory.

"'Cause they are!" she interjects. A soft chuckle comes from Jasper while Stafaan is openly making fun of her, repeating 'muscled beasts'. "Wait until Jupiter comes out. You'll see. He's huge!" Her hands raise to the sky, slightly lifting onto her toes.

I slide my arms around her. It's good time because Maple nearly hits her with her nose when whipping around to see what her son is doing. Zily falls back into me with a gasp. Gently, I right her on her feet on the floor.

"Thanks," she whispers.

Hooves clomp down the aisle. Jupiter is brought out first. Pebbles and Pax are not far behind. I take the reins to Jupiter from the handler. Turning, I gesture to Pebbles, looking at Jasper to say she's for him.

"See? Look! Look at how big he is compared to me." Zily speaks before I get the chance, standing beside Jupiter's shoulder. We all stare at her short stature next to the large stallion. A burst of laughter echoes in the building. It consumes all of us, prolonged by the pout on Zily's lips. Her eyes sparkle like midnight.

"As I was about to say, Jasper, the mare is for you. Her name is Pebbles. Stafaan, Pax is for you. Make sure to keep a tight grip." They nod, going to grab the respective reigns.

Turning to Zily, she is already waiting for me, looking at me expectantly. A smile creeps across her face as I place my hands on her hips, lifting her up into the saddle. Stafaan's deep laugh has me looking back with my foot in the stirrup. Jasper is swatting him away, seeming like Stafaan was trying to lift Jasper into the saddle the same way I'd done Zily. I smirk, swinging my leg over.

Zily doesn't react to my presence behind her. Her gaze is on the ground, looking lost in her own little world, a small frown on her lips.

"Zily," I breathe. She turns her head to look at me with distant eyes. "Is something wrong?"

She shakes her head, the ends of her hair brushing over her shoulders. Leaning against me, her head rests against my chest. "Worried," she whispers.

I understand. She's thinking about her friends. She can't elaborate more than that with the company we have, even if we're becoming good acquaintances. My chin rests on top of her head, an arm wrapped around her waist giving a gentle squeeze. I hope to alleviate some of her pain, even for this moment. My fingers brush along her side, wondering how her wounds are doing. Zily pushes herself up to peck my cheek in response. Good. They're not hurting her.

Leading the trotting horses outside, I glance over my shoulder. "Shall we be off?"

The hooves leave impressions in the grass as we go around the stables, heading south. Jasper's guards weren't thrilled about him going on this day trip with us. It's understandable. A few of mine weren't either. I saw it in their eyes as they passed us leaving. Stafaan ordered his men about, reminding me a lot of Kai. The guards didn't dare go against his words.

We enter the forest, though the trees aren't thick and become thinner as we shift more east. The sun shines bright overhead, the heat of the day at its highest. My fingers fumble to roll up my sleeves while holding on to the reins and not knocking Zily off. She helps, shoving my hand out of the way as she does it for me. She rolls them to the exact spot I like my sleeves. I kiss the top of her head as my thanks. She smells like strawberries today.

Jasper rides up beside us. "You mentioned the ruins we're visiting once belonged to Arcadia?"

"Yes. This was once the manor in which Arcadia and her lover Peyard built. My ancestors offered her this piece of land to do with as she pleased after the incident with the Betheba Kingdom. The magics she possessed weren't like that of other elves with a similarity to a Witch's magic." I absently stroke Zily's ears as I regurgitate history lessons. She's completely relaxed against me, making me wonder if she's dozing off.

"Arcadia never ventured down to Zeneth, so we're not taught much of her history," Jasper says, excitement in his voice. If I've learned anything about this man, he loves to learn about history.

My head bobs, pulling words to the forefront of my mind. "I'm told she came here and offered her services of magic and herbology." I glance down at the one it makes me think of. "After the devastation in the Betheba Kingdom, she and Peyard sought to get away. They wanted to live without the constant bounty that always seemed to be on their heads, particularly on her. Starting from scratch, they needed a way to earn money."

"My dedushka was around when the skies turned dark. I've heard and read the story of the devastation hundreds of times from different people who were there, yet it never goes into detail on who Arcadia was, and what she was doing there. I know she was a very powerful elf, and that her powers were used in summoning the beast that caused the devastation." Jasper adds what he knows.

"Didn't Betheba hunt her down for decades?" Stafaan chimes in from behind.

The area isn't quite wide enough for three horses to ride side by side. I have to steer Jupiter around some tree, swerving back to keep talking with Jasper. Streams of gold and green cross over Zily's hair, vibrant against the white. Birds chirp, wings fluttering to fly away. This part of the forest doesn't get many visitors. The animals aren't used to trespassers passing through.

"Arcadia was on the run when she ran into Peyard. He was one that was meant to turn her in to the Betheba King of the time. After getting to know her, finding out what they had done and were intending to do to her, he changed sides." Zily tilts her head back, peering up at me with a cute little smile on her face. I kiss her forehead. "It's funny how their names are still spoken of today while the King's name has been lost to time."

Another few minutes pass in comfortable quiet. We break through the trees into a large, lush, green meadow. What's left of stone walls two stories tall erect in the distance. Jutting out from the grey stones is a massive tree, larger than any other I have ever seen. It reaches for the sky with leaves like fingers, enormous roots protruding from the ground in waves.

We dismount at the front of the building. I hold my arms up for Zily. She slides down, dropping into my arms. I squeeze a small giggle out of her, her head tilting back to stare up at the decaying mansion shading us even from the trickle of light cascading from the green canopy overhead. One of the side walls has collapsed, revealing part of the second floor. Moss and vines slither up the wall. I give the group a moment to take it in while I tie off the horses to metal rings lodged in the stone. Jasper looks around in awe, mouthing something inaudible to my ears, though Stafaan smirking beside him makes me believe he's not simply mouthing words.

"Welcome to the manor of Arcadia! She lived here till the day she died. Presumably. There's no record of when she passed." I throw my hands out, walking backwards through the door-shaped gap in the wall, following the path of tall grass, some with fluffy, feathery tops.

Remnants of furniture lay scattered through the rooms. The first room is open, covered in a bed of tall weeds. What is left of a table lay crumpled to the side, a root looking like a bench to sit on beside it. A bookshelf carcass press against a half wall. Moss clings to the edge of a window outline. Rotting planks of inner walls separates the rooms.

Motioning for Jasper to follow, I leave Zily to wander on her own. Open palms glide over the feathered top grass. She's completely captivated by the nature here.

"As I mentioned, Arcadia came to Yuseaa seeking a more peaceful life with her lover. A few years passed before my ancestor realized who she was. She helped their child when they were seriously sick. For that, and her part in stopping Betheba when she could have simply ran for what they did to her, they gave her this land to do with as she wished. She and Peyard built this home themselves. I think it's her magic that has seeped into the ground that has made the grass so thick, and the tree grow so tall." As we go through the room, circling back around, I discuss what was in each.

"It's a gorgeous home, even as it is now. It's still hers even if it's not hers anymore. I can almost picture what the rooms looked like, how they would have been set up." Jasper's hand runs down the cold stone, eyes wide with wonder. An easy smile creeps across my lips.

Zily stands a mirror to Jasper behind him with her hand on the wide tree's thick bark, head back, staring at the green canopy above. "There are pictures of what the inside and outside of the house looked like back then. If you're interested, I could see about bringing them out for you to look at." I can't pull my eyes away from Zily.

Jasper turns to me with excitement written all over his face. He follows my gaze. We share a smile of understanding. He returns to Stafaan leaning against one of the solid stone walls. His arms are crossed, head back, mesmerized by the tree that shields us from the sun. His gaze drops as Jasper approaches.

My arms envelop Zily, her body melting against mine. I snake my hand down her arm, covering her hand pressed to the tree.

Setting it beside hers, I feel what she feels; life vibrating through the trunk. Squirrels skitter up and across branches. An orange fox darts around to a burrow at the base. Birds sing spring time songs overhead. This place is still a home, now belonging to these creatures.

"This tree was planted by Arcadia. It's said she wanted something that would be here long after she has gone. It's magnificent, isn't it? She didn't intend for it to grow into the house like this, but I like to think it wanted to preserve her memory as well," I quietly tell her.

Her head falls back, ears flattening as she peers at me with the tiniest smiles. "Is this another secret hiding place?" She matches my whisper.

I chuckle. "No. I like to leave this place to the critters that call it home. I like to believe that's what Arcadia would have wanted. But I come to visit at times like this, especially when a guest is a history scholar." We glance at Jasper rambling on about all the new information I told him to Stafaan who nods along, but definitely not invested in the words. His eyes are soft, tenderly staring at Jasper.

Lowering my chin to her shoulder, she tracks me, turning her head. I brush my nose against hers. "You want to go up?" Zily's eyebrows scrunch together. A wicked grin spreads across my face.

In a smooth, quick motion, I slide a hand under her legs, scooping her up into my arms. A yelp catches Jasper's and Stafaan's attention. I simply nod with a smirk, releasing my large, black wings. With a strong beat of them, we shoot into the sky. Air rushes through my hair. The feeling of freedom instantly takes me as it often does when I fly. Zily stairs up at the green clouds as we ascend. She's relaxed, an arm over my shoulder and around me.

We spiral up and around the thick trunk of the tree. Green to yellow glow crosses Zily's face from what light breaks through the leafy ceiling. I hover near a wide branch, thinking it's a perfect sitting spot. I start to set Zily down on it. Her body tenses up, clinging to me in horror. Laughing, I squeeze her to me. Turning, I sit on the branch myself with Zily on my lap. Her body relaxes, smiling at me, more pleased with this decision.

Zily's eyes drop, peering down at the ground far below us. Brushing my finger down her cheek, I hook it under her chin, forcing her to look at me. I will never get tired of counting the stars in her eyes. They're infinite, ever changing sparkles. My lips brush her, soft and lovingly. Her lips curl into a smile against mine, birds chirping around us. My hand moves from her hip to her ass briefly, stroking down her tail. The soft fur silken beneath my fingers. She pulls back, a shiver runs down her spine, bringing a grin to my lips.

Leaning in for another peck, Zily jerks back, smirking with a raised eyebrow. Slowly, she comes close, brushing her nose against mine, her lips trailing along my jawline and down my neck, sending my heart ablaze. A low moan reverberates from my chest. She shifts in my lap until her breasts are pressed against me, hands gliding down my back. I keep one hand on her ass, holding her safely in my lap. The other lightly running up her spine. My head tilts, intending to kiss her neck.

I suck in a sharp breath, her fingers caressing along the top of my wing. She giggles at the way the feathers ruffle with the tremble that goes through me. *Now she's done it.* My fingers tangle in her hair, lightly tugging it back until her face is in front of mine again. I capture her lips with mine, letting the heat of want, of need course through my veins. Her moan is muffled by the kiss, our tongues dancing together.

Her fingers of her other hand find their way into my hair, raking along my scalp and pulling out till the strands fall. Then she repeats the process. I groan, moving to kiss the spot where her neck and shoulder meet, knowing she loves it when I suck right there. The way her body tenses, pressing against mine shows how much she loves it. My fingers dig into her ass, dragging down her thigh, searching for the bottom hem of the skirt.

Her hand wraps around my wrist before it has a chance to slip up her skirt. I pull my hand back, lifting it to caress her cheek as I tenderly kiss her. Gentler, softer than before to try to calm myself. My breath comes out ragged, resting my forehead against hers.

"We should go back." Her voice comes out shaky.

I groan, knowing she's right. My thoughts try to reason out how much time we can take to ourselves up here alone. The things I want to do to her. I know she can feel me. Sighing, I drop my head to her shoulder.

"I need a minute," I whisper.

Zily runs her fingers through my hair again, a different kind of feeling to it, soothing my desire. I take slow deep breaths, calming my racing heart. She smells so good. It's not helping. I need fresh air.

I slip my hand back under her legs, looking into her eyes. She cocks her head to the side. I smirk, sliding off the branch, letting gravity do its thing, my wings folded in against my back. The short free fall is the change of adrenaline that I needed. Zily squeaks, clinging to me, but I would never let anything happen to her. My wings fan out, catching the air. We glide back down to the building of grey and green, landing on the second floor. I lower Zily's feet to the patch of moss and grass growing on the creaky flooring.

The second floor has less to it than the first. The only distinguishable furniture left is the rusty metal remains of a large bed. Grass and flowers cover every surface of the floor, beautiful and thriving.

Zily's tail swishes excitedly, gazing at the pink and purple flowers. She crouches near a small bushel, the floor bowing slightly under her. I stand close enough just in case the floor gives out under her. Turning her head, she beams up at me with a small bouquet in hand. I would do anything for that smile. Raking my fingers through my hair, I return the smile, chest warming.

"Ready?" I hold out a hand.

"Yes!" She stands, gripping my hand tight when the ground seems to shift under her. Fear flickers in her eyes.

I lead the way to the stairs, reassuring her the floor won't give out by walking in front. My wings stay out until I get halfway down the stairs as a precaution. Rounding the corner at the bottom, I stumble back, turning to push Zily back up the steps, my hands on her hips. Stafaan has Jasper pressed up against the wall, his fingers laced in the tendril of his short blond strands. Jasper's hands clutch the back of Stafaan's shirt in fist fulls. Stafaan growls, pulling back, turning to us, one hand dropping to Jasper's waist. Jasper's face is deep red with wide eyes, mouth hanging open as he sucks in breath. There's no way they didn't hear us even if we were quiet.

Stafaan's and my eyes lock. A knowing look creeps across my face. *We should have stayed in the tree.* I press my palm to Zily's lower back dangerously close to her tail. "Are we ready to head back?"

Jasper nods while Stafaan responds. "Definitely."

Zily curls into my chest as we ride back, my arms corralling her in. I let the horses gallop through the pasture, a mini race. Jasper and Stafaan seem to enjoy the little burst as much as the horses do. Jupiter snorts in protest when I slow him again. We trot at a little faster pace to keep the horses happy.

Zily stares up at me. I glance down periodically. Her fingers find their way into my hair. It's like it's her favorite thing to do. It makes me never want to wear a ponytail again, though I love when she undoes it too. The corner of my lips tugs upward.

"Maybe you should grow your hair out." Stafaan's voice reminds me of their company.

"Should I?" Jasper runs his hand over his hair, smoothing out the mess Stafaan left.

Zily giggles, a sweet ringing song. Slowly, dramatically, she plays with my hair. I roll my eyes, casting them down to look into the night sky. In them, I can see a shining future.

Though we walk from the stables back to the mansions together, Jasper and Stafaan are eager to return to their room to "freshen up." I assume to finish what was started at the ruins. I would love to do the same, my hand outstretched towards Zily, but she's skipping down the hall with her little bouquet in hand. She left, joy glowing on her face, so I couldn't object and ask her to stay with me. I should get cleaned up as well, my appearance disheveled with fresh wrinkles in my shirt from where Zily clung to me and who knows what my hair looks like after her fingers had been in it all afternoon.

Kai passes by, talking with Brawns. Brawns respectfully bows his head while Kai meets my eyes, giving a subtle nod. Everything is going according to plan. Tomorrow morning, Jasper and Stafaan will leave and that'll be one less thing to worry about. It's gone surprisingly easy. I did not know what to expect from King Jasper. He's good at wearing a mask, though that didn't affect our talks. We've agreed we want to discuss more details at length in the future, but for now we have an alliance and a trade system set to be put in place as soon as he returns to his own home.

It was fun to see Zily shatter his and Stafaan's walls. I'm glad she took a liking to them. It'll be good to help mend the awful shit Vampires have put her through in the past. I hope they take up the invite to my coronation. But, until then, we'll start preparing for whoever Zily thinks this Colin Eyler will send.

Dad catches me as I reach the top of the steps. He flags me down. I comb my hair back hoping it's not too much of a mess. Dad doesn't comment often on my appearance, but there is a limit to everything. His brown eyes give me a once over, an eyebrow twitching. Shaking his head, he sighs, but bites back his words. The corner of his lips tilts upward.

"I only wanted to know if you've considered reaching out to the Viararia Kingdom."

The thought has crossed through my mind, though I wasn't sure how good an idea it is to reach out to two kingdoms we haven't previously had relationships with. We haven't interacted with Viararia Kingdom since my mother was a young girl. The records as to why are a little lackluster, leaving me with mostly rumors. Something about a mishap between the families, and my grandmother cut off connections. It's where the prejudice against Kitsunes came from. It hasn't been that long in the grand scheme of time, and it may be good to rekindle our friendship espccially if there's more Kitsune like Zily stuck in that place. They will need a place to go and not all will be comfortable here. But if the next Queen is a Kitsune… I mentally shake my head, getting far too ahead of myself.

"Perhaps it would be good to invite them to the coronation?"

Dad gives his approval. "Invitations need to go out soon. I'd recommend writing this one yourself and to have it ready in the next couple days." He puts a hand on my shoulder, moving around me. "I'm proud of you, son. Proud that I get to be alive to watch you take my place."

I don't have time to respond before he's descending the stairs. It takes several moments standing in the quiet of the hall to recompose myself.

A maid carrying a laundry basket down the hall brings me back. I dip my head, hurrying to my room. A bath is exactly what I need right now. A moment to myself and to relax with all the thoughts that have been swirling round, running rampant in my head.

When I emerge from the bath, a towel draped over my bare shoulders, catching the dripping of my hair, Zily is sitting on the short couch by the little book shelf, back against the armrest, tail curled around her. Book in hand, she turns the page slowly, holding it up as she consumes the last few words, continuing on to the next page. I plop down beside her, taking the towel to ruffle dry my hair. I peek at her. She doesn't even seem to notice my presence. I dip my head down to get a look at the book she's reading. It's not her usual plant book. It's an actual story book. There's a woman in a red cloak, sword in hand on the cover. I haven't read this one yet, but it seems to have captivated her.

I lean close, wondering how close I can get before she looks up. Touching my nose to the cover, peering over the pages. Her deep night eyes finally lift, the corner of her lips twitching up. She pulls the book slowly closer, simultaneously leaning in as well. I chase after the book. She plants a kiss to my forehead, giggling. I chuckle in response.

With the book lowered, my hand reaches up to caress her face, my lips gently touching hers. Sweet and tender. I rest my forehead against hers, allowing myself a moment to get lost in the vast night sky of her eyes, stars shining in their depth.

She shifts to mark her spot in the book while I finish getting dressed. She sticks her tongue out when I tie my hair back into a ponytail. I grab her face, stealing that tongue. A soft moan escapes, making me grin. Her face burns a beautiful bright red, like a rose.

"Ready for dinner?" I breathe.

Her ears perk up, tail swishing as she switches gears. "What kind of dessert do you think we'll have today?"

I laugh. "I don't know, but I bet you'll love it."

We walk hand in hand down the hall, a little bounce to Zily's steps. We run into Stafaan and Jasper making their way down as well, hands loosely clasped together. Jasper glances around warily, while Stafaan appears more confident in their appearance. Both of their hair is damp.

Dinner is pleasant. Mom leads the conversation as she often does. There's a quick briefing of how the meeting went. Jasper and I share friendly, excited glances. We tell her about our trip to the ruins of Arcadia. My mind drifts to the tree top, ghosts of fingers scratching my scalp, the soft feel of her breasts pressed against my chest, her mouth on mine.

I shift in my seat, shoving the memories away. Zily peers at me, raising an eyebrow. With a shake of my head, I dismiss the look, heat rising up my neck. The little smirk that creeps across her lips is knowing. I hope sliding my little slice of cheesecake to her distracts her. Her tail wags happily, though she only takes a few small bites and slides it back.

The things I would do for this woman. The better question would be what wouldn't I do for her.

Chapter Nineteen
Marshmallow Plant

Althaea officinalis root is used to relieve sore throats and cough. The food item, "marshmallow," was named after the flower and was once an ingredient to it, though the sap is no longer used to make marshmallows today.

Zily

It's early in the morning, before breakfast, when Jasper and his entourage leave. The royal carriage is waiting with his guards mounted on horses around it. The knights are giving Stafaan wary looks, eyebrows drawn down. Stafaan's face is schooled into its serious expression, glaring at everyone with his arms crossed. I can almost see the daggers flying from his eyes when he meets the other guards' gazes. They quickly look away. *Good luck.* I silently send my wishes to him.

I'm trying not to yawn when Jasper walks up to me. A yelp escapes when he wraps me in a hug, lifting me off the ground. "Thanks for everything. Hope to see you on our next visit."

"The coronation." The words come out raspy, Jasper squeezing a tad too hard. He chuckles setting me back on my feet.

"Yes. We'll see you at the coronation." His gaze shifts to Sylas. I half expect them to hug as well, but they only give a firm handshake.

Stafaan stands near Jasper as he enters his carriage. We lock eyes briefly. His serious guard mask cracks when he smirks at me. I roll my eyes, grinning back. He gives a short nod once on his horse.

We stand there until the carriage is out of sight, hidden by the trees of the forest. Sylas rests his hand on top of my head, ears flattening. I peer up at him curiously. "You did good." He praises, setting a fire in my chest.

I force a smile, though my thoughts have already moved onto the next agenda. There's something I want to do to prepare for assassins. If they choose a different method other than poison, I won't be of much help, but I want to be useful in the way I know I can be at the very least.

"Do you know where I can get a few small jars?"

"Jars?" Sylas repeats, eyebrows scrunching together.

Turning to head back inside, I keep my voice neutral, hoping to keep the fear of the coming days out of it. "Yes. I want them to put antidotes in."

"For poisons?"

I pause, peering up at him, my heart picking up speed. Reaching up, I press my hand to his chest over his heart. His hand covers mine, staring down into my eyes. I suck in a breath.

"I can't predict fully what will come for us. Even if we never use them, I will feel better having them ready." There are so many variables and unknowns, and there's only one thing I'm good at.

Sylas cups my face in both his hands. Soft lips brush mine in a tender kiss, calming my anxious heart. His forehead rests against mine. "Do it if it makes you feel better. You could try asking Dr. Burgess. He may have extras."

I wrinkle my nose remembering the way he looked at me. "He doesn't like me very much."

Sylas straightens, taking my hand. "It'll be fine. He's a good man. I'm sure he'll help if you tell him what you would like them for." My head bobs.

After breakfast, I walk Sylas to his office, splitting off to go to the infirmary. Dr. Burgess wasn't exactly rude to me before; not like the chefs that gave me the nastiest looks and refused to help me. His eyes did reveal the distaste he felt for me. Still, I knock on the door to the infirmary. This is more important.

The woman, Sonya, who brought me food that first day opens the door. Her soft wheat hair is pulled back into a high ponytail, warm brown eyes widening at the sight of me, a smile tugging at the corner of her lips.

"Oh! It's you. It's been a while. How are you doing? How are the stitches?" She's kind with her inquiries, genuinely interested and concerned. The first who was kind to me here.

A smile forms on my lips, genuinely happy to see her. "Quite well actually. The stitches have begun to dissolve already. The salve really helped to speed up recovery. I would like to know how to make it some time." I get a little distracted.

Dr. Burgess, sitting at his desk in the room behind Sonya, turns toward us with not as hateful eyes as I expected to see. It's a relief and bolsters my confidence to ask for what I need. Perhaps he'll keep the finished products with him. Being a doctor, he'd more likely be the one to administer the antidotes. I'm sure he already has knowledge of how to do so and in what quantities. I hope. Well, I can write up instructions, just in case.

I step past Sonya in the room that smells like cleaning alcohol, eyes trained on Dr. Burgess. "Actually, I'm here to see if you have any empty jars I could use?" My tone pitches into a question.

He leans back, the chair squeaking with the motion. "What do you need jars for?"

"For antidotes for poisons. To be prepared, unless you already have some ready?" I slightly tilt my head, ears twitching with the possibility I hadn't considered. Nerves prickle under my skin.

Dr. Burgess' eyebrows shoot up above his glasses. "And why would you need that?"

"Because someone will come to kill Sylas, and the possibility of poisoning is a strong one. And, I was hoping I could leave the antidotes with you." Dr. Burgess stares at me with unreadable features, though Sonya gasps behind me. She crosses the room to a cabinet against the wall. I swallow hard, trying to figure what is going through their mind with the information I gave them.

"Very well then. I believe Sonya is already gathering the jars, but I am curious, how do you plan to make these antidotes?" His tone is suspicious as expected, his finger tapped the end of the arm rest. He'll probably double check anything I bring him. The fact that I said I wanted him to hold onto them probably earned me this favor.

Sonya holds a box of small glass jars, more than I expected to receive. My heart flutters with excitement. "Here. These are all the empty, clean ones we have." The glass rattles together, making me cringe.

I take it carefully, bowing my head in gratitude. "Thank you. I'll be back with whatever I can make in a few days." I turn to leave, careful with my precious cargo.

"Wait." Dr. Burgess stops me, pushing up out of his chair. "Let's take a look at those stitches while you're here."

I gape at him, while Sonya pulls the box back from my arms, setting it on the table near the bed I laid in when I first arrived. Behind the pulled white curtain, she brings me a loose shirt to change into, covering me with a white sheet. She draws the curtain back. Dr. Burgess adjusts his glasses.

A shiver runs through me when his cold fingers brush my bare skin, lifting the shirt up enough to look at the wound. He gives me a sharp look when he notices I'm no longer covering them with bandages. As I told them, the wound is healing nicely. Some of the stitches have started to dissolve, fading mostly on the bottom and top scars, a dark maroon color. The skin around each crescent shaped line is pink. He presses around them, checking for infection, though I knew what to look for. I've cared for more injuries than I'd like to admit.

Dr. Burgess' sharp eyes glare up at me. I turn my head as if I don't notice, pretending not to know about the tug on the edges of the rugged lines. Recent movements have caused tension on the stitches. The salve has kept it clean and from reopening. It doesn't hurt much anymore either, except when he presses around it like that. I flinch.

He sighs heavily, pulling my shirt down. "They look to be healing well enough, faster than even I expected, but whatever you're doing that's straining your abdomen, stop it. The edges could still be reopened, and the chance of infection is still there."

I nod, my face flushing, knowing exactly what it was that strained it. Sonya gives me an eyebrow raise while standing behind Dr. Burgess. I avoid eye contact. The curtain is pulled around the bed again, and Sonya helps me back into my dress. Bowing my head, I thank them again. They don't have any idea what this small favor means to me. I take my box of jars, carrying them as carefully as possible, trying not to skip, and make my way back to my room. Sylas' and my room. A concept I'm getting used to that fills me with joy.

I leave them on the bed, heading straight to my next destination. Yesterday, I made a request to Leona. She said it would be ready sometime this morning. I knock, poking my head inside. Once again distracted, Leona sits at her desk, feet up, sewing something by hand. With a snip to the thread, she's done. She holds up the bag, examining her work.

"Hi, Leona," I call to her as I cross the room. The room doesn't smell as strongly as dye today. There's a hint of coco butter the closer I get to her.

Her head falls back, looking pleased to see me. "Zily, good timing. I just finished." She swings her feet down, spinning herself around in the chair, holding up her creation.

It's a small, auburn shoulder bag with a brown sun embroidered on to the front of the flap. She shows me the inside, flipping the sun over revealing two small pockets in front and the main pocket with a zipper holds six small sections with padding in all the walls. Slinging it over my head, the bag rests against my hip, at the spot where my red dress starts to flare out.

"It's perfect! Thank you! I knew I could count on you." I beam, swaying with my hand on the bag.

Leona matches my grin. "Of course. It's been a while since I've had a request like this. It was a nice break."

I dip my head again in thanks. Wandering out to the garden, it's the second time I've caught a gardener out there. She's tending to a different section today than she was yesterday, pruning a rose bush. Some humming fills the air.

"Excuse me, June." Not wanting to startle her with the shears in her hand, I call out. It's a little awkward as I've only spoken to her one other time. She wasn't out right rude to me, but she didn't seem super nice either. It was obvious I made her uncomfortable, though it lessened a little when she found out we had a shared interest in the flowers.

June straightens, looking over her shoulder, her long brown braid swaying down her back. She neither smiles nor glowers at me. I want to tell her I*t's alright. You make me uneasy too.* Lowering the shears, she turns fully around. She's in a plain dress as many of the female workers wear, this one a forest green. A bark brown, thick apron covers the front. I force a smile to my lips.

"Hey, uh, were you able to get an extra pair of pruning shears and gloves?" Her head bobs, hands slipping into the large pocket of her apron. She pulls out both items I requested, quietly holding them out to me. "Thank you!"

Rushing off around the bend, I pick my first target. The most obvious: angel's trumpet. The gloves are small and fit perfectly around my fingers. I flex them a couple times, testing movement, amazed they aren't stiff. It'll make work easier. Taking the little pruning shears, I clip off what I need in such a way to not hurt the plant as a whole. There's a gasp behind me, but I don't look until I've taken a step away from the flower.

June is watching me with large brown eyes. "What are you doing?" Her voice is steady, though it hints at curiosity.

"Gathering supplies." I simply answer. Her eyebrows furrow together. I wait for her to ask more, to say anything but she doesn't. Just stares at me. "For antidotes."

Her eyebrows shoot up. "How many?"

"All that can be made from here." I gesture around me. *As many as I can make.*

She nods once, pointing back behind her. "I'll start over there." She's off before hearing a reply, leaving me standing with my mouth hanging open.

After a couple of hours of work collecting herbs, I have a large bouquet of useful flowers. It's more than I expected to get on my first round of gathering, especially since I wasn't sure how many there are here. I've never counted them. With June's help, I have a little of every plant that can be made into a poison, even if they are not outright poisonous themselves, to make into antidotes. I can't thank June enough. Her face turns a deep red when I keep bowing with my thanks. Eventually, she says "that's enough," and walks away.

I run up to my room to drop the flowers off, laying them on the dresser. Setting the glove and shears beside them, I write a quick note for no one to touch them.

Realizing it's lunch time, I head back down stairs wondering how many more times today I will be doing so. I hope Zachary is there; I have a favor to ask of him.

With luck, he's cleaning up while waiting for the oven to go off, garlic and thyme wafting in the air around him. He gives a short, acknowledging nod while I slide on to the stool behind him by the island. Discarded bits of cheese, potatoes, carrots, onions and thyme are swept off the cutting board into the trash, bits too small to be used. He does a quick rinse of the cutting board and the bowls, leaving them to be washed by other hands later.

Zachary spins to face me, hands on his hips, broad smile on his face lighting up his hazel eyes. "Come for lunch? It'll be ready shortly."

"Could I have Sylas' too? I'm going to take it up to his study for him. I'm sure he hasn't left all morning."

He rolls his eyes, taking a seat next to me, leaning back on the island. Completely relaxed in his environment, he doesn't care about the stares the other chefs give us, gives me. My fingers brush the moon hair clip, reminding myself that I have claimed this place as my own and I will not be scared away by meager scowls.

I shift on the stool unsure how to ask. "Hey, Zachary?" His head cocks as my voice pitches. I swallow, blush threatening to rise. "If I gave you a list of ingredients and tools, do you think you could get them for me?"

"You want to cook something?"

"Not exactly." I lower my voice from eavesdroppers. "I'm planning on making antidotes, as a precaution and to ease my own anxiety, but I don't have access to a lot of things on my own." A quick glance is given to the other chefs pretending to mind their own business. "I need a stove as well, if you don't mind. I promise to thoroughly clean up after."

He blinks, staring into my pleading eyes. "Of course. I don't mind. I'll help if I can." Uncertainty and worry lace his voice. "Do you think it's necessary?" I simply nod. "Alright. Just tell me what you need."

The tension in my shoulders ease, the corners of my lips tugging upward. The offer of help warms my heart. Sylas is an amazing man. He has to be to have all his subject respect him so. Sometimes I think he's too nice for his own good, but that kind heart is what drew me in. It's what allowed him to accept me. I will do anything in my power to protect that heart.

"I'll bring a list later. I'm hoping to do the work tomorrow."

His head bobs. We sit in companionable silence, watching the seconds tick on the stove.

"How is His Highness doing? Are you keeping that desk of his in order?"

A giggle bubbles up. "Yes. Hopefully he's keeping it organized while I'm not there. He gets off track and starts on something else so easily. I don't know how he manages to keep it all on the desk." Hands up with a shrug, I shake my head with an exaggerated sigh.

"I've seen it travel to the floor. I'm hoping it was simply a really bad day and it's not the usual."

My head snaps to him in slight horror. Zachary throws his head back and laughs at my wide eyes, earning glances from the other chefs. "Sir Sylas Ambrose is a good boy. He's kind to everyone and is as fair as he can be. He'll make a great king. I believe that's why His Majesty is stepping down. Sir Sylas Ambrose simply struggles with the neat and orderly of paperwork, but it's nothing against his character." The oven dings.

Zachary hops off the stool, using mitts to pull out two metal sheets holding different dishes. An easy smile forms on my lips, watching him work, serving the food on four plates, separated onto two platters. The scent of herbs and meat comes from individual round dishes with a creamy potato topping roasted to golden brown. Rolls are on the other sheet, fluffy and shimmering with butter brushed over them. He tosses salads together as the final plates to the platters.

Sliding off the stool, I smooth out my dress. He whirls around to the fridge, pulling out a glass pitcher and a couple glasses, adding them to the tray I presume to be for me and Sylas. With a glance in my direction, Zachary disappears around the corner. He comes back with a bowl of tiny chocolate chip cookies. My tail starts wagging involuntarily. He winks.

"You got it?" He sets the tray in my hands carefully. I grip the twisted handles, nodding once. He releases it fully to my care. He holds the door open for me as I step out into the hall. A few steps away, he speaks again, "You take care of that boy now, k?" As if he not only handed me lunch for the day, but his prince as well.

My chest tightens, but I pause long enough to glance over my shoulder. "I will." It's a promise.

I use my foot to knock on the study's door. Shuffling feet make me step back. Sylas opens the door, his blue eyes shining like the midday sun when they meet mine. His hair is a mess from fingers running through it over and over again, deep black strands falling across his forehead. The sleeves that were down for breakfast are rolled up, tight against his toned biceps. They flex as he takes the tray from me.

"I hope you're hungry." I skip into the office after him.

"I needed a break." He gently sets the tray on the table while I stare at his desk.

"Why is there more than the two piles?" I point indignantly at the papers sprawled across his desk.

He flinches, a rare blush seeping across his sun kissed skin. Right on cue, his fingers find their way into his hair. I stroll over, raising to my tiptoes, my hand following the same path. My hand glides down to his face where he covers my hand with his, pressing his cheek to my palm. He peels it away to kiss my fingers. I roll my eyes.

"I'll take a look after lunch."

He pulls me down beside him on the couch. "I'd have it figured out eventually."

I push a spoon through the potatoes on top, releasing the steamy meat and vegetables underneath. A delighted moan escapes with a mouth full. Sylas chuckles beside me.

"I have no doubt. You've done it before, but you don't have to do it alone anymore." He leans in, caressing the back of my head as he presses his lips to my temple.

"Do you want to join me when we grant citizens an audience?"

"What?" I stammer even over the single word.

"We have a set time to allow citizens to come speak their grievances or ask for assistance a couple times a month. It's that time again tomorrow morning. Truthfully, I typically find it boring, though necessary to make the people happy, but I think it'd be better if you were there beside me." He looks at me in a way that makes me think he hasn't thought about what it would look like to have a Kitsune next to him. The image and idea it would send. It would be permanent.

I blatantly stare at him, lost for words, a swarm of emotions trying to sort themselves out. Honor that he trusts me so much, cares for me deeply enough that he wants me with him even during moments that are crucial for his image, one my presence could damage. The implication has me shifting in my seat, his stare boring into me.

"Are you sure that's a good idea?" My voice quiet.

Sylas plays with my hair, tickling the back of my neck, sending goosebumps down my arms. "Yes." Simple and punctuated with a smile.

Chapter Twenty
Cutleaf Toothwort

This little cluster of white flowers symbolizes hope and renewal. It has a spicy flavor and is often used a culinary condiment. The roots can be washed, chopped and ground in vinegar to be used as a horseradish substitute.

Lily

I manage to get his papers back in order, organizing by importance. There's a half written letter, an invite started on three different sheets. Those go on top to be finished first. It's to the Viararia Kingdom. From the little written there, it's an invite to his coronation. Sylas sighs leaning back in his chair. I grab his wrist before he can rake his fingers through his hair, lacing mine in between his instead, pulling him back to me. A smile tugs at the corner of his lips.

Facing him more than I usually do while sitting on the corner of the desk, the finished pile, small right now, rests stacked behind me. "It's alright. We can get this done before dinner." I sooth, encouragingly.

Sylas leans in, wrapping his arms around my waist, his head resting against my chest. Running my fingers through his hair, I stare at the ceiling, pretending not to know what he's doing. He squeezes before straightening, pushing his hair from his face.

"Right. Let's get this done." He picks up the first pages on top, groaning when he sees it's his attempt at an invite.

"Didn't you have to write others? Can't you make this similar to those?"

He shakes his head. "No. A scribe is writing the other invites." I'm genuinely shocked learning this. It reminds me how much I don't know about a royals life and customs. My heart thumps a little faster thinking I may have to learn. "I wanted to do this one. It's a bit more personal. We haven't spoken with the Celyce family in…" He sighs.

My ears twitch, head tilting at the name. I comb my memory to place the name. It's like an itch at the back of my head. Eyebrows knit together, unable to recall how I know the name. It doesn't hurt like when I start to tell Sylas about Sir Eyler Colin and Gateswood, but there's that same foggy feeling, preventing me from remembering.

"Who are they?"

Sylas blinks at me. "They're the royal family of the Viararia Kingdom. They're Kitsunes like you. We actually used to have friendly relations with them a few decades ago. We thought it'd be good to rekindle that friendship, because…" He trails off giving me a once over.

I feel my cheeks beginning to burn. He's making political decisions for my benefit. It's sweet, but I hope he's thinking hard about all these changes he's wanting to do at the start of his reign. It could cause the people to hate him. I push the thought from my head.

"I didn't know there was a kingdom like that."

I've seen the name Viararia on maps before, but jobs have never sent me that direction, so I haven't been given information on that region. Sir Eyler Colin has probably kept us away. Some of us could be from there. I could be from there. I could have family out there that I don't know about, that don't know I'm alive. The possibility is nearly heart stopping.

Sylas cups my face, bringing me back to him. He touches his forehead to mine, keeping me grounded. He must have seen the thoughts in my wide eyes.

"We could ask," he whispers. "One thing at a time, alright? We'll get it all sorted, I promise."

I breathe out a long slow breath, closing my eyes. "Okay. First, let's write the invite, so that we can ask them questions."

The invite takes an hour to write even between the two of us. I don't know the formalities of a letter, especially between royals, suggesting what should be in there. The bin is filled with crumpled up drafts. Finally, we have one that we're satisfied with and can move on. I'm able to speed us through the rest of the work on the desk, more so on the ones I went over before and made notes on, leaving us a short bit of time before dinner to relax.

I curl up on his lap in his chair, soaking up his warmth and comfort. He pets my head, casually asking about my morning. I inform him I got the vials from Dr. Burgess, collected the flowers I want to use and warn him not to touch them. Tomorrow, I'll go to the kitchen to use Zachary's station to create as many antidotes as I can. It may take me a couple of days. We'll see. I've gotten the process down and with the proper tools and equipment, it shouldn't take me too terribly long.

"When did you get into poisons? How did you learn about them?" Goosebumps prickle on the back of my neck as he plays with my hair.

Biting the inside of my cheek, I run a hand over my arm, debating on telling him the truth. "Remember when I told you I picked flowers once and the doctor taught me about the properties of the flowers?" He nods, staring into my heart, looking so interested in what I have to say. "I began to secretly look for more information myself, stealing books for a time, trying to return them before anyone noticed they were gone. I also didn't stop picking flowers." Sylas frowns. "When I was sent on my first jobs, the kind the Callie still does of gathering information, I would bring back different plants that I found that looked interesting or sounded like something I read."

"When was that? You said you started making your own lotions around eleven right?" A smile forms on my lips, warmed that he remembers that.

"Uh huh. Poisons, admittedly, came before lotions." His eyes grow wide with concern, sitting up straighter. I glance at the clock. "Should we start making our way down?"

Sylas' turns me more towards him, caressing my face, his thumb stroking my cheek. "There's time. Tell me more."

I swallow hard, getting lost in the sky of his eyes. "I would test out new poisons on myself, usually on my arms. I ended up making lotion to help with the rashes I would get. It's also how I got caught messing with poisons, though it did take a couple of years before Sir Colin… Eyler found out and another year before… he sent me on my first assassination job." I shake my head, pain throbbing with attempting to say his name.

Sylas pulls me in, my head resting against his shoulder. "Do you still like to experiment?" He speaks gently, rubbing the top of my head, my ears in the way I like.

"I have thought about it. Not with poisons specifically, but…" I pause, a little embarrassed by my aspirations. "I have thought it'd be nice to make a new discovery."

"That sounds wonderful. We could set up a room for you. A lab, if you like. I only ask that you don't experiment on yourself."

I giggle. "Those days are long gone. And we have to get through a lot before I can think seriously about something like that." It's a distant dream, but it's a possible one with him. I put a hand over his heart.

His fingers curl around my hand, lifting my hand to his lips. "One day at a time." I nod with a little smile. "Shall we head down now?"

I hop off his lap. "I need to make a list for Zachary. I nearly forgot!" Going to his desk, I start opening drawers to find a blank paper. I leave a note at the bottom about when I'll be there; after lunch. Sylas peers over my shoulder, squeezing my waist when he sees I left the morning open for the audience meeting.

He holds onto me until he's pulling out the chair for me at the dining table. Sylas waits until delicious smelling food is placed in front of me before speaking with his parents. Only the knowledge of the chicken in my mouth keeps my mouth shut when he informs his mom and dad that I'll be joining them in the morning.

Eleanor lights up to my surprise. "Wonderful! I'll make sure a chair is ready for you." I attempt to match her beaming face, failing miserably. Anxiety at whatever that even means grips my heart.

Reuben doesn't disagree, and the only sign that he's shocked by the declaration is a raise of an eyebrow. He takes a moment to eat a bite. "Have you written the invite to the Celyce family?"

Both Sylas and I groan. We share a glance. "Yes. We have one written. I'll give it to the scribes to put with the others tomorrow."

Tomorrow is a busy day with constant moving parts. We walk to the throne room directly after breakfast at a slow, lingering pace. Sylas and his dad are discussing something an adviser brought up. I think it's about the Viararia Kingdom. It could be about Jasper and the Zeneth Kingdom. It's hard to concentrate on their conversation while having my own with Eleanor.

"I'm so pleased you're joining us. I haven't seen the seat yet, but the carver assures me that it's ready. Hopefully it suits you and is to your liking." She's talking more at me than actually conversing with me. I smile politely, periodically looking at her, so she knows I'm listening. "The first time may be a little anxiety inducing. You don't have to speak, but feel free to if anything comes to mind. We do more listening than speaking. Sometimes the people need to vent and don't really need our interference. They like to feel heard. Everyone does." She glances at me with a warm smile that reminds me of Sylas'.

I nod along, watching the way she floats across the floor. Her gate is so smooth, I can't even tell she's walking. With her chin up, shoulders back, hands folded neatly in front of her, she is the picture perfect image of elegance. Walking beside Sylas, the future King, I attempt to match the current Queen's appearance, feeling like a foolish child in comparison. My eyebrows scrunch, glancing at the floor, trying to figure out how she does it.

Eleanor lifts her skirts briefly as we pass a man in deep blue robes bowing. Sylas and Reuben bow their heads slightly. The man peeks up, eyes narrowing at me. I give a little smile, not having a clue who he is. With the moment her skirt was lifted, I notice Eleanor takes quick small steps. I change to doing the same, finding myself slightly on my toes. It reminds me of sneaking through a building. My smile grows as the familiar feel takes hold and my skirt doesn't shift with every step as much.

The room is large and well lit, feeling open and spacious like the sky. Warm and welcoming. Three large chairs -thrones- sit beside each other of equal size. Each is unique to the person it belongs to. Reuben's with a sword through a crown. A ruler through and through. A protector. The seat is cushioned with a deep green padding. Eleanor's has a fiery bird etched into the back of hers. Burning freedom. Strong and outgoing. Red lace creates a swirl pattern over a blue so dark it's nearly black pillow seat. Sylas' throne has wings spread open in flight in the clouds. Gentle and free. The tiniest hint of lightning comes from the cloud. His strength and willingness to protect if other means don't work.

Now, there is a fourth chair. A little bit smaller than the rest, but in no way less extravagant. Moonstones follow the ridge of the head rest, changing colors with the reflection of the light. A soft blue cushion rests on the seat. A bouquet of flowers, all poisonous flowers I note, tied together with a ribbon is etched into the back, a single small star in the top right and a crescent moon in the top left, matching how I wear my hair pins when I will inevitably sit in the chair.

My gaze darts to Sylas, my heart thundering like a storm inside my chest. I can't sit there. Being here implies too much as it is, but this chair, this throne, *my throne* will absolutely send a message. It's too soon. I don't even know what it means. However, Sylas looks as stunned as I am, though he appears quite pleased by the surprise. He turns his grin on me as he gives me a wink.

Hands land on my shoulders from behind, making me tense up on instinct. "I had it crafted last night. Not bad for being last minute. I think I will have to reward the carver more for his excellent, hasty job." Eleanor's voice sings with approval. I expected a simple chair when she said she would have one ready for me.

She takes her place beside the already waiting Reuben, both of them sitting with straight backs, feet planted on the ground. It's the first time I have seen any of them wear a crown, but they are the picture perfect image of a King and Queen.

A silver circlet of intricate filigree, weaving up into a pattern of short and tall points, wide like leaves, rests upon Reuben's black hair. Petite emeralds, matching those in his throne, shine at the base of the points. The metal is unpolished as one would expect it to be, giving it a darker tone. Gold and green thread embroiders the high collar of his dark, royal blue coat, matching that on his chest. More green peeks out in the slashes on his sleeves. Loose black trousers are tucked into polished boots. A decorative sword rests at his side. He holds his head high, cool gaze sliding to his wife. The hint of a smirk tugs at his lips, reminding me momentarily of his son.

Eleanor casually moves her hand from the armrest of her throne to his, her hand laying on top of his, fingers lacing together. Her ruby lips curve into a pleasant expression. Her dress matches that of her husbands with a more vibrant royal blue, silk fabric, forest green thread swirling around her bodice down to a solid line around her waist, the skirt flaring out, laying perfectly in the seat. Her crown, resting upon golden brown waves, is a sparklier silver, the base much the same filigree with teardrop eyelets around the top, encompassing large rubies.

Sylas takes my hand, escorting me to my seat when I don't move forward on my own, his broad shoulders covered in the lightest blue, black embroidery detailing what the tattoo of his wings look like on his back. They look like his wings, but I doubt they are as soft. The thread loops and knots down his chest, round felt buttons holding the coat together. His pants are tighter than usual making it difficult to keep my eyes from wandering, the muscles fighting against the fabric.

His midnight black hair is combed neatly back into a low ponytail, not a strand out of place. Yet. The circlet on his head looks more grey than silver, darker than even his father's. The design around the base looks like a mixture of feathers and leaves woven together with cloudy white stones placed evenly apart. The points around the top are a combination of that of both his parents, thin eyelets ending in sharp points with sapphire stones in the eyes.

I pull my hand free after taking my seat, partially because I need it to push myself back into the chair. Despite it being smaller in both width and height, my feet don't touch the floor. The short black heels I chose this morning thankfully have a strap over the top to keep them from falling off. Shifting till my spine is pressed against the backrest, I discover a pleasant little detail. There's a gap at the base where it connects to the seat, large enough for my tail to slip through easily. It swishes a couple times before relaxing.

Sylas' chuckle brings my attention back to him. His sword, more decorative than his usual one with a mix of sapphires, rubies and emeralds in the handle, rests in the gap in his chair. He's watching me carefully, a guarded worry in the depth of the blue of his eyes. If he's going to worry the whole time, he shouldn't have invited me. It's too late to back down now. I smooth out my long dress, the color of the forest at dusk with blue flower outlines in the skirt, hooking my ankles together, doing my very best to look as regal as the others while feeling like a child in this chair.

Guards line the room, all in the same black uniform. Colored thread on the shoulders indicates their rank, though I don't know the order. I assume the blue swirls, that of which is the main family color, is one of the higher ranks as it's on Kai's shoulder standing nearest me, face unreadable. What does he think of all this?

The first citizen to come in blatantly stares at me, jaw slack, eyes wide, frozen in place and everything. He's in a loose neutral tone shirt and breeches, a dark brown belt cinched at the waist. Calloused hands cling to the parchment with whatever he's come to request. Keeping my face impartial doesn't stop the heat creeping up my neck into my cheeks, my heart constricting.

King Reuben clears his throat, startling the man out of his stupor. His gaze shifts to the King, taking a moment to close his mouth. He opens and closes it several times like a gulping fish before dropping his gaze, remembering to bow and reading the request.

It proceeds like this for many more visits. Shock and confusion freezing the citizens to where they stand until a deep voice breaks them from the spell. I want to sink into the comfy cushion, but I can't hide. Instead, I find the flowers in my dress extra fascinating.

"Zily," Sylas whispers my name.

I peek at him. He leans towards me, sapphires glimmering on his head, the coat straining with the movement. I school my expression in an attempt to reassure him, though my smile is weak. I don't want him regretting this. I don't want him being judged for this decision. I want to be by his side. It's like I told Stafaan; he chose me and I will not let what others think of me scare me away.

With a few blinks, smiling becomes easier. He must see the change, his eyes softening. Casually, he moves his hand to the arm rest, flipping it over in offering. I consider it as the next person comes into the room. My hand slides onto the arm rest, hesitating to cross the gap between our thrones.

An old man with thin, matted silver-grey hair tied up into a little bun stops before us. The wrinkles on his face make his eyes squint when he smiles. He folds his hands in front of him over classic farmers' attire.

"Your Majesty." His voice is low, gruff with age. "Your Majesty. Your Highness." He bows, addressing each. His kind hazel eyes don't waver when they turn to me. "My Lady." He bows his head respectfully to me.

My face burns. I don't know if I'm supposed to acknowledge him back or not. I haven't paid close enough attention, so I give a short nod in return. Sylas is grinning at me like a fool, sparkles glittering in his eyes. His hand crosses the distance to take mine. A sigh escapes. No more holding back.

"-It's affected nearly half the village, Sir." The old man is saying. I've missed the first half of what he's said. "They only have days after the first sign of illness. My grandson… He's just a babe. Please. Could you send a doctor?" His voice cracks with pain, tears blurring his eyes.

Reuben and Eleanor share a wary glance. "Of course. We'll send a few of our best doctors back with you right away."

"This is most troublesome." Eleanor whispers, squeezing Reuben's hand.

"What are the symptoms?" My voice rings off the walls, sounding stronger, louder than expected. It's really startling considering I had no intention of speaking; it came out unbidden.

"It starts as a rash, usually on the legs that spread. A fever with cold sweats quickly follows, along with a cough. Puking is a common occurrence, though it seems not everyone does before… passing." Talking about those who have died already is difficult for him.

My eyebrows knit together in thought. The symptoms are common for a lot of diseases. I could help with the fever and puking, but I doubt only treating the symptoms will keep them from dying. They'd only pass in less pain.

Sylas gently squeezes my hand. My gaze flickers over to find that not only Sylas is staring at me, but so is Eleanor and Reuben, hope and expectations in their eyes. It's a lot for a girl who is more used to killing than saving lives. My expertise is poisons after all; medical uses are a byproduct of my research. *Poisons*. My mind races through all the ones I know of, imagining the plains the old man most likely lives in to raise horses, cows and pigs and fields for crops.

"Can you tell me anything else? Has any of the animals been affected?"

The old man's grey eyelashes flutter with a slow blink. "Yes. Now that you mention it. We've lost several of our pasture cows. They started acting strange, confused before passing. The villagers also seem confused in the days leading up to their passing. I always called it fever talk."

It's not fever talk. "Are there little white flowers with long, thin leaves around your village?" Sylas squeezes again, knowing I've, *hopefully*, figured it out.

Again, the grey eyelashes blink. "Yes, we've always had them. The children like to pick them, and the women sometimes use them in their cooking."

Please tell me they pick the right ones. "Those are cutleaf toothwort. What I'm afraid of is that toothbane has creeped in with it. They look very much alike, except the toothbane has five white petals and the leaves are rough. They're extremely poisonous. It acts faster when ingested, but the rashes occur from touching them."

The old man gapes at me in horror. "We let the kids play in those fields," he whispers, his eyelashes catching on the tears in his eyes.

I slowly swing my head back and forth. "You couldn't have known. They look so much like that of what you've known and used for years. They do need to be uprooted to get rid of them for good. I don't recommend burning them lest the toxicity become airborne."

His head bobs along with my words, ringing the front of his shirt. His eyes stare at me wide, though they appear to be somewhere else.

"Zily, do you think you can make an antidote for those already affected?" Reuben's deep voice startles me. It's not often that he addresses me.

I feel my cheeks starting to burn again. My ears flicker and I nod. "Yes. If I can get my hands on the right ingredients. The question then becomes how much is needed."

"Whatever you need. We'll get it to you." Reuben returns his attention to the farmer, his back pressed against his throne. "I will arrange for an escort for you and the doctors I've promised. A party will follow once we have the first batch of antidotes ready with a supply to make more if needed."

Tears roll down the old man's face, shoulders shaking. "Thank you." He whispers, the words choking out. "Thank you." He bows again, knees giving out, hands flat against the floor. He could be bowing to any of the thrones, but the slight angle change indicates he's bowing to me.

The farmer is escorted out. Reuben talks to a soldier to tell Dr. Burgess and another name I don't recognize to prepare to leave as soon as possible. It makes me uneasy knowing he's going to be gone with the threat that'll be coming here getting close at hand. He turns his attention to me, leaning on his armrest, peering around Eleanor and Sylas. "Do you think you can have at least a few vials ready to go by the end of day and written instructions of how to make it?"

I want to tell him that's a lot of expectation. We haven't even gone over ingredients to know if we have them here at the ready. The wild thing is I need a poison to counteract the poison from the toothbane. A heavy sigh escapes. I lift my head, determined gaze meeting the King's.

"I assume the kitchen has turmeric, licorice, ginger, garlic, and elderberry, but I need to go hunt for the last ingredient."

"What's that?" Sylas asks, looking ready to get up even though I know this meeting with the citizens is far from over.

"Jimson weed. It's another poison."

"You want to poison them to get rid of the poison?" The skepticism is rightfully in Reuben's voice.

"Yes." I give no explanation. "I'd like to start right away, if I may?" I scoot to the edge of the seat ungracefully until my feet touch the ground. Sylas moves to stand. "You stay. You still have responsibilities here." He frowns, letting my hand on his chest push him back into his seat. "Zachary will be waiting for me, so I want to try to find the jimson weed before I meet with him."

Sylas sighs, slumping back. Eleanor giggles at our interaction. I leave the throne room, heels clicking down the hall. My mind churns with everything that needs to be done and there's a lot to be done.

Chapter Twenty-One
Calla Lily

This flower represents rebirth, charm, passion, and sympathy. They are highly toxic to consume, but have been used in some places to treat wounds, sores and boils.

Lily

The scent of oak and fresh air fills my lungs. Branches of brush scrape across my bare legs, wearing my old shorts for the hike. I duck under a branch, my fingertips dragging along the trunk of a tall, old tree. My eyes scan the ground for a soft violet, five pointed flower. My chest is heavy with the task I'm determined to complete without much hope behind it. It's not the right time of year for the jimson weed to be blooming, and they only bloom for a day, though I don't need them blooming to use them.

I think about the old man, the heartbreak in his voice when he mentioned his grandson, solidifying my persistence. Everything is so vastly green that any other color stands out, so I move swiftly deeper and deeper into the forest, tracking my time by the location of the sun through the green canopy above.

The similarity in which this hunt is like my previous scavenging stirs unpleasant memories in the back of my mind. I force them back with the sole knowledge that this is to save people, not to find another means to kill.

An hour, then two and three pass. Will they wait for me if I don't return till late? I refuse to think of the possibility of never finding it.

I stumble, needles pricking my calves. Wincing, I glance down, leg turned to get a better look at the pin poles where tiny trails of blood leak down my leg. I turn slowly, searching for the source. A round bulbous plant covered in spikes on a purple stem sticks out on the path I was creating.

Pulling my sword from its sheath, I cut a bulb off the stem, letting it roll on the ground. Carefully, the tip of the sharp blade punctures the thick skin, peeling it back to, thankfully, see white and soft violet. There's no time to gloat, I start cutting more until I have a pile of prickly dark bulbs. The venom from the needles bite into my hands as I transfer them into the bag I brought. It's a leather bag I found used and discarded in the back of the closet when I returned to the room to quickly change. I'm not too concerned having the resistance to most poisons built from the years I used to experiment on myself. I'll treat myself when I return.

I race back to the mansion, flying through the forest like my life depends on it. It's not my life, but others who are depending on me. Legs outstretched, I leap over a fallen tree with ease. My pace doesn't slow until the mansion is in sight.

Zachary is in the kitchen with the list of ingredients and items I requested on the island, plastic laid out to protect the counter top. Smart, considering I'll be using poison in the kitchen space where our meals are prepared. It appears that he's cleaning up lunch. There's a plate set to the side with a cover over it.

He turns around, smiling at me with an expectation that quickly fades when he sees me. "Girl, what happened to you? Sylas Ambrose was looking for you and said you went out to find something, but you look like you've become one with the forest."

I pant heavily from running the whole way, dropping the bag beside the island, finger outstretched toward it. "Don't. Touch." My lungs struggle to get enough oxygen in to support my body. I pull a leaf from my hair, double checking on my hair pins. Still there and in place. They held up to my frantic searching and have kept my hair out of my face. I love them all the more.

Thank the Moon. Zachary has the ingredients organized in alphabetical order making it easy for me to find the herbs I need, pushing the rest aside for later use. The jars are twist lids, releasing the scent of garlic and turmeric into the kitchen. My nose wrinkles, ears twitching. It's not a pleasant scent. I measure them out into the mortar and pestle.

A gentle hand touches my shoulder. "I can help. Tell me what to do."

My hands shake holding the pestle above the herbs. I stare at him, my racing mind struggling to process his words as I think about the process, the ingredients, the measurements. "I, uh, water. I need boiling water."

"Easy. I can do that." He winks, filling a large pot, and setting it on the stove.

I add in bits of ginger, mincing it in. The elderberry and licorice need to be mashed separately from the powder. "Could I have a pen and paper? I need to write this down, so it can be duplicated." I nearly forgot. I hope I have enough jimson weed for them to take to the village. How long will it take if I aim to prep all of them before sending the poisonous spiked bulbs to the doctors?

A paper appears beside the mortar with a pen on top. "What else?"

I blink up at Zachary. Slow. My brain is moving too slow. I've never had people counting on me like this before. How much should I make before calling it and sending it to them? My gaze focuses on Zachary's kind hazel eyes. I've also never had help before either.

"Could you keep doing this? Add more at this ratio." I gesture to the two mortars, taking up the pen. I scribble down the ingredients, the ratio and the consistency. I then describe the boiling, peeling and draining process of the jimson weed in case I don't complete all of them, emphasizing a caution warning while handling them. However, I have a new determination to finish prepping the jimson weed with Zachary working on the rest.

I turn to the boiling water. The pot is huge, ready to boil over. I'm a little less careful than one should be with the plants, the pointed ends nipping my skin. I fill the pot with as many of them as I can. My estimation is I have enough to do this about three times. *Do I have the time for it?*

Shaking my head, I wipe my hands on my shorts, taking in a long, slow, calming breath. The adrenaline starts to ease from my veins. Rushing and panicking isn't going to help anyone. That's how mistakes are made. Creating antidotes, dealing with poisons, require precision or it could not work. Or one could poison themselves. Like I have.

As if to remind me of the past, an itchy, stinging sensation begins in my hands. They'll start to get a red tint to them soon.

That's the worst it'll get. Part of the experiments I did on myself was to test the potency. Small paper cuts covered my arm. The number of times I threw up from ingesting things I shouldn't have, though it was on purpose. I'm glad Sylas didn't ask about details when I was telling him about my past. Finding cures or such to combat the symptoms were their own kind of experiments. Memories of Sir Colin Eyler finding out and ordering me to use my love of plants to kill people threaten to surface.

"Hey, Zily." There's a shudder to Zachary's voice, breaking me from my thoughts. "What you wrote here about the poky plants, is that what you're handling now?" I turn toward him, hands on hips, head tilted. "Shouldn't you be wearing gloves, or something?"

A confident smirk slips across my lips. "I'm fine. It won't affect me as it would you. That's why you're not allowed to touch them. And don't worry, I know how to clean up so it won't affect the pot or your space." Giving my hands a solid scrub, I leave them slightly damp, so when I rub turmeric into the tiny holes it sticks. I wait a moment, checking on the bulbs, before washing them clean.

Zachary continues to stare at me, momentarily paused in his crushing of herbs. There's a couple bowls filled with the mixtures lined up. The pestle starts moving again, his attention returning to his assigned job. "You've done this before?"

"You could say this is my kind of cooking." I take a long fat knife, poking at the bulbs floating. The points are flimsier, and the water is murky from the poison that has leaked from the plants. A couple more minutes and this batch can be taken out and peeled.

"Still, be careful. Sir Sylas Ambrose won't be the only one effected if something happens to you." His voice is lower than usual, the truth behind his words ringing clear.

It freezes me for a moment, staring at the murky water the blade stirs. Something tightens in my chest. Not an ache, but more like a warm blanket draping over old wounds. During the days of experimentation, I didn't know Callie or Decan. I met them around the time my experiments slid me into a new line of work. They had only seen the bandages wrapped around my arms, not knowing why. I told them years later. They were also not pleased. Zachary is a fine reminder that I have friends that worry about me. I need to take care of myself, so I can keep them safe.

"Right," I breathe.

I use a strainer to scoop out the bulbs, laying them out on a thick plastic, shaking out more from the bag instead of handling them individually. I move the plate of food to the corner of the island, intending to use the counter space beside the stove. While the second batch boils, I use two sharp knives to peel the deep green outer layer away from the flower. It's the center I want the deepest violet of the flower along with about a quart of the green layer, depending on the size of the bulb. Both have to be weighed to get the right amount.

When the pile of bits I don't need starts to invade my cutting area, Zachary pulls over a trash can. Upon request, he pulls out a double boiler, already heating the water underneath. He puts in the ingredients to the ratio I wrote, and I add in the jimson weed. Slowly it turns into a thick liquid. I thin it out with drops of water using small increments because I have always done this by sight, but I need to write it down. I've decided I can have all the ingredients prepped, but I'll only get this batch done, using only half the flowers from the first pot.

Zachary runs to get me jars before the antidote over cooks. He watches as I fill the jars, not fully, with equal amounts without needing a scale. He takes a few to check and the difference is a hundredth of a gram. Pride grows, happy with how much I was able to make.

I package the prepped jimson weeds, cleaning the area thoroughly so Zachary could begin on dinner. He doesn't say anything, but I feel bad that he's getting a late start because of me. I don't know when the other chefs came in, but they're staring at us and his area with wary eyes.

"Are you still in here?" A voice that warms me to my core calls.

Sylas strides in, hair a mess compared to how neat it was this morning. My hand reaches up to touch it without thinking. It's in a ponytail, so I can't freely run my fingers through it, but I pet him in a similar manner as he often does to me. He smiles, eyes lighting. My shoulders slump, exhaustion weighing in.

"I'm almost done. Zachary has been a big help." I glance back in time to see him grin and wink. "I need to finish jarring these and get out of his way."

"Do you want help?" Sylas stands beside me, picking up a jar.

"Sure. I've already packaged the poisonous herb, so it'll be fine." By the horrified looks the other chefs give me, maybe I shouldn't talk about poisons so openly. Oh, well. They didn't like me before and I'm too tired to worry about it now.

"Are you okay?" He asks, pouring powder into the glass. It clouds up, making it difficult to see how much is in there. Hence the scales.

"Mmhmm." I scoop the licorice and elderberry mixture into a jar.

"I was surprised when you weren't back yet when we finished with the audiences. I waited till lunch. I was getting worried." This is going a lot faster with his help. Now to figure out how to transport them.

"Do you have a box or something to carry these in? And you must have just missed me. I came in as Zachary was cleaning up." It reminds me that I forgot to eat, the covered plate sitting abandoned on the corner of the island. I wipe my hands on my shorts. Sylas' gaze follows the motion, staring at my shorts. No, my thighs.

His eyes are darker when they meet mine again. "We'll transport them in chests. I'll let them know it's ready and the men in charge of transport will come get them."

"Great!" A yawn suddenly escapes. Sylas pats my head before departing.

It's not long before three large chests are escorted in by Sylas. I hover around them as they fill the crates with all my hard work, fussing and worrying every time the glass clinks together, but the interior is padded, made for travel. When the men carry the antidotes away, I all but run to our room, lingering long enough for Sylas to keep up at a brisk walk.

Watching from our balcony, the carriage and its entourage speed down the path. A heavy sigh escapes, and I slump against the railing, bowing my head. Sylas rubs circles on my back.

"You worked hard." He commends.

"I just hope it's enough."

His arms slide around me, pulling me from the railing as his wings engulf me in his warmth. I lean into him, my eyes closed. Tomorrow, I'll be doing all of this again, only with different ingredients. Different poisons. Different antidotes. Different cause. I hope it won't be needed, but I'd rather take the precaution. I don't know any of the other assassins' track record, but if it's anything like my own, then every precaution should be taken to counter the unknown. The things one would be willing to do to avoid punishment is a dangerous factor.

I tilt my head back. The sky looks down at me with a kind smile on his face. His lips brush my forehead. My chest warms, spreading throughout my body. No one knows the pain I'm willing to endure to keep this man alive.

Chapter Twenty-Two
Monkshood

It represents chivalry, protection, danger and warning. This is extremely poisonous, so much that simply touching it requires medical attention. Symptoms range from the usual nausea, vomiting, diarrhea, and headaches, to paralysis, seizures and arrhythmia.

Sylas

Zily struggles through dinner. She can't stop yawning and doesn't finish her meal. My parents are unusually reserved as well, as if allowing her the peace and quiet. She put everything she had today into saving a village she may never see. Perhaps I'll take her to visit one day. I'm sure seeing those she's saved will be a joy. She deserves that.

I attempt to talk her into bathing in the morning, like I often do, but she insists on washing off the sweat, forest and herbs left on her skin and in her hair. She's so tired, blush doesn't even rise to her cheeks when I slide into the tub behind her. A moan escapes as I massage conditioner into her scalp, ears flickering.

I don't let her sit for too long in the hot water in fear she'll fall asleep on me. She can hardly keep her eyes open, swaying on her feet while I dry both of us. I kiss the tip of her nose after pulling a shirt, one of mine, over her head. It earns me a little smile and squinted eyes. I tuck her against my side in the large bed, finding sleep comes easier with her there.

The morning knock doesn't wake Zily. I let her sleep in for as long as I can. She mentions spending the day in the kitchen again, anxiety in her voice; counting the days until my next would-be-assassin arrives. I wish I could ease her fear. The antidotes she insists on making should help. I hope.

I'd rather her spend her days doing hobbies she enjoys, like reading or drawing in the garden or visiting Maple and S'more, though she has mentioned enjoying the work before. But it'd be nice if it didn't come with the anxiety.

Zily, to my joy, spends the morning with me. Unfortunately, it's spent in my study going over all the paperwork from the meetings yesterday. She guessed there would be a stack on my desk and has graciously decided to help me with it first. After we eat lunch together, she disappears to the kitchen until dinner time.

She's not as exhausted by day's end as the one previous. Zily's tail wags as she tells me how much she accomplished with Zachary's help, excitement sparkling in her eyes.

The following day is much like the last. During our time together in the morning, we visit Maple and S'more. I introduce her to a couple other mares, trying to get her up on one. It takes a lot of convincing, but I walk her around on Pebble in the field for a while, and that's only because she had seen how calm Pebble was with Jasper. Slowly, Zily becomes more confident, sitting up straighter. She's becoming more comfortable around horses, quicker too, than when I first brought her to the stable. One day, I'll give her own horse, and we can go riding together.

Once again, after lunch, Zily meets Zachary in the kitchen. Coronation formalities have me in meetings with my father. Along the same line, I end up in Leona's room with my arms out as she takes new measurements. I go to pick Zily up from the kitchen for dinner, but Zachary informs me she is delivering the box of jars to Dr. Burgess room. Sonya's probably there to grab them for her.

I wait for her by the stairs, a little impatiently. It's a comfort when her hand slides into mine and we walk to dinner together. She lets me know that she finished the antidotes she hoped to accomplish, and that she's carrying a couple for quick death poisons on her, along with a burn cream and a salve for cuts. She pats the little bag she started carrying, beaming up at me. She has her weapon and I have mine, my free hand resting on the pommel of my sword.

Mom keeps the conversation pleasant, talking about events that are coming up; how my cousin has requested a visit. I'm not thrilled about the timing of it with all that is going on, but we were close as children, making me excited to see him, nonetheless. Dad tries to bring up the farming village, but mom shuts that line down real quick. Dinner is meant for pleasant conversations, though Zily's ears perked at the brief mention. I promise her we'll see if there is any information available tomorrow.

Zily takes her nightly bath while I sit on the couch, reading. She comes out with only a towel on. Pushing my book away, she sits on my lap. Chuckling, I pull her in, giggles escaping her lips. My hand slides around to the back of her neck, bringing her head close to capture her lips with mine. I love the way I can feel her smiling in the kiss. I slide my hand under her legs, standing with her in my arms. I literally drop her in bed, a squeal echoing across the room.

I fetch her a nightgown from the closet, pulling it over her head, watching the way the silk forms to her body. The thin fabric hardly does anything to cover her. She raises an eyebrow at me when my hand runs down her side, I lift the blanket up for her to crawl into bed. Zily snuggles up against me, head on my chest. I pet her head, ears falling back with the motion, until she's asleep, hands clutching my shirt.

The room is dark, save for the moonlight coming in through the balcony. The curtains flutter with a breeze that should not be. Slowly, carefully and pretending to be asleep, I slip my arm out from under Zily, her body shifting with the movement. I roll over, draping my arm over the edge of the bed, hidden by the covers.

The intruder freezes momentarily as my fingers slowly wrap around the grip of my sword, tucked in its secret hiding place in the mattress. I'm waiting for them to get closer before striking. I want to catch them off guard. Feet shuffle across the carpet, inching closer. They're breathing heavily, a dead giveaway of where they're standing.

"Don't move." A familiar voice growls.

I sit up with a jolt, glancing at the empty bed behind me. Zily stands on her tiptoes behind the perpetrator, a Kitsune with short brown hair sticking out at every angle, with her blade to his throat. I didn't even feel her get out of bed, let alone sneak across the room to get behind him, footsteps as light as falling snow. The man glares at me, a dagger in his hand pointing toward the floor. His hand merely twitches up, a shift of his feet and a tiny sliver of blood trickles down his neck.

Swinging my legs off the bed, I stand, pointing the tip of my sword. I motion for Zily to join me. She takes a step back, the edge of the blade delicately sliding across his throat without breaking the skin more, until it's at his back. Slowly, she walks around him, never turning her back to him. I haven't seen her eyes this dark before. She's posed to kill if necessary.

He blinks, staring at Zily, his gaze running down her body and back up again. The realization hits him. "What are you doing, Snow?"

Zily flinches, grip tightening on her short sword. "That's not my name," she growls. "And I've left. You could too." An offering, to see if he could be like her.

He snorts a laugh, using the moment to slide his foot back. "You can't *leave*. There's no escape, you know that." Zily shifts beside me, put off by his words. "Wait till Sir Colin Eyler finds out about this. Do you know what he's going to do to you?" He grins wickedly. A shudder runs through Zily.

I step forward, moving her behind me. "Nothing. He won't lay a finger on her."

The man's eyes flicker between us, taking another step back. I debate letting him go. He could send a warning to this man that scares them so much, or it could cause more trouble.

"You think you can protect her from Sir Colin Eyler? You don't know what he's capable of, the leash he has us on. I know she can't tell you." He smirks with devilish amusement. *Why does it seem like he's enjoying this so much?*

I glance down at Zily, watching her reaction to tell me if I should stop him when he makes his move. Zily lowers her sword the moment his body twists to run for the balcony. So, we'll let him go, but he *will* deliver a message.

He's quick on his feet, but I stay right behind him. The moon glistens off my blade, cutting a deep gash into his arm using it to fling him over the balcony. He yelps in voluntarily, and a second cry escapes as he hits the ground hard. A moment later, he's running, limping across the yard to the forest. Perhaps I should ask Kai to clean the blood trail up. No need to frighten the servants.

I return to the room. Zily sits on the edge of the bed, staring at the floor, looking haunted. She brushes hair from her face only for it to fall right back, her hair clips resting on the nightstand.

Laying my sword on the ground beside me, I kneel before Zily, reaching up to cup her face. I force her to look at me. There's no stars in the night sky of her eyes. There's only worry and fear. So much fear.

"It's okay. It's going to be alright. We handled that just fine and we'll handle whatever else they send." I rub my thumbs across her cheeks. Her head bobs, though her eyes don't clear. I kiss her forehead.

"Do you think it was really okay to let him leave?" Her voice is small, all but a whisper.

"Would you have liked me to stop him?" She slightly shakes her head. "There's a chance that word will get around and maybe your friends will hear. They could come join you."

"What if Sir Colin Eyler or other Vampires decide to come instead?" Her fear filled gaze pierce me. Her hands curl into fists on her thighs. It's a quick motion indicating she said something she shouldn't have. I hate that she still feels the need to call that man "Sir." There's no reason to continue to be respectful of him.

"As I said, I won't let him lay a finger on you. As long as you're with me, he won't hurt you." I pull her face down until our brows are touching. Stars dance in her eyes. "I have to admit, you're one sneaky little fox."

A giggle escapes. "I *am* an assassin, you know."

I chuckle, getting to my feet. I run my fingers through her hair, her ears flattening with the petting motion. "Next time, trust me to take care of you. You don't have to do those things you don't like anymore."

Zily shakes her head, hair falling in her face again. "No, we take care of each other."

My lips curl into an easy smile. "Yes. I'll keep you safe, and you'll keep me safe." I press my lips to her forehead.

She smiles more, rubbing her eyes, reminding me it's the middle of the night. I release a sleepy sigh. "Alright back to bed." I wave my hand for her to climb back under the covers while I strap my sword belt around my waist.

"Where are you going?" She returns her sword to her side of the bed.

I scoop down to retrieve my sword from the floor, sheathing it. "Going to wake up Kai to tell him about the incident and have him clean up the blood left behind before it freaks someone out." She moves to get back out of bed. I put a hand on her shoulder. "It's fine. Get some sleep. I won't be long."

Zily lays down, though the concern hasn't left her expression. I kiss her gently, leaving the room.

Kai swings the door open quickly. He's in his underwear, sword in hand, ready for a fight. His gaze scans me, releasing a sigh. I give him another moment to wake up. He scrubs his face, raking his fingers through his auburn hair.

"Emergency?"

"No, they're gone."

He blinks, rubbing his face again. "What do you mean 'gone'? What happened?"

"A man came into our room. I sent him with a warning, though I expect others to come." I motion on my arm where I cut him.

"If you handled it, what do you need from me?"

"I'm pretty sure he left a blood trail. I don't want it to freak out the servants in the morning, and you may want to tell the patrolling guards before the whole mansion becomes panicked."

Kai groans, throwing his head back. "So, you're asking me to clean up after you."

"Yes, please."

"Fine." He grumbles. "Let me get dressed. How's the girl doing?"

"You can use her name, you know." He waves a hand dismissively turning back to his room.

It's smaller than mine, a bed big enough just for him on one wall, a book shelf and a reading chair in the far corner, and a desk by the window. He's been offered larger rooms, but this is how he likes it. He grabs a shirt draped over the desk chair, pulling on pants left on the floor.

"Zily was upset by it. I think the words he said got to her, but she's hopefully going back to sleep, and is alright."

"What'd he say?" Kai pulls on his boots.

"Just what you'd expect. Threats." I run my fingers through my hair, ready to return to bed, to return to Zily.

Kai mimics the gesture, forcing himself to be awake. "Go on. Go. I got this." He shoos me away.

"Thanks." I turn to stroll back down the hall.

"Yeah. Yeah. I have some men I need a word with anyways." His voice takes an edge of irritation, bringing the question of how did the Kitsune get past the guards in the first place.

I'm annoyed when morning comes and I find two guards outside my door. Kai assigned them to me. Apparently there's two to be stationed below the balcony at night now too. They make Zily nervous, her tail pointed down, as they walk, one in front and one behind us all the way to breakfast. They're smart enough to keep their expressions neutral whenever they so much as glance at Zily. The guards wait for us outside the dining room.

Over breakfast I inform my parents of the incident last night. Mom's gaze darts worriedly to Zily who hasn't lifted her head to look at them once, ears drooped. Her tail is curled around her, petting it nervously before the first dish is served. She pokes at her food.

"That explains the increase in security." My dad notes. Kai assigned a few to them as well, though we know the main target is me, and now I fear Zily as well.

"Yes. I woke Kai up soon after. It seems he has been busy."

"Are you doing alright, dear?" Mom leans forward, wanting to get Zily's attention.

Zily finally looks up briefly. Her hands drop back to her lap, stroking the fur of her tail. "I'm sorry," she says quietly. "I'm sorry. This is all my fault. I shouldn't..." She swallows.

"Oh, sweetie," Mom begins, though my dad surprisingly interrupts her.

"You're right where you're meant to be." I stare at my dad, his brown eyes focused on Zily. "If not you, it would have been another. There have been others. We're not unaccustomed to assassins, Zily, but your presence has made an impact, and I wouldn't change it." Dad gives me a glance.

I stare dumbly at him, my heart throbbing. My hand automatically reaches for Zily's. She blinks at him, tears on the tips of her eyelashes. Her lips part to speak, but nothing comes out. We eat in silence for a few moments, Zily actually digging in.

"You said she snuck up behind the man, correct?" Dad addresses me, Zily's mouth full.

"Yes. I didn't even feel her get out of bed."

She swallows, covering her mouth. "I woke to the door opening. I knew you were awake too when you started to pull away. So, I used you as cover and slipped out."

"Are there others that move as silently as you?" Dad asks, calculating.

"I don't know. I actually don't know many in Gateswood. I see them, like in the mess hall, coming and going, but I don't know them, their jobs or their skill sets. I do know one who can match me, but she's not an assassin." Her ears twitch uneasily.

Dad nods, contemplating, the hint of relief in his eyes. Mom finally changes the subject, wanting brighter topics to discuss over breakfast. Zily seems to appreciate it.

Waiting for us outside the dining room, Kai is with the other guards, standing with his hand on the pommel of his sword at his side. There's no news. He got everything from last night cleaned up and the details of what happened under wraps, keeping it among us and those who need to know among our guards.

He looks down at Zily. "What are your plans for the day?"

Zily looks up at me then back at him. Her shoulders rise and fall. "I don't know."

"Why don't you take your book out to the garden? It's been a while, hasn't it?" I suggest one of her favorite hobbies, hoping it'll help her anxiety. "I have a few meetings today. Boring stuff."

She frowns, dark eyes full of worry watching me. "Are you sure?"

I tangle my fingers in her hair, bringing her close to kiss the top of her head. "Yes. Do something you enjoy and try to relax. It'll be fine. I promise."

"Great. Let's go." Kai takes a few steps down the hall, staring at Zily expectantly.

She reluctantly pulls away. "What do you mean 'let's'?"

"Isn't it obvious? I go where you go." Kai looks impatient.

Zily makes a face, nose wrinkling, tail dropping with a slow swish back and forth. She looks at me for help. I shrug, gesturing to the two guards I have tailing me as I head toward my first meeting. She grumbles, walking past Kai. He falls in line right behind her. I know I don't have to worry about being separated from her when my best friend is there to protect her.

Chapter Twenty-Three
Oleander

This known poisonous plant symbolizes protection and caution.
Ingesting any part of the plant can cause severe symptoms, including
nausea, vomiting, abdominal pain, and irregular heartbeats, potentially
leading to fatal cardiac arrest.

Lily

Kai follows me all the way into our room for me to pick
up my book. He's right on my heel all the way to the garden. When I
settle down to draw, he stands not three feet away, towering over
me, though he's angled away from me. I know he's doing it to bug
me. I ask him for space, and he shifts ever so slightly away. He
smirks without a word to my scowling.

Sylas must have put him up to this. I can't imagine him
choosing to be my personal guard on his own. Perhaps no other
would agree to do it. No. The ones from this morning seemed to take

their duty seriously. They're disciplined, making me doubt they'd disobey direct orders.

Sighing, I lean back against a pillar with a vase on it, adjusting my bag to rest on the grass beside me. It feels like forever since I last drew in my book. I flip through the pages, seeing what I've documented thus far, deciding what I should draw today, glancing at the different hydrangea in this section of the garden. The pencil glides across the page. It's quiet out here, the only sound being the shifting of leaves and petals whenever the breeze passes through. It's easy to get lost in the art.

Kai reminds me of lunch. I can't believe he stayed standing the whole time. Heading back inside, I consider dropping my book off, deciding to take it to the library with me after lunch instead.

Zachary is at his station, dancing back and forth on his feet. He stirs a pan with orange tinted rice with the smell of spice and cheese. My tail betrays me, forgetting Kai is by my side.

"Hey, Zachary! Is that lunch?"

"Yup. Almost done." He grins back at me. Doing a double take, hazel eyes growing wide at the sight of my shadow. Eyebrows raised, he turns back around.

I look up at Kai. He purposely turns his head, now staring at the other chefs gawking at us. Short time later, Zachary is plating the rice, paired with broccoli and chicken. One tray has three plates, and another has two. He hands me the one with two.

"Sylas…"

"I was told he's having lunch with his parents. Sorry, hun." He gives another quick glance at Kai.

My tail droops, turning to leave. Kai takes the tray from my arms. In the hall, he looks down at me. "Where do you want to go?"

To wherever Sylas is. I sigh. "The sitting room just down the hall."

He nods, marching off down the hall. I roll my eyes, trailing after him. I sit in the cyan chair that Sylas sat in the first time we ate in here. It's amazing the collection of memories I've gained since being here. So many more happy ones than I can recall in my twenty-three years. It's strange to think how the compilation of good moments, all consisting of my friends Callie and Decan, are smaller than the ones growing with Sylas.

I close my eyes, lost in thought, missing my friends and wishing they could all meet. How wonderful would it be to have all my favorite people in a room together. The thought includes Zachary as well, and Leona. A smile forms on my lips. When I open my eyes, Kai is staring at me mid bite.

"What?" I ask, picking up my plate, digging in, suppressing a moan of delight. Delicious, as always.

He shakes his head, finishing the bite. "Nothing."

Silence that I'm starting to get used to with him washes over us. It's not until we're done and I'm grabbing my book that I speak again.

"Do you plan to follow me everywhere?"

"Yes." Simple.

"You don't have to." I debate leaving the tray. I know the servants will come clean it up, but I pick it up anyway.

"Yes, I do." Once again, Kai takes it from my arms, eyebrows knitting together.

I roll my eyes. "Did Sylas ask you?"

"Yes." He follows me out. I lead him back towards the kitchen. "I made a promise, and I keep my word."

I hold the door to the kitchen open while he walks in to drop the tray off. Zachary looks shocked to see Kai again, eyes darting to me as he takes the dirty dishes. He looks mystified as to what is going on. Tilting my head, I wonder what else I can get Kai to do. A smirk forms with a little half laugh.

As we walk toward the library, I peer up at him, my hand gripping the strap of my bag. "Could you make me a promise too?"

His gaze slides to me. "Depends," he drawls.

"If something happens to me…" I don't even know how to put my thoughts into words. "You'll take care of it?"

Kai's eyebrows scrunch together. I sigh. "You know it's my job to keep Sylas safe. Not to mention, he is my best friend."

"I know. I just wanted to make sure. I'm still not safe."

His hand suddenly presses to the top of my head, my ears flattening. He rubs roughly, and I glare at him. "Don't worry; I'll keep you safe as well."

"That's not-"

"I know what you meant." He pulls his hand back, returning it to the pommel of his sword.

In the library, I pull down a couple of books one by one, flipping through to find hydrangeas. Settling down in the chair, legs tucked up and dress draped over them modestly, I begin copying down information in small print, little dots indicating a new note. Kai strolls around the library a couple of times, acting like he's browsing the books. It surprises me when he pulls one from the shelf.

He sits on the couch, angling himself against the arm rest facing me, sword hanging off the side, one foot on the ground the other crossed over his knee. I angle my head, attempting to inconspicuously peer at the cover of the book. There's a picture of a man holding a sword to the sky, a dragon in the background. I didn't take him as a novel reader, but I'm not terribly surprised by his choice either.

Engrossed in the book, I forget about taking notes, simply enjoying the peace reading gives. I'm learning to take my time while reading. My ears twitch, picking up voices, but trying to drown them out as I finish the page. I glance up.

Sylas leans on his forearms over the back of the couch casually, the posture making muscles ripple under his rolled up sleeves. His dark grey shirt is tucked in tight against his finely toned back, black strands of hair falling across his shoulder, tucked behind his ear. Whatever he did today must have stressed him out enough to take it down. It makes me worry, but damn, do I love his hair down. He chuckles at something Kai says, his face glowing. Kai's eyes flicker to me.

"Someone's staring." He quirks an eyebrow, noticing where I'm staring. My eyes have drifted down to Sylas' pants.

I glare at Kai, face burning. Sylas turns his midday blue eyes on me, a laugh on his lips. "Did you have a good day?"

"Mostly." I give Kai another pointed look.

He shrugs, setting the novel down on the table. Standing effortlessly, he stretches his arms up, black shirt threatening to come untucked. He rakes his fingers through his hair like fallen leaves.

"Now that you're here, I'm off duty. See ya tomorrow." He waves without looking at me though I know he's telling me he'll be following me around again tomorrow.

Sylas saunters over, offering me a hand. I unfold myself from the cushioned chair, using his hand to pull myself out. A hand caresses my waist as I regain my balance, legs needing to wake up. I lift onto my toes. He dips his head in response, brushing his warm lips against mine. Sweet and tender.

"Ready for dinner?" He rubs his nose against mine, speaking softly.

"Mhm." I close my eyes for a moment, breathing in the scent of trees, paper and leather.

Dinner is pleasant. There's talk of Sylas' cousin visiting next week. Apparently they were really close when they were young, but it's been a few years since he last saw him. He'll be coming to the coronation, but this visit is purely social and has been talked about for months. It's finally happening. Sylas is excited. Even while talking about it, he can't sit still.

"I can't wait to introduce you." His eyes shine down on me.

Blush rises to my cheeks. "Make sure to take time with just the two of you too, alright?"

Retreating from the conversation, falling into the darkness of my own mind, I calculate the days. His cousin will be here during the days I consider some of the most dangerous. We have maybe six days before there's a possibility of another assassination attempt. Would they think to hurt his cousin to get to him? The last went straight for him. I go straight for my targets. But things have changed with me on Sylas' side. Eventually, I believe Sir Eyler Colin will come himself or maybe he'll send another Vampire general. Either way, I'll be in trouble then and I can't even warn Sylas about it. About me. I chew on my cheek.

A strong hand squeezes my knee, pulling me from the darkness. Bright skies fill my vision when I turn my head. I smile, letting the warmth flood me. I have no choice but to trust him to do what's needed to stay alive.

Kai follows me all around the mansion once again the following day. After breakfast, Sylas goes to his study while I take Kai to the garden. It's one of the rare times I see someone tending to the garden. A girl I've seen around a few times, petite with a warm smile, humming to herself prunes the marigolds, thick garden gloves covering her hands.

The girl turns to me, face glowing. She dips in a polite curtsy, bowing her head. "My lady." My face burns as I stumble to respond, doing a quick dip. Her eyes drift to Kai standing like a statue behind me. A soft giggle escapes. "And a good day to you, Sir."

I glance back at Kai who gives a short nod in response to the girl, keeping his gaze out across the yard to the forest. She excuses herself, picking up a basket of gardening supplies, tossing her gloves on top. I feel bad for interrupting her work, going to inspect the flowers. She takes tender care of the flowers; I can tell.

"Who was that?" I turn completely around to face Kai.

His back is to me, now staring at the mansion, where the girl had gone. "Hmm? Oh, that's Marie."

"You're blushing." A grin slips onto my face, spotting the red rising from under the collar of his uniform.

"What? No, I am not." He glares, but the red has consumed his face.

I laugh, throwing my head back. Peering at him, his expression makes me laugh more, doubling over. I make a note to tell Sylas about it, see if he has information about Marie. There's a sense of power having something to tease Kai about. His fingers twitch, hiding them in his back pockets. His facial feature school into a straight lines.

Sitting on the ground, we take up our position of yesterday. Instead of drawing the flowers around me, I draw Kai, adding him to the ones of Sylas in the back of the book. I think I would like to sketch Zachary too, while he's cooking. Then Leona with a needle in her mouth and one of her dresses on the mannequin in front of her. When Callie and Decan are here, I'll draw them too. Then one of everyone together. My secret collection. My collection of friends.

Kai is the perfect model. He stands completely still, hardly moving except when he glances at me, like silent little check-ins. He keeps his hands in his pocket for the most part, every now and then lifting one to run through his hair. It must be hot in his uniform standing in the direct sun light.

When I'm satisfied with what I have, rough sketches of the flowers around him, I get up stretching. Time for lunch. Sylas is in his study working today which means I can take him lunch. I skip back inside, heading toward the kitchen, happy by the thought.

"Oh, Zily." A sing-song voice calls my name. I turn to find Eleanor gliding down the hall, two guards on her heel. She moves with elegance and grace, hands folded in front over her soft green, floor-length gown. Heels barely make a sound as she walks.

I try harder with this curtsy, lowering myself slowly, bowing my head. "Your Majesty." The words are weird on my tongue, making me lick my lips as if to get rid of the feel.

She giggles lightly, brown ringlet bobbing with the motion. "I would hope you know by now that you don't need to address me as such." I quietly sigh in relief, relaxing at the words. It feels weird, since I haven't been formal before, but this is the first time I've had to address her solely. "If you're not busy, I would like to have lunch with you."

I contemplate how rude it would be to refuse a Queen. My Queen? Am I a part of this kingdom now? I'm with Sylas, so I suppose that puts me in this kingdom, but since I'm his partner, where does it place me in the hierarchy? What is the Queen to me?

"I was just coming in for lunch." I push all the thoughts away.

"Lovely. I've arranged for lunch to be sent to us already. This way." Eleanor hooks her arm with mine, jasmine drifting off of her.

Kai falls in with the other two guards, walking behind us. Eleanor leads me to a room I haven't been in before. It's larger than the sitting rooms I've been in. There's a long cream couch where the back has three hills, the middle poking up higher than the outer two. Decorative pillows sit at angles on either side. Two matching chairs face the glass rectangle table between all of them, gold filigree legs holding it up. A platter of food and a tea set already sits waiting. There's a fanciful glass cabinet against one wall displaying a variety of valuables. A large painting of a girl under an arch of flowers covers a good portion of another wall.

The guards, including Kai, wait outside the door. Eleanor sits on the couch, patting the open space beside her. Less gracefully, I plop beside her, crossing my ankles. She leans forward, pouring each of us a cup of tea. I get the feeling that I should be the one doing such a task.

"I've been wanting to speak with you for a while; have a little girl time." She holds the cup out to me delicately with one hand caressing the handle and the other cradling the bottom.

I force a smile, nervously taking the cup. She takes a sip. I take a sip. She begins on the salad. I follow suit. She continues smiling with ease. My tail curls around, forcing my lips to hold the same smile, my gaze darting everywhere except directly towards her.

"I know what brought you here isn't the most pleasant topic, but I hope you believe me when I say I'm glad you're here. I'm glad my son found you." She turns her blue eyes, not like the sky like Sylas', but like the ocean, on me.

My face heats up, hand moving to my side. All this changed because a beast of a forest attacked me and I fell into a river. I remember how accepting of death I was; how I almost wished for it in that moment.

"Me too," I whisper, setting the salad plate down and going for the main dish.

"Have you been adjusting well to life here?"

"It's a change, that's for sure. There's still quite a bit that I'm unaccustomed to and moments that take me by surprise."

"There's a lot to get used to. You could ask Reu; he didn't come from royalty either. How has everyone been treating you?" Eleanor cuts her food delicately.

"Reuben hasn't always been King?" The words spill out quickly, too quickly to format my question properly. My face flushes. Eleanor giggles, understanding what I meant. Hopefully, she doesn't realize I'm avoiding her question.

"He was simply a stable boy; took care of my Delilah. It's how we met. You could imagine that my parents did not approve." She sighs, a sad sound. "They tried to marry me off several times. Somehow, I managed to hold them off. When the crown passed to me, I finally married my love. We knew we wouldn't pressure our child like that." Her gaze trails to me.

I take slow breaths, failing to keep the heat in my cheeks at bay. "You've raised a kind man," I say quietly.

"And he's found himself a lovely lady." She looks at me warmly. I keep my gaze on the plate of half-eaten food, my heart fluttering. "How have others been treating you?" She revisits the question.

"Well, Leona is friendly and Zachary is amazing."

Eleanor nods knowingly. "They're a couple of amazing people. Zachary's dishes never disappoint." She takes a bite, humming with delight. "What about the others?" She's persistent. I'm beginning to think she already knows the answer.

"They tolerate my presence." My shoulders shrug nonchalantly.

She sighs heavily, touching her cheek. "That's what I was afraid of."

"It's not that big of a deal. Sylas has talked to a few and I've met a few who are naturally nice as well. You can't expect everyone to change their prejudice within days."

"I wish they hadn't developed in the first place. It occurred during my parents' reign. When I was a small girl, I remember having a Kitsune friend from the Viararia Kingdom."

"Do you think they'll be one of the ones who'll come to Sylas' coronation?"

Eleanor blinks. "I hadn't thought about that. Yes. She should. Oh! How wonderful that would be!" She claps her hands together, face lighting up. "I would love to become reacquainted with Mari."

I smile, setting my empty plate beside hers. We sip our tea. Eleanor stares off, getting lost in her thoughts.

"I had many tutors when I was a girl. Sy didn't have quite as many. I did my best to teach him myself when he was small. I had

289

tutors for everything; history, sewing, playing instrument and dance, to name a few." Eleanor decides to tell me.

"Sylas has offered to teach me to play piano. He also offered to teach me to dance once, but I had declined at the time." I smile enthusiastically.

"That sounds like him. Are there other instruments you would like to learn to play? I could see about getting you tutors if you like for all you may need to know or would like to learn." Her eyes watch me curiously.

I gasp, eyes growing wide. My tail struggles to hide my excitement. "I would love that. I adore learning. I would like to learn the violin, and if I could have lessons on etiquette, so I'm not guessing at what's appropriate."

Eleanor softly giggles. "Lovely. I'll find you some teachers to come to the manor after we take care of a few things." She sets down her empty tea cup. I take another sip, savoring the last in my cup. I know what she's referring to. "Did you have any teachers as a child?" It's the first time she's inquired about my childhood.

My smile slips. "No. I've had to teach myself what I know."

Eleanor nods sympathetically. She gently presses. "Did your parents not teach you to read and write?"

"I taught myself to read by secretly taking books back to my room. I taught my friend, Callie, to read. I… don't remember my parents well," I confess.

My memories from before Gateswood are a little more than hazy. There's fuzzy images of who I assume are my mother and father. I get my looks from my dad. I don't know what I got from my mom. The image I have is of long, reddish brown hair cascading around a heart shaped face with a loving expression. I can't picture her eyes.

Vaguely, I recall my first days at Gateswood. There was a lot of crying. My pretty dress replaced with the dark neutral colored shirts and pants. Pain and scars came soon after for disobeying the simplest orders. I lightly shake my head, bringing myself back to the present. That was nearly fifteen years ago.

"We should do this again." Eleanor's voice brings me out of my mind. She smiles at me kindly.

I return the smile, agreeing; it was a surprisingly pleasant experience. I nearly forgot Kai has been waiting for me in the hall. He stands to one side of the door, back straight, staring at the wall across from him. His gaze slides to me. With a nod, I lead the way to Sylas' study.

Kai does not wait in the hall when I enter the study. Sylas' head rises from his work, a hand in his hair. His eyes brighten, standing and moving around his desk to greet me. I hold my arms out for him. He slides his arms around my waist, lifting me up briefly. I steal a quick kiss.

"How's your day been?"

"Good." I glance at his desk to assess how his has been. I'm so proud to see his desk mostly in order.

"She had lunch with your mom." Kai plops onto the couch, lounging sideways, an arm draped across the back, one leg bent on the seat, the other hanging off.

"Oh? Did you have a good time?" He tries to hide it, but I can hear his curious concern.

I cock my head. "Worried about what she may have told me?" He chuckles. "We had a good time. She talked about getting me some tutors. I'll be able to actually play the violin someday." The shared grin tells me he remembers that day as well. "I'm also going to have history, etiquette, and dance lessons." It fills me with excitement.

Sylas turns, returning to his chair, holding my hand. He pulls me onto his lap. "You don't need an etiquette lesson."

"That one was my idea," I say.

"You have a lot to learn." Kai smirks.

"Says the one getting ready to take a nap in my study." Sylas laughs, gently squeezing my waist. "Have you had lunch yet?"

Kai shrugs, sinking farther in a lying position, hands behind his head. "You could add swordplay to your lessons."

"Oh? Are you going to teach me?" I arch an eyebrow, though I am serious in my inquiry.

Kai shrugs. "Why not if I'm going to be watching you daily?"

Sylas frowns, ready to speak up, but I cut in. "Alright. You teach me how to properly wield my short sword, and I'll teach you how to identify poisons."

"I did not agree to that."

"Oh, well." I shrug.

Kai groans, throwing an arm over his eyes. Sylas laughs, kissing my neck. I grin at him.

The lessons with Kai start the very next day. Tutors for what I discussed with Eleanor will be hired in the next few weeks, hopefully after a certain situation is dealt with. We start with basic exercises. I get to impress Kai with how much body weight squats, sit ups and push-ups I can do. It crumbles as soon as he adds any sort of extra weight that's heavier than my old backpack. I can barely do a couple squats while my legs shake. The weight distribution isn't great, but he's making it up on the fly. Kai pinches his nose when he sees my hold of the sword. Apparently, it's amazing I've survived traveling through the forest. Every muscle is sore by the time lunch rolls around.

We have lunch with Sylas. I help him through some paperwork before dragging Kai to the garden. I've never tried to teach someone before, so during the first day, I rattle off facts about the different poisons that the garden has in it. It's a bit overwhelming. The next day, I take my book outside, using it to help pick out the most important facts to know. The most dangerous of the local plants first. Kai grumbles when I make him repeat what I've told him. I shake my head.

Days continue like this. Kai brings out weights to strap around my wrists, ankles and waist. I make him put it over the strap of my bag, so it doesn't swing and bump it. Don't want to risk breaking the vials I carry even if the bag is padded. He makes me do the same number of squats, sit ups and push-ups that I can normally do with extra weights. Alone, they're not heavy, but the longer I have them on and the more I do, the more they tire me.

Once those basic exercises are done, he instructs me on proper stances while holding my sword. The shock on his face when he first lifts my sword stays for several moments. He swings it a few times, eyebrows furrowing.

"I was about to tell you it's too light to do any real damage. However, the shape and sharpness make up for it. It's quite agile. Suited for you." He hands it back.

"Thanks! My friends made it for me." I beam. His eyes narrow at the way I hold it, nearly hugging it. Rolling my eyes, I spread my feet apart, changing my grip, blade pointed out. He nods with approval. He won't spar with me until I get basic stances and movements down. My arm begins to shake, sore from the exercises and the wrist weights.

Eventually, he has me sheath my sword and tells me to run. My eyebrows shoot up. He nods to the side, a 'get going' gesture. Groaning, I put one hand on the pommel of my sword and the other on my bag to hold it still. I am sweating through my dress by the time he lets me stop. My lungs burn as I suck in air. He ran the whole time beside me. It makes me feel better when I turn to him and see his hands on his head, chest rising and fall as he also works to steady his breathing.

"You're faster than I expected." He admits.

"Thank you," I breathe, grinning.

"I need to get more weights for the running."

"No!"

"Yes." His voice lowers. I scowl at him.

Kai takes the weights back and we detour to the soldiers quarters to drop them off before heading inside. I need a shower. Only a quick one to freshen up a bit and clean clothes before I go to Sylas for lunch. I return my sword to its slot in the bed.

We pick up lunch and I'm grateful Kai carries the tray because the stairs are becoming my enemy. My legs burn with every step. When we make it to Sylas' office, and he gets up to greet us, his arms wrapping around me, I all but collapse on him. He glares at Kai through lunch. Kai appears completely unbothered by it.

We all sit on the couch to eat, Sylas in the middle. The food tastes extra good as I feel like I'm starving. I down two glasses of iced tea. Sylas rubs my back, slowly eating his meal with one hand.

"You're not pushing too hard, right?" Sylas inquires, voice low. I don't know which one of us he's addressing.

"Of course not." Kai answers nonchalantly.

Sylas turns his gaze on me, wanting to know if I agree. I nod my head, my mouth full. He waits. "I am very much sore all over, but it's to be expected. I'm fine." His eyes search mine, making sure I'm not lying because Kai is in the room with us.

Sylas is reluctant to let me go when we finish eating. I can't blame him. It's hard to leave the warmth of his side. However, it's my turn to torture, I mean, teach Kai. Sylas kisses my forehead.

We head back down the dreaded stairs and out to the garden. First, I drill the names of the most poisonous plants within the garden into his head. Then I take him to them, pointing at it, repeating the name a couple times. He raises an eyebrow.

"You have to know what the flower looks like and be able to name it. So, look." I throw my hand pointing at it again.

Kai rolls his eyes stepping closer. "Okay. Purple droopy flower is an angel."

I toss my head back closing my eyes. "Its name is angel's trumpet. It's a type of bell flower, that's why it hangs like this. They are not only purple. Some are white, orange, yellow, red, or even pink. They are highly toxic, resulting in hallucinations, seizures and even death if enough is used."

Kai pulls away from the flower, wrinkling his nose. "Why are these even in the garden?"

"Because they're pretty. Come on. On to the next." I wave my hand, moving down the path to a shrub with pink flowers. "These are oleanders, also known as rosebay. You have to look carefully. Flowers can be easily misidentified, just like the case in the village. One can be perfectly harmless while another can make you severely sick or kill you. This pretty little thing can cause vomiting, diarrhea, convulsions, respiratory distress, a few other minor things like headaches, but will lead to death. The more concentrated it is, the quicker it'll kill. Mine is very concentrated. You have minutes to administer the antidote."

"You don't carry those around with you still." He says it like a statement, but there is a question behind it.

"No, I carry the antidote now. I do still have it in my old bag in the back of the closet." I turn, moving on to the next.

After I've gone through the top five most dangerous plants in the garden, I take him back through, testing to see what he remembers. He gets some of the symptoms and the time it takes them to kill mixed up, but he did remember three of the names.

By the end of the week, I am still sore after my workout with Kai, but I am able to complete the exercises. Kai says we can start sparring next week. He normally wouldn't start sparring this quickly, but I may have been pestering him. Sylas gives me massages at night. He reminds me that I don't have to indulge him. Even though my body aches, the workout feels good to do. I love learning too.

Kai is also a fast learner. He likes to pretend he's uninterested, expression set into that of annoyance. However, he will answer almost perfectly when I quiz him. He knows enough that if one is used he can find the correct antidote or tell the doctor. I'll work to expand how many he knows.

During dinner, Reuben tells me the antidote I made for the village worked and those afflicted are on the mend. They're being cautious, but there's a group dedicated to weeding out the invasive plant. The old man who came with the request for help sent a personal thank you letter to me. I read it in our room, my tears staining the paper, the edges crinkling from holding it so tight. I tuck it safely inside my book.

The thought of actually being able to save lives hadn't ever crossed my mind before this. For so long, I've only known death. I was the bringer of death like a cold winter storm, blanketing the world in a silent coat of snow. However, snow melts, making room for new growth to bloom.

Chapter Twenty-Four
Deadly Nightshade

To no surprise with the name, this flower represents danger and deception and is highly poisonous. They cause a long list of symptoms including blurry vision, rash, slurred speech, confusion, delirium, convulsions and death.

Sylas

We all know about the impending danger; it hangs over us like a dark cloud. It's closing in on two weeks since the brown haired Kitsune slipped into our room at night. I know the thought of another weighs on Zily, though I'm glad to see her smiling daily, tail wagging as she speaks excitedly. She's developed her own routine, becoming more comfortable in the mansion.

Mom found and hired a violin instructor for her. She'll start lessons in another two weeks. Mom says they'll work on finding other instructors as time goes on. She's being hopeful this will all be resolved soon. I hope so too, though the scouts we send out to search for Gateswood keep reporting back that they haven't found it.

Zily, impatient to learn, started reading history books on her own. She's the only person I know who reads textbooks for enjoyment. I'm not terribly surprised, and her buzzing about what she's learned is like a refresher course for myself.

We don't get to spend as much time as I would like together, work keeping us apart. During our nightly baths, we tell each other about our day. After the bath, I rub lotion into her skin, massaging the tight muscles she worked that day. I adore the little sounds of pleasure that escape her, my hands exploring her body. Zily often brings me lunch after her morning workout with Kai. It's not an activity I would have expected from her, but she always shows up bursting with energy. Kai says she's a fast learner, if only she could execute the moves the way she knows it's supposed to be done. She proudly tells me about the vital parts of the body and how shifting a centimeter could be fatal in certain spots.

More work and meetings often fill my afternoons. I haven't mentioned it to Zily, but I've had several arguments with the King's advisers. They're supposed to be mine in a few short months, and yet I'm struggling to accept them with their judgment of Zily. I glance at dad for help, but he simply raises an eyebrow and nods for me to handle it. At one meeting, I told Dressen that maybe it was time for him to retire and that I would find a replacement by the time of my coronation. He blanches at the threat. Some call it a bluff. I'm honestly unsure if I'm bluffing or not. Only time will tell.

Some meetings are the usual ones with our treasurers. We have a big meeting with them once a month. They're a sibling pair, Maxime and Justine, twice my age. They have always done good work, taking our kingdoms finances seriously. We have small meetings with one or both of them if something comes up that they feel should have the King and Queen's approval.

This town is struggling after a tough winter and they're afraid they don't have enough to get crops in the ground to make it through the next winter. However, if we give them financial aid, we'll have to up the taxes which could still hurt them in the following year. I put forth the suggestion of loaning them what they need this year with the agreement that in three years we'll start to collect on the loan at a reasonable rate to not ruin the town. Secretly, it was a suggestion Zily made when I told her about it one night, grateful we were able to end the meeting early for dinner.

When I'm at my desk, dropping off a stack of papers from the morning and early afternoon meeting, a three toned chime comes from my desk. Pulling open the top right drawer, the blue and white swirl cahmo crystal I have in it rolls to the front. I pick it up with one hand, fingers straining to keep hold of it. The chime happens again. I run a finger over it with the intention of answering the call while dropping down into my chair.

"About time," a familiar voice chides.

"Hey, Philip." A grin spreads across my face, the excitement of seeing my cousin soon surfaces.

"I tried to contact you earlier before leaving, but now we're a day away from home. So, I hope you're ready."

I laugh, relaxing in the chair for a moment. "Yes, yes. We have rooms, your room, ready and waiting for you and your men." I rotate the crystal in between my hands.

Philip huffs a chuckle. "Good. It's been too long, though I don't miss the ride there. I wanted to fly, but both mother and my guards insisted on the carriage."

"We'll have to ditch them in the air when you're here like we used to." I turn in the chair to face the window.

"Yes." A muffled sound comes through the crystal. "We're stopping for a late lunch. I'll see you in a couple days."

"Can't wait," I say quietly, standing and staring out the window. Zily and Kai are walking through the garden. A hand is clutching the bag's strap across her chest. The other pointing at flowers. It looks like they're finishing up their lessons as they head towards the edge of the garden. I run a finger over the cahmo crystal, giving the intention of hanging up the call. I truly can't wait to introduce Zily to Philip.

In the afternoons for Zily, she turns the tables on Kai, teaching him about plants. It almost sounds like he enjoys it. Originally I thought he tolerated it because I asked him to look after her when I could not. However, with a grin on her face, Zily tells me how Kai can repeat information back to her and point out the plants she's testing him on. I'm glad they're becoming friends. It warms my chest to see my favorite people getting along.

My dad invites Zily to attend a few of our meetings that occur in the afternoon. She squeezes in her lesson with Kai before returning to my office, so we can walk down together. After the arguments I've had with them, I smirk at their annoyed faces when we walk into the room, Zily on my arm. Dad explicitly states that he invited her here. They don't argue with him. It does take several dark looks of warning before they start speaking normally in her presence. She holds her head high in the seat beside me, though an undertone of pink in her cheeks gives away her nervousness. She mostly listens, telling me her thoughts when we're alone.

Zily leans on me, holding my hand on our way to dinner. Dad strolls along on my other side. Zily seems exhausted, though her tail swishes slowly behind her. The smile on her lips lets me know she's had a good day over all.

She giggles as I pull her seat out for her. Her tail thrums against the chair beside her thigh, ready to eat. I remind my parents that Philip will be here in two days, informing them about the brief call. We don't have any particular plans. I will be expected to keep up with my work, but I plan to take time to relax. I hope Zily will too, let some of her anxiety go, even for a few days.

Soup is brought out as our first course of the night. It's a white, creamy mushroom soup, small slices of bread on the side. Zily sniffs it as the butler places the bowl in front of her, tail wagging excitedly. I chuckle, looking up to thank the one standing between us, leaning down to set my bowl down.

The man stumbles. The bowl tipping over and pouring all over the table. He instantly begins apologizing, beginning to clean up the mess, keeping it from running off the table onto my lap.

"It's alright. Don't worry too much about it. It didn't get on us, right Zily?"

"Right." That's when I notice her staring at me with wide, dark eyes. The man shoots her a quick glare before scurrying off.

"Zily." I lean in, my hand resting on her thigh.

"It was poisoned," she says simply, fear swirling around in her dark orbs. Her hand clutches her bag's strap.

I run my fingers through her hair, an attempt to comfort her. "Thank you, sweetheart."

"How could you tell?" Dad doesn't often sound impressed.

"It smelt different than mine." She wipes a finger through the spilled soup, bringing the finger to her nose.

"So, you think we have an unwelcome guest somewhere?"

"Yes. I'm sure they're already inside somewhere. They have to be, to be able to poison the soup, Sylas' soup specifically. We have to be extra careful with a poison user."

"Speaking from experience?" I tease, hoping it lands well.

It earns me a small grin. Then she licks her finger, and I can feel the blood draining from my face. Mom gasps from across the table. I grab her wrist, though it's too late. "Why would you do that?"

"I wanted to know what kind they used." She cocks her head, staring at the soup.

I cup her face, forcing her to look at me. My heart thrums out of control. She looks fine, but I also know not all poison is fast acting. My eyes search hers. "Are you ok?"

Her lips curl into a little smile. "Yes. I'm fine. It's a slow acting poison, but it wasn't enough to affect me. My body is used to toxins like nightshade." She picks up her spoon. "Would you like to share my soup?" She peeks at me with genuine curiosity.

I sigh, leaning back in my chair, raking my fingers through my hair, messing up the pony tail. Mom and dad stare at her in disbelief. Dad clears his throat. "As grateful a I am that you kept Sylas from eating poison, I'd rather not watch you risk ingesting it."

Blush coats Zily's cheeks as she looks at each of us staring at her. Her ears droop and she lowers her head. "Sorry. I didn't think."

Reaching over, I glide my fingers through her hair. "It's alright. Let's enjoy the rest of our meal, and then we need to speak with Kai about this."

Zily nods her head. She does share her soup with me, though I could have simply had another brought out. To ease everyone's fear, I let her sniff my food after it's been placed in front of me and the servants have left the room. She samples it, declaring it's safe to consume. I watch her out of the corner of my eyes, worrying that she'll suddenly clutch her stomach. I don't like her using herself as my food tester. What if other parts of the meal had been poisoned? She can't be immune to everything. She continues eating as if it were any other dinner, confident there's no more poison in our meals.

Her tail drops when I ask her to wait in the dining room while I fetch Kai. We explain what happened. He clicks his tongue, annoyed. Father shares his sentiment. It's not looking good with these Kitsunes slipping past as they have been. Zily gives Kai a little test, describing the poisons properties, including the subtle bitter taste and sweet after taste.

Kai's gaze flickers to me briefly. His eyes narrow on her. "Please tell me you did not consume the nightshade."

"Deadly nightshade, but you got it!" Zily's tail swish, eyes sparkling with pride. I glance at her when she says the full name.

Kai pinches the bridge of his nose, mumbling a few choice words. "Alright. We'll investigate."

"Thanks. Let me know what you find." I put an arm around Zily's shoulder, gently ushering her out.

"Send the others in to help, would you?" Kai calls, heading through the servants doors leading to the corridor that goes directly to the kitchen.

Zily looks a little wary as my guards go into the dining room. Mom and dad say their 'goodnights', their own guards following them down the hall. Zily hangs on my arm as we walk down the hall, slowly making our way back to our room. Her gaze darts around, looking small and timid, but I know better than to think that.

"Are you sure it's alright to be without the guards?" Her grip tightens protectively. I squeeze her hand.

"It'll be fine. I'll keep you safe." Her acute gaze says *I'm* the one she's worried about. I roll my eyes. "We'll keep each other safe, right?"

Her eyes soften, a small smile forming on her lips. "We should check your food regularly from here on out. Zachary is going to be mad his food was tampered with."

"He's going to be mad you licked the poison."

Her nose wrinkles, the little point of her tongue sticking out at me. It makes me chuckle, though it's a little louder than natural. I slow my pace, holding Zily against me. Her shoulders tense, letting me know she also heard the creek of a door. Her grip on my arm loosens and I slink it across to grab my sword.

"Zily?" A small voice comes from behind.

Zily spins around. She stares as a girl with curly brown hair, ears pressed down to the side, steps out of a closet wearing a plain brown shirt and loose black pants. Zily's excited squeal puts me at ease. She lights up, doing the cutest little happy dance I have ever seen before she leaps towards the girl.

"Callie! Callie, it's you!" Zily nearly knocks the girl down, throwing her arms around her.

Callie, not much taller than Zily, manages to stabilize them, a nervous expression on her face that instantly has me on edge again. She embraces her back, holding tight like someone who thought they'd never see them again. I keep my hand resting on the pommel of my sword, letting them have their moment.

"What are you-" Both girls start to speak, stopping simultaneously to let the other go first. Callie quietly laughs, glancing at me nervously.

Zily looks between the two of us. The realization crosses her face. Subtly, she steps between her friend and me. Her tail lowers.

An ache stabs at my chest that she may have to choose between me and her friend.

"Callie, this is Sylas. Sylas, this is my best friend, Callie." She formally introduces, angling her body as she motions with her hand, though she remains a barrier between us.

"Pleasure to finally meet you, Callie." I offer my hand with a tight smile, moving to Zily's side. I do mean it; I'm pleased to finally meet one of Zily's friends she's told me so much about. However, I can't be sure she'll be on our side with the way Callie's eyes dart between us. She takes my hand.

"Hello," she says meekly, her hand sliding in to my for the quickest handshake she can do. "Zily, what's going on?"

Zily loops her arm with Callie. "It's a lot. Let's talk somewhere else."

"Your old room is still available." It does seem like a good idea to move my would be assassin out of the hall. I suppose I'll be alone in a room with two assassins. Kai's head is going to explode one of these days with the safety measures I take.

"Perfect."

I walk slightly behind them. Zily's tail gives away her nerves. It curls and swishes back and forth a couple times before dropping, tucking in against her legs. Callie's remain down, slightly curled around the inside of her leg. I close the door behind us once we're in the room. Callie peers back at me, looking like a trapped animal. Slowly, she turns to Zily.

"I thought you were dead," she whispers.

Zily gapes at her. "What? Is that what you were told?"

"Sir Colin Eyler told us Misha discovered that he killed you." Another glance in my direction with an attempt at a glare from brown eyes. Despite Zily standing right in front of her, it's like she still believes I did something to her.

Zily laughs, a little strained. "He actually saved my life." Callie's eyebrows scrunch together. Zily waves her hand through the air, bringing it down to run over the strap and smooth out her dress. "I nearly drowned, but that's a story for another time. For now, a quick summary. I tried to follow orders, but I couldn't because I… Well," Zily's face turns a deep red, a shy smile on her lips, stars sparkling in her eyes. Her fingers curl around the fabric of her skirt. Callie's eyes grow wide in understanding before Zily even continues. "I fell in love." My heart skips a beat at the verbal declaration. I step forward, sliding my arms around her, wanting to feel her against me.

Zily sucks in a deep breath. "So, now, I'm actively going against Sir Colin Eyler to the best of my ability with… you know. There's limitations, but they're looking for Gateswood, and now that you're here, you can stay. We'll get Decan too. We're going to save all of them." Zily steps out of my arms, taking Callie's hands, hope echoing in her words.

Callie's muddy brown eyes are sad. They don't hold the hope or the faith that Zily's does. "Are you sure it's even possible? You know what that does, what they can do."

"That's just a rumor. We haven't seen it done before." Fear edges Zily's voice. I wish I could ask about it, but if they're being vague, it's a subject that brings pain to speak of.

"Zily…"

"Stay a few days. I can show you the library and the garden, oh and the music room! I'll introduce you to Zachary; he makes the best meals. And Leona would love to make you a dress. Kai has been giving me sword lessons. It hasn't been too long, but I've gotten better." The words come rushing out, desperation cracking her voice. She's giving every reason she can think of for her friend to stay, to desert like she has. The look in Callie's eyes makes me worried it's not working.

Callie sighs, pulling a hand away to tug on a curl. "Alright." The one word has Zily bouncing, tail swishing quickly behind her.

"You can stay here. We're just across the hall. I'll get you when it's time for breakfast. I'll bring one of my dresses over for you until we get you to Leona."

Callie glances around the room, looking Zily up and down. "The dress suits you."

Zily giggles, grabbing the skirt of the red dress, twirling around. "Ok. Rest up. See you in the morning!" Zily grabs my arm, leading me out. "Oh, and check out the bathtub!"

Her face glows as she skips around our room. I approach her, sliding my arms around her waist, pulling her against me. My lips lightly brush hers. A little happy sigh escapes her lips.

"I love you," I whisper, wanting to make sure she heard it even if it is obvious.

Her face turns beat red, ears flickering, eyes wide. I chuckle, stealing another kiss. She slides her arms over my shoulders, pulling herself up so that her body is flushed against mine and her head resting on my shoulder.

"I love you." Her breath tickles my neck.

"That went better than expected when you first noticed the poison, didn't it?" I don't want her to know the worry inside my chest that persists.

She hums, nuzzling her face in the crook between my shoulder and neck. "Yes. I'm glad it's her, though I worry Sir Colin Eyler sent her on purpose because of me. She's normally sent on information gathering jobs. Assassin jobs are rare for her. Her tactics are similar to mine because I've told her how I do it when he first gave her this kind of assignment." She drops back to her feet, peering up at me. "I'm glad you get to meet her though."

"She's the one you were referencing when you said there's one as sneaky as you."

"Yes." She turns, tugging me toward the washroom. "I'm hoping I can convince her to stay. If she goes back, and she lies," she shakes her head, a shudder running through her, "I don't want to think of the consequences she'd face."

"I'll inquire if we've made any progress on finding Gateswood tomorrow."

"Should we warn your parents about Callie?"

"She'll come with us for breakfast. It'll be fine. She's a friend of yours, so she is a guest of ours." Though I think I will ask Kai to be a little more cautious of her. There's just something about the look in her eyes that leaves me unsettled.

Zily runs her hand through my hair as I unzip the back of her dress. I lean down to kiss her neck. I hope for her sake, Callie is everything Zily believes her to be.

Chapter Twenty-Five
Snapdragon

These have a range of meanings, including strength, protection, desire and good luck as well as deception and mystery. They are technically edible but have a bitter taste.

Zily

Deciding which dress to take to Callie to wear for the day is more difficult than anticipated. I'm thinking of taking her to Leona right after breakfast. I wonder if Kai will let me off the hook of training for a few days. I pick out a red with black polka dots dress for Callie, grabbing the cloak she let me borrow from the back of the closet.

Callie's eyes grow wide upon seeing the cloak. They dart between it and the dress in my other hand. Taking the cloak, she stares down on it. "I didn't think I was getting this back."

"I promised to return it, though it's not exactly how I said I would."

Her head bobs, slowly striding to the chair at the desk to drape it over. Returning to me, she reaches for the dress to put it on. The bottom hem falls above her ankles, and the waist is a tiny bit loose. She trades her boots in for a pair of flats. She seems nervous, fidgeting with the dress, tail down.

Holding the door open for her, she peers into the hall. "Is this really alright, going to meet the Queen and King? I did attempt to poison their son."

"I was also sent to kill him, too. Eleanor and Reuben are really nice. Reuben looks intimidating, though." I look around, wondering where the usual guards are, fiddling with the strap of my little bag across my chest.

"Hey," Sylas meets us in the hall. "Ready?" His gaze flickers over me, then to Callie. They cloud slightly when looking at her.

I loop my arm through Callie's as if she may disappear. "Yup!" I cheer. Callie looks between us.

Kai's waiting for us at the bottom of the stairs, back against the wall, hand on his sword. He does a double take looking at us, raising an eyebrow. I hold tight to Callie, keeping a smile on my face, though I silently convey his suspicion is correct with a subtle nod and flick of my ears.

Sylas walks around, putting an arm around Kai's shoulders who glares at him. "This is Kai; my best friend."

"And this is Callie; my best friend. Don't worry Cal. He always looks angry." I tease him, grinning, hoping to ease the tension. He grumbles rolling his eyes. "Unless Marie is around." His eyes narrow on me. He may not let me off the hook for a few days after all.

Kai finishes escorting us to the dining room, talking quietly to Sylas. They linger back far enough that I can't hear exactly what they are saying. Neither man looks particularly pleased with their conversation. Guards outside the dining room glance down at Callie suspiciously, but with my arm hooked with hers, they don't object to her presence. One opens the door for us. I give my thanks.

"Morning!" I beam catching Eleanor's and Reuben's attention. A hand brushing along my back lets me know Sylas has joined us.

Reuben's eyebrows twitch, gaze shifting to Sylas pulling out a chair for Callie. Eleanor smiles politely, looking between Callie and me. Silent conversations all around. Yes, this is the one who tried to poison him last night. No, we don't have to worry. *I hope.*

"This is my best friend Callie." I pull free so we can take our seats, waving at her.

Her face flushes. After a moment, she suddenly dips into an ungraceful curtsy. "Your Highness."

Eleanor gently laughs, Reuben pulling the chair out for her. I motion for Callie to sit as I take my seat, Sylas pushing me in.

"You don't have to be so formal, dear. You're a friend of Zily, which makes you welcome here." My chest warms with Eleanor's words.

Callie shifts uncomfortably. I show my thanks, smiling at Eleanor. Conversations are as they were when I first arrived; light, vague and pleasant. Sylas mentions a morning meeting with his father and Kai. If it's with the two of them, there's a good chance it involves Gateswood. I wish I could be a part of it, but my current duty is entertaining Callie. I want to give her the hope that I've found. It's perfect. With Kai busy, I don't have to worry about morning training.

However, he assigns one of the other guards to follow me around. I roll my eyes. Sylas wordlessly asks me to deal with it for his own sanity, conveying it through a kiss to my forehead. I sigh, motioning for him to follow.

I take Callie on a tour through the mansion. Mostly I point out rooms as I lead the way to the library. This room is a sitting room. Down that hall is the kitchen. Up the stairs. This whole hall is filled with bedrooms. I pause in front of my favorite painting on the wall, a field of flowers at dusk, a single tree to the left side of the canvas. After a moment of admiration, we continue on past our rooms. Turn down another couple halls and gesture to the infirmary.

Sonya steps out as we're strolling past. I raise a hand in greeting. She gives a friendly smile, gaze drifting to Callie. Of course I introduce them.

"I'm glad to see you made it in a better condition than how Zily showed up here." Her gaze is teasing and genuine.

Callie shoots me a horrified look. I shrug casually. "I told you I nearly drowned."

"With a few holes in you." Sonya points, drawing circles down her side where my wounds are. They're nearly completely healed. The itch is finally gone too.

"You didn't mention that." Callie accuses.

"I'm fine. I'm here, aren't I?"

"Good thing, too. I couldn't imagine what we'd have done without you. A whole village may have been wiped out." Sonya lifts a hand, waving goodbye with her last statement.

I fight the flush creeping up my neck. Callie stares at me wide eyed, waiting for an explanation. A sigh escapes. "A village had an invasive poisonous plant that was killing them. I made an antidote. They're doing fine now, and the flower has been weeded out." I turn continuing down the hall. "It's not that big of a deal."

"Don't think for a moment that you haven't made an impact here." The deep husky voice of the unnamed soldier startles me, halting my progress. He appears to have made Callie uneasy as well. She stands closer to me, staring up at him. "I doubt there's a soul here that hasn't been affected by your presence." He strolls past us casually, back straight, hand on his sword. The picture perfect guard.

"Sorry?" My feet follow after him. I don't know how to respond.

"She's always had a tendency to do her own thing," Callie says, quietly.

"It's not necessarily a bad thing."

"No." Callie agrees, bobbing her head, though her eyes appear murkier than I'm used to.

"She even got Neil to come to training and actually put in effort to work hard. I know you don't know Neil, but he's a lazy drunk, so it was quite the feat." The man glances back over his shoulder, emerald eyes flashing to Callie with a grin.

"You forgot 'womanizer.'" I add. "I also didn't realize our little interaction affected him so much."

"You left a mark." He taps his cheek.

An unexpected laugh bursts out, remembering. We finally reach the library. I move around the guard quickly, shoving the doors open. I skip to the middle of the room, standing behind the couch. Turning back to them, I throw my hands in the air.

"This is the library. Look at all the books!" My tail swishes behind me.

Her tail curls up for the first time since coming here. Finally, she appears to be relaxing, even just a little. "How much time have you spent in here?" She starts to roam around the room, fingers brushing along book spines.

"Quite a bit. Oh! I've started making my own book. Kind of. Sylas gave me a leather book with blank pages that I've been filling with pictures of flowers, mostly, and adding notes around them."

Callie peers at me over her shoulder. "You draw?" I shrug. "I always wondered why you packed sheets of paper."

"You could have asked. It's how I paid for things like rooms to sleep in while out on a mission." I explain. I'm itching to grab my book and show her, excited to share a part of me I've kept hidden for years. I can add a drawing of her to the back.

"I take it, we'll be going to the garden next?" His husky voice pitches into a question. He leans against the door frame, staring down the hall.

I stare at him, feeling awful for not knowing his name. "Yup. I think I've spent as much time there as I have here. Probably more actually." Walking back around the couch, I get close enough that I have to lift my chin to look up at him. "I'm sorry. I don't know your name." I say quietly, embarrassment threatening to turn my cheeks pink.

He chuckles, straightening. "Tarren Ashwood." He holds his hand out to me.

I slide my hand into his, shaking it. "Zily. Just Zily."

"I know." Tarren smirks, eyes glowing like jewels.

"How would anyone not know who you are at this point, Zily? You kind of stick out." Callie comes up behind me, putting a hand on my shoulder. I sigh.

"She's right. I'm sure word about Miss Callie has spread already too."

Callie blushes, eyes widening. Tarren waves for me to continue with my tour. As expected, I take us down to the garden. From there, I point out the window to Sylas' study, rambling on about his messy desk for a moment. Tarren hides a laugh by clearing his throat.

We stroll through the garden. I rattle off names of plants. Callie is used to me going on about herbs, flowers and poisons. Some of them she knows from what I've taught her for when she would get jobs like mine. It's a comfortable companionship. Tarren remains quiet, though I see his eyebrows raise from time to time.

A whistle breaks through the giggles. I'm so happy she's here and I get to share this little piece of the world with her. Seeing her has given me hope that we can do this, have a new life, though she doesn't seem to believe it yet. Her shoulders aren't as tight, but her lips struggle to smile and her eyes remain muddy. Turning, I see Sylas and Kai walking toward us. Sylas raises a hand. Grinning, I lift the skirt of my dress, running to greet him. He stops, holding his arms out for me. I nearly knock him down when I jump. We laugh easily. Kai rolls his eyes, meeting up with Tarren to get a briefing and relieve him of duty. He nods once, though there's disappointment in his eyes when he peers back at Callie and me.

"It's about lunch time. Should we all have lunch together?" I suggest, taking a step back to address everyone, my hand finding its way into Sylas'.

Kai slides his hands into his pockets. "Sounds good to me. I'm starving."

Sylas shoves him playfully. "That's because you have a tendency to skip meals." Kai shrugs.

"Tarren can join us too," I say quickly when he starts to leave. His emerald eyes flash his thanks. Kai's eyebrows scrunch together. Callie shifts uncomfortably. She's gone quiet again.

We walk back into the mansion with Sylas and I leading the way. "How's it going?" Sylas leans down to whisper in my ear.

"Good." I glance back at Callie, walking nervously beside Tarren. Her hands are folded in front of her. "She's still anxious about all this."

"I can't blame her." His eyes flicker to her as well. In a more normal voice, he says, "I'll summon one of the servants to bring lunch for all of us to the drawing room."

"Actually, I want to introduce Callie to Zachary, so we can pick it up."

"Then we might as well all go because you can't be left alone and what would the point be of having just two of us wait in the room?" Kai speaks up.

I shrug, hoping they don't mind us crowding the kitchen. The other chefs pay their respects to Sylas, bowing and addressing him formally. Sylas waves a hand dismissively. Their gazes travel to me, sharpening and then falling on Callie. Eyes widen in shock. I have the urge to stick my tongue out at them.

Instead, I stroll up behind Zachary, sliding onto a stool. I pat the one beside me for Callie. The men wait on the other side of the island the stools are against. Sylas leans across it, blowing air against the back of my neck, sending a shiver through me. He chuckles, catching Zachary's attention. He does a double take over his shoulder. Finding a moment he can turn away from the cooking food, he faces us with a pleasant smile, hands on his waist where the apron is tied around him.

"Now who do we have here?" His eyes roam over all of us, landing on Callie.

I wave my hand back and forth with the usual introduction. "Zachary, here, makes the best food. It's always amazing."

Zachary gives a humbled shrug. "It's just what I love to do."

Callie tilts her head, like the words ring a bell for her. "I look forward to trying it."

"How many plates am I making?" He turns back to the pan with chicken and pasta.

"All of us here, if that's not a problem." I gesture behind me, settling back with my hands on my lap, shifting toward Callie. "Zachary also helped me make antidotes. The one for the village Sonya mentioned and others like the ones I'm carrying." I gently pat the bag hanging at my side.

"Is that what's in there? Why am I not surprised?" Callie shakes her head.

"She's a bit paranoid," Sylas says behind us.

Callie stares at him. Words go unspoken. It's fine. We all know why she's here, why I was sent here. The danger we know is still out there hangs over our heads like a dark thunder cloud ready to burst. Her tail droops behind her.

Zachary fills two platters with plates of food, and another with a tea set and pitcher of iced tea. The men carry them to the drawing room for us. I tried to take one, but Sylas slips his hands undermine, pulling the tray from me.

Settling into chairs around the glass table in the room I ate lunch with Eleanor in, I watch Callie take her first bites. She pauses with the fork near her mouth, eyes flicking to me. I wait patiently. Her face turns red under my stare. She covers her mouth, finishing the bite. Chewing, she closes her eyes, a soft moan emanating from her.

"This is great!" It's the first time her voice pitches with excitement. It's slow, but it's only day one.

"Right!" I dig into my own plate of food. Sylas's shoulders silently shake beside me, holding back laughter.

It's a casual meal. I tell Sylas where I took Callie during the morning. He's unsurprised about the amount of time we spent in both the library and garden. He offers to continue the tour with us. Kai tags along since he's supposed to be my guard. Tarren sticks with us as well, Sylas' usual two guards nowhere in sight.

Sylas takes us to the ballroom, the crystal chandelier glittering overhead. The tables have been moved around since the last time we've been in here. The floor shines from recently polishing. Callie has the same look of awe and amazement as I felt the first time I'd seen this room.

I spin around, the bottom of my dress flaring out, arms outstretched. I paint an image for Callie of a room full of people, dancing to music, us swaying along with partners. My gaze briefly passes over Sylas, smiling at me with bright eyes, picturing it himself. Me and him dancing together in front of hundreds of eyes on us. Blush rises at the mere thought of it, heart racing and yet, the idea doesn't scare me as much as it would have before.

As we walk to our next stop, Sylas asks if we should pay Maple and S'more a visit as well. I'm delighted by the thought, skipping beside him. He stops us before the doors to the throne room. He pushes it open for Callie to enter first. The marble floor glistens under the light.

Our heels click as we walk into the room, Tarren and Kai waiting by the door. Callie moves closer to the thrones while Sylas explains what happens in the room. She folds her hands behind her back to keep from touching the seats. She leans forward, staring at the engravings. She moves down to the smallest seat, eyeing it. She swivels, looking back and forth between all the seats, her gaze turning to me in the end. Heat rises in my chest, up my neck into my cheeks.

"Why are there four seats?" She asks the obvious question.

Sylas walks over behind my throne, resting his arms on the back of it. "This one here is Zily's."

"I thought so." She points to her head where a moon and star hairpin is on mine. I can't read her expression. She's neither smiling nor frowning and her eyes are darker than I've seen them before. Trying to explain this might be too much right now. She doesn't ask anything in front of the boys. I can feel the void growing between us, my hearts starting to sink.

"Anyway, would you like to meet Maple and S'more now?" Callie's eyebrows draw together with my attempt to change the subject.

Sylas chuckles. He returns to my side. I shoot him a glare. He returns it with a kiss to my forehead. The afternoon bleeds into evening as we cross the field to the stables. Sylas is enjoying retelling my first experience with horses and our first ride. It seems to be his favorite story to tell. I wish we could go back to that little place by the creek again.

S'more has grown more than I expected in the short time since I last saw them. Callie is nowhere near as nervous about being around the muscled creatures than I was. She even asks if she could enter the stall with them, something I have yet the courage to do. That is their space, their home; I didn't want to invade.

Sylas opens the door for her. She walks slowly, calm with confidence to Maple who's munching on some hay. Callie holds up a hand, palm out. Maple presses her snout against her hand, letting Callie pet her. S'more whinnies for attention, bumping his head against her side. She laughs, shifting to pet them both.

"Have you been around horses before?" I question, watching her interaction with them.

"Yes. I've rode a time or two." The way her lips curl into a smile makes me believe she's rode quite a bit. I suppose we all kept secrets from our time beyond the walls. It's a different world out here.

Kai and Tarren wait outside the stall, speaking quietly. Sylas keeps a firm grip around my waist for comfort as we follow in behind Callie. S'more recognizes me, trotting up for my attention. We feed them some carrots. Callie seems the most comfortable here than she has been all day.

We take a trip farther into the stables than I have ever been to see Jupiter. Callie doesn't blanch at his size, approaching him in the same manner as she had Maple. Once again, the stallion dips his head for her. She's like a horse whisperer.

Callie retreats back into herself as we make our way back inside for dinner. Tarren and Kai stand outside the dining room doors as we go in. I greet Eleanor and Reuben. Callie tips her head, nodding a 'hello' when Eleanor addresses her. I speak to Callie directly to incorporate her into conversation, showing her that it's alright to speak casually. Eleanor and Reuben are nice.

I hope she understands why I chose to stay. Why I love this place so much. Hoping she'll like it enough to stay as well, that she won't hate me for my decision. It's only been a day. There's more time to convince her tomorrow.

Chapter Twenty-Six
Sunflower

It symbolizes adoration, loyalty and happiness. Sunflower seeds are a common snacks. Additionally, the flower can be used to produce a yellow dye while mature seeds can produce a purple dye.

Sylas

Zily is enthralled by her friend's presence. I leave them alone as much as I can. Callie seems anxious whenever I'm around. It's unclear if it's because she attempted to kill me or if it's because I'm a prince. I don't want to hurt Zily or make her worry, but some of the looks Callie gives concern me. The few times I've seen her smile, it never reached her eyes. She always looks nervous, like a caged animal. Sad. I hope it's different when it's just the two of them.

However, my cousin is almost here, and I want to introduce Zily to him. I hope neither mind too much if I separate them for a few. Unsurprisingly, they're in the library. The two girls stand chattering near the tall bookshelf against the wall, Zily holding a book, beaming. The stars are shining bright in her eyes, like a guiding light of hope. Callie tries to match her glow, but there's no spark in her murky eyes.

Kai sits crooked in the chair, leaving the little couch to the ladies. Even with a book in hand, he's fully aware of his surroundings, oak brown eyes meeting mine momentarily without shifting his position. I need to find a moment to ask him how the girls are when I'm not here. He was shocked when I confessed my paranoia about Callie, asking him to keep an extra eye on her.

Zily turns around as I get close. She grins and I have to make an effort not to reach for her, fingers twitching. My hands slide in my pockets. Callie shifts, tail dropping, though her ears don't droop like Zily's does when something is bothering her.

"Sorry to interrupt. Do you mind if I borrow Zily for a little?" I address Callie while also making sure it's alright with Zily. Zily cocks her head, a cute, curious gesture. "Philip will be here soon. It's custom to greet guests in the foyer. I would like you to be there."

"Oh! Your cousin. Right." Her white fluffy tail swishes once. "Will you be ok? I'll come back soon after." She promises, staring at Callie.

She shrugs, waving a hand around the room. "I think I'll be fine."

"Do you love to read as well?" I ask.

"Not the same as Z, but yes, I enjoy a good book." She rubs her hands down her skirt. I think that's the most she's said to me.

I nod my thanks, sliding an arm around Zily's waist. The warmth of her body against mine is an instant comfort. I give her a gentle squeeze as we walk down the hall. Kai stays in the library with Callie. Two guards follow me and Zily at a respectable distance.

Curiosity and concern get the best of me. "How's everything with Callie?"

"Good." She gives the same response as last time, pausing with hesitation. "I think she's having a hard time. It's an adjustment from where we come from. It feels like she's still being pulled back there."

"I'm sure it'll be fine. I think we're getting close to finding Gateswood. Kai marked on the map the places that have been searched so far. We're only sending out small search parties right now, but we'll find it. You both are safe here in the meantime." I kiss the top of her head.

Her tail flicks, curling up. "Keep each other safe." She repeats my words.

"Exactly." I grin down at her, though her eyes look distant, staring ahead.

"I wish Decan was here too. I think she's worried about him being left behind." Zily whispers, her voice matching her eyes.

We enter the foyer before I have a chance to respond. I give her another squeeze instead. My parents are already waiting for us, waiting for Philip. Mom greets Zily, pulling her in for a hug. Surprise crosses Zily's face, eyes widening, but she returns it with ease.

The carriage comes to a stop outside. A few moments later, a butler announces my cousin's arrival, opening the grand doors. His men enter first before I see the familiar goofy grin and piercing blue-grey eyes. He strides in with confidence, raising his arms.

"Sylas! Finally. It's been too long."

I break away, going to meet him halfway. Our hands clasp together, and I pull him in for a hug. As he starts to back away, I put him in a headlock, ruffling his shaggy wheat hair. He laughs, shoving me to break free.

"Good to see you too, Philip." I slide my hands in my pockets.

His fingers comb through his hair, straightening the mess. He addresses my parents. Father gives him a firm handshake while mom gives him a warm hug. Then his gaze lands on Zily. He hides his confusion well, but I've known him since we were small boys. His eyebrow twitches, and the corner of his lips curving in a sly smile.

Zily dips into a nearly perfect curtsy. She's practiced, the movement becoming smoother and more natural. Her smile is broad and bright, snow white waves bouncing against her shoulders.

"Hello, Philip. It's a pleasure to meet you."

Now his eyebrow truly rise. I walk around, placing my hand on the small of her back. "This is Zily. Forgive me, I've talked about your arrival, so she already knew your name." *And she tends to skip titles and surnames.* Mom mentioned she used her title once, only once.

"Well, Zily, the honor is all mine." He holds out his hand. She delicately places hers in his. He brings it up to kiss her fingers while he does a partial bow. Blush creeps into her cheeks, eyes of starlight glance over at me. A warm feeling of pride that I get to call this woman mine fills me, happy I get to introduce her to Philip. I just know they're going to get on well.

Father and mother exchange a few more words before excusing themselves. Zily dips her head, also intending to leave, anxious to return to her friend. I nod, waving Tarren over to escort her back.

"We'll have lunch together, but Zily has a friend here waiting for her." I explain to Philip.

"Until next time." He winks at her.

A soft blush coats her cheeks and she giggles. She squeezes my hand once before spinning around with Tarren. I turn my attention back to my cousin.

"So, fly?"

A broad grin sweeps across his face. It takes a moment to narrow down the guards that'll stay near us. Philip is giving me looks as to why this is an issue to begin with. We've flown off on our own plenty of times before. I literally have to argue that I've only had two with me this whole time, we'll be fine with just them. However, the veteran guards know better than to let me and my cousin out of their sight when we've had several breaches in our security recently. We settle on four and they'll follow at a respectable distance.

Outside, Philip releases his golden brown wings, shooting into the air. I follow after him, my large black wings batting at the air, wind ruffling through my feathers. We soar through the sky enjoying the sun beating down on us.

"So, what's up with the extra security?" Philip begins, gliding over the trees at the border of the forest. "Does it have something to do with the Kitsune?"

"Kind of. It's a long story." I sigh heavily. "It's nothing to worry about at this moment. Tell me about you. How have you been?" I do a slow barrel roll, feeling the rush. Strands of hair break free from my ponytail. I pull the band out, letting the wind blow it. I'll need to brush it later, but it feels great.

"I, well, I started seeing someone." It's unusual to hear him nervous.

"Oh? Tell me more."

"We met during the summer solstice festival in the village near home." A smile forms on his lips as the memory glosses over his eyes. "Without knowing who I was, she grabbed me and forced me to dance around the fire with her. I went back to see her, visiting her more and more frequently."

A chuckle comes out as I playfully shove him. "And? I take it it's been going well."

His ears turn red, a small grin on his face. "Yeah. I've taken her on quite a few dates. My favorite was when I carried her to the lake for a picnic. We stayed until after the sun set." I want to tell him about the horse ride and picnic with Zily. "We've kept it somewhat a secret. I've met her parents. They're nice and seem accepting of our relationship. My parents found out about her, and believe I'm simply playing around with her. We've talked about moving in together.

"She sounds wonderful. You should have brought her with."

Philip half laughs, rubbing the back of his neck. "Thanks. She is. I haven't told father how serious I am about her yet, about our plans for the future. She's… She's a Witch."

"I suspected something of the sort," I say. Having mentioned that he carried her to the lake gave away that she's not a Corvum. Philip remains oddly quiet, drifting with the wind. "Is something wrong?"

"Well, it's a bit strange, wanting to marry a Witch." He speaks softly.

I snort, thinking about Zily. "I don't see a problem with that. You seem happy simply talking about her. If you love her, you should do it."

Philip stops, his powerful wings beating the air to keep him hovering, facing me. "My parents don't realize the extent of our relationship."

"And you're worried about what they'll do."

"Yes." His eyes are sharp, staring at me, asking for help.

I contemplate it for a moment, thinking of my uncle. My aunt and uncle are ones for tradition. They've tried to marry him off when he came of age, but father stepped in. Now, it's my turn. "I'll see what I can do, but you shouldn't let them stop you from marrying her if you really love her."

Philip sighs, running his fingers through his hair. "It's really a relief to hear you say that. I thought if I could get your approval, then they couldn't argue."

I put my hand to my chest, feigning hurt. "Is that the only reason you came to visit after all these years?"

Philip rolls his eyes, slinging an arm around my shoulder. He ruffles my hair in the same way I did to him earlier. "You know that it's not. Hey, when did you start letting your hair down?"

I shove him, the wind making him dip before fanning his wings out to bring him level with me again. "Someone suggested it, so when I don't have to be extra presentable, I take it down."

He laughs, carefree. "I like it. It feels more you."

I grin. "Thanks."

We fly around, not too far from the mansion, catching up. It's relaxing and playful, like when we were kids, trying to tackle each other out of the sky. We scare the men keeping an eye on us when our wrestling lands us in a tree. When we finally touch the ground, breathless, I send one of the guards to get Zily and Callie and another to request lunch to be sent to the drawing room.

I lead the way down the hall, pulling leaves from my hair. Philip manages to shake the leaves from his head without much trouble. The man must have ran, because Zily and Callie are walking down the hall with Kai and Tarren behind them when Philip and I reach the room. It's her giggle that catches my attention, making me pause at the door.

Zily glances up, her eyes shining. She crosses the distance with a combination of sprinting and skipping, tail swishing behind her. I welcome her into my arms, squeezing more giggles out of her. She reaches up, running her fingers through my hair. It feels nice. I lean into the touch.

"Did you have fun?" She leans around to peer at Philip around me. "Hi, again, Philip." He stares at her, lips parted as if to speak but too stunned to find words. Callie joins us, hands folded in front of her, tail between her legs.

"Shall we go in?" I push the door open, walking into the room, holding Zily against my side.

We take the couch. Callie sits in the chair closest to Zily. Philip lowers himself into the other chair opposite. Most of the guards wait outside, but Kai joins us. He and Philip do a quick hand shake as he passes to fetch another chair by the window, dragging it over.

Philip's eyebrows are drawn together, staring at my arm around Zily. Zily sweetly does quick introductions for Callie and Philip. He shoots her a polite smile. Callie returns it with her usual anxious one.

"So, you live here?" He asks the words slowly, putting a puzzle together. The corner of my lips quirk.

Zily's ears twitch, blush creeping into soft pale cheeks. "Yes."

"And you two are… together?" Her cheeks turn a darker pink. I nod. "Publicly?"

"I've only been here two days, and I think they're a little too public." Callie suddenly speaks up.

Zily's mouth hangs open while I chuckle. Kai snorts from his seat. A knock tells us lunch is here. Servants bring in the trays, setting them down on the glass table. Callie remains quiet throughout lunch, shifting in her chair. I feel a little bad putting her in this situation. I'm being selfish, wanting to have lunch with my cousin, my best friend and my love.

"Is it alright to ask how you met?" Philip raises an eyebrow, taking a bite of his meal.

I share a glance with Zily. Her hand is against her cheek, enjoying the food. "A forest beast got to her, so I brought her here."

"I was sent to kill him," she says casually, covering her mouth after taking another bite. Her tail thumps happily beside her.

Callie stares at her, mouth agape. Kai chokes, coughing hard. He has yet to hear her admission like that. Philip's eyes grow wide, darting between each of us. "Is that an inside joke I don't understand?"

Zily shakes her head. I run my fingers through her hair, answering. "No. She does mean it quite literally. We're working to find the man who sent them."

Philip leans back, eyebrows scrunching together. "That explains the increase in security."

"There's been a few that's slipped past us. As head of security, it's frustrating to hear about." Kai's gaze drifts to Callie. "No offense, but you should not have made it in, let alone been capable of what you did."

Callie stares at her plate, picking at her food. I want to kick Kai. "Callie is just extra sneaky; she's had to be." Zily defends. "It's not our fault the guys like to talk."

Philip laughs, breaking the tension. Zily's eyes shine with gratitude. We finish lunch. Kai gets up to follow the girls out to continue their day. Zily gives me a quick peck on the cheek before skipping down the hall. I won't see them again until dinner. Philip leans forward, inquiring more about Zily, these supposed assassination attempts and what is going on with them. I'm open and honest about everything, though it won't extend to his parents when they'll eventually meet her. The light hearted talk grows grim as I explain the little we know about Gateswood and Colin Eyler. He offers his own men to help with the search, and when the time comes, the sieging of Gateswood.

Philip sits beside my mother at dinner seeing as the seat beside me is permanently occupied now, with her friend beside her. Callie doesn't say a single word for the duration of dinner. Philip enjoys teasing Zily and me. It makes her face burn red. The sparkles in her eyes are an indicator that she's alright with the teasing. Dad has an amused look on his face, contributing to conversation from time to time. Mom is bright, laughing all the while.

"It's good to have you around again, Philly." She calls him by his childhood nickname, earning an eye roll.

We say goodnight at the top of the stairs, Philip turning down a different hall to go to his room. Kai leaves us too, seeing the other two guards that'll stand outside our door at night fit enough to escort us back to our rooms. Zily starts to say goodnight to Callie when she grabs Zily's arm.

"Can you come in for just a minute?" Callie glances up at me warily, returning her pleading gaze back to Zily.

"I'll wait for you." I kiss the top of her head, referring to our nightly bath together, letting her go. Zily smiles, stepping away into the room with Callie.

I should have given her an extra squeeze, a reminder that I love her.

Chapter Twenty-Seven
Foxglove

All parts of the digitalis are poisonous. Ingesting can lead to nausea, vomiting, and visual disturbances. Chemicals are taken from this flower to make medicines that can help strengthen the heart muscle contractions. This flower represents healing and harm.

Zily

"He has Decan."

As soon as the door is shut, her soft words fill the room. I blink. Her ears lie flat against her head, tail woven between her legs, tears stinging her eyes. She sucks in a shaky breath, ringing the front of her dress in her hands. My mouth gapes open, words lost and ears unsure they heard correctly.

"Sir Colin Eyler is holding Decan hostage. If I don't return, he'll…" Her words break off, shaking her head. "If I don't complete the task, he'll hurt us both. He's already… Decan… his hands." Large tears roll down Callie's face at the confession. My heart drops into my stomach, my body going numb. She sobs, "I'm sorry. I'm sorry. You've found happiness, and I debated not telling you. You deserve this; all of this. The joy and love and happiness after everything. But I don't know what to do. I tried thinking of another solution."

My mind reels with the information. He punished my friends because of my decisions. He knew I defied him and found a way to hurt me even here. He sent Callie as a warning. If she didn't tell me, what would have happened to them? Would I have ever seen them again? When Sylas' men finally find Gateswood, would we have found their bodies?

My feet drag as I step toward Callie, wrapping my arms around her. She's covering her face while she sobs, shoulders shaking. I don't say anything, stroking the back of her head. There are no words that could bring comfort. Saying "it's okay" would be a lie. Nothing has been okay since we entered Gateswood as young children.

"How much time were you given?" My voice doesn't sound like my own.

"A week," Callie meekly responds. I feel like I'm going to throw up, doing the calculations in my head. She should be heading back *now*.

"We'll leave tomorrow," I whisper.

Callie gasps, jerking back. "Z, you can't. What about…"

I shake my head, cutting her off. "I'm not obeying him. I'm not returning to Gateswood. I'm going to bring it down." Her eyes grow wide. "No more. I won't let him hurt you, or Decan or Sylas ever again. Even if it kills me; I will stand up to Eyler." I growl his name, rage slowly boiling deep inside, fighting against the prickly feeling in my head for having these thoughts.

Callie shakes her head in disbelief, clutching the front of my dress. "You can't. You know how strong he is. He'll kill you, or worse."

"I won't simply do as he says without a fight. No more. I can't." I wipe my dear friend's tears from her cheek, running my fingers through her curls. I wonder what bruises she's hiding under her clothes. "Try not to worry. We'll leave tomorrow. Get some rest." I turn to exit the room.

"I'm sorry," she whispers once more as I open the door.

Nodding to the guards in the hall and entering my room, I start formulating a plan. Sylas sits on the chair by the book shelf, leg crossed over his knee, quietly reading. A warm smile forms, eyes flickering to me. I hope he can't see how cold I feel, plastering a smile on my face.

I lift my bag over my head, setting it on the nightstand. He puts a bookmark in between pages, shelving the book and meeting me halfway. His arms slide around my waist, pulling me against his body. Safe and warm. "How is Callie?"

He asks this periodically. Can he read the worry on my face? As long as he misinterprets it. "She's… having a hard time." It's as honest as I can be.

He hugs me tight, fingers tangling in my hair, his head dipping down to my shoulder, breath tickling my neck. The smell of fresh air and pine fills my nose. "I'm sure she just needs time." I nod, biting the inside of my cheek.

If I tell him what's going on, he'll help. He'll have men, and we could simply show them the way instead of their blind searching. He wouldn't be happy about me being out there, but it'd be the only way for them to find it. It'd be great to have the numbers against the unknown number of Vampires, and the Kitsune that may still fight for Eyler. However, what would he do to Decan if we showed up with force? Decan is already in his grasps; he'd torture and possibly kill him in front of us. The time it would take to get the men there is not in our favor either. We need to get in there quickly and quietly if possible. Who'd be better than the two most stealthy Kitsunes I know?

I tilt my head back, lifting onto my toes to kiss Sylas. I slide my fingers into his hair, enjoying the way it feels gliding through. His arm tightens around my waist, hand balling with a fistful of my hair. A soft moan escapes when I nip his bottom lip, sucking on it.

He presses his body flush with mine, shuffling us back till my ass touches the bed. The warmth of him covers me like a blanket, heating my insides, allowing me to forget tomorrow momentarily. It feels like I'm melting under his touch, gasping for air. I want to remember him, every muscle, every divot in his skin, every scar. He's never asked about mine. Maybe one day I would have told him where they came from. Which ones were placed upon me in punishment. Which ones I did to myself with experiments. And the ones I got from days like the one he rescued me. A different kind of intimacy.

A small flickering flame in my heart still hopes for a day like that. Hoping to be here for his coronation. What a great King he's going to be. I'd love to dance with him. Then to meet the Celyce family of the Viararia Kingdom. I wonder if I could learn where I came from.

Sylas's lips trail down my neck, placing tender and sweet kisses. My chest flutters with every little peck, rising and falling with heavy pants. He growls, with want and need. Pleasure builds up. I cling to him, feeling ecstasy take over both our bodies.

We're hot and sticky. His grin has me giggling while he plants more kisses across my body. He carries me to the bath, washing me with loving caresses. I hold on to the night, wishing tomorrow never comes.

Tomorrow does come with a knock and the usual greeting of the maid. When we meet Callie in the hall, the guards are smirking. If my thoughts weren't already spinning with today's plan, I certainly would blush.

Callie remains quiet, head down, shame written in her eyes. I have to smile, have to hide my thoughts, fears and anxiety. Laughing through breakfast to Philip's jokes. I'm grateful for his presence, his distraction.

Sylas is reluctant to let me go, but I insist he spends the time he can with his cousin. He doesn't think anything of it. Leading the way up the stairs, Callie stares at me wide eyed. Kai is right behind us. My personal bodyguard. I will miss him too. Hopefully he can keep Sylas here and safe.

"Callie, come look at the dresses Leona made me. You can get a feel of what you like, and we'll visit her later. She'll love having a new model." I put as much cheer into my voice as I can, bounding up the last few steps.

"Alright. Yes, sounds fun." Callie squeaks.

I pull her into my room -Sylas' room- closing the door. Kai tries to enter, but I put a hand on his chest. "We're going to be changing. You stay out here." I quirk an eyebrow in challenge. He rolls his eyes, turning to lean against the wall, arms crossed. I pause, holding onto the door, glancing at the bag at my hip. Pulling it over my head, I hold it out to him. "Hold this for me."

"Why? Can't you just put it on the bed or something? Where do you keep it at night?" He eyes it.

Groaning and rolling my eyes, I make a show of it. "I just wanted it to be safe while we changed a few times. If you're going to be a baby about holding it for a little while, I suppose I can set it on the bed." His eyes narrow on me, not liking the insult. He snatches the strap from me, grumbling. "Careful! I worked hard on those antidotes. Keep it on you and keep it safe." I beg before shutting the door.

I duck into the room. Callie is pacing. She opens her mouth to speak. I put a finger to my lips, shaking my head. Walking to the closet, I make sure the doors opening and us shuffling about is loud enough for Kai to hear, to convince him of what I want him to believe we're doing.

In the back of the closet, I whisper my plan to Callie, pulling out my old clothes along with the extra in my old bag seeing that Callie's is still in her room. I'm short a shirt, the one they had been torn and bloody when I was brought here. The light blue one I was given hadn't been returned since the last time I wore it, though my shorts have. I pull a black, short sleeve shirt from a hanger on Sylas' side. It's huge on me, but I tie it in the back, tucking the extra fabric under the edge. In a way, it's like I'm taking him with me still. It's dumb, but it makes me feel better.

Slinging my old trusty backpack over my shoulder carrying my box of poison vials and strapping my sword to my waist, I'm nearly ready to go. I pull my book out of the nightstand drawer, flipping through it one last time, pausing on my secret drawings in the back. I didn't get to finish adding to them.

"You really are good at drawing," Callie says over my shoulder.

I hug the book to my chest before setting it on the nightstand. My precious hairpins are laid on top, a plain brown headband replacing them on my head. Should I leave a letter? No, there's no time. I can only hope for one of two scenarios; I somehow manage to save Decan on my own or survive long enough with my friends for Sylas and his men to find us.

I loudly make a comment about a blue dress. Callie's eyebrows scrunch together until I point my thumb at the door, remembering what we're supposedly doing. She manages to fake a giggle.

We stand out on the balcony. I glance at the sky while Callie surveys the ground. There are guards making their rounds. If we can get to the ground, we could easily pass them. They're not going to question me roaming around, but they would be suspicious of me scaling down from the balcony. It needs to be timed perfectly. Callie points at some bricks jetting ever so slightly out of the wall. I cringe, wishing we had a rope.

As soon as the overhead guard has his back to us, her leg is over the rail, hand reaching for the first handhold point. Callie makes it look easy. I've scaled walls before, but not with the same grace as she does. My limbs burn from clinging to the bricks, though not as much as I expected. I'm not sure if it's the adrenaline seeping into my veins or that the training with Kai is already coming in handy.

We pass a few guards who nod to me, casually asking what I'm doing. I simply tell them I'm taking Callie to see the horses. It makes our attire less strange with the suggestion that we may be going horseback riding. They don't know I wouldn't approach the horses without Sylas, let alone go riding without him. We sprint the distance between the stables and the forest.

"Are you sure about this?" Callie glances back, eyebrows scrunched together.

"Let's go save Decan and anyone else that we can."

My chest clenches around my heart. Tears threaten the back of my eyes. I know they'll fall if I so much as glance back. However, Decan needs me. He was my first real friend. He found me curled up and sobbing after the first time I killed someone. He introduced me to Callie. I won't abandon him.

We move faster than we took to get to Sylas' mansion. There's no time to waste with the time frame Callie was given. I force us to keep moving at a steady, quick pace. There's a few times we have to duck into hiding, a Corvum flying overhead. It amazes me how close they've gotten. When we are nearing Gateswood, a sensation prickles my skin. Suddenly I realize why they haven't found Gateswood yet. Never have I thought too much about the sensation till now. There's a magic barrier around the area, detouring those who don't know it's there from discovering its location.

Back tracking until I feel I've passed through the barrier again, I draw my sword. Callie gives me a crazy look when I start chopping at branches. Unless I point the way, they'll never find it. It's a half-baked plan, but if I fail, we will need their help. Feeling satisfied with the outside of the barrier, I cut clear markers on the trees until the wall is in sight.

Crouching in the brush, I dig into my bag, pulling out my poison collection. I've always been picky about what job to use my personal collection on. This one seems fitting. Sliding my fingers carefully along the blade, I lace it with poison, returning it to the sheath. Staring at the tall, smooth walls with wires coiled at the top, I've come to realize and accept over our couple day journey that there's no other way in except through the gates. *So much for sneaking in.* I keep my hand on the pommel of my sword like I've seen Kai and other soldiers do, like I've seen Sylas do, walking with my back straight and head held high.

The men on watch sneer at my return, eyes glittering with darkness, knowing what Eyler is going to do to me. I don't think about it, ignoring them. Kitsunes going about their jobs stop to stare. So many of them that I never paid attention to. They whisper and gawk.

"Snow is back."

Yes. I've returned, but I am not the little snow fall they all knew before. I am stronger and colder than ever. I have more to hold on to; the small moments of joy my two friends and I stole. I will return to my peace, my love and the life I found and claimed for myself. I will be a blizzard, wiping out this place of dark negativity.

At least that's what I tell myself.

I stride to Sir Colin Eyler's study with a confidence I don't deserve to have. Callie scurries behind me. I hold my hand up, motioning for her to stay behind me. The knock on Eyler's door echoes down the hall. I don't wait for a response, silently scolding myself for knocking in the first place. This man doesn't deserve respect.

He sits at his desk, fingers folded together, propped up on his elbows. The dark walls and the bookshelves soak up the bright light, making the room feel small and dark. He has a dangerous smirk on his lips. I leave the door open behind us as a route of escape, giving a false feeling of security.

"Welcome back Snow. You've done well Canary." His grin grows wider.

"I don't go by that name anymore." My hand curls into a fist, trying to hold my nerves together.

"Ah, yes, Zily then." A chill runs down my spine. He stands, strolling around his desk without care. "I knew you'd come back; you always come back."

"Where's Decan?" I growl, gripping the sheath, thumb pressed against the cross guard.

"He's fine. I could take you to him if you would like to give him a hand." I grind my teeth at his sly remark. He takes another step towards us, too close for comfort. The self-preserving instincts give me goosebumps.

Taking a quick, deep breath, I move forward, closing the space between us. Running with weights has increased my speed when I don't have them. Just as Kai had taught me, the blade glides from its sheath the moment I lunge at him. He dodges with his vampiric speed. Reading his moves before he makes them, I swing again, barely missing. Kai taught me that a person reveals their next move in the way their eyes shift, the way the place their feet and in the angle of their shoulders. All I need is one little scratch.

Eyler avoids the blade, not even touching it when he shoves my arm to the side. The couple weeks of training I received doesn't keep him from knocking the sword from my grasp. It clatters on the floor, spinning until it hits a bookshelf. A fist connects to my gut, air being forced from my lungs. Before I have a chance to suck it back in, his hand is clamped around my throat, holding me up against the bookshelf.

I kick wildly, clawing at his hand. I change tactics, reaching out to gouge out his eyes. He leans back, out of range, eyebrows raised.

"You've turned into a fiery little one, haven't you? What put that spark in you? Or should I say 'who'? That prince? Would you like to see him again?" My eyes narrow. Fighting is futile, but it doesn't stop me from thrashing about.

Sir Colin Eyler pulls a device out from his pocket. He holds it in front of my face, a turn dial and a button in the middle. "I think it's time to remind you how to be obedient."

He presses and holds the button, slowly turning the dial with his thumb. My head starts to spin. I think it's from my lack of oxygen until it starts to hurt. My vision blurs, thoughts becoming muffled, like a cloud forming inside my head. He releases me and I drop to my feet.

"There we go. I'll give you your punishment later. Let's collect Canary and go meet up with your other friend. We have preparations to make." He turns, picking up my sword. Carefully he slides it back into the sheath.

Now would be the perfect time to stab him. My fingers don't so much as twitch. I can't move; not of my own accord. He crooks a finger, telling me to follow. My legs move on their own, obediently. The hope that the rumor of their control over us was false vanishes with every step. I'm trapped inside my body, watching without control.

Callie succumbs to the same fate. It even makes the tears streaming down her face stop. We pass other Kitsune that step out of the way, head bowed. Their gazes catch on us, shock and fear filling their eyes.

Eyler takes us to where Decan is. It's a room we're familiar with, though I haven't been here in years, not since the last time I tried to defy him. The walls are smooth dark grey with chains and handcuffs spaced evenly apart. There's a stone slab that sometimes we're pinned to in the center of the room. Stains of captives past cover the floor in blotches, going up the walls.

Decan is chained to the wall, hands -*oh his hands*- are held by metal cuffs that he probably made at some point above his head.

His fingers are purple bruised, twisted at odd angles. Blood trickles down his arms from where the cuffs bite into his milk-chocolate skin. The rest of him is not much better off than his hands. Burns and cuts from hot rods and whips I know well lacerate his body. His clothes are torn, scraps sticking to his skin where the blood coagulated.

My heart throbs with the pain he must have endured, though my face doesn't express it. It remains neutral, walking into the room, kneeling on the floor, hands up. He clasps cold metal around my wrists, unstrapping the belt holding my sword to my waist. He hangs it out of reach.

Once Callie is secure to the wall, he presses and holds the button on the device again. A ringing in my head makes my ears twitch, but my body is my own again. I blink hard, trying to rid myself of the fog.

"While I get things set up, you will remain here. Donovan has missed you. Why don't you get reacquainted?" Eyler smirks, closing the heavy door behind him.

My body slumps, the cuffs digging into my wrists. My chest heaves, sobs wanting to escape. Tears build up in my eyes.

"Do you think he'll come for you?" Callie quietly asks.

I shake my head, lowering it. It's not a no. I know he'll come, but I don't want him to. It's too dangerous. Knowing what I know now and the things that I don't know scares me. He knows about my relationship with Sylas. He can control my body. Sir Colin Eyler will get his wish, and Sylas will die, and I will have to watch.

Chapter Twenty-Eight
Red Spider Lily

These pretty flowers represent death, afterlife, and final goodbyes.
They are highly toxic, causing diarrhea, vomiting, abdominal pain,
convulsions, difficulty breathing, and ataxia.

Kai

Zily's bag hangs limply by the strap in my hand, dangling just above the ground. I know about the jars it holds and take care not to let it hit anything, but I will not wear this thing as she does. She's carried it on her since the day she worked hard creating antidotes for possible poisons to be used against Sylas. She's been drilling the names and symptoms of those poisons into my head for the past couple weeks after I push her to her physical limit with training.

No one could argue that she's a hard worker, and her love for Sylas is written in her eyes. It's all over his face as well. I saw it early on when he'd look at her. Glad it worked out, though it came with some complications.

Sighing, I shift my stance, leaning against the wall beside the door. My gaze drifts back down to the bag brushing against my calf. In her constant fear and worry, I haven't seen her without this bag of hers. She might think I haven't noticed, but with all the time we've been spending together, I've seen she has a habit of grabbing the strap that goes across her chest. Whenever she spaces out for just a moment or something makes her nervous, her hand automatically reaches up.

I think back to our little argument. She could have left the bag on the bed while they played dress up. She sets it to the side in the grass when we get to the sparring part of her training. I don't see why she would be insistent on me holding it now.

I straighten, gut tightening. Knocking on the door, panic begins to swell. No answer. I open the door, not caring if they are supposedly in there changing. The room is empty, the closet door left open as is the glass door to the balcony where the curtains flutter with the light breeze coming in. I curse.

"Zily!" I call, just in case, roaming around the room.

My fear is confirmed when I see her precious hairpins set on top of the leather book. I throw my head back groaning, raking my free hand through my hair. She tricked me. Now I'm going to have to tell Sylas that I failed him. I don't understand why she would leave, not without Sylas. We're searching for their base. She's been helping us the best she could with whatever that makes her faint.

Then Callie showed up. It's no surprise that I didn't trust her. I was surprised when Sylas also didn't trust her. She constantly looked sad, something bothering her. Is that why they left? Some secret she held? I wonder if they left a trail to follow so we can help.

Sliding the strap of the bag over my head, I leap off the balcony, my golden brown wings fanning out to catch me. I hold the bag against my hip to keep the bottles inside safe. It doesn't take long before I run into a few guards who saw Zily and Callie walking across the yard. Supposedly they were going to visit the horses. I start my search near the stables. They couldn't have gotten too far; the room hadn't been quiet that long.

On the ground, I pace along the forest's edge, looking for any sign of where they could have entered. These damn sneaky foxes haven't made this easy on me. Taking to the sky, I let out a string of curses. Sweeping over the trees, I don't see any disturbance on the ground. Not even a deer running or a bird fleeing the trees.

Eventually, I give up. I'm not one to give up easily, however, I've been out here for hours and I need to report back. I order a few men to search for them, or at least some kind of sign of where they went. Thanks to the map Zily pointed to, we have an idea of the direction they took. I have hope to fix this, already imagining scolding her for pulling such a trick when she could have easily asked for help.

For now, I need to disappoint my best friend.

A maid passing by informs me he and Philip are getting settled for lunch in the sitting room on the ground floor. She gives me a funny look, seeing the bag over my shoulder. My hand reaches up, running down the strap.

I knock and enter the room with two cyan chairs and a cream little couch where Sylas is sitting. The moment of excitement when Sylas looks at me damn near breaks my heart. I've known this man since we were boys. He can read the grim expression on my face. *Damn that girl.*

"Where's Zily?" His voice is low. Philip's eyes fill with concern, darting from me to the door behind me.

My fingers curl around the strap across my chest. "They left."

"What do you mean they left?" Sylas stands, as if there's still a chance to stop them.

"She said they were going to try on dresses and when I checked on them, they were already gone. Out through the balcony."

"Why?" He whispers, dropping back to the couch, a hand finding its way to his loose black hair.

I mimic the gesture. "My best guess is something to do with Callie. She shows up and Zily disappears? It's not a coincidence. Even you had a strange feeling about her, and don't say it's because she tried to poison you. Obviously, you don't hold your life in high regard." Sylas glares at me. That's fine. It'll be easier if he's more angry than he is depressed.

My mind churns, attempting to come up with a logical reason behind her sudden actions. That girl doesn't know logic; from the little I know of her, she's all emotion.

"Why couldn't she have come to me? If something came up, she knows she could have asked for help. I'd do anything I could to lend a hand." Sylas' voice wavers. His logic is fighting with his emotions. I know he would like nothing more than to go look for her himself. Maybe he would catch something I missed.

I sigh, shifting my weight. "I don't know."

"Perhaps the situation was -is more dire than you know and she had to leave right away." Philip leans forward, arms resting on his knees. "Is there something they'd risk going back for?"

Sylas sits up. "Decan. They have another friend there. If something was wrong involving him…" The pieces begin to fall together. He shakes his head. "I still don't see why she wouldn't have come to me for help. They could have led the way instead of us wandering aimlessly.”

I stare at him. On this matter, I understand Zily. The danger I would put myself in if I found out something had happened to Sylas, even if he wasn't my future king. She called Callie her best friend. If Decan is a part of that friendship, then I could see her running off to try to save him. Even then, she's smart enough to know Sylas would chase after her, so why couldn't I find a trail?

“We need a plan,” I murmur, growing frustrated.

“Do we have a direction to start looking in?” Philip fidgets in his seat. He seems ready to go right now, determination burning in his eyes.

Sylas and I exchange looks. I'm unsure what he's told his cousin or how much he's willing to get him involved.

“Yes. We've been sending out small scouting parties daily. We haven't found hide nor hair of this place.” I roll my shoulders, feeling the weight of the words on them. “I checked around where I believe the girls entered the forest. There're men currently sweeping the area. We'll follow after them the best we can, as soon as we can, but they're slippery and she did not leave a trail for us.” I reiterate this for Sylas' sake.

A heavy sigh comes from him, leaning back against the couch. He stares at the ceiling as if that will give him some idea of what to do.

“I will help,” Philip says with conviction, reminding me when we were boys and Sylas had the bright idea of exploring the forest near the gorge when none of us could fly for long yet. He insisted on tagging along.

“Philip.” Sylas turns his attention to his cousin.

"You can't stop me. I've seen the two of you together. She's good for you. I couldn't imagine how I'd react if Mira was gone. I'll help you get her back." There's no arguing with him.

Sylas stands. "First, we need to inform my parents. Then we need to make a plan."

I nod in agreement. "I'll check in with my men to see if they've come up with anything and then meet you in the war room." I stride toward the door.

The poor maid standing on the other side with her fist in the air ready to knock flinches away from me. Expertly, she's carrying a tray of food with her other hand. Their lunch. Sylas easily dismisses her, asking if she would like the food instead. Flustered, she babbles about how she couldn't possibly eat it. Sylas is already moving down the hall, calling back to tell her to take a break and enjoy the meal.

Philip chases after Sylas while I make my way outside. Taking to the sky that's turning grey with clouds, I catch up with those I asked to search the area. One found a single footprint in mud, but that's it. No broken branches. No markings. No trail. My hand tightens around the bag, keeping it from jostling too much. I wonder how Zily could move around without worrying about breaking the glass.

When I get to the war room, His Majesty and Her Majesty are standing around a table, peering at a map along with Sylas and Philip. The King is pointing out places that we've already searched to Philip. Sylas looks up at my approach. I wait to interrupt.

Setting my finger on the map, I tell them what was found. "They entered the forest here. Based on what Zily managed to tell us before, and where Sylas met her, my assumption is to go this way." I drag my finger south-west.

"Haven't we looked there already?"

"Yes, and we should look again." My tone may be a little too harsh to be addressing the King. "We're chasing someone now. They may be stealthy, but it's the forest; they can't cover all their tracks." I hope he doesn't mind my rudeness.

The King nods, touching his chin in thought. "We'll send out men right away."

"You may use mine as you wish as well." Philip offers.

"I want to go too," Sylas says to no one's surprise.

"No." His father takes on his Kingly tone.

"Why not?" Sylas demands, eyes darkening to storms.

His mother moves to his side, resting a hand on his shoulder. "Because you'd take off on your own if you discover even a trace of her. I know you're worried; we all are, but we need to go about this methodically."

Sylas' shoulders slouch. He doesn't object. I volunteer to be in the search party. It feels like my fault that they were able to leave so easily.

It turns into a long day with nothing to show. The clouds in the sky grow darker, the scent of rain on the horizon. It's after dark when I return to the manor. There's nothing to report, so I head straight to my room. I know the wait, the anticipation must be killing Sylas, but I don't have the heart to be the one to disappoint him twice in a day.

Groaning in frustration, ready for a hot shower, I fling the bag onto the bed, only for it to slide off the edge to the floor. I drop to my knees, quickly pulling it to me, checking the contents. All the glass bottles are safe and intact. It's the first time I've actually looked at the antidotes. They're clearly labeled with paper glued to the bottle where she hand wrote the names. There's a small amount of liquid in each compared to the size of the vial, maybe a quarter of the way filled. Scoffing at my reaction, I carefully hang the bag on the chair instead. I can't believe how this one woman suddenly has all of us wrapped around her finger.

      Sylas squints at me with bags under his eyes early in the morning. I shake my head and his gaze drops. I walk him to breakfast, slipping into the kitchen to grab myself a little bite before I'm out the door and in the sky again.

      Picking up where I left off, I drop to the ground, landing in mud. It rained straight through the night, only ceasing a short time before we set out. I curse our luck. The rain would have helped before the girls took off. Now it may have helped to cover their tracks. They're so subtle as is that there's no way we'd be able to see them from above. We have two parties in the search; those in the sky and those on the ground. The ones flying are more like lookouts.

      I move slowly through the brush, making note of where I've stepped and what I've touched to not get it confused. A broken branch nearly hides a half footprint. A flicker of hope sparks, but I can't find anything after.

      Another day is gone, and I return frustrated, exhausted and starving, and yet I don't have much of an appetite. Sylas is waiting for me. I bow my head, moving past before he has a chance to ask. I can't stand seeing the let down in his eyes.

      The next day is no different, and neither is the one after that. Sylas is going mad inside the mansion. He has guards on him, not for his own protection, but to keep him from going off on his own. I've never heard him fight with his dad like I have these recent days. Philip's been missing with a few of his men the past couple days.

We know it takes approximately three days to walk from Gateswood to the mansion, but his missing cousin doesn't help Sylas' anxiety.

Then, on the fifth evening, I hear someone calling my name. Philip flies overhead, a bit frantic searching for me. Releasing my large golden brown wings, I shoot into the sky. Philip flinches, not seeing me coming. The men that have also been missing are with him. They look exhausted, like they've been flying for a while.

"What? Did something happen? Did you find something?" I don't really have hope for the latter, doing a headcount to make sure they are all truly there. Philip's hair is a mess, coated in dirt, and the smell coming off him is pungent, but they all appear unharmed.

A big grin grows on his face, stoking embers of hope. "Yes. She left us a trail."

I blink, throwing my arms out wide. "Where?" I don't mean to snap.

Philip points directly south. "It's over a half of a day flight, but we came across trees that have clearly been chopped at with a sword. We followed it until we came to a structure surrounded by a large wall. We didn't get too close, not wanting the Vampires to spot us."

I stare at him, mouth hanging open, ears ringing. He found it. I can't believe he actually found it. I swear we've had men look in that direction before, but it doesn't matter. Philip has found it.

"Let's get back. We need to tell Sylas and prepare everyone to leave." The words are barely out of his mouth before I'm flying back, wings beating hard, propelling me forward. I leave the others behind.

It's the middle of dinner when I stumble through the foyer doors, finding my footing. My wings return to the tattoo on my back as I all but sprint to the dining room. The men standing watch look at me like I'm crazy. I feel like we're all going crazy. It's fine.

I ignore them, pushing the door open. Sylas picks at his meal. It takes him a moment to turn and look at me. His eyes grow wide. Calm and collected is just not going to happen. I grin wildly.

"Philip found it. He found Gateswood."

Chapter Twenty-Nine
Bluebonnet

This flower symbolizes resilience, sacrifice, hope, renewal and bravery. All parts are poisonous and can cause nervous system issues.

Sylas

Kai is my best friend; I am always happy to see him. But I've never been so grateful for his sudden presence as I am when he interrupts dinner. My chest hurts too much to flutter with hope, until I hear the words.

"Philip found it. He found Gateswood."

The rest of dinner is excruciating. Mom forces me to sit back down and finish my food instead of running off to make a plan right away. She says I'm going to need my strength, but I still don't like sitting still now that there's something to be done. Philip returns as I'm scarfing down the last bit on my plate. Dad requests plates to be made for him and Kai to be sent to the war room. The men with Philip are ordered to eat and relax after the long flight.

We stand around the table, map splayed over it with little markers of where we've previously looked decorating it. Philip, eyes heavy, is more than happy to point where he found the chopped up trees that led to Gateswood. It's right near a marker. It doesn't make sense how it could have been missed. Philip insists that's where it's at.

I don't want to wait another day or night to go after Zily, fearing what she may be facing on her own right now. I promised her that I wouldn't let him hurt her. The thought of what kind of punishment he'd give her for actively going against him makes me sick. It's late, though and we need to gather the men, decide on a formation and strategize how we're going to attack.

Mom sends Philip and Kai away, telling them to get some rest. She hugs them both, thanking them for all their hard work. She walks over to me, making me think she's going to send me to bed as well. Instead, she rests a hand on my shoulder.

"Let's take a seat."

We formulate a plan, going over it for hours, late into the night. There are factors we don't know about. Too many. We don't have time to scout and collect information. We do the best with the knowledge that we have.

There's a few unknowns that scare me the most. First, what is that Colin Eyler man doing to Zily? We have not talked about them, but I've seen the scars littering her body like silver stripes. Second, what power does he have that prevents her from even talking about him and the place he runs?

I get little rest, though I try to force myself to sleep. The bed feels cold and empty without her by my side. Hugging the pillow is a poor substitute.

When dawn breaks, I dress quickly. I don't have much of an appetite, but mother once again forces me to eat something. Philip looks anxious to move as well, but he doesn't object to the food. As the plates are being hauled off, dad tells me to get my gear.

It's been some time since I've donned my armor. The rack it's on is toward the back of my closet. The aketon is stiff, though the hauberk covers it with ease. The surcoat is a deep blue, my family's main color, with a small triangular cut in the front and the back. Bracers cover my forearms and grieves protect my shins. I strap my sword belt around my waist, before making sure my hair is secure in a ponytail.

Noise comes from outside drifting in through the window of my balcony. I walk out seeing my father's, no, my men, lined up, wings out ready to fly. My heart swells seeing how quickly they formed, knowing my dad commanded them. Soon it'll be my job.

My black wings spread out as I hop on to the railing, letting gravity tip me over. Air catches in my wings, gliding me down to where Philip, Kai, and my parents wait. Mom is hanging on dad's arm whispering to him. Kai and Philip are suited up like I am, Philip in borrowed armor as he did not come here to fight. Kai looks a little funny with Zily's small bag draped over his shoulder, across his chest, standing out against the silver chain mail. His sword belt is wrapped around his waist, holding the straps of the bag down.

I'm informed that each of the lieutenants, including Kai and Philip, have the experimental earpieces with small cahmo crystals in them. Kai hands me mine, pointing at his ear to show me how it goes on. It loops around the back of the ear, curving down to a cushioned piece that goes in the ear. Kai taps it once, a tiny blue light glows. He taps it again and a second blue glow appears, turning on the talking piece. With a double tap, he turns it off. Got it. I hope these work.

My parents are in the same attire as they wore to breakfast. Sorrow and worry fill my mother's blue eyes, like a cloudy sky preparing to rain. Dad's face remains neutral, but I can tell he's hiding his own anxiety. In a few short months, commanding men, making decisions won't be his duty; it'll be mine. This is my first task. After all, Zily is mine. I should be the one to save her. Just like I know she's done for me.

Hovering in the air above the awaiting soldiers, I project my voice. "You should all know by now about Zily, the Kitsune girl that's made herself at home here, and if you don't already know, I'm telling you now that this girl means the world to me. Right now, she's in danger. *Her* people are in trouble." I pause, sucking in a deep breath as I gage the reaction of the men. There is none. They continue to stare at me with unchanging determined expression, ready to fly into battle.

"We don't know what we'll be flying into. There are many unknown factors. The facility is surrounded by a large wall. That won't be able to keep us out. Delta and Echo squad, I want you to come around the back. Bravo and Charlie will flank from the sides. Alpha, we'll be going in from the front. The enemy will be using the Kitsune against us. You are to do as little harm to them as possible while keeping your own lives as a priority. There is a man, a Vampire by the name of Colin Eyler who is the leader of this organization. He is to be taken out and Zily is to be retrieved."

With a uniformed stomp of the feet, the soldiers fists slam to their chest. With a nod, Philip and Kai join my side and we fly out, leading the way. Philip flies slightly at the head as he's the one who knows where we are going. We're bringing the King's Guard, my personal men and Philip's with us. It's a small army. I may not know what we're flying into, but I doubt they'd expect this kind of force at their doorstep.

If I could, I'd make us fly through the night and following day to get there faster. We rest in the forest, scattered by the trees. We don't make any particular sort of camp, finding patches of grass to lay on or sleeping against trees. The ground has dried from the rain earlier in the week. The grass is thicker thanks to it. I forgot how uncomfortable it is to sleep in armor. It's not like I was going to sleep well anyways. I take whatever kind of rest I can get.

The men don't complain when I push them to move a little faster the next day. The late spring sun beats against my back. When our wings tire, we march on the ground. We have to be on the ground to find the spot where branches of trees are roughly cut and scattered. Seeing it for myself, I can picture her chopping at the branches and the brush, creating a clear path, reaching as high as she can with her sword to cut down branches. She's expecting us and it's taken us days to come for her. *Hang on. I'm almost there.*

Once the wall is in sight, the sun is starting to set. I'm drenched in sweat, and nobody smells particularly great. It doesn't matter. We do a quick test of the ear devices, making sure each can hear me. Then the squads part to their designated positions. I itch to move, but I need to wait.

Word comes that everyone is in position. It's pitch black out now in the dead of night, the stars above reminding me of Zily's eyes. Soon. Soon I'll gaze into them again. There's dim light coming from inside the walls, most likely from a few light posts.

I give the order and as one, we fly over the wall.

We don't have the element of surprise as I had hoped. Vampires are scattered around the open dirt field inside the wall wielding swords, fifteen or twenty of them. There's a tan building that seems too small to house all of them and the hundred Kitsune fighting with them.

I drop down, drawing my sword and engaging in combat with the first Vampire I come across. Blades clashing in shrill clinks and battle cries echo all around in a sudden burst as the two sides collide. The Vampires are trained with a sword. Most of the Kitsunes are easy to brush off with their lack of skill in battles.

My blade clangs against the sword of the Vampire. He presses hard, having more strength than I. I direct his sword down, blades scraping against each other. Twirling my wrist, I bring my sword around in a circle, destabilizing his stance. I try to take the opening, but the Vampire is too damn fast. He recenters himself, swinging at me once more. I jump back, my wings flapping to push me back further.

His dark eyes narrow on me. He closes the distance in a second. Bringing my sword upward, I block his attack. I have to concentrate, anticipate his next move to keep up with him. He jabs the blade forward, I spin out of the way, feeling it grazes my feathers. In my rotation, I get closer, sling my sword at his neck. He starts to move, but it's too late to save his life, though it keeps his head from coming clean off. Blood drips off my blade as I turn to my next opponent, shoving the attacking Kitsune away.

It takes me a while to notice as I'm searching for snow white hair in a sea of browns, blacks, and golds, but there's a murkiness to the Kitsunes' eyes. A fog clouding them, and all their expressions are the same. They don't show any reaction to being shoved or even cut.

Kai's back presses against mine. "Have you found her?"

"Not yet." I growl, shoving another Kitsune off of me. They tumble backwards, rolling. I don't want to hurt them, but they certainly make it difficult not to.

"I hate to say this, but it doesn't look good. We're outnumbered, massively and the Kitsune's just keep coming." He grunts, the sound of metal hitting metal coming from behind me as his presence leaves mine for a second.

"I know." I touch the head piece. "Something is off about the Kitsunes. Focus on the Vampires." I order, turning the mic part of the communication device back off.

"Sylas." Kai's voice is low, disturbed.

I spin, glancing at him then following his gaze. Across the battlefield, I catch glimpses of white. She comes more into focus, getting closer and closer, walking beside a tall man with slicked back blond hair, brown eyes tinted red and a malicious grin on his face. A hand is placed on her back, guiding her seemingly gently.

Her hair is a knotted mess with blotches of rust from dried blood in it. Her clothes are tattered, torn and stained. A simple pair of shorts like the ones she wore when I found her and a black shirt that is obviously too big for her. No bandages hide the fresh and days old wounds covering her body. Cuts, burns and purple bruises mar her pale skin. She's holding her short sword, finely crafted and decorated by her friends in her hand, the tip pointed at the ground. The night sky full of stars I long to see in her eyes are clouded over with the same milky film as all the other Kitsunes.

I grit my teeth, trying to keep it together. My blood boils beneath my skin, flowing fast and hot, shaking my body. It burns like the sun, and I am ready to scorch this man for what he's done.

The man stops, Zily by his side, a couple meters in front of me and Kai. The battle ensues around us, seeming to forget about us and them.

"Look here, Snow, I told you your prince would come." His eyes glisten wickedly. I bare my teeth, scowling at him. She hates that name. "Hello, Prince Sylas Ambrose Caraway. So kind of you to come to my humble home. Are you enjoying the party?"

A Kitsune is flung through the air between us, a small gasp escaping upon impact. Their chest rises and falls with harsh breath, but they lay unmoving, unconscious.

"What have you done to them?" I growl.

"Oh? Do you want her back?" He looks down at her. He has the gall to brush hair from her face.

My body moves on reflex. I'm going to cut that hand off of him, so it won't be able to touch Zily ever again. He will never hurt her again. I swing my sword, finding another blade in the way. Zily has stepped in front, blocking Eyler from me, protecting him. Her expression, her eyes don't show any recognition when they look at me. My chest clenches, stepping back.

"It seems she doesn't want to return to you." His smirk is like a snake's.

I attack again, seeking to get around her. She's swift on her feet, not as fast as the Vampire from earlier, but she stays between us. Though our blades clash, I can't use my full strength on her. She shoves my sword to the side, moving in for her own attack. I dodge, the tip of her sword tearing a hole in my surcoat.

Kai groans in frustration, having moved around in an attempt to flank with me. Callie's there, a dagger in hand, though she isn't actually using it. With her arms outstretched, she's basically a meat shield for Eyler. She looks almost as bad as Zily does only with more bruises and less lacerations. She won't let Kai get close.

He knocks the dagger from her hand, picking her up and throwing her over his shoulder, deciding to remove her from the scene completely. Before he could attempt another attack one handed, more Kitsune swarm him. His wings take him to the sky, Callie still over his shoulder as he moves to a less crowded area.

I try to pull a similar tactic, reaching for Zily's hand when her blade is coming toward me. She yanks her arm away, jumping back on her toes. Without hesitation, she lunges for me again. I block her.

"Come on, Zily. Come back to me, sweetheart." I whisper when our swords are pressed against each other. "Fight it. I know you can. Come on, sweetheart." I search through the fog for any sign that my words have reached her.

She pulls back and swings again, her stance of one that Kai has shown her. This is not the time to be impressed by how much she's learned in a short time. This fight is beginning to feel hopeless. I can't do anything with her in front of me. I told her once that I couldn't fight her.

So, I stop.

The sharp bite of metal piercing through my armor into my abdomen comes with the clatter of my sword hitting the ground. Her midnight eyes grow wide, staring up at me. The clouds are fading from them. A smile forms easily on my lips, my hand reaching up to caress her face, my thumb wiping away tears rolling down her cheeks. I can't help myself. Leaning down, I brush my lips against hers, tender and light.

"Welcome back," I breathe the words out, unsure if they form properly.

Her eyebrows shoot up, becoming aware of herself again, eyes clearer than ever. Her grip loosens on the sword. I cover her hand with mine, making her squeeze the handle as I take a step back, the blade slipping from my body. The taste of copper fills my mouth.

"Sylas!" My cousin's voice comes from behind, his feet thudding against the hard ground behind me. My foot shuffles back a half a step before my legs give out. "Sylas. Sylas, hang in there!" Philip begs, his arms around me, lowering my body to the ground. My eyes feel heavy, but I don't want to take my gaze off Zily. I want her pretty face, eyes of night, to be the last thing I see. It's a shame there's no stars tonight.

Chapter Thirty
Poppy

These pretty flowers represent remembrance, sacrifice, and death. The seeds have been used for pain relief, but too much of it can be deadly.

Kai

"No!" I scream in horror dropping down beside Philip. He's kneeling on the ground with Sylas in his arms. He's pale, looking like he's going to be sick as blood soaks his arms, hands and lap.

Zily stands not too far off, staring wide eyed, short sword in hand, Sylas's blood dripping off the tip. Her head snaps up at the sound of Colin Eyler's vicious laugh. Our eyes meet. They're not like they were moments ago. Her eyes are a dark storm I would not cross. A swirl of emotion swim in them.

Eyler calls her back to him. Zily's lips press into a tight line, the grip on her sword tightening. She turns back to him in a quick fluid motion, her head tilted down, making me doubt he can see the deadly expression on her face. I take a step after her, ready to back her up. One of our men fights a Kitsune through the space between. I throw a few that get too close to Philip and Sylas.

"What a fantastic job you've done!" Eyler praises, laughing more. "I suppose you can still be of use." He reaches up to pat her head.

Zily's ears flick back, ducking under to avoid his touch. She plants her feet apart, both hands on the handle of her sword. She swings with incredible speed. The Vampire appears startled, taking a step back, raising his arm to block the attack. It slices across his bicep, the full length of the blade cutting through muscle. She moves back, adjusting her stance to defend. A little sense of pride bubbles up, seeing her use what I've managed to teach her so far.

"You wanted his blood, now you have it," she growls.

Eyler fills the distance in a blink. He back hands her, sending her sprawling on the hard ground. Scowling, he clutches his arm. "Foolish girl."

His hand slides into his pocket. Suddenly, Zily shrieks in pain, as is a few other Kitsune around us. Her fingers claw at her head, body writhing on the ground. I have to hope the Kitsune are distracted enough by whatever is happening and trust that Philip can protect Sylas in his state.

I lunge forward, flapping my wings once to lift me over a set of wailing Kitsune. Eyler jerks back, avoiding my slash down. Pressing, I reverse the trajectory, cutting upward. He pulls his hand from his pocket. Something falls out. He draws a small dagger, using it to block my next attack. It doesn't help. I knock it from his hands. As I shove my blade forward, going for the finishing blow, I feel a little guilty that I'm the one doing it when it should have been Zily or Sylas.

Sacrificing his hand, Eyler manages to get out of the way. He backs up, submerging himself in the battle around us. It's getting more difficult to focus on him and not the Kitsune throwing themselves at me. Another Vampire steps in between us, a sword in hand.

With the clash of blades, the familiar sound of metal clinking against metal, I lose track of Eyler. I curse at the man in front of me. He smirks, swinging his sword down at my shoulder. I take the moment to lop off his head. The blade hits my shoulder piece, though there is no weight behind it.

"Kai!" Philip's voice brings me back to them.

A couple of guards are surrounding them, fending off the crazed Kitsune. I'm getting tired of this. My foot kicks a hand held device. The thing that fell out of Eyler's pocket. Plucking it up, I press the only button on it, messing with the dial. The shrieking around me stops. The fighting around me stops. Kitsune stand perfectly still, breathing heavily, confusion in their eyes. A few drop to their knees, sobbing. Our men don't know what to make of this.

I rush to Zily's side, dropping down beside her. She lays on her back, chest rising and falling as she struggles to catch her breath. Her eyes have a different kind of glaze to them, eyelids fluttering. Carefully, I slide my arms under her. She tries to sit up, despite being unable to keep her eyes open.

"Hey. Hey, now. It's ok. I've got you. You let your stance slip, but you didn't do terrible for how little training you've done. We'll get back to your training soon, so you have to hang in there." Sylas should be the one holding her. My gaze drifts to him. Philip and another are getting Sylas' armor off to tend to the wound.

"Sylas." Zily's voice is but a weak whisper.

"He… He's alright. Philip is seeing to him." He has to be alright. There's no way I can believe he won't recover from this.

Her hand slowly slinks across her body. She reaches up, fingers curling around the strap of her bag that I've faithfully kept on me this whole time because she asked me to take care of it. The damn girl should never question the kind of impact she's made on all of us.

She pulls on the strap with a force I didn't expect from her in this state. "Oleander."

My body stiffens, recognizing the name instantly. It's a pretty pink flower where every part of it is toxic. Is she saying it's in Sylas' system? How? Her sword? I set her back on the ground, pulling the bag around to the front. She whimpers softly, curling into a tight ball. Bottles clink together as I lift them enough to read her handwriting, then putting them back until I've found the correct one.

Wishing I could do this on my own, I put my hand on her shoulder, needing directions. She squints at me. "How much do I give him?" My voice comes out calmer than I feel. My mind is trying to calculate how much time has passed since she stabbed him.

"All of it. Now." Her words come out with heavy breaths. "Put some… wound directly… with water. Have water?"

I stroke her head. "Yes. I'll take care of it. It's going to be okay."

She doesn't say anything more. Labored breaths pass through her lips, her arms wrapped around her legs. She's out. It's now up to me.

Standing, I order a man to bring me water. I drop back to my knees beside Philip holding Sylas' head up. He doesn't ask when I unscrew the bottle and start pouring the thick liquid into Sylas' mouth. He jerks in his unconsciousness, making both Philip and I jolt. He swallows, making a face. It's probably bitter as most medicine is.

A bottle of water is handed to me. I splash some on the wound before dribbling the rest of the antidote into the wound. Philip wrinkles his nose when I start to rub it in, using water to thin it and press it into the wound. Together with the soldier that brought the water, we wrap the wound up, laying Sylas on the ground to rest.

I stand stretching, muscles aching from being tensed up in a kneeling position for so long. I take a peek at the chaos around us that I've been ignoring. All fighting has ceased. The soldiers are rounding up the Kitsune. Most of them look drained, in a state of shock. A few are crying. Across the dirt field, I spot some soldiers standing guard over some Vampires tied up. I need to deal with that.

"What was all that about?" Philip gets up with me. He looks like a mess, covered in blood that's not his own. I hope none of it is his, though the thought that all of it could be Sylas' blood makes me nauseous.

"Zily's sword had poison on it." I stare down at Sylas like he'll start convulsing. He doesn't, making me believe we got the antidote into his system in time.

Philip stares in horror. "He's going to be alright now, right?"

"Zily insisted on carrying antidotes around." I pick up the bag, slinging it over my shoulder again. Philip rakes his hand through his hair. "Keep an eye on them. I'm going to see how the rest of our men are doing and figure out what to do next." Before I turn away, Philip slides his arms under Zily, bringing her closer to Sylas. She remains curled in a ball like she may still be hurting.

I walk past some soldiers out of their element. They're attempting to comfort a group of confused and scared Kitsune. The soldiers glance at me for help. I turn my head away, continuing on to the tied up Vampires. There's four of them. The soldiers keeping watch over them put a fist to their hearts in salute. I nod back, eyes narrowing on the Vampires. None of them are the one that hurt Zily and Sylas. Tsking, my gaze sweeps across the field, searching for that man.

One of the Vampires spits at me. I clutch my sword, resisting the urge to cut his head off right there. Turning my attention to him, I crouch down. "Where's Colin Eyler? What have you done to the Kitsune here?"

The one in front of me laughs hysterically. "Wouldn't you like to know?"

"He probably made it out in the chaos." The woman behind him responds. It's hard to tell if she's mocking me or if she's bitter.

"Sir Rehn." A soldier drops down from the sky. "We saw a man making a run for it in the forest." He points in the direction he flew from.

The Vampire in front of me cackles. I spread my wings, purposely sending a gush of air at the Vampires as I take to the sky. The soldier leads the way. Eyler is in fact attempting to run away. However, he's not running fast or straight. He's stumbling over himself, clutching at tree trunks as he moves, leaving a blood trail from his missing hand. We drop down behind him, swords drawn.

Eyler spins to face us. His eyes are wide, face pale. A hand clutches at his chest, ripping buttons off as if that would help him breathe. Taking a step toward him, his fingers dig into the tree trunk beside him, clawing the bark off. His lips move as if pleading for help, but words don't make it out. His eyes roll back as his body contorts, seizing. Doubling over, he throws up more than I thought possible. His body tenses, jerking back. His knees hit the ground, the rest of his body following. Dead.

A shiver runs through me. That could have been Sylas. My hand runs along the strap going across my chest. If I hadn't held on to it… No. Can't think of what ifs. Need to finish up here and get them both help. I'm pleased I'll be able to report to Zily that the poison did its job.

Back inside the walls, a squad emerges from the small building. They report there's a whole underground system. They came across a Vampire kept in a dungeon as well as a few other Kitsunes. Small children, scared and crying, clinging to one another. The Vampire woman doesn't look much better, eyes darting around. She flinches whenever someone gets too close.

The woman's eyes, a caramel brown, meet mine. She purses her lips together, failing to hide her fear. I do my best to appear approachable. It's not my strong suit. Sliding my hands into my pockets, I show her I don't mean her harm. There's bruises on her wrists.

"Hello." She speaks first, voice like a song bird.

I nod a greeting. "I'm Kai Rehn. For the time being, I'm in charge. Could you tell me about this place?" I need more information, but I don't even know what questions to ask.

She blinks slowly, glancing at our surroundings. Her eyes soften on the youngest group of Kitsunes, around six to eight years old. "They haven't been touched yet." I follow her gaze. "They don't undergo surgery until they're going through puberty."

"What surgery?" Small bumps rise on my skin, getting an eerie feeling from the comment.

She raises a hand to the back of her neck. "There's a chip implanted here, connected to the nerves leading to the brain. Sir Col…" She clears her throat. "Eyler made me put it in, so he could control them." Her gaze travels over the unconscious bodies, and the frightened Kitsune scattered in huddles.

My eyes flicker to Zily. It explains so much. I didn't know that kind of technology existed. A scary prospect. "Can you remove the chip?"

The woman blinks slowly. "I've never tried."

"Could you try?"

Her head slowly bobs up and down. Turning back towards the small building, she peers at me over her shoulder. "I'll show you my lab."

I grab two soldiers to come with. She leads the way down several flights of stairs. The men weren't kidding when they reported a maze-like underground system. The halls are lit by many dim lights. All the walls are a mustard color. It's difficult to keep track of where we're going.

The woman opens a door that's not too different than Dr. Burgess' infirmary, only a lot smaller. There's a desk built against the wall with cupboards surrounding it, a chair tucked under the desk. A table is in the middle of the room, covered in white linens. A second chair is pushed up against the wall.

I send one of the men to bring a Kitsune down to be the first to have the chip removed. I'm not about to let Zily be the first she experiments on lest it goes wrong. Sylas would have my head if something happened to her after all this. He carries down an unconscious girl with dark brown hair.

As soon as the woman takes a small scalpel to the back of the neck, I leave. The others stay to guard her. She may have been found in a cell and volunteered to help, but it doesn't mean we can trust her.

I check back with Philip. He's dabbing a cool cloth to Zily's forehead. She's relaxed a little, no longer curled in a tight ball, though her legs are still bent and her arms are tucked in close. Sylas remains unconscious beside him, though he doesn't appear disturbed by his wound or the poison that accompanied it. That's a relief. I rake my hand through my hair.

We're going to be here for at least a day, if not a few. I need to create some semblance of order. Soldiers need to rest, and we have to figure out food. Everyone is going to be hungry after a fight like that. Then there's the blood and dead bodies mixed in to deal with as well.

A bonfire is built in the middle of the enclosure. The children scream and run around it, playing. It's an oddly comforting site after the events of the night. A couple of Sylas' personal guards are chasing them, laughing. It's a nice picture after spilling blood.

I help with removing the dead from the enclosure. No one wants to stare at dead bodies. We don't want them around when the sun rises and the heat of the day sets in either. Dirt is stirred up to cover the majority of the blood splatter.

The woman, Vilma, sends for me a couple hours later. She has successfully removed the chip. She wants to wait until the girl wakes up to check for side effects before continuing with others.

"I need to know as soon as possible when you're able to proceed." I slide my hands into my pockets, hiding balled up fists. How long this is going to take is frustrating, but there's a few that'll be at the top of the list to have the procedure done. "Do you think it's possible for other doctors to be able to remove the chip without leaving permanent damage?"

She cocks her head, contemplating. "A skilled doctor might be able to, but I wouldn't trust simply anyone."

There's only one doctor I know of that's skilled enough. With the amount of Kitsune's here, it's going to be a painstakingly long process. Where are they all going to go anyways? We certainly can't house all of them. Would they be alright if we said "you're free to go and do as you like" and then left? Should we send them to the Viararia Kingdom? These are Sylas questions.

Light creeps over the wall from the rising sun when I finally settle down beside Philip. I give him a quick briefing of everything I've learned, including Eyler's death and the chips. It concerns me that neither have woken up yet. Just as I'm laying down, using an arm as a pillow, Sylas stirs. Of course, the first thing he says is Zily's name.

"She's right next to you." I wave my hand, struggling to keep my eyes open. Philip gives me a concerned look. He'll take over for me.

I'm glad my friend is awake. I didn't worry too much seeing how his body didn't seize like Eyler's had, Zily's instructions working. She wouldn't let him die if she could help it. I can't wait to tell her that she killed Eyler. Now that Sylas' awake, I don't have to worry about her either. There's too much to think about; so much to do. I need to conserve energy and get some rest while I can.

Chapter Thirty-One
Nasturtium

This flower is associated with conquest, victory and patriotism. It has been used to add color to salads. Some would consume it for antibiotics.

Sylas

Philip's hands are on my shoulder, pushing me down when I attempt to sit up right away. I heard Kai's voice somewhere to the left of me, saying Zily's right next to me, but her not responding herself sends a bit of panic through my veins. Sharp pain shoots through my body, radiating from the hole in my abdomen. I suck in a breath through clenched teeth, a hand flying to press against the wound. Giving up on forcing me back down, Philip's hand moves to my back, helping me up instead.

Zily is indeed next to me, lying unconscious, lips slightly parted as soft breaths pass through them. She's curled up. I reach for her, merely wanting to touch her, feel that she's here. Her skin is like a burning flame, my fingers brushing across her forehead, moving strands of hair out of her face.

"She hasn't shown signs of waking yet. I've been trying to break her fever." Philip lays a wet cloth across her forehead.

"What happened?" I lower back down onto my elbow, turning toward Zily, shifting slowly until I'm laying again, an arm draped around her waist. I bring my wings out, covering her like a blanket. Her features soften, looking more relaxed, bringing a smile to my lips.

"After you went down? She turned on the guy. She cut him, but only on the arm. Kai says that her blade was covered in poison, however, and he fell sometime later to it, trying to escape. She managed to warn us before passing out herself. Luckily, Kai's been carrying that bag around and we were able to administer the antidote." He sits back, leaning on his arms. He looks tired.

"Thank you." I whisper, kissing the side of her head.

"Kai also managed to find out how he was controlling all the Kitsunes. There's a chip implanted in the back of their necks. They're working on getting them removed."

I frown, watching Zily sleep. It explains so much, all she couldn't say and their eyes glazing over. The number of times I've seen her rub the back of her neck comes to mind. Philip gets to his feet, brushing his pants off.

"Since you are awake. I'm going to see how the procedure is going and take over for Kai." He walks off.

I really should get up myself, show everyone that I'm alright and figure out what to do next. Reluctantly and painfully, I sit up again, looking around. Slowly, I make it to my feet, swaying a little.

I don't stray far from Zily, keeping her unconscious body in sight at all times. The bright sun doesn't seem to disturb her. I hover

over the ground, trying not to disturb the ground too much when my wings flap. It's less strain on my wound to fly than it is to walk. Philip, shocked to see me up and moving around, offers to introduce me to the one removing the chips, another Vampire, a woman named Vilma. He, thankfully, brings me a shirt to wear as well.

Vilma comes out to meet me. She's a quiet girl, eyes absorbing everything around her. There's scars and bruises on her wrists from where she's been held captive. There's a sort of distance to her, the way she refuses to look at anyone, gazing off into the distance. The first Kitsune Kai had her do the surgery on has woken up and is doing well. There doesn't appear to be any short term side effects, though Vilma, of course, can't be sure of long term. She's already done a second.

I glance at Zily, wondering if it's really safe to let her proceed with her. Most of the Kitsunes are waking now. The injured are being tended to. We'll need to continue with the chip removal, and I don't particularly want to make Zily wait.

Striding back to her, I crouch down, sliding my arms under her. Soft groans escape as I pull her against me. I groan too, struggling to stand with the movement pulling on the wound. Philip looks at me annoyed, taking her from my arms with ease. Recomposing myself, subtly covering my wound, I turn back to Vilma.

"Could you do her next?"

Vilma's gaze drifts from where my hand presses against my abdomen to washing over Zily. Her lips press into a tight line, pity filling her eyes. She nods once, spinning on her heel to head inside.

It's my first time inside the small structure that turns out to be not so small. It goes underground, spreading out in a series of long halls and closed doors. The walls are a plain, light mustard color and every door is the same slate grey. I don't know how she remembers where she's going when everything looks the same no matter the turns we take or the floor we land on.

How did Zily get around here? Does one of these doors lead to her room? Is this all they knew? Zily told me once that most don't leave the compound.

Finally, Vilma opens up to a medical room. It looks like Dr. Burgess' infirmary, but smaller, simpler and plain. There's no color, only whites and greys. She motions with her hand to lay Zily on a flat, barely padded bed. There's a round hole at the end shaped for the head. She makes a twirling motion with her finger when Philip sets Zily down on her back.

Philip pulls a chair from the wall. I plop down, slouching in pain and panting. Blood is trickling from where Philip tried to bandage me up. Vilma stares at me, clean rubber gloves on. In a whirl wind around the room, she collects a couple supplies. Needle, silver spider thread and alcohol. She pauses before me.

As if contemplating what to do, she kneels before me. Without a word, she points at my injury. I glance at Zily, then back to Vilma. Her steady eyes say she's not moving until this is done. Sighing, I slide to the edge, leaning back while lifting my shirt. The gauze there is completely soaked through. There's a stain on the new shirt Philip just gave me.

I flinch when she peels the gauze away. The alcohol stings as she cleans the area. My body jerks, sucking in air through gritted teeth with the first puncture of the needle piercing my flesh. I clutch the thin arm rests. She's skilled, quick with her work. When she's done, I slump back in the chair, beads of sweat rolling down the back of my neck. I almost think that hurt worse than being stabbed, though I was a bit distracted at the time.

Vilma changes gloves before getting to work on Zily. She gives her a shot directly into the side of her neck. She pins Zily's hair out of the way. I flinch when the sharp blade of the scalpel pierces and cuts into Zily's skin. A trickle of blood seeps down the side. Vilma wipes it quickly before it has a chance to touch the bed.

It takes a couple of hours of slow and gentle probing. Philip excuses himself early on, saying he needs to look after what's happening above, his face pale and looking sickly. The little blade meticulously strips away layers until the chip is exposed. It makes tiny slices at the muscles and nerves connecting it. When the chip is free, Vilma starts stitching the inner layers together, working her way back out. I don't watch the whole time, mostly staring at the prestige white floor.

Vilma taps my shoulder to get my attention. "I'm done," she says in a monotone voice.

I stand and she turns, watching me, waiting for me to take Zily off the table. It's difficult picking her up. I roll her off the bed into my arms, grunting in pain. Zily hums softly in her sleep, ears lying flat against her head. She nuzzles into my chest, settling in. It gives me hope she'll wake soon.

"Thank you. Are you alright if I send another? I'm sure they're all pretty eager to get those things out."

Vilma nods slowly, eyes on Zily. "Take care of her. She's a special girl."

I don't disagree, but my eyebrows scrunch. Vilma doesn't seem inclined to elaborate, turning her back and cleaning the tools in preparation of the next procedure. Guards follow me back to the surface. Tarren offers to carry Zily for me when I start panting. Sweat from both the heat of the day and pain rolls down my back, but I refuse to let her go. It feels too long since I've been able to hold her. I'm not ready to let go.

My legs are shaking when we finally reach the surface. Tarren and Malder are on either side of me, helping me up the last few steps, there to support me in case I collapse. If I could, I would keep her with me, but I need to set her down for both our benefits. I lay her in the same spot I woke up. Zily curls in a ball where I leave her beside Kai, the two sleeping back to back. Needing to keep things moving, I start my search for the next Kitsune to send to Vilma. Continuing being selfish, I hunt down Callie.

Callie sits against the wall, knees up to her chest, arms wrapped around them, tears streaking her face. Her tail is curled around to her lap. A man sits next to her, one leg stretched out, and an arm draped over the bent knee. He's talking, waving his hands, attempting to comfort her. He leans forward, peering at her face, the bottom of tight braids swaying. Callie wipes her eyes, sniffling.

"Hey," I say when I get close enough.

Callie blinks, quickly getting to her feet. She has similar markings as Zily covering her body, dried blood stains her clothes. Her eyes are wide, staring at me expectantly, nervous, clutching the bottom of her shirt. The man slowly rises too, pushing off his knee with his wrist, bringing my attention to his hands. They are various shades of red, black and purple of healing bruising. His fingers are mangled. They twitch, flexing. His gaze travels over me, assessing, judging.

"You must be Decan." The corner of my lips tug upward, finally meeting Zily's other friend, the one she came to save.

He raises an eyebrow. Callie takes an unsteady step forward. "Zily, is she…" She can't finish the question. Her whole body trembles.

"She's fine. Unconscious, but we're looking after her." Relief visibly washes over the two, shoulders relaxing. Callie sighs. "She just had the chip removed." Callie gasps, hands flying to her mouth. Decan's eyebrows raise together. "I thought you two would like to be next."

Tears swell in Callie's eyes. She slowly nods. I lead them back to the building, curving around to check on Zily and allowing them to see her as well. Kai shifts, waking up. I suppress a chuckle when he glances back in confusion, nearly rolling onto Zily. He rakes his hand through his hair, blinking against the sun.

I leave Callie and Decan with Vilma, telling them to find me when they're done. I'm hoping they'll be able to help organize the other Kitsune. Many are wary of us, and a few have had to be separated due to wanting to fight us still. I don't blame them. They're scared and confused.

Sitting down next to Zily, I watch the calm chaos around me, a hand pressed against my throbbing abdomen. Word is spreading about the chip removal. You could see when one is hearing it for the first time, the way joy lights up their face. I'll need to make an official announcement soon, create a listing and a schedule. Even if Dr. Burgess could also do the surgery, only six to eight can be done daily. Max. We don't want to exhaust the doctors either. Not knowing the exact number there are, it'll be at least two weeks to get through everyone.

My shirt shifts, a soft tug, catching my attention. I glance down, meeting starlit eyes and a faint, quiet smile. Returning it, I slide down beside her, giving a quick kiss to her forehead. The fever hasn't broke yet, but she's awake. That's progress.

"You okay?" She whispers, voice raspy. I need to fetch her some water, I note, and some food if she can handle it. Come to think of it, I haven't eaten either and it's already mid-afternoon.

"I'm not the one with a fever." I pet her head, ears smoothing back with the touch. She closes her eyes momentarily, quietly sighing.

"Kai followed instructions." I don't know if it's possible for her voice to become any softer.

"That he did. Thanks to you, he saved my life."

"He wouldn't have had to if it wasn't for me."

"I told you I couldn't fight you." She sighs again, exasperated with me. I can't stop the grin forming on my lips. "Let me get you some water. Are you hungry? Could you stomach some food?"

Zily curls up on her side again, shaking her head. I stroke her ears back once more before getting up. Putting a hand on my wound, I hide my discomfort of the motion. Asking around, I'm able to get a couple water bottles and a bowl of soup brought out. I'll see if she wants a few bites, but I'll eat it if she doesn't.

She gulps down the water, taking three sips of the soup. With her head resting on my lap while I basically drink the soup, I tell her about what the current situation is. Her head turns, peering up at me when I tell her that the chips are in the process of being removed. Her eyebrows scrunch together, and she blinks several times.

"The one in me is already gone?"

"Yes. Kai asked the lady to do it on another while we were both still out. When the results of that came back positive, I took you down." She nuzzles my leg affectionately, making me chuckle. I set the empty bowl beside me. "Callie and Decan are down there now. After them, we'll create some sort of sign up list and schedule. We can't stay here; I'd like to head home tomorrow if at all possible. I don't know what we're going to do with all of them, but at least at home both Vilma and Dr. Burgess could work on extracting the chips."

"Home sounds wonderful," Zily mumbles. I think she's falling back to sleep. I adore hearing the word 'home' on her lips knowing it's the same as mine.

I leave her undisturbed as much as possible, wrapping a wing around her. Flagging down a soldier passing by, I ask him to leave with a message for my father, mostly about the number of Kitsune we'll be bringing back. He flies off right away.

Zily wakes a few hours later. Kai checks in. He tries not to show it, but I can see the relief written all over his face upon seeing her now sitting up, leaning against me. She's been quietly telling me what it was like for her, being in the fog of her mind, watching the world around her but unable to control her own body. My arm stays wrapped around her waist, comforting her when her voice cracks. Seeing as Zily's fever isn't going away, Kai runs down to find some medicine.

When Kai returns, Callie and Decan are right behind him. Decan's hands are all wrapped up, as well as his other wounds covered. Callie looks better as well, even has more color in her cheeks and her eyes are sparkling with joy. Zily sits up, holding out her arms. I shift away so her friends can embrace her. Callie takes one side, and Decan takes the other, smooshing her between them.

"Here, take a couple of these." Kai tosses a pill bottle on her lap, sounding like his usual gruff annoyed self, though his eyes betray his concern.

Standing, I offer to fetch the trio food. Zily makes a face like she still doesn't have an appetite. I'm led down a couple flights of stairs, down the never changing hall to a pair of double doors. The mess hall is filled. A line forms along the wall to get food. The soldier escorting me takes me to the front of the line. I over hear a few commenting about how food the food is; the best they've ever had. It's merely soup and bread.

The soldier carries the tray of food up for me. Moving my hand away from my wound, I take it from him once we're outside again. When I hand Zily the dish, she eats more than half. It doesn't seem like I'll be getting Zily back anytime soon, so I occupy myself with my duties.

I spread word that I want to leave tomorrow, giving tasks to collect supplies we can carry over the next several days. We can't simply fly home as much as I would love to. A few are given the task of collecting Kitsunes' names. I pay Vilma a visit. She's sitting in a chair, staring at the wall. She's apparently waiting for the next Kitsune to be sent down.

"Get some rest for now. We'll be leaving in the morning." I pause at the door. "Pack anything you would like to take as well. We'll have tools and supplies for you to use, but if there's something you would like from here, bring it."

I pause on my way out the door, gaze lingering on a couple books in the corner. They're the kind Zily loves to read. Glancing back at Vilma, who simply continues to stare at me, I wonder if she's the doctor Zily told me about. I leave her alone.

It's late when I finally return to Zily. Callie and Decan are asleep a short distance from her. I'm silently and selfishly grateful they didn't all sleep together. Zily sits with her knees pulled up, head resting on top of them, angled toward Philip lounging next to her.

"I'm glad you found my trail." I catch her saying to Philip. Her gaze drifts to me, stopping in front of her.

"You could have left a longer one," Philip says teasingly.

I take my place on Zily's other side. She instantly leans into me. Wrapping an arm around her waist, I plant a kiss to the back of her head. She sighs at Philip.

"Well, things didn't go as I had hoped." Her head turns to glance at her friends, ears drooping.

"You're okay now. Everything is okay now," I whisper. She nods along.

"Honestly, the only reason I started a trail there is because I discovered a barrier that I assumed had been detouring others from finding this place." She shifts, curling into my side more. Her dark eyes peer up to me. Tired. She wants to lay down.

"I think I know what you're talking about. I felt something when we passed by the broken branches leading the way." It only takes a look for Philip to understand. The conversation is coming to a close and we're going to sleep.

He stands, stretching. "I'm glad you're alright, Zily. I'm going to make a round and turn in for the night as well."

"Night, Philip," Zily says, turning to rest her head on my chest while I slowly lower to the ground. I don't let her see me wince.

"Sylas?" She tilts her head back to peer at me.

"Hmm?"

"I want to grab my things before we go. It's not much, but there's some stuff left in the drawer in the room Callie and I shared. And I want my backpack."

I press my hand to her forehead, stroking her hair back. I don't know if it's my wishful thinking, but she doesn't feel as hot as she had before. "Sure. Of course, sweetheart. You can show me the way in the morning, ok?"

Larisa Blackledge

Her head bobs, nuzzling my chest. Her breathing quickly settles into a deep, heavy rhythm. She mumbles, fingers curling, clutching my shirt. Holding her against me, I sigh, ready to sleep and ready to go home. My mind starts to drift to all that's to come. It's a mixture of stress and excitement. There's a lot to deal with in the immediate future, but there's plenty to come that'll bring joy and excitement. I can't wait to dance with Zily.

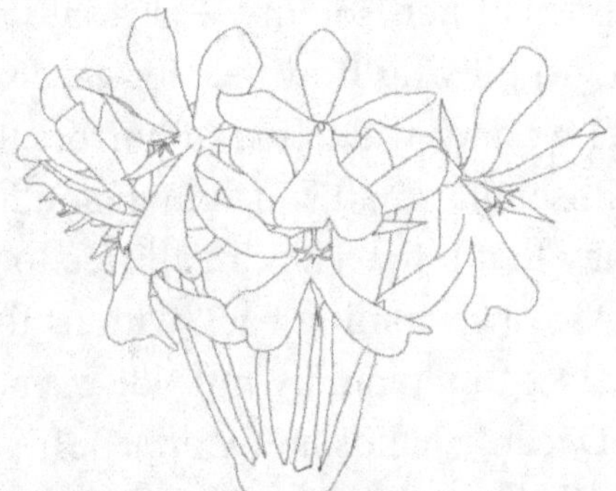

Chapter Thirty-Two
Ivy geraniums

In the language of flowers, these represent loyalty, companionship, and favor. It is also considered to symbolize a request for a dance or a proposal. The leaves can be eaten and have a tangy taste. The petals can be used to make a bluish textile dye.

Lily

Home is only another day's walk away. I'm exhausted. Everything hurts, though I don't want to worry Sylas. He has enough on his plate and he fusses over me so much already. I see the look in his eyes when he has to leave my side to deal with something or another. His hair is a frayed mess, pulled back into a ponytail. His eyes are sharp and voice thick, deep, commanding. I haven't seen him kinglier as I have these past few days commanding and organizing the mass of people we're seeking to lead home.

Our departure was delayed, half the Kitsunes opting to stay at Gateswood for now. Even though the Corvum saved them, there's distrust and wariness. Vilma decided to stay behind as well, removing the chips from the Kitsunes staying. She's an odd one. I have vague memories of her from my early days at Gateswood, when I was just a girl picking flowers. Her gaze seems more distant than I remember. I wonder what kind of horrors they put her through. Sylas will send a small squad in a month to check on them if any decide to stay that long. They're all free to go and do as they please, including the ones coming back with us for now.

Callie and Decan remain by my side even as Sylas, Kai and Philip rotate out. Decan's hands are wrapped. It's unknown what kind of permanent damage they have, but he's hopeful with the way he flexes his fingers. I tell him all about my adventure and finding my place in the Caraway mansion. I'm hoping it gets him to stop glaring at all of them. He stands between Callie and I, protective in stature. He scowls especially hard when Kai starts to poke fun at him which I know he only does because of the looks.

My fever has a slight presence even after all these days. The medicine has helped, but it's fighting against the exhaustion and wear of travel that makes it worse. I rake my fingers through my hair, getting stuck on clumps of dried blood and dirt. I cannot wait to bathe. Shower first, then a nice, long, hot, relaxing bath. I sigh in my daydream.

Philip drops down where he was scouting above. "Almost there." He encourages. "Only a few more hours."

I groan. "Do you want me to carry you for a while?" A sweet, deep voice asks behind me.

I wet my lips, glancing back. "No, I'm fine. I was just dreaming of a bath."

He chuckles, coming up on my other side. His hand finds mine, giving a squeeze, while his other arm is wrapped around him, pressing against his wound. Vilma had stitched him up, but I worry about him reopening it. Dr. Burgess should take a look when we get home. The salve he gave me should work wonders on his wound as well. I continue to daydream about home.

"You should see the baths, Decan. They are really something." Callie attempts to help me.

He side eyes her. I snort. "The one in our room is like a pond." Sylas rolls his eyes, a warm smile on his lips. I'm glad I get to see it.

"It's not like I'm not excited about getting cleaned. I just think you're being ridiculous." His gaze drifts past me to Sylas. He at least doesn't glare at him anymore. "And you're sure it's fine bringing back fifty plus Kitsunes?" It's the third time he's asked this. I can't blame him for being anxious. Maybe the reason he's between Callie and I is it's the place he feels safest.

"Yes. My parents are expecting all of us. Rooms are ready and waiting as well. Everyone will have to double or even triple up in a room. Except you two." Sylas seems unbothered answering the question again, dropping new information with it.

"Us?" Decan sounds shocked.

"I have a room already." Callie declares. Her eyes dart to Sylas for confirmation. He nods. The room she stayed in before is permanently hers.

"We had one picked out for you too, Decan." I beam up at him. "We'll all be in the same hall."

"Actually, I made some arrangements to get the room next to Callie's cleared out, so he won't be down the hall," Sylas says. I squeeze his hand lovingly.

Decan stares, speechless. He flexes his fingers, slowly crossing his arms. Staring at the ground, he seems lost in thought, so I proceed to tell him more about the mansion. I talk about dinners, and Zachary, and Leona. I wasn't able to introduce Callie to her before. Now I can introduce both my best friends to her. I go from fantasizing about baths to about Zachary's meals.

The smell of something delicious hits me long before I can see where it is coming from. It's a very sudden difference scent to the stale sweat I've been smelling for days now. Callie's tail swishes and Decan's ears twitch. I know they smell it too. There's a subtle surge moving the march faster. Nobody complains seeing as it's been the Kitsune holding everyone back.

Finally, we break through the trees to the field leading to the mansion. The grass is littered with chairs and tables. The farthest away and closest to the mansion, covered by a canopy, is a kitchen set up. Eleanor and Reuben are standing nearby, waiting for us. I swallow hard at the sight, gaging if my body has enough energy to sprint the rest of the distance.

Sylas lifts his hand high above in greeting to his parents. Then he lifts the one holding mine as far up as my hand will go. Eleanor puts a hand to her mouth. I'm too far to see it, but I know she's crying. Tears sting my own eyes. Reuben puts an arm around her.

I'm home.

The marching mass disperses, spreading out to find seats to collapse into. Kitsunes stay clustered together unsure of the new environment or what they should be doing. They do take seats, eager to be off their feet. The soldiers remain standing, scattered around until they are ordered to sit and enjoy the meal that's about to be served.

Sylas walks me to a table near the kitchen set up, intending to leave me there. Callie and Decan settle down, stretching out tired legs. Philip goes to make sure his own men are taken care of, the stubbornness showing when they don't sit. Kai drops into a chair opposite Decan. Decan glares. Kai smirks.

I don't sit even as Sylas pulls a chair out for me. I see a familiar looking stool behind a familiar figure. Sliding onto it, my feet are relieved to not have to hold my weight anymore. Bright hazel eyes glance back over broad shoulders, the blue straps of his apron tied around his neck.

He turns with his hands on his waist. "Welcome home, darling."

"Good to be back." I'm beyond happy to see him.

"You look as lovely as ever." He winks, moving to check a different pot. He sticks a thermometer into a chunk of meat.

I snort a laugh, touching my disgusting hair, and down my dirty, tattered clothes. "Thanks. What are you making?"

"Oh, just a whole welcome home feast." His grin widens. "There's roast, chicken, duck, soup. There's pasta boiling down there." He points where another chef is, checking the noodles. The chef glances over, giving a respectful nod toward me.

"Sounds wonderful. Smells amazing." I sigh, closing my eyes momentarily, letting my other senses take it in.

When I open them again, Zachary has a small plate held out to me with small slices of a couple different meats, some beans and corn on the cob. "First plate for my favorite girl. Don't tell Her Majesty."

I laugh again, a bubbly warmth filling my chest. I hop down, ignoring the protest of my feet, taking the plate to the seat Sylas had pulled out for me at the table of my friends. Jealous glances eye my food. Sylas touches my shoulder, simply for the contact before getting up. Waves of people make their way to line up for food. Sylas, Kai and Philip are the first due to who they are.

Leona surprises me, dropping by our table. She takes the chair beside Callie, golden brown eyes glittering with excitement, hair up in two messy buns. It's strange not seeing pencils sticking out of them. She startles Callie with her questions, asking about fabrics and dresses. It makes me giggle, remembering how nervous I was when we first met. This is nice. It's perfect.

Decan brings Callie a plate of food, though he doesn't look at her or the table as he sets it down. I turn in my chair to see where he's staring. Zachary turns back to the stove quickly, ears turning red. Decan's ears twitch at my snicker, gaze flickering to me briefly then back to the kitchen. He takes his seat, poking at the food. I can't keep the smirk off my face.

"What?" He finally asks, though he can't look me in the eye.

"Nothing." I take a bite, savoring the juicy meat. "He makes the best meals in all the kingdom."

His eyes lift, looking past me to the kitchen again. He fidgets in his seat, acting like he's not stealing glances at Zachary. I grin.

It's nice to be home surrounded by my friends, with my stomach full. The table is generally quiet as everyone enjoys the hot meal. It feels like forever since I had a nice hot meal. I had spent years without food like this, and yet it feels apart of normal life now. How my life has changed. A smile forms on my lips watching the clash of my old life, my best friends, with my new life, my new friends and my love.

Zachary sits down with us, next to Kai. It forces Decan to look towards Kai. Decan attempts simple conversations. Zachary is more than willing to oblige, grinning while he talks about cooking and food. I get Decan to talk about his blacksmithing. Different elements, but both passionate craftsmen.

Leona budges in, question Decan about fabrics he likes. His eyes grow wide, staring at her dumb struck. Zachary waves his hand, regaining his attention, explaining the textures of certain fabrics. I didn't know he knew clothes too. Leona bobs her head along, staring eagerly at Decan for his answer.

Sylas' hand remains on my back throughout the meal, rubbing from time to time. I love the constant contact. It keeps me grounded, reminding me that he's with me.

Eleanor and Reuben make their rounds, apologizing they didn't come see us first. Reuben has taken charge of the men, giving out orders and requesting reports to be made. I stand to greet them, excited to introduce Decan to them. Eleanor pulls me into a hug. A heavy, relieved sigh escapes in our embrace. It surprises me when Reuben swoops me up into a hug as well.

"Welcome home," he says in a gruff voice in my ears. My face flushes, tears welling in my eyes.

He stands to the side while Eleanor is talking to my friends. She's praising Leona's and Zachary's work while making strong suggestions for Decan and Callie as they'll be living here now. She mentions the rooms Sylas told them about. My friends look a bit overwhelmed.

"Thank you, your Highness." Callie trips over her words, trying to bow while still seated. There's a moment where it looks like she's going to get up.

Eleanor giggles sweetly. "You can simply call me Eleanor. Finish your meal; I won't bother you longer." She gives a little wave, turning to leave. Our gazes catch. She smiles warmly, and I lip a 'thank you' to her.

After the feast, we make our way inside. Finally, we have some privacy. Sylas helps to detangle my hair in the shower. He's extra gentle, washing blood and grime from my body. As his hands glide over scars, new and old, I think about how I'll be able to tell him about them. When I'm ready. We have time. Lying in bed feels like heaven. I sleep deep and long, waking up alone halfway through the next day.

Days begin to pass quickly. Philip returns home, promising to bring Mira, his love, to Sylas' coronation. Decan does a double take the first time he sees me in a gown. It takes a couple weeks before he gets used to eating supper with the King and Queen, though after some time he starts opting to have dinner with someone else, a certain hazel eyed chef.

Callie adores Leona's room. She loves being a model for Leona. Soon Leona starts teaching her how to create patterns and to sew. Callie is a natural at it. I have the honor to wear her first dress, and she's going to be making my dress for the coronation. Leona says it's great to have the help with all the outfits she needs to make and send out.

The Kitsune that came with us from Gateswood, slowly start to leave after having their chips removed. They're given a small map and a few supplies to take with them. Freedom is a strange concept of which many are excited to explore while others seem wary by the prospect. Word from Gateswood is that it's been cleared out too when Sylas' men returned from checking on the place after a month as promised.

The lessons Eleanor promised begin soon after I make a full recovery. My tutors tell me I'm the best student they've had with my eagerness to learn everything I can. I have a great memory as well. Learning to waltz takes longer. It soon becomes clear that it's an insecurity issue.

My confidence grows with every passing day. I attend more meetings with Sylas and sit on my little throne during the bi-weekly audience with my head held high. Eleanor jokes about having a tiara made. I turn it down instantly, my face heating. Sylas watches me all the while, a slight tilt to his head.

The coronation is fast approaching. The mansion is buzzing with energy. With it getting close to the date, Sylas is dragged around being asked a million questions about minute details. The panic in his eyes has me giggling. Squeezing his hand, I help him through picking out colors of napkins, tablecloths and centerpieces. That's my favorite. He lets me go on about what kinds of flowers should be in the middle and what vases, mirrors and rocks should be used to compliment them.

Two weeks before the ceremony, Sylas and I escape for a day. He has a meeting in the morning while I have dance practice. I go down to the kitchen, to ask Zachary if he can put our lunch into a basket for a picnic. It's no surprise that I find Decan in the kitchen as well. I sneak up on them, making Decan jump while Zachary simply greets me with a smile.

Sitting on my usual stool, I watch Zachary at work. He's teaching Decan as he goes. Decan helps with the same look in his eyes that I used to see when he worked with metal. His hands are completely scarred from what happened to them. Sometimes, they shake. I'm glad he found a new way to create. It may be because of a certain someone. Whatever makes him happy.

I recognize the basket they pack the lunch in, my tail wagging in anticipation. Tarren walks in, fetching lunch for two ladies that hardly leave a brightly colored room. It's a habit he developed soon after Callie started learning to sew. He's often busy with his own duties, but he always makes sure Callie has lunch. I give Zachary and Decan a kiss on the cheek when they hand the basket over. I wave bye to Tarren before skipping to meet Sylas in the foyer.

Jupiter is ready and waiting for us in the stables. Sylas lifts me onto his back, handing the basket of food up next. I lean into his warmth when he hops into the saddle. We follow the river to our secret little spot. I eye the water warily, but maybe I could actually learn to swim next year.

The spot is as beautiful as it was the first time, though it has changed with the seasons. Thick green grass cover where we lay out the blanket and set up the food. The flowers have changed and there aren't as many, but they're just as pretty. The varying shades of green have been replaced with a thinner layer of yellows and oranges above.

Sylas sits opposite me, leaning back on an arm, sleeves rolled up his toned muscles. One leg is outstretched, and the other is bent where his other arm drapes across it holding one of the fried macaroni and cheese balls from our lunch in hand. His hair is down, but it hasn't gotten to the messy stage from having his fingers run through it all day.

I sit on my ankles, cradling a mini quiche with both hands. My emerald green dress flares around me, covering my feet. I feel like a flower with the way the bottom hem is fanned out. A giggle escapes at the thought, tail lightly swishing.

We're able to relax, enjoying each other's company in silence. His stare has my cheeks heating. When we finish lunch, he pulls me to him, his back against the tree and my back against his chest. I sigh, sinking into him. He pets my head planting a kiss there.

"It's almost here. The guests will start arriving before we know it."

I angle my head to peer up at him. "Nervous?"

He chuckles, his hand finding his way to his hair. My fingers follow his, earning me a real laugh. "I was raised knowing this day would come, but it's still hard to believe it's time. Yes, I may be a little nervous, thinking about all those who depend on me and even more once this is over."

"You're a great king." I'll show him all the confidence I have in him. I've already seen it. It's a matter of fact.

Sylas eyebrows raise, surprised by my declaration. It's not every day I can make the man blush. I cherish when I do. Shifting, I stare out into the forest, listening to the trickle of water from the creek, the birds chirping overhead. Sylas gives me a gentle squeeze.

"Are you nervous?"

"Hmm?" I turn to look at him again. "Why would I be nervous?"

"Because all eyes will be on you too." He watches me carefully. I open and close my mouth several times, the realization of the truth behind the words washing over me.

"No, they won't." I deny it, thinking of any reason they won't be looking at me. I'll be beside Sylas for most of the celebration, though I'm suddenly wondering where I'll stand during the ceremony.

His laugh is rich, strong arms giving me a loving squeeze. "They most certainly will be watching you as much as they'll be watching me. You'll be by my side through it all after all."

"Where will I be during the ceremony?"

"By my side."

"I am not getting crowned with you." Eleanor mention of the tiara suddenly has me scared, but as we're having this conversation, thoughts I've neglected run wild in my head. Sylas is about to be King. What does that make me?

He rolls his eyes. "Fine. By my mom's side, then." He caresses my cheek, holding my gaze. "But I'll be reaching for you as soon as that crown is placed upon my head and once dad introduces me to the people as their new king, I would like to introduce you," My heart thunders in my chest, wanting to escape its cage. I fall into the sky of his eyes, the world around us fading away. "As my future wife." He breathes.

My hammering heart flutters on the last word. Butterflies beat their wings in the pit of my stomach. Warmth that not even the sun can cause envelops my body. Joy. Pure joy that a future I have never seen for myself shines brighter than ever. I get to stay with him, be with him, and love him for all my life. Knowing he wants the same, can see the same future has me smiling and fighting back tears.

"Okay," I whisper.

Sylas lips press against mine, capturing and sharing the smile. He holds me, forehead resting against mine while we simply stare into each other's eyes. I turn to face him, my knees on either side of his thighs. He reaches into his pocket, pulling out a small black box. I watch him curiously. He opens it in one hand with a single finger.

Beautiful silver twirls like vines into a circlet. Two diamond shaped like leaves spout out from the aster flower with a larger diamond as the center of the flower.

I gasp, unable to believe my eyes. "No."

"No?" He teases, quirking an eyebrow.

"I mean yes, but really? For me?"

He chuckles, a hand finding their way to the back of my neck, pulling me in for another kiss. "Yes, for you. Of course, for you. Can I see your hand?"

I hold it up. He slips the ring onto my finger, the diamond glistening in the light peeking through the leaves. Excitement bubbles up inside. I can't wait to tell all our friends.

Chapter Thirty-Three
Snow-in-Summer

This white as snow flower symbolizes purity, innocence and hope. It's
a small, ground covering plant, spreading like hope.

Lily

Sylas holds our clasped hands up to show his parents the
ring on my finger. Eleanor squeals, moving around the dining table
to hug me.

"It went well? Can I see the ring?" She lifts my hand up to
examine the ring closer.

"Did you know he was going to do this?" I note how
unsurprised she is.

"Of course we did." Reuben smirks. He surprises me by
joining us and wrapping me in a hug.

"But he wouldn't show me the ring beforehand," Eleanor
says. She's beaming, staring at her son lovingly.

Dinner proceeds with going over what the following week is
going to look like. We have an estimate of when each of the guests

will be arriving. We'll be expected to greet them. Leona will have a lineup of dresses for me to wear each of the days. I also need to pay her and Callie a visit for last minute adjustments on both my ceremony dress and my ball gown.

I pop in for the tailoring the next day, excited to show them my ring. Unsure how to bring it up, I wait until Callie catches sight of the sparkle on my finger. Her head snaps up, pinching the piece of fabric on my hip where my hand hangs. Blush coats my cheeks as I can't stop the smile growing on my face. Callie steps back, gasping loudly with her hand over her mouth. Leona comes around after fanning out the back of the dress. I hold up my hand so she can see what Callie is freaking out about. A shrill shriek nearly has me covering my ears. She dances around the room before grabbing Callie by the shoulders.

"Do you know what this means?"

"My best friend is going to be Queen?"

I sigh, having pushed that thought to the back of mind to deal with another day.

"That too, but we get to design a wedding dress!"

Callie's ears perk and her tail begins to swish back and forth. It makes me laugh, watching them jump around in a circle together. The knock on the door doesn't disturb them. Tarren pokes his head in, carrying a tray of food.

"What's all the excitement about?" His kind green eyes scan over all of us. "Sorry, Zily. I didn't know you were here." He sets the tray on Leona's desk.

"Quite alright. I'll be going to have lunch with Sylas soon."

"They're getting married!" Callie beams, spinning toward Tarren.

"Congratulations." He nods.

"Thanks." I look down, smiling sheepishly.

"We have to finish this before we can break. Don't to come back and try on the dresses for the week." Leona goes back to adjusting the back hem.

Giggling, I promise. They hold me in the room all day. My face burns as I retell the event of the previous evening.

Sylas' family are among the first to start coming in. Aunts and uncles, Dukes and Duchesses prim and prop. They don't look pleased to see me, glancing down at Sylas' and my joined hands. Sylas lips remain in a thin line, his eyes dark with challenging storm clouds. They don't outwardly say anything, not willing to defy the soon to be King.

His cousins all seem more laid back, like Philip. It's good to see Philip again, and to meet his fiancée, Mira. We click instantly, bonding over shared situations. The other cousins have fun teasing the two newly engaged family members. Sylas has a constant smile on his face, clear skies watching me.

Days leading up to the coronation, royals from other kingdoms arrive. I notice Stafaan isn't wearing his guards uniform. He's in a deep navy suit, hair smoothed back and a hand steady on Jasper's lower back. I smile at them. Jasper grins and Stafaan winks.

I'm nervous and excited to meet the King and Queen of the Viararia kingdom. We found out that most of us were kidnapped from that kingdom when we were just children. I'm eager to learn more about where I came from.

Lady Mariam Celyce is gorgeous. She strides in, head held high with ringlets of apple cinnamon hair framing her round face with the rest of her long hair pinned up like ribbon behind her head. Her eyes, so blue they're nearly black, like the deepest center of a lake, scan the foyer, taking in its beauty. She wears a brilliant cobalt blue gown, hugging her torso in a heart shaped top and sheer short sleeves, the bottom swaying like waves as she drifts towards us. Her tail, a slightly lighter shade than her hair, stays curled up in a pose of perfection.

His Highness, Sebastian Celyce, walks beside her with an air of authority. He reminds me of Reuben with his calculating eyes, as dark as night with glitters of gold. It's probably why I don't feel as intimidated by him as I normally would. He has short straight hair, combed back out of his face with ears slender into points on top of his head. It's white, like my own, making him the only other white haired Kitsune I've met. He wears a tailored suit matching his wife in a darker shade.

Mariam's gaze finds mine. She grabs Sebastian's sleeve, lightly tugging on it while staring up at him. The look of shock and panic on her face has my stomach in knots. Sebastian nods, putting a gentle hand over her hand, pulling it from his arm and lacing his fingers with hers. Mariam returns to staring at me.

I peek at Sylas for comfort, but his darting eyes, moving from King Sebastian to me, doesn't help the prickles of nerves in my chest.

Eleanor breaks the silence, stepping forward, arms outstretched. "Mari!"

Mariam's eyes snap to hers, a smile growing on her face. "Ellie! It's been so long!" The two embrace, grinning like children. "This is my husband, Sebastian"

He bows gracefully, hand over his chest. "How do you do?" There's a bit of mischief in his eyes.

"A pleasure. I trust you've been taking good care of my childhood friend." Eleanor curtsies. The look Sebastian gives Mariam is one of love and devotion. "This is my husband Reuben, and my son, Sylas." Eleanor introduces both in kind, each bowing as their name is said.

"And who?" Mariam asks softly, staring at me again. Blush begins to blossom on my cheeks.

"This is Sylas' fiancée, Zily."

I dip, one ankle behind the other, slightly lifting the skirt up. I've practiced a lot for this occasion, knowing I would be meeting many royals. The quick glance between Sebastian and Mariam doesn't go unnoticed. After introductions, they're swept inside with the other guests milling about.

I spend the following day, the day before the event, leading a tour for the ladies who haven't been here before. Mariam joins the group asking what feels like the most random questions throughout the day. Some made sense, like how did I meet Sylas? Many were curious and I spoke of those weeks like a fairytale, overall, being vague in my telling of things. I go from talking about being saved in the river, that I was sent to kill Sylas, to finding a home here. I've always been open about the assassination attempts. It gets me the wildest looks, but their eyes soften as I continue my story. I speak of Callie's visit and our failed attempt to save Decan. Sylas bringing the King's guard and the fighting that took place.

"I finally did stab him." I grin wickedly, earning lots of giggles and chortles.

"You've been through a lot," Mariam says, sorrow in her eyes.

I soften my expression, hoping she believes my words. "It hasn't been easy, but I don't think I would change a thing. If anything was different, even the smallest thing, I may not be here. I wouldn't be with Sylas." A few young girls' wistful sighs make me blush.

Mariam's tail swishes once, lips curving into a warm smile. "I'm glad you found happiness, Zily."

From there, her questions became more personal, asking if I know how to play an instrument. I'm learning to play the violin and a little bit of piano when Sylas and I have a spare moment. In the garden, it's what's my favorite flower, which also led me to telling her about my book. I've decided to call it my book of favorites. I've added pictures of all my friends to it and so many of Sylas. At lunch, it's about the kinds of food I like. That question is both hard and easy as I love so many foods, finding new foods to enjoy all the time. Randomly she asks about my favorite color and what else I like to do in my spare time. I joke with "what spare time?" Many laugh. I do tell her about reading and my love of the library.

Ever since guests started arriving, we've been having dinner in the great hall where a long table is filled with people from all over. Reuben sits at the head on one end while Sylas sits at the other end, both Eleanor and I sit to their right, respectfully.

Breakfast remains small and intimate. I like it, especially before a busy chaotic day. As we're finishing up, Eleanor goes over the schedule for the day. When we leave the dining room, we'll be whisked away to get ready. Leona and Callie will be helping me into my dress and doing my hair. I won't see Sylas again until he's making the long walk in the throne room surrounded by nobility and those with power. It's supposed to be a five hour ceremony which seems like a long time to me. Afterwards, we'll return to individual rooms to change again for the ball this evening while all the other guests arrive and are shown to the ballroom.

Leona helps me step into the sky blue dress, the fabric glistening in the light, the top hugging my curves, a thin layer draping over my shoulders. The back dips low with ribbon crisscrossing down. The bottom is loose and lifted over a not too bell-shaped hoop skirt. Shiny white, short heels are placed before me.

Callie combs out my hair, splitting it down the middle. She twists the pieces up into two low buns on the back of my head, adding my hair pins just above them. Soft, small brushes tickle my face as she adds a touch of make-up.

Standing before the mirror, I can feel the excitement seep into anxiety. It's been fun letting them dress me up, but soon I'm going to have hundreds of eyes on me, and when the ball starts, that number will grow to well over a thousand. I don't know if my little pounding heart can take it.

Kai comes to escort me to the throne room. Besides the line of guards, I'm the third one there. I stand beside Eleanor, a sheepish smile on my face. She gives a subtle nod, face warm and kind toward me. I try to copy her posture; shoulders back, head held high with false confidence, hands folded neatly in front. Her bronzy brown hair is braided and pinned in a circlet on the back of her head, her crown resting on top. She wears a long elegant, emerald green dress, slender all the way down.

Reuben stands off kilter from her, wearing an emerald embroidered tunic, cinched at the waist with a matching belt. His crown glistens on his head, his hands down by his side.

Eleanor leans in, whispering something. He nods with approval. She waves a hand at Tarren who brings her a black felt box. He gives me a wink, a broad grin on his face. With excitement growing on her face, she turns toward me, holding the box. My eyebrows knit together, watching her open the box.

"No." I instantly say, seeing the sparkling piece inside.

Her eyes shine excitedly, lifting the tiara, handing the box back to Tarren. He dips his head respectfully before returning to his spot in the lineup. The tiara is the same shade of grey-silver as Sylas' crown. There's a larger, round, soft blue crystal in the center with smaller ones shaped like diamonds throughout, surrounded completely by white crystals.

"Nonsense." She sets it on my head, adjusting it with pins to hold it in place, the long slender sides disappearing into my hair on the outside of my ears. "There. It looks perfect on you." She beams. My face burns. I open my mouth to object, but then the throne room begins to fill.

The King and Queen readjust their stance, looking like the regal royals they are. I pale in comparison standing next to them. Closing my eyes, I suck in a deep breath. Yes, they're all staring at me, but soon their gazes will shift. Today is Sylas' day and I can't wait to see him. Music starts and I know the true ceremony is about to begin.

Sylas, slowly, in time with the music walks before all the guests from all over who've come to see him crowned. He's in a dark grey tunic with black pants. Sky blue thread embroidering down the front and his shoulders. A slightly darker blue belt is wrapped around his waist. His eyes meet mine, the corner of his lips twitching into a little grin. His hair is down, though not in its usual messy form. It's combed neatly out of his face.

I roll my eyes at the look he gives me, a genuine smile on my lips. Thankfully, all eyes are now on Sylas, as they should be. It's clear that everyone in the room holds some kind of admiration for Sylas in one way or another. He walks with the confidence of a King. I can't help shifting under his gaze. He hasn't looked anywhere else.

Eleanor sighs like a mother watching her boy grow up. Reuben watches with pride in his eyes. My chest warms, swelling with pride as well. The room may be filled with hundreds of people, but there's only one I can't take my eyes off of. He's mine, regardless of titles and situations.

As he reaches the front of the room, up the steps to the stage, he breaks tradition, reaching for my hand. He only gives it a squeeze before letting go and facing his dad.

With that, I don't care who all is watching us, what they think about our relationship. I know everything is going to be fine, as long as we have each other. The Assassin and her King

Acknowledgments

Years ago, I made a goal. I didn't accomplish it and was very discouraged. My husband, Cameron, said something about how goals aren't there to bring you down. They are a guide to get you to where you want to be. A year later, I wrote the first draft of this project within the time goal I set. This story is very different than what it once was. I want to say thank you, my love, for being there through it all and for being my constant support. All the writing I'm able to do is because of you, your love, and your hard work.

Thank you to my best friends, Chelsea, for putting up with all the times I turn to you to ask for help with names, spelling, song ideas and to run an idea by you. Thanks for listening to all my ideas.

A special thanks to Fountain for being my first beta reader, and reading it twice, helping me make it better every step of the way. All your little notes are a delight, and I will cherish them forever. I'll always giggle about "Fade to Feathers" and "Salad Dressin'" as my favorites.

A huge shout out to my beloved Poets. You have no idea how much of an impact you all have had on me and my writing. Viscera, my chaos partner in crime. Twist, Epic, and Pixel, keeping me going with sprints. Whisper of support and encouragement. Nova, sharing all your wild knowledge with me. Zephyr, helping with formatting.

You all have given me the courage to go from simply talking about publishing, to actually doing it.

Last, but certainly not least, thank you, the one reading this right now. Thank you for giving my world a chance to be your own. I hope you enjoy it. I can't wait to share more of it and other stories with you.

About the Author

Larisa is just a girl with hundreds of stories ready to burst out. When she was little, she would tell her mom bedtime stories instead of the other way around. A part of her always knew she wanted to share her stories with the world. Now she survives with her husband, two wild kids and dog. When she's not writing, you can find her playing with the kids or doing some kind of craft project.

Join her on

Instagram: @larisab.author

TikTok: @larisab.author